IT HAPPENED IN THE HOLLOW

BRENDA STANLEY

OLIVERHEBERBOOKS

For my family

At sunrise, everything is luminous, but not clear.

— NORMAN MACLEAN, *A RIVER RUNS THROUGH IT*

PROLOGUE

The weight of the body was not any different than most young men of that age. Not short, not tall, and certainly not overly muscular or fat. It was a normal-sized body, but when slack and being dragged over the uneven ground of the woods, it felt like something with much more heft.

Maybe it was the emotional weight of what had happened that made him so difficult for the two girls to haul. Only one of them had used a large stone and smashed him from behind. But neither felt bad about her doing it, and now they had to remove the evidence of what had happened that night.

"My hand is slipping. I need to stop," whispered Evelyn.

The girls each held a leg and were tugging the body backward towards the awaiting watery grave. They stopped, and each dropped the leg they were pulling.

Both of the heavy boots crashed down onto the dried brush and leaves, but the girls weren't concerned about the noise. The night air was already filled with the sounds of the bonfire just over the ridge. The yells and laughter rose into the sky like a tribal war party getting ready to strike.

Evelyn felt like they were gearing up to track her down, and her fear heightened. She knew getting the body into the strong, deep current of the canal would need to be done before anyone realized he was missing.

After a short moment, Ramona reached down and grabbed a leg again. "Let's go," she directed Evelyn, and she, too, picked up a leg, adjusted her grip, and the two resumed their grisly mission.

The dried leaves and grass of the trail helped them slide the body along, but Ramona had to turn, with the small flashlight in her mouth, and try to guide them.

"What if someone comes looking for him?" Evelyn whined.

Ramona shook her head. "Shtop," she tried to say, with the flashlight between her teeth.

"Are you sure no one saw you come over?" Evelyn said with a soft whimper.

Ramona tried to answer her by nodding, making the light flash up and down through the trees.

Even with what had happened to her, Evelyn was letting the horror of what they were doing seep into her, and along with the strain on her body, her mind began to break, and tears blurred her eyes.

Ramona heard Evelyn softly crying and stopped. She took the flashlight from her mouth and, for a moment, let Evelyn release her sobs in the dark.

"I'm sorry I made you go with me. This is all my fault," Ramona called over to her friend.

Evelyn wiped her eyes and nose, stood straight, and took a deep breath. "This isn't your fault. He's the one who did this, not you." Her voice was no longer sad but angry.

Ramona listened and began to worry that Evelyn's newfound defiance would make her want to abandon their plan and confess the truth.

"You're right," Ramona tried to assure her, "but we can't stop now. No one can know about any of this."

Evelyn was silent, and Ramona's heart raced with worry.

"Yes," Evelyn finally said definitively. "I don't ever want to think about this night again, and I don't ever want to talk about it," she then turned to Ramona and squared her shoulders, and even in the dark, soft glow of the moon, Ramona could see her resolve.

She gave a nod, hoping that would spur Evelyn on and allow them to continue up the hill to a place where no one would be able to see what they planned to do.

When she stood at the top of the steep embankment looking down on the deep and rushing water, she hoped everything about that night would be washed away forever. But what lingered was something that would not only bring back the horror of that night but fill her with conflict and a churning sense of guilt that no amount of water or time could wash away.

Chapter 1

It was the last thing I still see clearly. Chopped down and hanging in ruins, it is now a source of both suspicion and blame, neither of which is warranted, but only from this side of the veil do I see that.

It was a bridge that linked our two sides. Constructed years ago of boards and rope, it wasn't sturdy and certainly not safe, but it somehow lasted for decades. It was a vital access to a precious commodity we defended with our lives. That is why the person who stands accused of destroying the bridge is also facing accusations over my loss. The grudge is deeper than the water in the canal it once spanned.

They still don't refer to me as dead. I'm missing, but after over a year, most have lost hope of finding me, but they keep those thoughts to themselves, thinking they are allowing my parents to hope.

There is finger-pointing along with the pain, and this stretch of water hidden deep in the woods is the source of the conflict, just like before.

The first tragedy was thirty years ago and resulted in death, and that began a bitter feud between two families that soon festered and spread to the rest of the small valley. And now, with the supposed connection to my loss, the pointed fingers and passionate pleas for justice have only fueled the smoldering.

Death is never easy to accept, especially when it's your own. Maybe that's why I continue to hover, to watch, and to hope that somehow, I'll find the answers as to why this happened to me.

Being alive for only fifteen years, I feel unfinished. How can I not? I have no choice any longer. My life is over, and while the warm and inviting light calls me to leave this stagnant space of gray, my desire for closure is stronger. Yet I'm not sure if finding it is even possible.

And it's not just for me that I seek this resolution. The existence I have now has me seeing what took place and the actions that led up to it in a completely different light. The people involved were present and moving forward with me during my life, but now I remain, and they go on. I know their origins, issues, and pasts. How different life looks when you see what came before. Even though I realize much more on this side, there is still so much I don't yet understand. And if this loss is a mystery to me, my soul hurts for what it's been like for her.

She's the reason I stay and sift through the clues. I have to help her let go. It's the only way I, too, can make my way out of this limbo. I can't move on until she can.

It's usually the cold that is most prominent when I relive my death. I'm not sure if it's the actual physical sensation of when it occurred or the feelings of loss and regret that have come from it.

What a change from what I once had. I still see my life. It comes back to me in quick flashes of remembrance. Some of the scenes are significant, some mundane, and yet I cling to them like precious little gems that will fall through my fingers if I don't hold them tightly. I looked forward to what was to come and felt good about what I had already done. When I let myself drift back to what I had in life, I see warm, glowing sunsets hovering above the sparkle of the water. I hear the rhythmic wash of the river and the mechanical ticking of the reel as I bring in my catch. My chest fills with the breath of contentment and calm. And the other souls—those who created my life and made it what I miss—are who I must redeem and allow to live in peace.

I have to find what brought it all to an end. I know it won't change anything or bring me back to what I once had, but there is still a need for justice, or at least closure, even on this side of the veil. I know that is what is keeping me from following the glow that draws me toward some other place and away from this dark space of flux.

Flashes of what took me are all I have, but I know it was violent as I remember the frantic attempts to thwart what was grabbing me and eventually snuffed out my breath.

Her face comes into view, and the emotion of crying fills me. She's still in pain. I know that she probably always will feel loss, but the trauma hasn't lessened, even with time. I feel the push to wrap around her and protect her. How can I possibly leave when she's still looking for me?

I was an only child. Now she has no child, and yet she also has no evidence that I'm dead, except that I'm gone.

Some people may have felt I was indulged and pampered. That may be true, but I wasn't spoiled—I had chores and was expected to help with the farm and animals while also keeping up with schoolwork.

My ventures into the woods and along the river were what I lived for. I did everything I could to be able to be in that place. It was my escape and reward to make my way back to where I felt free and most at home.

I felt the weight of being the only one, and seeing things now, I know my parents had wanted more children. It never happened, and now it only adds to my mother's feelings of failure and loss— emotions heightened by what happened to me. She blames herself for my demise—not that having other children would make her feel better, but having only one child has emphasized that loss.

The guilt is overwhelming because she sent me away. It's true, but like so many things in life, it was a moment of anger—one that she would forever regret.

I want to relieve her guilt and let her know it wasn't her fault, but I can't do that until I know where to lay the blame. Why can't I see that? There is so much now that has been revealed about my life and the past of those I knew who are still living. So much has opened up to me and yet the one thing I want revealed refuses to step out from the shadows. If I could just find the truth, then I could help my mother see that her shoulders are free from that burden.

I've learned how to creep into her dreams. I've been able to breach that curtain between consciousness and sleep, and yet I can't comfort her. I've tried to journey into the others who were part of my life, hoping I can glean something that would break the shell of secrecy around why I'm here, but the demon who caused this is keeping me from the truth.

The life I lived is with me always. Every moment, from my birth, until I took that fateful walk back into the woods, is clear as if I'm still experiencing it. All of it except what led to my demise. That I still don't see.

CHAPTER 2

I was told to call her Aunt Vera, but even at five years of age, I knew she wasn't really my aunt.

She was nice enough but the first to make fun of my smile. She tried to act like she was harmlessly teasing me by lifting her upper lip to expose her teeth. She did it when I laughed or grinned widely. It's when I realized my smile was something to hide. Once, my mother scolded her, but instead of apologizing, Aunt Vera just looked at me and rolled her eyes. I knew we were a burden, or rather I was.

My mother and Vera worked at a Bob's Big Boy restaurant near the interstate. We stayed in a small room that had one twin bed. I slept in a sleeping bag on the floor, which I thought was a fun thing, not realizing how hard and dirty the floor was.

"No going outside, no making noise, and don't answer the door for anyone," my mother would warn me. She said the same three things every time she left for work, but on that day, she added something. "And don't go snooping around. Vera already thinks we're stealing from her."

"Stealing what?" I asked, truly curious. There was nothing in that tiny, rundown house that I needed or wanted, and I had never stolen anything.

"Don't you worry about it. Just do what I say, watch cartoons, and be a good boy," she said, ruffling the top of my head as she slid out the door. "Lock it!" she called from outside, and I flipped the deadbolt.

I peeked through the sheer curtains of the kitchen window as she walked down the street toward the bus stop. It was the last time our lives would be happy.

I knew I wasn't supposed to use the stove, but I was hungry, and I'd seen my mother make macaroni and cheese many times, so I found a box in the pantry and began the process, just as I had seen her do it.

I turned the knob of the stove, and after two clicks, a blue flame burst from the burner. I smiled at my success. I filled the pan with water and set it on the flame, and when it began to bubble and hiss, I poured in the noodles and gave them a quick stir.

I wasn't completely sure how long to let them cook, but I knew it would take a while, so I sat at the small table to wait. I became bored and was trying to draw a picture of a mouse on the inside cover of the telephone book when a knock came at the back door.

I slid off the chair and under the table so if whoever was there tried to look in the window, they wouldn't see me.

After a moment, a second knock came. It was louder and more urgent.

"I want my shit!" the voice yelled. It was muffled from the door, but I could clearly tell they were mad.

Soon, there was another round of knocking and more yelling. I darted out from under the table and quickly turned the light off in the kitchen to better hide myself. Then, I crawled toward the hallway so I could run for the closet in our room. It was small but deep and a great place to bury myself under the pile of dirty clothes on the floor.

"I know you have the stuff! If you don't open this door, I'm going to break it down!"

What stuff did he want? I wondered. There were others who came to the door, and my mother or Aunt Vera would exchange small packages with them. My mother would go to our bedroom and take them from the secret drawer where she kept her money and her treasure. But she never allowed anyone in the house, and no one ever came into our room.

There was a loud bang as the man at the door slammed into it. He was trying to break it in. From the crack I heard, I knew it wouldn't take much for the entire door to give way.

I ran to our room and to that secret place. I pulled open the drawer of her small nightstand and reached behind it. My mother had to remove the drawer completely to reach what was there, but my thin arm and small hand were able to slip behind and grab the small satin pouch that held her treasure and the envelope she had stuffed with cash. When I pulled it all free, I saw there were several plastic bags with the cash and assumed they were valuable if my mother felt the need to keep them in her secret stash. I took them as well. She would be glad that I saved her stuff.

There was another loud slam against the door. I knew I needed to run to the closet and hide, so I tried to shove everything down the front of my pants, but the envelope was too thick. The money and some of the bags spilled out onto the floor.

I dropped to the ground and frantically tried to gather it all up. I then heard a smash, and I knew he was in the apartment.

"What the hell?" I heard him say.

And then a loud, blaring siren came from the kitchen. It echoed all through the house. What was that noise? Did we have an alarm on the door?

I ran to the closet and closed myself inside. I then burrowed under the clothes, deep into the back. I lay completely still and waited. The scream of the siren was so loud I couldn't tell what part of the house the man was in, but I stayed still and continued to wait.

After several minutes, I peeked up from under the clothes. The alarm was still going, but if the man had been in the house, he surely would have come into our room to search, and the closet door was still closed. I pushed the clothes away and sat up. I put my ear to the door and could only hear the siren's scream. Then I stood up and grabbed the door knob of the closet; I barely cracked the door and peered out.

"Oh no," I said, seeing smoke filling the room. Fire. I needed to get out.

I walked out of the closet and across the room to the bedroom door. I carefully peered out but saw only smoke. I ran through the blare and haze, through the kitchen, and toward the door. That's when I realized it was the pan I had put on the stove. It had been on the entire time and was now burning.

My mother had told me never to touch the stove, and now I had caused all of this. I began to cough but knew I had to try and stop it.

I grabbed a large glass from the cupboard, filled it with water, and then went to where the pan was burning and poured the water on it. The flash of steam hit my hand and arm, and I fell back. The money and bags spilled onto the floor, but I knew I didn't have time to retrieve them. On the floor, I could see my way to the door, but when I put my hand down to try and crawl, a streak of pain coursed through me, and I screamed out.

"Who's there?" I heard a voice call above the blare of the alarm.

Then I felt large hands grab my arm, and I flinched back, not only from fear but excruciating pain. It felt as though my skin was being torn off of me. My head began to buzz, and soon, the smoke turned dark.

I WOKE up lying on the grass outside. I was wrapped in a blanket, and there were people all around, and a police officer was standing over me. I knew then I was in trouble. I had used the stove and had started a fire.

I tried to sit up, but someone else sitting beside me put their hand on my shoulder. My hand throbbed.

"Were you home alone?" the police officer asked. He was so tall, and I could barely make out his face because he was blocking the sun.

I nodded.

"Where's your mom?"

"At work," I answered. "At Bob's Big Boy."

He looked up at someone else and nodded.

I then remembered the treasure, and my stomach clenched, worried I had lost it.

I reached down under the blanket and felt the pouch where I had placed it in my underwear, making sure it was secure. But where were the money and the other bags?

———

THAT WAS ALMOST ten years ago. I haven't seen my mother since that day. We used to talk on the phone every week, but the older I got, the less she had to say, and the calls became fewer.

We used to talk about when she was going to be free and what our life would be like when she came to get me. But lately, she just says happy birthday, asks if I'm doing good in school, and then tells me to be a good boy. I don't think she realizes I'm not a child anymore. I'm short for my age and don't have many of the attributes others have at fifteen, but I'm no longer the little boy who was taken away.

I didn't understand why I was sent to live at a stranger's home, and the first few times, it was like a new adventure. I would miss my mom, especially when I was alone in bed, but during our calls, she would always assure me she would be coming to get me soon.

"It won't be long. Be a good boy, and I'll come and get you real soon," she'd tell me.

I used to wait each Sunday night for the phone to ring. The man at my third foster home would accept the charges and then let me sit alone in a small room he called his den so I could talk in private. I appreciated this when I went to the other foster homes because the noise in the kitchen, where the phone usually was, made it hard to hear, and my mother would often get annoyed and cut the calls short. But the call I got on my tenth birthday was the best. It's why I know my future is on a lavender farm.

"There's a place I used to live with no crowds or smog," my mother mused. "It was a lavender farm. It was just mine, and I can still smell the flowers. Someday, we'll go back." Her voice was light and dreamy, as if she were envisioning herself there at that moment.

My heart swelled hearing that she had plans for us. I wanted to be anywhere with her, and if she wanted to live on a lavender farm, I wanted to do that, too, and it quickly became my obsession.

I checked out books at the library that were about the flowering bush and where it was grown. I read about soil and rainfall and all the different things that were made from the fragrant buds.

England and France grow the most lavender worldwide, but in

America, the state that grows the most is Washington. I'm assuming that's where we'll go. I don't see us moving to another country, and Washington is just a few states over from California, where we are now.

I have so many questions about our plans for when she's free. When she calls, there isn't a lot of time, so I don't pester her with questions like I used to, but I always reaffirm that her release date is still the same—September 9th.

And the timing will be just right. I still have the treasure she entrusted me with, and we'll use it to buy our farm. She's getting out at the end of summer, and soon after, the lavender will be in full bloom and ready for harvest.

Chapter 3

Her name is Laura, and she still lives in the house on the other side of the river. She was the most beautiful girl I'd ever seen, and she's only gotten prettier. I miss her, and I feel she misses me, making it a bit easier.

I was thirteen, and she was fourteen years old when we met, and even though I know that is too young to really fall in love, it felt that way. My grandfather always said, "Perception is reality." I didn't know what he meant by that until now. However, what I perceived my feelings to be was what was real in my life regardless of what was reality. That all-encompassing, even painful ache is what I felt was love.

Her long hair is what I noticed first. It was black and shined like the wings of a raven. She was with several girlfriends swimming at the trestle bridge. I was surprised I'd never seen her before. Our town was so small, I couldn't believe this was the first time I'd noticed her.

She looked at me with large, dark eyes. No smile, but something in her face made me feel like she was drawn to me, too. My friends all noticed her as well and did their best to get her attention. They laughed too loud, pushing and shoving each other. Even my best friend, Jeremy, couldn't help himself and made a Tarzan call as he leaped from the tall bridge into the water below.

The boys' antics had the other girls whispering together in their giggling huddles, but Laura was quiet and didn't acknowledge their clowning, which drew me to her even more.

It was 1982 and the summer before my first year of high school. Which meant all the kids my age in Bingham County would be under the same roof. In our earlier grades, we may have been able to keep to ourselves—stay on our own sides of town, in our own schools, but when we reached high school, we were all brought together.

Of course, I had no idea what was to come, yet I felt my time with Laura was limited and precious. I often wonder what I would have done differently regarding us. The only thing I would change is something I had no control over, so why do I even dwell on it? I hope she thinks of me. It's a selfish thought. I don't want her to feel sad. I don't want her to be lonely. It's how I feel now, and I would never wish this terrible ache on her.

It's only been a year since I left, and I have to keep myself away because I know it would only make my pain worse to see her. I miss others as well, but nothing compares to what I feel I lost with Laura.

I'm not sure why I linger. I feel other things keep me close and watching, but the prospects I felt for her are unfinished. I'm guessing that pain will leave once I accept what happened. I wish I could, but there is still so much left undone.

I want to apologize, but that can't happen. I've tried to tie the loose ends that I left behind, but I can't seem to find the missing pieces. And so, I continue to search.

I would have married Laura if we had had more time. I know it sounds childish to say that at my age, but I genuinely believe it would have happened. Maybe that's why I stay away. She probably feels she's to blame.

———

WE SAT under the cottonwood trees in a shaded and secluded corner of the woods we felt was our own.

When the worry of our parents and others finding out became too much, I would try to convince her it wasn't as bad as she thought.

"Who cares what side of the river we live on. We didn't start that stupid fight. Who even knows what it was all about? It doesn't matter anymore."

For months, we hid in the trees, held hands, and stole kisses. The time went by so quickly, and I often forgot about my chores until I noticed the sun was beginning to fade.

I would have to drag myself from her and then run to the gates, hoping that no one would notice and make a fuss that the water had flowed longer than it should have.

It all seemed so perfect until our secret got out. When it did, both our families were on us like hens pecking corn. It was as if we had committed a terrible sin, and they did all they could to convince us that what we felt for each other was wrong.

"You don't know her," I told my mother as she shook her head in frustration.

"I know where she comes from, and that's enough," she balked. "They have told terrible lies about our family for years."

"Laura didn't say those things," I scoff. "How long are you going to hold a grudge? Why are you taking this out on her?" I demand.

My mother rolled her eyes and leaned back in frustration. She had no good answer. Never would she reveal the reason for her deep-rooted fear and aversion. How could she have ever told me the truth when it would have destroyed everything she had tried so diligently to bury? I see now exactly what took place and why I could never be with Laura or know the reason behind it.

The fierce determination coming from both our families to keep us apart only swelled our desire to be with each other. They may have discovered our love, but they hadn't yet found our secret place deep in the woods or how we got there.

With even more stealth, we each made our way back into the hollow and, seeing each other, embraced more fervently than we ever had before.

"We won't let them do this," I told her. "They can't keep us from seeing each other."

"But my brother says he'll kill you if he sees us together."

I scoffed. "Kevin's all talk. Besides, no one will find us. They don't even know the bridge exists." I then looked at her to assure myself she hadn't said a word.

She nodded but still looked unconvinced.

I took her face in my hands. "Don't let them do this. We can hide back here. They'll never know."

She closed her eyes, looking as though she was about to cry.

"But then what? We can't hide forever."

I pulled her close. "We won't have to hide. Someday, it won't matter."

Laura leaned back and looked at me. "But when? They say my grandfather died because of what your family did."

I shake my head. "They're wrong about it all," I said.

Through wet eyes, she peered up at me. "But my grandfather died, and my mother says your grandfather got away with it."

I flinch back. "My grandfather? That's not true," I told her. I had heard that there was a fight over water, but I'd never heard that my grandfather was accused of killing anyone. "He would never do something like that. It's a lie."

Her face fell. "Why would my mother lie? She said they were fighting about the water and that your grandfather used a shovel to hit him and knock him into the river. She said you're the grandson of a murderer."

"What?" I said, leaning back. "My grandfather is no murderer. He's one of the best people I've ever known."

Laura looked at me like I was a stranger. "I never got to meet my grandfather. He died before I was born."

My chest sank. I felt like she was blaming me for her loss. I took hold of her shoulders and made her look at me. "Laura," I begged. "Don't let them do this to us. No matter what happened, it has nothing to do with you and me. It's in the past. Please don't give up on us."

Her eyes were heavy, and she slumped into me. We sat holding each other with nothing but the sound of water slowly rippling past us. I began to feel the weight of what seeing each other really meant. At school, we would pass each other in the hall and at lunch, but during the summer and any other time that we weren't in school, our only hope would be the secret bridge in the hollow.

"I love you," I told her, still holding her close to my chest.

She looked up at me with red eyes. "I love you too. But it's so hard. I feel like I'm hurting my family, and I also feel like I'm hurting you."

I tightened my embrace and kissed her forehead. "The only thing that could hurt me is if I lose you."

CHAPTER 4

LANDIS

They always say the same thing when they drive up to the house where you'll be staying. "Well, here we are." I've heard it eleven times and from almost as many different people. I've had many case-workers. They are the people who know why you're in this situation and make the arrangements for where you're going to live. Some of these people last a few months and others a couple of years, about the same amount of time I spend in each home I'm sent to.

The homes aren't always terrible, but I've never been sad to leave. The last place they told me was just temporary, which was weird. Aren't all these places just temporary? And yet, I'd never been told that before. It didn't matter because I didn't stay there even a week. It was a group home, and I was sent there for something I didn't do.

The boy who shared my room at the house before stole some money from the woman's purse. He denied it, and I didn't rat him out, so we were both suspects. We were put in a place called The Idaho Home for Boys. Two states away from where I'm from. They said it wasn't a jail, but there were locks on the doors and men with uniforms and badges who told you what to do. I thought I'd be there awhile—at least until my mom could come and get me—but now I'm going on move number twelve. I hope she'll be able to find me.

The drive out to the new place is longer than I expected, but at least it isn't a thirteen-hour bus ride. I'm still confused as to why I'm in another state. The longer I wait, the harder it is for them to find someone willing to have a boy my age live with them. I'm old for a foster kid. I'll be sixteen in two weeks. I don't know if anyone knows my birthday is coming up, and even if they did, I don't expect anything. I've never wanted a birthday party or presents, especially now that I'm older. It's just a date, and in just two months, I'll no longer have to worry about where I live.

"Landis is a cool name," says my new caseworker, Marge. I don't usually call adults by their first name, but she insisted. It's her attempt, along with using words like "cool," to act like she's not the old lady she is. She continues to annoy me by trying to get me to talk the entire drive. And instead of finding out about where I'll be living, it's just mindless chatter.

"I've never heard that name before. Where does that come from?" she asks.

I shrug like I don't know. But I do know. It was my grandfather's name. I was named after my father, and my middle name comes from my grandfather. I never met either of these men, but that isn't so strange, figuring I've never met anyone in my family except, of course, my mom. I haven't seen her since we lived in Sacramento. She got us out of Los Angeles and moved us up north when I was three. She said there was too much crime in L.A. Somehow, it finds her wherever she goes.

As we drive, I see large fields dotted with cows, and the houses are sparse and spread out, with farm equipment and large red barns. The other places I've stayed in are apartment buildings or side-by-side houses surrounded by concrete and chain-link fences.

I've read books about places in the country, but I've never really been there until now. I can't imagine I'll be staying at one of these farms. There's got to be a city coming up soon.

The farther we drive, the less evidence I see of people. Why was I taken so far away from my mother? I have such a short amount of time until she's able to come and get me. I don't understand why I couldn't have stayed somewhere closer until then.

I'm tired of all the moves. You'd think I'd get used to it after eleven different times, but I don't. The other kids who I've lived with have similar stories. There have been dozens of them. Some have parents who died, some have parents who are in prison like me, and others don't know or just don't talk about it. That's what I do now. What's the point of anyone knowing? I'll soon be free of this. I have a date—September 9th. It's fitting. It's the day of the year that more people are born than any other day. It was the foster dad at home number seven who told me that. He said it was an actual statistic. He worked at a mortuary and said the day with the most deaths is January 6th, and the day with the most births is September 9th. The day I'll be able to be back with my mother—to be home. It will feel as though I'm reborn.

Some of the houses I've stayed in weren't all bad, and at one, I had my own room for an entire week. The room was a converted closet, but I enjoyed the seclusion. It was my retreat from the mob of other kids. But none of those houses was ever really my home. And that's just fine. Once my mom gets out, I'll go back to living with her. It's supposed to happen in just over three months.

It's not like I'm counting down the days; I've made that mistake before. And even if they don't release her soon, I only have a few more years of staying with strangers—the "paid parents," as my mother refers to them. She hates my situation and never wants to hear anything about the homes unless it's terrible. She wants to make sure I'm still planning to be with her. Of course, I am. None of these other places will ever be better than being with her.

———

We pull into a narrow laneway lined by thick spruce trees. This isn't it. It can't be. All the way out here in the middle of nowhere?

Then I see it. An enormous home. Large gray stones cover the entire structure, and tall carved rock spires reach up into the cloudy sky. A castle. That's what it looks like—something from out of my books about knights and dragons—but sitting in the middle of farm fields.

Marge turns to me and lifts her brows. "Well, here we are," she says.

"This is it?" I ask. I wonder if it's even a house.

She smiles brightly. "The Frosts have been waiting to meet you. They're such nice people. I think you'll really enjoy it here."

I look at the house and wonder how many other boys will be living here, too. Considering the size of this place, I'm sure there will be a bunch.

I nod, but I have nothing to say. I don't even have questions about this new place. It doesn't matter. I don't have a choice. If I mess up, I'll have to pack up and move again, and I'm just putting in my time, just like my mom.

"It looks like the river is just over there," she says, pointing out in the distance where a long line of large craggy trees sways in the breeze. They look like tired old men unable to stand up straight. "My father and brothers used to go fishing. Do you fish?" she asks.

I look at her oddly. Do I fish? She acts like I'm going to summer camp. I shake my head and look out the window. She can sense that I already hate it here. Why wouldn't I? None of these people want you in their home, not really. It's a money thing for them. They get paid for letting you live there. Initially, they may have done it to help out the poor kids without homes, but none of them would do it without the government's money. And they need it. The houses are usually cramped and cluttered with junk and too many kids. There will have to be over twenty to fill this place.

I look up at the ornate cornices and tall windows. The space around the house is preened and clutter-free. A huge red barn sits just behind and to the left, and there are corrals filled with horses and cows. The house looks as out of place as I feel.

My shoulders sink as I realize what this really is. They've run out of options for where to store me, so it's their last resort.

"What is this place? Is this another group home or a ...?" I sigh, wondering if I've finally worked my way through every possible foster home and am now at an orphanage. I was sent to that home for boys after some money was taken. Maybe they decided I really did steal it, and this was their only option.

"Do these people know why I went to that place?" I ask, convinced that is why I've been taken here and irritated that I'm being blamed for something I had nothing to do with. They even searched me, and that was the worst part. I obviously looked guilty. How could

I not? While I had no part in what was taken from that purse, my racing heart knew what I was hiding.

I have two items that could ruin everything for me. One is a library book I wasn't able to return, and the other I've carried with me for almost a decade—the opulent treasure I have hidden in my underwear.

Cocking her head, Marge turns to me. "Landis, this is your new home. This isn't a punishment."

"Then why was I put in that jail?"

She lifts an eyebrow. "That wasn't a ..." she tries to find a word for it, knowing that's precisely what it was. "That was a home for boys, and you were only there because we needed some time to get things arranged for you to come here. The Frosts have been wanting you here for some time, but some things happened, and we needed time to get everything arranged."

I huff. "It doesn't matter. My mom is out in a couple of months anyway."

She scratches her head, searching for words, and I wonder if she knows something I don't.

"Her release date is still set, right?" I press her. I feel my face begin to sweat. It's happened before. I'm told she'll be out, and then some judge changes his mind and ruins everything.

Clearing her throat, Marge sits up straighter. "I don't know about any of that." She looks out at the large, looming house. "Give the Frosts a chance. I think you'll be very happy here."

At this point, I've stopped listening. I can't even think about the possibility of my mom not getting out this time, and I'm tired of listening to the "what ifs."

I sigh loudly as a sign that it's time to get this new home introduction over with. I open the car door and then retrieve my bag from the back seat. It's a black plastic garbage bag. I had to leave so quickly; I barely had time to find a bag at all. It's far too big for the number of things I need to carry—two shirts, two pairs of underwear, and five mismatched socks. I was supposed to get new shoes and a coat last year, but I ended up starting school without either of those things. I wonder now if I'll be going to school at all since the year is almost over. I look around. It's hard to imagine where the school is. This place is so far out of town.

The yard surrounding the house is just starting to show the effects of spring. The grass is beginning to turn green, and tiny purple flowers that look like short tulips fill planters that border the walkway. The house and yard are incredibly clean. I don't see toys or other evidence of little kids and wonder about the other boys with whom I'll be sharing a room. The usual number is three, but there are some houses where I've slept on the couch. At that house, I could hear the little kids in the other room crying, and I remembered the first places I stayed where I thought my tears might bring my mother back sooner.

The sound of a rooster crowing shakes me from my thoughts, and before we reach the porch, the large door opens, and a woman stands looking tentative. When she sees me, her mouth falls open as though I have horns.

"Hello," she says, still studying me. She is tall—much taller than I am, which isn't saying much because the last time I measured, I was still just under five feet.

I've always been small, which can be a good thing as it helps me stay under the radar, but it also has people thinking I'm much younger than I am.

"Landis, this is Mrs. Frost," says Marge.

Hearing Marge's voice seems to shake the woman from a daydream.

I've never met a woman this tall before, and yet she isn't big. She is thin and pretty with shoulder-length brown hair and blue eyes. I can't tell if her eyes are big or just look that way because of how oddly she's staring at me.

"Hey," I say. It's almost a question.

"Come in," the woman says, stepping back and motioning us inside. She then studies me again, and her eyes become wet. Is she starting to cry? I'm feeling awkward, and I look back at Marge, wondering if we are at the right place and hoping we aren't. Then, a heavenly scent wafts from inside the home. It smells like bread and something savory, and it reminds me that I haven't eaten since last night.

As we walk into the foyer, I take a quick sweeping scan of the home. It is spacious and immaculate. The walls are covered in muted designs, and some have textured flowers or birds. There is a stairway that swoops up to the left with intricately carved banisters.

The house looks like something from long ago, and while everything seems antique, it's a different kind of old. I see no sign of wear and tear. I've stayed in many other places that are far newer and yet look as though a light wind could topple them. I think about the tale of the three little pigs—a house of straw, a house of sticks, and a house of bricks that not even the big bad wolf could blow down. This house of stone is not only sturdy but feels like it could stand up to anything, including time.

We follow Mrs. Frost from the foyer and into a sprawling area furnished with large leather chairs and thick oak bookcases. A real deer head with huge antlers hangs above a fireplace that stretches from the floor all the way to the top of the high ceiling. It's made with the same large earth-colored stones.

Mrs. Frost clears her throat and takes a deep breath. "Gordon is out back, but he'll be here soon."

I'm assuming Gordon is her husband, and I wonder if he'll be overly interested, gruff, or just absent. It's always one of those three when it comes to the men in the homes I've lived in. I've always watched them closer and been more interested in who they are and what they do. I have my own mother, but my father left before I was born, so I've been curious my entire life about that role.

As we all wait, Mrs. Frost motions to the garbage bag in my hands. "Are those your things?" she asks.

I nod.

"You can set that down. We'll take it to your room later."

I slowly lower the bag to the ground but keep it gripped closely. It may look like garbage, but I can't allow what's inside to ever be out of my control.

She motions for us to come farther into the house, and I notice her hand. Two of her fingers are stubs. Missing digits just above the knuckle. I try not to stare, but then I see her notice, and I look away quickly.

I rub my own scarred and damaged fingers with my good hand,

feeling the hardened and uneven skin that covers each finger and my entire palm.

"Here, have a seat," she says as we enter a large room.

The house seems to expand as I see even more space, and again, I wonder where the others are. Are they in the backyard or another part of this big house? And it's so quiet.

I sit in a large, high-back chair and try not to look like I'm casing the place, but I'm intrigued by everything from the wallpaper to the floors. Above one of the bookcases is another animal stuffed and appearing to be alive. It's smaller than a cougar but looks fierce in its frozen stance. It has a speckled coat and pointed and tufted ears. Its back is hunched as though it is about to pounce. And on the wall across the room is a massive and colorful fish. It looks over two feet long and has brilliant stripes of color the entire length of its body. I look at Marge and wonder if she already knew something about this place when she pointed out to the trees and pondered about a river.

Marge and Mrs. Frost sit on the sofa and exchange some paperwork. Mrs. Frost acts like she is afraid I'll see this, as though I don't know I'm just another kid being transferred from one place to another. I've seen it done so many times. However, this part is usually done while I'm pestered by the other kids I'll be sharing the house with. Today, I sit and wait.

When they've finished, they chat aimlessly about the weather as I continue to study my new surroundings. I'm surprised at how little I see that shows other children are living here. I usually step over plastic toys and half-eaten sandwiches before I even meet the parents at the new place.

After several minutes, Mrs. Frost gives a quick, disappointed sigh. "He knew you were coming, but he must have lost track of time."

"It's not a problem," says Marge. "I'll let you two get acquainted. I have everything I need." Soon, she is out the door. I'm hoping this is the last time I see her before my mom gets out. Everything needs to go smoothly until then. I just want to stay put while I wait. No more moving and certainly no more trouble. I have to be free and able to go when my mom gets here.

CHAPTER 5

I'm now alone with Mrs. Frost in the massive and silent house.

She turns to me. "Would you like to see your room?" she asks.

"Okay," I answer and retrieve the garbage bag that holds my life.

She leads me up the long flight of stairs, and they creak, each one with a slightly different tone and volume. Some are silent, just like the woman I'm following.

When we reach the top, I look out over the large living and dining room area. The ceiling is so high, and again, I wonder where the other children are.

She walks down the hallway, and I follow along. There are no photos or wall hangings. There is no clutter or signs of life. Everything is stark, almost sterile. The air feels cold, and a breeze encircles me. A window must be open.

I see a door and assume it's the room I'll be staying in, but she keeps walking, directing me past it and then stops at another door at the end of the hall.

"This is your room."

I stop and then, without thinking, look back at the first door we passed. She notices and comes around to that side, blocking off my gaze.

"That room is off-limits." Her face and voice turn dark. The change in her demeanor is so abrupt that a chill goes over me. She has obviously heard that I was accused of stealing that money and is hoping to keep me from robbing her. I can't help but flinch back, and when she sees this, she tries to soften.

"There is nothing in that other room that you need to worry about."

Of course, I don't believe her. Does she have any idea that what she's said has only made me more curious? There must be something very valuable in there for her to act this way.

I nod to let her know I've heard her, but my head is spinning with how strange this day has become.

She takes a deep breath and opens the door to the other room.

"Everything you need is here. This is your room," she says, stepping inside, but before I follow, I can't help but look again toward the "off-limits" room. It's just another door. What could be so valuable in there that she would need to make her point so clearly?

As I enter my new room, cool air rushes around me, making me gasp. I turn back and see her severe tone has returned. I don't know what to say, so I try to brush it off by feigning interest and purposefully looking around. With this, she gives a strained smile.

There's a queen-sized bed, a large dresser, and a small television— a television in the bedroom.

There is only one bed. It's been a long time since anyone expected me to share a bed, so I figure they must have cots or other mattresses that they pull out at night. From the size of it, this room can sleep at least four.

Mrs. Frost goes back toward the hallway and motions outside the door to yet another room across the way. "This is your bathroom."

My bathroom. This can't possibly be just for me. I have to ask, so I do. "Where are the others?"

She cocks her head, confused. "Others?" she asks.

"The other boys who live here," I say.

Her face falls as though a cloud has moved over us. It seems like a harmless question, and yet the look on her face makes me want to reel it all back in.

"There are no others," she says sharply.

I shake my head, perplexed. "No other boys live here?" I ask again. It just doesn't make sense and yet, why do I care? I should be thrilled that I have all this without a bunch of others trying to shove their way in and claim it as their own.

She looks both perplexed and sad. "Why would you think there are other boys here?"

"Because they always are," I answer.

She swallows and straightens, making her seem even taller. "There is no one else." Her voice is quiet.

A tiny gust of wind twirls around me as sunlight spills in through a large window. A window that is closed. I feel the breeze again and look for the source but see nothing.

She turns and motions to the closet. It's a change of subject, and I'm thankful for the reprieve.

"If you have anything you need me to wash," she says, looking at my bag, "there is a hamper in the closet."

I nod and stand there, feeling awkward and trying not to look stunned by it all.

"I'll let you get settled and cleaned up. Dinner will be ready in about an hour, and Gordon should be here soon."

I have nothing but a few items in my garbage bag. There is nothing I need to do to get settled. I will never be settled until I'm back with my mom. I look out the window over the vast pasture and out to the stretch of lush trees and brush.

"Is there a river back there?" I ask, remembering what the caseworker had said as we drove up to the house.

She doesn't answer, and I look back to see if she may not have heard me.

She stands staring out at the woods and then snaps from her stupor. She blinks and looks at me. "Yes. There is a river."

"That's cool," I say. It sounds like an apology. I'm feeling uneasy and wonder if my questions are annoying her.

Her lips go thin as though she's angry. "You're not to go near there."

My heart clenches, and I flinch. Another place she's deemed off-limits, but why?

"Why not?" I ask and immediately wish I hadn't.

She throws me a look that's severe. She begins to speak but then stops and, after a moment, straightens.

"You don't know what's back there. It's unsafe." She continues to stare out at the woods.

I take a step back, not only from her tone, but now I'm wondering if I'm barred from the river because she knows I can't swim. But how could she know? It's another of my failings, but one I can usually keep hidden.

"Okay," I say.

"I don't want you to go back into those woods at all."

My face flushes, and I stand perplexed as an awkward silence fills the room.

She turns and begins fidgeting with some folded towels on the dresser. It's then I notice she's missing another part of a finger on her other hand. I study it and wonder if she was born that way or if they were cut off.

She begins to turn back to me, and before she can catch me staring again, I pretend to look out the window but then quickly look away. I'm afraid of even glancing at the place she's deemed forbidden. I'm on edge, not knowing what to say or do. I wish I could leave the room, leave this house. I was planning to live under the radar—just getting through these months without having to move yet again—but being the only one here, I'm now front and center. Every move I make is seen.

"Are all those horses and cows yours?" I blurt out, hoping to direct her attention away from me.

"Yes," she answers. She takes a deep breath and is now smoothing the bedspread.

It may have worked. "So, is this a real farm?" I continue.

She glances up at me with eyes wide. She cocks her head, surprised at my question, and I feel foolish. There are too many questions, like some little kid, with their "whys" and "how comes."

"Didn't she tell you anything about us?" she asks.

I shrug. I think about the long drive here, how little I was told, and how few questions I asked. Why would I? The caseworkers rarely say anything about the foster parents before I get there, even when I do ask questions.

"Not really," I answer. "We don't talk much."

Her face scrunches up in thought and what seems like disappointment. "You don't talk to her?"

Not talking does seem strange when I'm with these people for
hours at a time. I don't want Mrs. Frost to look at me like I'm an inso-
lent child who won't speak when spoken to.

"We talk, but she just didn't say much about where I was going.
She must have thought I already knew or something."

I wonder if there is something I should know, something that
might explain how strange things feel. This huge, old house, the farm,
no other children, and the way she forbids me to go near the woods.

She lifts her eyebrows and seems satisfied with my answer, but I
still feel like she can see through me.

I can't help but stare out the window toward the long stretch of
thick trees. The window is at the back of the house, where a large barn
sits.

"Can I go out and see the barn?" I don't know what I plan to do,
but I'm curious about this new place, and I want to free myself from
this room.

"The barn?" she asks, surprised. She thinks for a moment as
though allowing me to go outside is a major decision.

"I've never been on a farm before," I say, urging her to say I can
go. And it's true. Even with my mother's talks about our future life on
a lavender farm in Washington, I've never stepped foot on a planted
field or been near a real cow or horse.

"Yes," she relents. "Put your things away, and then you can go.
But stay close. Don't go past the chicken coop. Gordon will be home
soon, and we'll have dinner."

I nod.

She turns and is out of the room, leaving me standing there
holding the garbage bag that contains my life. I lower it to the ground.
Besides the book, what's in that bag would all be considered trash
anyway.

I own nothing of value, but I possess something that is worth
more than I can imagine. It isn't mine, but I've held it close for
years now.

I tap my front pocket, feeling for the thing that will allow me and my mom the life we both crave. The solid circle is there, as it always is, but I don't feel the relief it normally gives. Instead, I feel the rush of coldness that came over me before, along with a weight that makes the air seem thick.

I have a bedroom and bathroom all to myself, and there's the warm and savory smell of food that is waiting for me. So, what is this blanket of dread that is making me feel like I should run?

Chapter 6

―――――――

Benji

I wish she could smile and know that what she thinks happened didn't. That is the reason I can't move on. Her pain is understandable, but her reasoning is what's making it all so difficult for everyone, especially her. There is a need to blame when it comes to loss. It helps ease the pain when you shift the anger toward something or someone else. The only person she should blame is me, but even when she learns the truth, how can she possibly blame her dead son?

My mother's name is Evelyn, but her dad started calling her Evie when she was young, and that's what most people in our small town know her by. However, now she's gone back to Evelyn. There is a lot that she's changed, trying to remove the pain, and that has ended up causing even more of it.

She was a girl who grew up with a sense of loss, and what happened to me hasn't helped that any. I understand that now that I'm able to see more. It's what happens when you leave the living. Hindsight is clear and relentless. And now I see the retrospect of others, too. My mother's pain from loss started long before my death. It began even before I was born.

She lost her own mother when she was very young, and while she knew very little of her mom, she felt the loss regardless.

Her father was the town doctor who, like many in rural Idaho, lived and worked their land along with their jobs.

Her older brother, Wesley, was someone she both idolized and resented. He was larger than life, making Evelyn, shy and introverted, feel small next to him. Wesley was tall with wavy blond hair and sky-blue eyes, which had all the girls swooning. But it wasn't just his looks —he was athletic and intelligent. He knew he would inherit the farm but refused to sit back and be given the family business. He wanted to earn it, grow it, and make it even more productive.

Evelyn loved him but inwardly longed for the attention Wesley garnered from their father. The pride and love she saw her father openly express regarding his son was something she aspired to as a child but eventually felt her efforts were fruitless.

"That's a pretty dress," her father said as she came downstairs one morning. "Is it new?"

My mother rolled her eyes. "I made it. I've been working on it all week. You took me to buy the zipper for it." Then she sighed. She felt he never paid attention to anything she did, especially her sewing.

She had become so proficient at it that girls at school and women in their church asked for similar pieces that Evelyn had made and worn. They even paid her, although the money was never her incentive. Having them admire her creations and seeing her handiwork worn by others was what she desired.

"I asked her to make my shirt for the state finals," Wesley piped up.

She scoffed. "And have it drug through the dirt?"

Wesley was a rodeo star. He'd been winning belt buckles and trophies since he was young and now was a stand-out in the high school circuit.

"That's only if I get bucked off," he said, grinning. "Besides, a little dirt won't hurt it, and imagine all the people that will see it."

He was right. Of course, he was. Thousands flocked to the grandstands to watch the competitions, and the attire the competitors wore was as much their calling card as their performance. Evelyn wanted the opportunity to have her work spotlighted. She knew the attention it would bring, but she had no desire to let her brother know that.

"I'll make it if I have time. I'm still working on other things. Mrs.

Sherman asked me to make her dress for her son's wedding," she said dismissively.

"Family comes first," her father piped up. "Your brother's shirt for the state finals should be the priority."

Wesley looked at her, both surprised and apologetic. "I was just teasing you, Evie. If you don't have time, that's okay."

"Family comes first," her father repeated.

She huffed, the jealous anger roiling. "You mean Wesley comes first," she spat and then turned on her heel. She was now irritated with herself as well. The last thing she wanted was for them to know she felt slighted and worse—that she cared.

Whether it was real or not, her perception of that time in her life was that her father favored Wesley, and she was overlooked. He wasn't interested in her life. She didn't work the cattle or help to irrigate the fields. She was adept at cooking and other activities that women and girls did but felt he saw no value in, so her resentment grew.

What I see now are two people who were unable to see how much they needed the other because their similarities got in the way. My mother and grandfather are both stubborn and proud. It's a shield to deflect what could cause them pain.

I watch them both needing the other but allowing their stubborn pride to keep them apart. My death drove the divide even deeper.

My own father tried to reason with Mom regarding her anger toward her father. "Blaming him isn't going to change what happened," my father pleaded, seeing her festering condemnation.

Evelyn ignored what he said. She felt she had lost everything, and if she gave in, who could she blame besides herself?

As she rubbed the stubs of her fingers, the pain of her past came to the surface, and the face of the mother she barely remembered filled her mind and had her convinced that earliest of losses was somehow connected to my own.

The loss of her mother and now her son, even in the dry heat of summer, had her feeling the chill of that night from long ago.

Chapter 7

Landis

The back porch of the house spreads out to a grassy and groomed yard with a short stone wall surrounding it. The barn sits to the left, and a large gravel and dirt pad leads to it from the back of the house. It is just like the barns I've seen in pictures. It's bright red with a tall pitched roof and a pointed overhang, and the wooden slide doors have a white "X" on each.

A corral stretches out from behind the barn, and even more, fences made of wood and wire encircle the vast fields. I can see cows and horses out in the distance. Their heads hang as they graze. From here, they look smaller than what I had imagined. I wonder if they'll be friendly or if I'll be able to touch them.

Some chickens peck at the ground, and there are two old trucks and a green tractor parked to the side of a smaller shed.

This is a real farm with actual crops and barnyard creatures. With my mother's talk of a lavender farm, I wonder if she had something to do with my placement here. Is this where I'll learn how to care for the flowers that will be my future life? It feels like a stretch, but nothing since I've arrived at this place has felt anything but strange.

I breathe in the air and take a step off the porch. To the right of the house are wide, open fields except for a tall, thick willow tree alone in the foreground. A tire swing hangs from one of its limbs, and wooden blocks are nailed to the trunk, inviting me to climb into the spread of branches. If there are no other boys here, why would they have this? I can't imagine Mrs. Frost out here swinging and climbing.

I walk to the tree, and from the looks of the tire and the weathering of the planks, I see that this isn't something that was done recently. Others have obviously played here before, but where are they now?

I'm under the umbrella of leaves and branches, and I feel the breeze again, yet the tree and everything else are still. There is no rustle of leaves or other evidence of wind. That wisp of cool keeps following me. It's strange and unnerving being alone out here with nothing but this silent whisper. Its subtle nudging annoys me, and I turn my attention back to the tree. I give the tire a push, and as the rope attached to it creaks and complains, I feel a presence. My eyes take a quick sweep back at the house, expecting to see someone, but there is nothing. I look out over the fields and pastures and see only the uninterested cattle and horses. It's so void of the crowds and noise I'm used to. Even with the sun bright in the cloudless sky, the silence and space intensify the chill that surrounds me.

I look up into the tree and take hold of one of the weathered wooden blocks. I put some weight on it to see if it moves or if it's still solid enough to hold me. It must have been sturdy enough to hold someone at one time.

The block is firm, and I gingerly step and reach for the next one. I check it before I continue, and soon, I'm up to where the canopy begins to spread. The higher I get, the stronger the breeze becomes, as though trying to dissuade my climb. I reach over and cling onto an outstretched limb and then pull myself up so that I can swing a leg over. As I do, I see how high up I am and have to grip the branch to keep from swaying from this dizzying height.

As I'm clinging onto the tree like a giant, leggy, praying mantis, I see something carved into the bark. Someone else has been up here, high up in this tree. I right myself and sit solidly on the large branch, but my heart is still racing, and I'm wondering why I decided to do this. Hidden in the cover of new budding leaves, I feel an odd sense of accomplishment that quickly turns to embarrassment. Who climbs trees when they're almost sixteen? And yet, I am somewhat proud of myself.

I take a deep breath and face the trunk. The carvings on the tree are letters that scar the bark. "B" and "F" and the year that whoever has those initials sat where I'm sitting now. 1979. Five years ago.

I trace the letters with my finger. B. F. Who could that be? Possibly one of the Frosts, but neither of these temporary parents has a first name that begins with a B. The breeze that lingers turns ice cold. It's such a change that I shiver as I wonder who else was here and where they are now.

I turn my body carefully and adjust so I can look out over the expansive pastures and fields. How did I end up at this strange place so far away from where I'm from? There is no sign of other kids, so why bring me here? What could they possibly want with me? Nothing makes sense. I take a deep breath and settle with the thoughts I often have—what does it matter? I just have to get through the next few months. It's such a short amount of time, and yet, because I'm at the end of this long and exhausting pursuit, the wait feels like a standstill.

My mind wanders back to the boys at the place I just left and what they'd think if they saw where I'm living now. This castle-like house, with my own room, a farm with animals, and those woods. The lure of that thick, dark grove of trees is so strong that I find myself lost in thought about what could be in there.

I know there's a river back there, but also something else. Something that has Mrs. Frost on edge. But is it a real concern or a futile fear? In just this short amount of time, I can see that she seems to worry about everything. I wonder if it's her usual demeanor or because I'm now here.

The new parents in the other homes are normally unaffected by my arrival. After the first meeting, I usually fade into the routine and am rarely noticed until something goes wrong. Something always goes wrong. It's either a fight, someone is caught stealing, or they get caught with booze or pot. I've never done any of those things, but I'm part of the group, and after denying things for years, I finally gave up and realized it didn't matter. I got moved again, and until this last year, I didn't care. The only reason I do now is because my mom will soon be coming to get me. If I'm caught and sent to the juvenile jail,

I'll be serving time just like her, and I can't risk not being able to go with her and finally be back to normal again.

Maybe now, without other boys to stir things up, I'll have a chance that they'll let me stay until the last day of my sentence.

But then I realize it may be even worse. If I'm the only one here, I'll have a much harder time staying under Mrs. Frost's radar as I wait things out.

I can't do anything that could cause issues or even bring attention to myself, which is why I need to do what she says and stay away from the woods.

I study the elusive mass of brush and trees from my vantage point, hidden in the fluttering green of new buds. It's as though the woods call to me. Funny how when something seems out of reach, it becomes the thing you want most. Like being with my mom.

Just a few more months. I tap the treasure and find it secure in the tiny front pocket of my jeans. I'm still surprised and relieved that it wasn't discovered during this last run-in with trouble. What drove me to move it from my pocket into my underwear is still a mystery, but I'm so glad I listened to that voice in my head. Being accused of taking that money had me at that home for boys, and the first thing they did when I arrived was take my clothes—my shirt, pants, even my socks. But my underwear was allowed to stay, and with it, my treasure.

I huff at my good luck. It's something I rarely experience, but I've been afforded a few good breaks in life, and that was the biggest one yet.

A loud clang, clang, clang echoes from the house. I envision a large bell being rung to announce that dinner is ready. It's like the old Western shows I've watched, and I wonder if I've been taken back in time as well.

Clang, clang, clang, the bell rings out again, this time with more urgency. Is the ringing for me? I take a deep breath, not wanting to leave this hidden perch, but decide I should see if I'm being summoned.

Gingerly, I transfer my body from sitting to lying over the large branch as my foot searches for the wooden block below. When they meet, I push myself carefully off and scale down, block by block, and finally to the base of the massive tree. I feel my breath release when I reach the ground, soft but solid. When I come around to the back of the house, Mrs. Frost is standing on the porch, peering out over the fields. She looks frantic. She reaches for the rope connected to the bell, ready to make it call out again, but then she sees me. She gasps, but then her face softens, and she forces a smile.

"Where did you go?" she asks, trying not to sound upset.

I begin to speak, but for some reason, I hesitate to tell her about the tree. "Just looking around," I say.

She doesn't say anything, but I hear the relief as she exhales and directs me into the house.

———

THE TALL GRANDFATHER CLOCK CLICKS, its long arm swinging, as I sit alone at a table set for three. I've always been one of many and longed for the solitude of when it would be just us two, but now it has me wishing I had others to take the attention away from me.

I hear plates clattering in the kitchen. Two large swinging doors separate me from the noises of cooking. They are like saloon doors but bigger, with a dark lacquered finish.

I asked if Mrs. Frost needed help—it's usually expected of me at the homes, but instead, she shuffled me to the table.

"Gordon will be here soon," she said and then told me to sit and relax.

That's a joke. I haven't felt my shoulders settle from their tense scrunch since I arrived.

My stomach rumbles, but my appetite has left as I think about having to sit at the table with two strangers. I've done it so many times before, but there are usually so many other kids I never felt the pressure I'm feeling now.

If I'd known I'd be staying in a house like this with its grand ceilings and posh furniture, I wouldn't have believed it, and yet now I'm sitting here wishing I was somewhere else.

The crowded spaces and constant battles for privacy at the other homes I've lived in are annoying but inescapable. It's why I've slid into my own world, relieving me of being the focus of anything. I don't need or want attention. I have too much to hide. That may be why I can sense that Mrs. Frost is hiding something as well.

When she walks through the swinging door of the kitchen, she's carrying a platter. I see meat, potatoes, and carrots covered in gravy. Steam rises and drifts up in soft swirls, and my hunger returns with a vengeance.

Setting it in the middle of the table, she places a large serving spoon in front of me.

"Mr. Frost will be here soon," she says, and then she leaves, and I wonder if that means I'm supposed to wait for him or start eating. Before I can decide, I hear the front door open and voices in the foyer. I turn in my chair as two men come into the large living room. One is young and thin, with a short beard and tan cowboy hat. He follows the other man, who is taller and older, with a dark hat that he removes and hangs on a hook on the wall. The younger man notices me at the table.

"Oh, hey," he says, not expecting to see some strange boy in the house.

This makes the older man turn.

Suddenly, I feel awkward sitting at the table as though someone is supposed to wait on me. I push back the chair and stand up.

"Hey," I answer back, then I suck on my teeth, unsure what to say next. I'm relieved when Mrs. Frost appears at my side.

"Hi, Jesse. This is Landis," she says quickly. "Landis is ..." she stumbles on what to say next. I look at the ground, feeling her pain in trying to explain my pathetic place in this world. "He's living here with us," she blurts out.

Jesse lifts his eyebrows, confused.

She nods confidently as though that is exactly what she meant to say. "So, you'll probably be seeing Landis around here quite a bit," she continues. "He'll be living here."

It's as though she's still trying to accept it herself. I wish she'd stop. It's getting more awkward with every word.

I'm used to this painful dance of how to explain who I am and why I'm living in their home, but I understand why they do it. How would people react if simply told the truth? "This is Landis. His mom is in prison, and his dad is dead, so we're getting paid to let him live under our roof." Obviously, the truth would be far worse, so instead, they side-step around in an attempt to hide my shame.

Some foster parents go so far as to refer to me as their child; some even tell me to call them Mom and Dad. This never works because I refuse to do that. They're not my parents, and I'm not their son. They all eventually look at me as someone taking up space in the house, and I do my best to fade into the background like old, dull wallpaper.

Jesse smiles and walks to us. "Landis, it's nice to meet you." He puts his hand out, and I shake it. His grip is firm, and his hands are like leather.

"Landis, this is Gordon," says Mrs. Frost.

He nods but is silent as he studies me.

"Hello, Mr. Frost," I say.

He looks at Mrs. Frost and then back at me. "Welcome. And my father was Mr. Frost. My name is Gordon."

"Yes, sir."

He cocks his head, and I immediately correct myself. "I mean Gordon."

He gives me a nod and a half smile.

Jesse starts to stir.

Mr. Frost gives a tiny grunt. "I'll get the keys," he tells Jesse and goes toward a hallway on the opposite side of the house. I watch and wonder if that area is off-limits as well.

"Would you like to stay for dinner?" Mrs. Frost asks Jesse.

He shakes his head. "No, thank you. It sure smells good, but I just came to get the keys for the shop so I can get to the tractor while Gordon is gone."

Mr. Frost comes back into the room with a set of keys in one hand and a newspaper in the other.

"You're leaving?" Mrs. Frost asks him.

I'm still standing, looking from face to face, unsure what to do or how to act.

Mr. Frost takes a deep breath. "I told you I need to take those heifers down south."

"When are you going?" she asks.

"Tomorrow morning."

"But what about Landis?" she says, disappointed. "He just got here."

He smiles. "He'll be here when I get back, or he's welcome to come along," he chuckles jokingly.

She huffs, unamused. "You know he can't do that. He has school."

School? I look at her, surprised. There can't be more than a week or two left until summer break. I've rarely finished an entire school year, so why would I need to go to some strange school for just a few weeks? Besides, why do I matter in all this? Just let me exist here for a few months, and then I'll be gone.

He scoffs at her. It's obvious he's an ignorer and will simply put up with me until I'm gone. And while I hope he's not upset that I'm here, I'd be more than happy to be shelved and out of the way for the next few months. They can collect their checks as I wait for my mother to return.

I glance up, and Mr. Frost cocks his head at me. The blood has rushed up into my face, and I wish I could wiggle my nose like in Bewitched and disappear.

"Your being here is good timing," he says.

It is? When has my arrival ever been good?

"Jesse needs to turn over the fields in Mooreland, so I'm sure Landis won't mind helping out with some of the chores around here while I'm gone."

Mrs. Frost huffs. "He just got here. He doesn't need to be given a list of chores," she snaps.

I look back and forth between the two, and even Jesse shuffles uncomfortably.

"I don't mind," I say, hoping to end this. I'd much rather be doing something than sitting around with the silent echoes of this house.

"Can you pitch hay?" Mr. Frost asks, ignoring his wife's scorn.

Pitch hay? I raise my shoulders, unsure of what he means.

"I can show him," says Jesse.

My breath releases with appreciation.

"Then it's all figured out." Mr. Frost says.

Mrs. Frost scrunches her lips and raises one eyebrow.

Mr. Frost hands Jesse the keys, and they walk away toward the front door.

"I'll come by and show you what to do tomorrow afternoon," Jesse calls back to me and waves as he leaves. I wish he were staying. Everything feels cold in this house, and he was a fleeting bright spot. I shiver and continue to stand there, waiting for a cue as to my next move.

I hear Mrs. Frost sigh as she stands next to me. It's clear all of this is a burden to her. I'm just surprised she didn't fake it for the first week or so like the others. Again, I wonder why I'm here alone. There are usually at least four or five other boys. I never thought I'd miss the crush and chaos of others.

When Mr. Frost walks back to us, Mrs. Frost stays quiet but stares at him.

"Let's eat before it gets cold," he says, dismissing her irritation and motioning toward the table. He gives me a smile. "I'm surprised Landis hasn't already eaten the entire platter."

I try to smile back but worry it will look like I'm siding with him. I feel like a mouse caught between a cat and a trap.

I'm still standing, and he tips his head as though telling me to take a seat. I wait until he pulls out a chair for himself. I've learned that the foster fathers always have a specific seat at the table, and the foster mothers are usually seated to their left. I've taken note of this over the years, and now that I'm older, I see how they react when I take the space that is theirs.

"It looks good, Evie," he says. "And smells even better." And that is when Mrs. Frost's shell seems to loosen a bit. She blinks and takes a breath as though coming back to life. She nods and then takes a seat.

I marvel at everything on the table. Not just the platter of meat but plates and bowls filled with rolls, a colorful salad, and two different kinds of jam. I've never seen anything like this, even on Thanksgiving.

Mr. Frost reaches with his large and rugged hands for the serving spoon and dishes up large chunks of meat onto his plate.

He then passes the platter to me, and I look at Mrs. Frost. I begin to hand it to her, but she puts a hand up, directing me to keep it.

"Do you like pot roast?" Mrs. Frost asks.

"Yes," I answer as I dive in, scooping up almost as much as Mr. Frost, and then pass the platter to her.

My mouth is watering just looking at the food. For the last few months, I've lived on hot dogs and jelly sandwiches. The people at the house before didn't cook unless it was frozen dinners. An actual meal with gravy and real meat and potatoes is something I haven't had—I have to stop and think about it—it's been that long. I've never gone hungry at any of the places I've lived, but the food has never been a high point. I'm not picky. There really isn't a food I don't like. I'll eat anything—except macaroni and cheese.

It doesn't happen often, but when that is what I'm offered, I always avoid it. It's the one thing I just can't eat. No matter how hungry I am, I'll go without rather than eat macaroni and cheese.

I've been called foolish, ungrateful, and rude when I've refused to eat it. I'm not picky. I like noodles, and I like cheese. But I just can't eat macaroni and cheese. I don't want them to know why I won't eat it. I've even lied and said I was allergic.

"No one is allergic to macaroni and cheese," one of the foster mothers snapped at me. And when I started to gag as I brought it to my mouth, she slapped it away and made me spend the rest of the night in the bedroom while the rest of them watched The Wonderful World of Disney.

When Mrs. Frost finishes serving herself, she sets the platter down, looks at me, and nods as a sign that I can start. Mr. Frost is already eating and reading the newspaper he brought to the table.

With every bite I take, I can feel her watching me. I feel like I'm on display.

The room is so quiet I can hear myself chew. Where is the television droning in the background, the chaos of rowdy kids, the noises of my usual life?

The flavors of this meal are amazing, and the meat is so tender it falls apart on my plate. I want to ask for seconds, and before I can, she's offering the platter to me again. I hesitate and look at Mr. Frost as though I may be taking what is his.

He feels my gaze, looks up from his paper, and squints at me. "You don't need my permission," he smirks.

I feel I do, but my hunger removes that, and I dig in again.

He watches and then grins. "I forgot how much boys your age can eat," he says.

I look up and smile back, beginning to relax, and then I hear Mrs. Frost let out a tiny gasp, and his smile vanishes.

I turn to her as her face fades into one of despair. The air in the room goes still, and I stop mid-chew. What just happened?

I swallow hard, the food sticking in my throat. "It's delicious," I say to her. It sounds like a plea—an apology.

Mrs. Frost bites her top lip, trying to regain her composure.

Mr. Frost shakes the newspaper to straighten it, and I jump. He sighs and goes back to reading.

The harsh silence is like a sheet of ice, and I feel I need to break it. "Thank you for the meal," I blurt out.

She looks at me, confused. She nods. "Of course." She reaches for the platter. "Would you like some more?" she asks.

"No," I blurt, then quickly say. "I mean, no, thank you." Inside, I groan. I sound like a beaten puppy—pathetic and shaken. I'm trying too hard. I should have just stayed quiet. Where are the other kids who annoy, badger, and distract away the attention?

"Are you finished?" she asks.

I nod, and she stands and starts taking dishes from the table. I stand and begin to help her.

"That's very nice, but you don't need to do this," she says. "You can go watch TV or get things ready for school tomorrow."

"School?" I ask. It's the end of May. I thought the school year had already ended while I was stuck in that place that I didn't deserve to be.

"Yes. I know it's less than a month until summer break," she says. "But you should at least get started, and maybe you can meet some of the other kids."

My head is spinning with the idea of starting at yet another new school for just a couple of weeks. I won't be at this house next year. I won't even be in this state in a few months.

"The bus will pick you up right at the end of our lane. It will be here at 7:15. Unless you want me to drive you?" she asks.

"Drive him?" Mr. Frost huffs. "He doesn't need you driving him to school. It's hard enough being the new kid, right?" he says to me with a grin.

I shrug, trying to seem okay with it all but she must see my unease.

"I already have your class schedule," she says. "And I bought some school supplies if you need them."

"That's okay, I have stuff," I say, but all I have is a thin notebook and two pencils. I begin to regret not at least seeing what she was offering. Now I start to panic about yet another first day of a new school.

I excuse myself and go to my room. Rummaging through my bag of clothes, I hope to find something that doesn't smell or is too small. Even being as short as I am, I've still grown out of almost everything I own. Being short helps to keep me from standing out, so I don't need anything that would draw attention. I just need to stay under the radar. I will show up and do whatever I need to do as I wait until I'm finally back with my mom.

I pull out my other pair of jeans and a faded green t-shirt, lay them on the bed, and then try to smooth out the rumples. My socks are mismatched, but at least they have no holes, and no one should see them anyway. It should work. It should all work.

The book I didn't have time to return is what gives the bag its weight, and that is also why I keep this small bunch of worthless items close. It's yet another thing I would be accused of stealing. I carry this along with another hidden item, knowing it would destroy everything if I lost it or if it were found.

I take a breath and then pull the precious treasure from the front pocket of my pants. I've carried it for years. I rub the small silk pouch and feel for the hard circle and large stone inside. It's traveled with me all this time. I was so young when it was placed in my care, and I've been relentless in keeping it hidden and safe. I'm never without it. It's in my pocket, or my underwear, or on the side of the bathtub, never out of reach. It is the one thing that someday will allow us to breathe. I didn't steal it. It was entrusted to me, and someday, it will be used to save us.

I put it back in my pocket and look at the TV, hoping to distract myself from new-school jitters by finding a show to watch. It's Wednesday, which means Little House on the Prairie will be on. Being here so far out in the middle of these fields, I feel like I'm living in a time warp back to those days of living on the wide open plains.

I walk to where the television sits on the top of the large dresser. One that I won't need. My entire wardrobe won't fill even a quarter of one of its drawers.

As I pass the large window, I notice something far out in the distance. It's already dark outside, and I can see a flicker of light back in the trees—moving.

It isn't the headlights of a car but a single beam dancing and bouncing off the trees way out in the vast, dense woods. I watch it and try to figure out who or what is back there and why. It is so dark. There are no street lights. I can't imagine anyone just walking around alone in those trees.

As I watch, I'm convinced it's a flashlight and that someone is searching in those dark woods. But for what?

I feel a presence behind me, and I turn to find Mrs. Frost. I startle, and she cocks her head in question.

"What are you looking at?" she asks, coming to my side.

"I saw something," I say, still shaken. I feel like I've been caught doing something I shouldn't.

She peers out into the night. "What did you see?"

"I think someone's back there in the trees," I say, pointing out toward the woods.

For a moment, she studies the darkness, but the light is now gone.

"I saw a light," I say defensively, feeling like she thinks I'm lying.

She reaches up, pulls the cord, and shuts the blinds with a clap. Her face turns cold, and she takes a deep breath and stares at me. It makes me take a step back.

"I don't want you back there. Do you hear?" She looks upset and urgent.

What have I done? I feel like I'm already on her bad side, and it's only the first day.

"Okay," I say to appease her, but I'm perplexed and becoming annoyed. What is it with all these forbidden places? I'm not a child, and I'm not her child. Don't go in this room. Don't go out back. I hadn't even thought about exploring this place, but I flinch at her harshness. "Why?" I ask. "What's back there?"

"It's not safe. You don't know what might happen back there."

"Like what?" I ask.

"You don't need to worry about it," she snaps.

"I'm not worried," I say with a shrug. "It's not like I'm going to get lost or something."

As soon as I say it, I regret it because her face goes from firm to broken.

I sigh. My questions and talking have caused trouble in the past.

"Zip it, Landis, or I'll stitch your mouth shut," the father at house number five told me. I was ten and saw how he was with the other boys. I had no doubt he'd actually sew my mouth closed. And he wasn't the only one who became bothered by my questions. The mother at house number three made me sit facing a corner for over an hour when all I wanted to know was if we were having cereal for dinner again.

It's why I keep to myself and just bide my time. It took several houses before I learned that staying out of the way and under the radar was always the best plan. I don't need to know these people or about these different places. What does it matter? I'm eventually moving on to the next house. Soon, the only questions I asked were to my caseworker about when my mother would be coming to get me. I'm determined that this house will be my last.

I want to apologize, but wait for her to scold me for talking back. I'm not trying to be a smart-ass, but it sounded that way. After so many moves, my patience is running thin. Just stay the course, Landis, and get through these next few months.

The breeze that has followed me comes through the room and snakes through and around us. Mrs. Frost's cold stare, like a dark cloud, drifts away. I watch this strange transformation as I wait for her to lay into me. Instead, she stands for a moment in silence, and then, with confused blinking, she swallows and looks at the clothes I've laid out on the bed.

"Is this what you're wearing to school tomorrow?" she asks. She tries to hide her repulsion, but I see through it. She tries to smile.

"Well, it looks like you're ready for school. Is there anything you need before bed?" she asks.

I shake my head.

"The bus comes at 7:15. There's an alarm clock on your night-stand, or I can wake you up?" she asks.

"No. I'll be ready."

And with that, she nods again and leaves me alone in my room.

That night, as I lay in bed, I hear what sounds like footsteps. The noise is coming from the room next to mine—the "off-limits" area. The padding is rhythmic pacing.

I feel tempted to get up and see, but the urgent warnings of Mrs. Frost to stay away from that room fill me, so I stay still and listen.

I'm in a clean, warm bed in my own room. I've had one of the best meals I've ever eaten. This house is, without a doubt, the largest and nicest home I have ever stayed in, but as I lay here, instead of feeling fortunate to be in this place, I feel an ominous sense of dread.

CHAPTER 8

It's still dark. Only the faint, hazy glow of the moon seeps into my room, but I hear the sound of an engine outside. I go to the window and lift one of the slats of the wooden blinds, and in the gleam of a dim bulb at the top of a tall pole, I see Mr. Frost walking from the barn to a running truck. Attached to the back is a long metal trailer that I assume is filled with cows. I wonder how long he'll be gone. He said he was leaving, but why in the middle of the night?

I look back at the alarm clock on my nightstand and realize it's five-thirty in the morning. Is that when you wake up on a farm? Is this when I'm supposed to get up and start pitching hay?

I take a deep breath as I remember my night of fitful sleep and the dread of what I learned about my new home and parents.

Last night, I heard the two of them talking. They thought I was asleep, but I had sneaked out of the room into the hallway. They were at the kitchen table, and their voices were just above a whisper. I could tell they didn't want to be heard, so I assumed they were talking about me. I stood as close to the corner of the wall as I could to hear them, and now I know there is something strange going on that they're trying to hide from me.

"It's him. I know it. Just look at him," she said in an urgent whisper.

"You don't know that," Mr. Frost argued. "You said he was fifteen. He looks barely twelve."

Twelve? I thought. I'm always mistaken for younger. I'm short and my face barely has a wisp of fuzz, but twelve? No wonder they treat me like a child.

"I saw his records. His birth date," she countered.

"You still need to wait and see," said Mr. Frost.

I took a step closer to the corner of the wall, straining to listen.

"He's going to find out," she tried to appeal.

Mr. Frost hushed her. "Not if it isn't true."

Find out what? I wanted to yell it out. Why so many secrets?

"The kids at school are going to be curious. They'll ask who he is."

Mr. Frost huffed. "He'll tell them he's from Sacramento and staying with us. He doesn't know any more than that, and he doesn't need to. The only other choice you have is to keep him locked in this house. We need to make things as normal as possible. It will be fine."

There was a long pause, and I held my breath, hoping they hadn't heard me as I eavesdropped at the top of the stairs.

"What about what happened in the hollow? He keeps asking about the woods," she said in a soft whisper. "I told him he wasn't to go near there."

I leaned back, worried they suspected I was listening, but I strained, trying to hear more. Something happened back in those woods. My mind raced with what it might be.

"Eventually, he'll know," said Mr. Frost. "If he's staying and if he's blood, he'll have to know."

Blood? Did I hear that correctly? I gasped. Who are these people, and why are they trying to cover up something terrible? My mind raced with what it could be. And what did it have to do with my blood?

"Just be patient," Mr. Frost said.

"I know," she agreed. And then her voice became muffled, but I thought I heard the word September.

September? My stomach clenched. My mom is scheduled to be released in September. Is that what they're referring to? And what could that possibly have to do with the strange happenings at this place?

Then, my fears about blood and whatever happened in those woods turned to the thing I fear the most—she did something yet again, and now her release date will be pushed back. It's happened so many times before. Somehow it always gets screwed up. Why did I think this might be different? I refused to completely give up until I was able to talk to Mrs. Blaire. She had been my caseworker for several years, and I wished that hadn't changed. She would know what was going on with my mom. And I needed to tell her who these people are and what I've heard. I've been in strange and uncomfortable places before, but what I heard was terrible. Then I wondered if Mrs. Blaire would even believe me or even care. Did she even know where I am? She wasn't the one who brought me here. It was some woman named Marna or Marge. I can't even remember her name. And what if I did tell them, then what? Would they move me again? I feel that every time I get removed and placed somewhere else, it makes it that much more of a risk that I'll get lost in the shuffle, and it'll be harder for my mom to find me.

I instinctively dove my hand into my front pocket to feel for the hard circle that will save my life. The solid weight was there. I ran my fingers over the large stone, and it calmed me.

I then heard what I thought were whimpers. I peered around the corner to see Mrs. Frost with her face in her hands.

"It's like I actually have a part of him," she cried softly.

It was all so strange and confusing. I felt they were talking about me, but none of it made sense. And yet what surprised me most was when Mr. Frost placed an arm around her shoulders to comfort her.

His gruff indifference at dinner, made his tenderness with her at that moment seem out of character. However, nothing about this place seems anything but strange.

Now, I stand at my upstairs window, looking down at Mr. Frost. His breath rises up into the dark morning air. His gruffness seems to have returned. He shoos the chickens aside as I see another truck pull up. It's Jesse. They talk for a moment, and Mr. Frost motions to different places around the property as if giving him instructions. I wonder if I should go out and begin the chores he spoke of. He then points out toward the woods, and for a moment, they talk, both looking out into the vast dark field that leads to the trees. I lean closer to the window, wishing it was open so I could hear what they are saying. Then, both men turn toward the house, and Mr. Frost looks up toward my room. I step back away from the window, hoping he hasn't seen me in the dark. My mind returns to Mrs. Frost's dire warnings about those woods and last night's talk of my blood and whatever happened back there.

Again, I peek through the blinds. The truck's exhaust is heavy in the cold air, and I shiver at the thought of having to be out in it without a coat. I decide to wait until later to ask about what I am expected to do.

Mr. Frost has climbed into the truck, and he slowly pulls the trailer around a dirt path that loops back. Then, the truck and massive trailer chug off down the road.

Jesse is now carrying two large buckets and walking toward the barn and corral. I watch, wondering again if I should go out and help.

The morning sky begins to brighten, and my dread of the first day of school returns. I decide to take a shower and get ready for what lies ahead.

As I STAND under the steaming spray of water, my mind flips from the woods in the back of the house to worries about starting yet another new school.

I'll be relieved when I can be back with my mother and stop this continual migration. I think it's futile to start yet another new school, especially since I won't be here when the next school year begins. Just bide my time.

I wonder what classes I've been assigned when I'll be there less than a month. This is really just an attempt to get me out of the way. What's a couple of weeks of school really going to teach me? I shrug. It's not like my grades have ever really mattered before. Even though I have never earned less than a B, my records never seem to make it to the next school I attend, so the teachers all assume I'm behind.

I sigh and take in a deep breath of the hot, humid mist that surrounds me. There are two bottles on a shelf in the shower. One is shampoo, the other conditioner, and there's an unopened bar of soap. A clean, dry towel hangs on a bar within reach of the shower.

My own soap. My own towel. It's then I realize no one is banging on the door telling me to hurry and not hog all the hot water. Part of me wants to stay there for hours; the other part still feels odd about enjoying this luxury. But because I'm always on borrowed time at these homes, I don't take any chances of upsetting the Frosts and leave the warmth of the shower to start my first day at school number twelve.

I'm dressed and listening at my open bedroom door. When I can hear movement downstairs, I find my notebook, put the pencils in my back pocket, and leave the room. I go to the stairs but can't help but linger at the door that she was so adamant I stay away from. It looks like it's just another bedroom. What could be inside there that has her determined to keep me away? Blood. What happened back there? I can't shake the Frost's hushed discussion from my head.

When I reach the dining room, the clock above the table says 6:30 am. I stand wondering what to do. I can hear her in the kitchen. A half-empty cup of coffee and a small plate with crumbs sits on the table. I was hoping to have breakfast, but I may have to wait until lunch at school. At the other homes I've been to, there is usually a pile of kids already fighting over boxes of brightly colored cereal, making it easy for me to blend in and follow their lead.

Mrs. Frost comes through the swinging doors of the kitchen, and when she sees me, she startles, but then she rights herself and smiles. It isn't beaming, but it's real, and it may be the first time I've seen her do this.

"Good morning, Landis." She's sincere, but her voice is soft. "How did you sleep?" she asks.

"Good," I answer. It's a lie, but I'm certainly not going to tell her about the strange noises coming from the "off-limits" area that kept me awake most of the night.

She looks at my clothes and then tries not to look.

What I thought would keep me from standing out has obviously drawn her attention, and I sigh inside.

"I'll get your breakfast," she says quickly, trying to distract both of us from my worn and wrinkled clothes.

She's already pulling out a chair for me. "Would you like pancakes or waffles?"

The look on my face has her flustered. I'm used to cold cereal, and I'm used to getting it myself.

"Or eggs?" she asks.

I'm flustered by the attention and respond to keep her from offering anything else. "Waffles are good."

Mrs. Frost nods.

"You don't have to do that," I say as she begins to walk off.

She turns back, forehead scrunched. "And have you not eat breakfast?" she asks stunned.

I shrug. I'm used to waiting for lunch in the cafeteria. In fact, unlike many of the kids at school, I enjoy it. I never let them know and have even chimed in when they complained, calling the food gross or disgusting. I never want them to know that what they scoff at is not only the best meal I have that day but often the only one.

"Sit," she orders, but her voice seems almost playful. "You have plenty of time to eat. You have over half an hour before the bus arrives."

She leaves, and I sink slowly into the seat, feeling awkward at being waited on but also looking forward to tasting what is creating the heavenly scent that already fills the room.

I hear the noises of the kitchen, and within minutes, she is back with a plate stacked with two golden waffles and another smaller plate with a heap of scrambled eggs.

"I wasn't sure what you like to eat," she explains. "So I made both. Only eat what you want."

She sets everything in front of me and then goes back to the kitchen and retrieves butter and syrup. She places them on the table and then sits in the chair across from me with her coffee.

Just like that first dinner, this meal is delicious. And just like before, I find her watching me. She tries not to be obvious by asking me questions—what's my favorite food, color, or TV show? I answer as best I can, but it's like she's looking for something in my answers.

She seems lighter than yesterday, not as tense, but I feel her stare with every bite. When I'm finished, she checks the clock. "It's almost time for the bus." Then she looks at my lone notebook. "Do you have a backpack?"

I shake my head. "No. I'm good."

"Are you sure?"

I nod. Then she looks at my T-shirt. "Don't forget your coat. It may be spring, but it's still freezing in the morning here."

I look down, unsure how to tell her I don't have that staple of clothing. But then she can read the predicament in my face.

"Do you have a coat?" she asks carefully.

"I left it at the last place," I lie. "But I'll be fine."

She stands straighter, cocks her head, and takes a deep, decisive breath. "Wait here. I think I have something." She goes to the kitchen. The swinging doors rock back and forth as she enters, and before they stop their rocking, she is back through them with a set of keys in hand. She lifts her eyebrows at me before going up the stairs towards my bedroom. I watch, wondering what she is doing that would need a key, but she disappears from view.

I hear the keys rattle and a door open. It has to be that door—the one she's forbidden me to enter. It's the only one that would be locked.

I try to sneak a glance, but the hallway is dark and too high for me to see.

I hear the door close and the sound of the keys again, and soon she is back downstairs. In her arms is a black letterman's jacket with thin purple stripes down the arms. She is holding it to her chest as though it's alive. She pauses and then hands it to me. "It should fit you," she says, holding it up.

I hesitate. "It's okay. I don't want to take his coat." I'm assuming it's Mr. Frost's. There is no one else at this house and certainly no one else this size.

Her face freezes for a moment, but then she lets out a breath. "It's not Gordon's." Then she hesitates, searching for words. "Please take it. You'll need it in this weather."

An odd tingle goes through me, wondering whose coat I'm being offered, but I don't want to look ungrateful. I put it on. I feel awkward and want to protest, but why would I? It's not only warm but covers up my tattered shirt.

I thank her, and she smiles.

I glance at the sleeves. Purple? It isn't my color; however, I appreciate this coat far beyond these sleeves.

When she sees me in it, her thoughts seem far away. After a moment, she blinks several times and then looks at the clock. "It's 7:10. Are you ready?"

I nod, feeling anything but ready, and she walks me to the door.

"I wish you had more time to settle in, but it will be good for you to go see the school and the other kids."

Going to this new school is a fruitless effort, but I do as I'm told, not wanting to rock the boat.

"Here is the paper you'll need to get checked in. Make sure you go to the office when you get there so they can give you your classes. And ... Oh!" she gasps. "I almost forgot your lunch money." She scurries off to the kitchen and returns, holding her purse. She reaches in and hands me a dollar. I take it, surprised.

"But ..." I stumble with the words. I've never had to pay for lunch. I get a punch card that all the other foster kids get. The kids at school know what that card is, so I do my best to hide it. I've even gone without lunch if I think someone might notice and make a scene.

I look at the dollar in my hand and then carefully put it in the front pocket of my pants alongside my other treasure. I find comfort in knowing it's still there and safe.

"I should be here when you get home this afternoon. If not, I'll leave the back door unlocked," she says.

I nod, and as I walk off toward the road, I feel the warmth of the coat as it breaks the chill of the wind. I'm grateful for it, and yet, it feels foreign and stiff.

When I reach the end of the laneway, I see the big yellow bus rounding a curve and heading my way. My stomach twinges with the thought of being the new kid yet again. That never goes away, but instead of being at the stop waiting with other parentless kids, I stand here alone.

The gears of the bus let out a loud screech as it lumbers to a stop. I wait for the door to fold open, and I look up to see faces staring down at me from the bus's windows. With my head down, I climb the stairs and onto the bus. When I glance up to try and find an empty spot, the looks of those already seated are ones of shock. Their eyes are wide, and mouths agape. Have they never seen someone new? There's an empty seat near the front, and I quickly swing into it.

The bus pulls away, and I feel a dozen pairs of eyes boring a hole through the back of my head. This is going to be a long ride.

CHAPTER 9

I can hear them whispering behind me, and what they say is both odd and disturbing.

"That's the house." "He looks like him." "They still haven't found him."

I keep facing forward as the bus bumps along the uneven and pothole-covered road. I have no idea what they're talking about. Do I look like someone? And who is missing? I want to know, but have no desire to ask.

Their voices don't sound necessarily mean. Instead, they sound confused and curious, and yet, it still feels like I'm being accused of something.

I face forward. In the seat up and across from me is a tall guy with almost white blond hair and a girl with dark eyes and brown curls. He glared at me when I first got on and continues to take disturbed and confused glances back. It's probably for the same reason I'm hearing the weird talk behind me, but the girl sitting with him smiled, and now I'm wondering if she's his girlfriend, and that's why he's mad.

I stare out the window, watching field after field pass by as the coat I'm wearing begins to feel too warm and smothering. I keep it on because I'm hoping that if I stay still, I'll fade into the seat of the bus and be unnoticed.

The paper Mrs. Frost gave me to check in is crumpled in my fist. My hands are clenched, and my shoulders are stiff. It's only a few weeks. I just need to bide my time. It's what I tell myself. It's what I've been saying over and over for the last few months. It's finally coming to an end. I have a date. All I need to do now is stay out of trouble and bide my time.

When we arrive at the school, I'm surprised at its size. For miles, the bus drove through nothing but barren fields and farmland, and then, out of nowhere, appeared the sprawling high school. Other buses and numerous cars are filling the parking lot as we pull in.

As soon as the folding doors of the bus open, I stand and step outside, away from the stares and whispers. I walk toward the main doors of the building and see a large sign. It reads Snake River High School, and I realize why my jacket is purple and black. Those are the school's colors. Mrs. Frost must have really wanted me to fit in, giving me this coat. Good luck with that, I think. No jacket is going to keep me from being the outsider I've always been.

"Hey, who are you?" says a voice behind me.

I turn, and it's the guy who was sitting on the bus next to that girl with the curly hair.

I try to act indifferent. "What do you care?" I'm used to them trying to intimidate me for being the new kid. It doesn't help that I am short for my age. However, I'm numb to it anymore.

He flinches back, surprised. He's taller and older than I first thought, and I wonder if he's going to tell me to keep away from his girlfriend. It's happened before. They see me as the new guy coming in and making the moves on the girls. Although it's never happened like that, they make it clear I'm not welcome. Girls will be friendly when you're new, but the guys rarely are. I'm not trying to make friends. I quit trying years ago, especially since I don't know how long I'll be anywhere.

"Are you living at the Frost's?" he asks.

I stop and take a step back but then nod. "Yeah, what of it?" If I stand up to them, they usually back down and then ignore me.

"Nothing," he says, putting up his hands at my defensiveness. "I saw you get on the bus at their house."

"Yeah, I'm staying there."

He doesn't seem to be trying to rile me, and I back down, realizing the jitters of another first day are getting to me. I'm so used to covering up my weird and unstable life with bluster.

Then the girl approaches us, and I feel myself stand taller. She seems hesitant and stands close to him.

"Are you related to the Frosts?" she asks.

The guy waits for my answer. I don't want to admit my situation, so I nod and lie, "Yes. They're my aunt and uncle."

"They are?" he asks. "Are you from around here?"

"No. I'm from Sacramento."

I'm used to these questions and I do whatever it takes to keep my circumstances a secret. I've used the aunt and uncle lie many times. However, I worry that they know the Frosts and will find out about my lie.

He doesn't press me for more. My story seems to work. Both of them nod. The boy still looks at me oddly, taking particular interest in my jacket.

A loud alarm sounds, and he turns back toward the school.

"That's just the first bell," the boy says. He rubs his hands together. It's cold, but no one is wearing gloves. "We still have ten minutes. Do you know where to go?" he asks.

"Not really," I answer, surprised he is trying to help me. "I need to go to the office first."

He points toward the main doors. "Follow me. I'll take you there."

I'm surprised by his willingness to help me, and we all begin to walk toward the school.

"I'm Jeremy," he says as we're walking. "And this is my sister, Nicole."

Sister. I immediately brighten at this revelation. I smile widely at her and then cringe, hoping she hasn't noticed how obvious I am, as well as the enormous gap in my front teeth that I've become an expert at hiding. I then cover my right hand with my left. I've learned to be stealthy about a number of things in my life.

Some kids walk past us and give me odd looks. They then whisper and scurry off.

Jeremy gives a huff.

"What's their problem?" I ask.

He sighs. "They saw you get on the bus at the Frost's. It's just kind of weird."

Weird. It certainly has been for me, but how would they all know about my situation?

"Haven't they ever seen someone new?" I ask.

I'm used to being the new kid; however, this has been even stranger than I'm used to.

He ignores my question. "What grade are you in?" Jeremy asks.

I hesitate. I should be a junior. I'm almost sixteen, but since I've rarely completed an entire school year, I've been placed two grades below. Being short has been a blessing when it comes to this because I easily pass for much younger, so no one knows that I'm behind.

"Ninth," I say.

He nods, not giving it a second thought.

"Nicky's a freshman, too," he says.

I instinctively look to Nicole.

She looks skeptical but gives a small smile. I smile back, and inside, I hope I don't look like the goofy, grinning idiot that I feel.

"I'm a sophomore," says Jeremy. "So, I won't have any classes with you, but Nicole might." He then turns to Nicole, who lifts her eyebrows. He then turns back. "Maybe I'll see you around." He leaves us at the office entrance.

"Okay, thanks," I call after him, almost too appreciative. Then I turn to Nicole, who has stayed behind.

"How long are you staying with the Frosts?" she asks.

My mother is supposed to be released the first week of September, but I don't want anyone to know that, so I give her my usual lie.

"My parents are in the Army. They'll be done soon, and then we'll be moving to Washington."

"Your mom is in the army?" she asks.

I nod confidently. "She's a nurse. They need her on the front line."

Nicole's eyes go wide. "Wow, that's cool."

It's the response I want, and I scrunch my shoulder and nod like it's no big deal. It's not a complete lie. My dad was in the army when he died, and saying my mom is too at least gives her a good reason for not being with me.

Nicole holds out her hand, and I almost take it with mine. Then, I realize she's asking to see the paper in my hand.

"Is that your schedule?" she asks.

"No," I say, feeling like a klutz. "I still have to check in and get that."

"I was going to see if we had any classes together." She shrugs one shoulder, then the bell rings and her eyes go wide. "I guess I'm late. Maybe I'll see you around," she says and then gives a small wave as she walks off.

"Sounds good," I call to her. I sound way too excited.

I sigh and head into the office.

Behind a long counter, a woman is seated at a large desk and pecking away at a typewriter. She looks up, irritated. "That was the second bell. What do you need?"

"I'm new. I was told I need to check in."

She walks over, and I hand her the paper. She looks at it and then up at me. "Oh, yes," she says. Her demeanor immediately changes. She then reaches into a drawer and pulls out some papers. "Your aunt came in a couple of days ago and got everything arranged."

My aunt? How is she already aware of my lie? Before I can ask, she has come around the counter and hands me a small paper card. "This is your lunch ticket."

I guess I'm still part of the program. I debate if I should tell Mrs. Frost that I'm getting free lunch or keep her dollar. Don't chance it, I tell myself as I add the card to my pocket. A dollar isn't worth being moved again or, worse, sent back to that juvie jail. I'll return the money to her tonight.

The woman signs my schedule and hands it back to me, and then she looks at my jacket. "You're already wearing the school colors. That's nice." She then reaches out and pulls at something on my chest. I step back, wondering what she's doing.

"You have a loose string here, but it seems to be attached," she says. She then gives the area a pat. "It's not that noticeable."

I try to look down at what she sees, but she motions me to follow her. "Let me show you how the halls work." She then proceeds to explain the alphabetical hallways and how they coincide with the room numbers.

When we get to my first-period class, two men are standing outside talking.

"Mr. Davidson," the woman says, and the two pause. One of the men turns toward us.

She continues. "This is Landis. He's a new student in your homeroom."

He nods at me, says hello, and she hands the paper to him. He then motions to the door. "I'll be in shortly. Take any open seat."

"Thank you, Mr. Davidson," the woman says. "And welcome to Snake River High, Landis."

She heads back toward the office, and the teacher goes back to his discussion, so I open the door to the classroom.

The loud chatter goes silent as a sea of faces turns to me. I'm relieved to see an empty desk only a few steps away, and I quickly slide into it, but before my butt even hits the seat, I hear the same strange murmurs as I did on the bus.

"That's the one I was telling you about." "He even looks like him." "He lives at that house."

I give them a look, and they stop for a moment, but as soon as I turn back around, they begin again. I try my best to ignore them until the classroom door opens, and the teacher walks in. The class goes quiet.

He sees me and remembers he has a new student. This part I dread. I don't need to be introduced, and I certainly don't need to tell any of these people about myself. I sit cringing, praying he doesn't ask.

"I see you found a seat," he says to me. He then addresses the class. "This is ..." he looks at the paper he was handed. "Landis." My entire body tenses when I realize I may be listed as Landis Frost. I've already felt the shock and repulsion they have toward that name, and I exhale in relief that he simply leaves it at Landis. It's not like I'm attached to my last name, but at least it's mine.

Again, to my relief, the teacher goes to the chalkboard and begins his lesson. I'm off the hook with the painful introductions.

The following two classes are equally odd and disturbing, with the same whispered talk and comments about "that house" and "That Frost kid." I'm not their kid. Are they freaked out because the Frosts have no kids, and I'm living there? That seems like a stretch, but I'm disturbed by what could make them act this way. I'm used to the "new kid" stares, but this is more than that.

By the final class of the day, I'm exhausted. My mind churns with questions about the disconcerting attention I continue to receive.

I have my notebook, and I bury my attention in it, pretending to take notes. My time at this school is short, and the summer break starts in less than a month.

I'm not concerned with the lesson, and I wish I'd brought my book. I'm bored, so I begin to doodle and daydream about how life would finally be normal if I could just hang on for a few more months.

At first, I'm just doodling, but then I see that the shading and thick lines of my pencil swipes are actually the rows of tall, craggy brush out beyond the fields of the Frost's house. The view from the window of my temporary bedroom. Something happened out there, but what? The question repeats in my mind.

CHAPTER 10

I get through all my classes, and when the bell rings, I quickly make my way out to the bus. There are several that are parked and waiting.

I can't remember which one is mine, and I begin to panic, thinking that I'll end up on the wrong one and be bussed somewhere across town. I don't even know my new address or phone number. I would have no way to contact Mrs. Frost.

"Landis," someone calls from a distance.

I turn when I hear my name, and it's her. Nicole's standing by a bus and gives me a half-hearted wave to join her. I'm relieved and grateful, but I also feel like a helpless fool. I walk over, and she looks around, obviously aware of the stares I'm still garnering.

"You look lost. We're bus number five, and it always parks here," she says and steps into the open door.

I follow, and when she takes a seat, without thinking, I sit next to her. She looks at me with a face that says I shouldn't have, and I immediately apologize. I then begin to stand up and move.

"Sit down. It's fine," she says.

I do, and I feel even more like an idiot. I sit back, and as every person steps onto the bus, they stare at us, and I want to apologize to her again.

"Hey," Jeremy says when he gets on. He takes the seat behind us.

As others board the bus, I get the same stares and whispers. Nicole clears her throat and looks out the window. I know she's hating the attention. When are these people going to stop?

Jeremy leans forward. "So, is everyone still acting like you're a ghost?"

Nicole looks at Jeremy with horror.

"A ghost?" I ask.

He rolls his eyes. "Ignore them. They'll get over it."

"Over what? Did I do something?" I turn to Nicole.

She shakes her head, "No. They're just being stupid."

When I begin to ask her what she means, she sighs in frustration and looks out the window, obviously wanting my questions to end.

The bus lumbers forward, and I sit back. The school's parking lot disappears behind us, and soon, we're out, away from anything but pastures and fields.

I sit back, realizing the girl I was admiring on the ride to school this morning is now the one I'm sitting next to. A lot has happened today, but I smile to myself and want the ride on this bumpy, smelly bus to last for hours.

We drive for a distance, and then suddenly, Nicole sits up straight and looks out the window as we pass something on the road. She looks up at the bus driver and then turns to me. "Don't worry, I'll let him know," she says.

My face must show obvious confusion because she rolls her eyes. "He missed your stop. Now you'll have to ride the whole way until he can turn around."

I look out the window and then back to her. "Oh." That's all I can say. I have no idea what stop is mine. I guess I should be annoyed, but instead, I just shrug.

When the bus stops, three students file down the center and descend the stairs. As we wait, Nicole turns to me.

"Are you going to be at your aunt and uncle's place the whole summer?" she asks.

"Yes."

"What are you going to do?"

It's not something I've given much thought to. "I think I'll be helping out on the farm. They want me to shovel hay," I tell her, but it doesn't come out right. Was it a shovel or throw or something else? I can't remember, but when she lifted an eyebrow and smiled, I could tell I didn't say it right.

Her smile fades, and she cocks her head. "Do you go back to the woods?"

Her question surprises me, and I immediately shake my head. "No."

"You don't?" It isn't a question but more of a confirmation.

I shrug. Mrs. Frost has made it clear that I'm not to go back there, so Nicole asking about it strikes me odd. I wonder why she's curious about the place I've been told to avoid. "No. Why?" I ask.

She lifts a shoulder. "No reason. Just wondering. I wouldn't think you would."

Now I'm really curious. "Why not?"

She squeezes up her shoulder. "With Benji going back there and all. Did you know him very well?"

This makes Jeremy lean forward. "Nicole," he scolds her.

"What?" she answers, annoyed. "I was just wondering. He was your best friend, don't you want to know?" she snaps back at him. She then turns back to me for an answer.

I have no idea who Benji is, but they act as though I should know. He's obviously been back in those woods, so he must know the Frosts. Is he the reason Mrs. Frost has deemed the woods off-limits? Inside, I begin to panic. If I say yes, they'll want to know more, but if I say no, they may wonder why not. I decide on the latter.

"No, not really," I say. I look away, hoping my lie isn't obvious.

For a moment, there is nothing but the rev of the bus and other kids chatting.

"I'm sorry," she says softly. "I didn't mean to bring that all up."

I'm so confused but also curious. I turn to her. Jeremy has leaned back and is trying to act like he's looking out the window and not listening to us. I know I should just keep quiet. The more I talk, the more likely I am to let on that I'm not related to the Frosts, which would out me as a fraud.

Bring what up? I wonder. But instead of asking, I simply say. "It's okay."

Whoever this Benji is, he was Jeremy's best friend and must be someone who knew the Frosts. But what happened to him, and why would she apologize for bringing him up to me? I want to ask her, but I obviously can't. I then wonder if this Benji kid has something to do with the strange comments I've heard since I first stepped onto the bus that morning.

The bus heaves to a stop. "This is me," says Nicole, needing to slide by me from the seat.

I stand to let her by. "See you tomorrow," I say.

She doesn't respond except to nod. I can't tell if she hates me or is just indifferent. She's obviously curious about me, which may help me talk to her more, but before I do, I'll need to find out about Benji and how he fits into my new life in this strange new place.

When Jeremy and Nicole are down the stairs, I stare out to see where they live.

I see fields in all directions as they begin to walk down a dirt and gravel road leading back to a white house. The house is much smaller than the Frosts' but similar in that it is surrounded by a barn and other smaller buildings. They must be farmers, too. That must be what all the kids on this bus do, as I've seen nothing but fields, barns, tractors, and livestock on the ride to and from school.

There are several stops, and kids get off at dirt turnouts and then walk off toward distant laneways. It makes me wonder why the bus has to stop right at the front of the Frost house, and then I ponder what it is about that house that has everyone talking. Are they jealous because of the size? Maybe, but I know there is something else that is causing such a stir. I've been through many first days at many different schools and have never felt or heard troubling things like I have today.

By the time the bus reaches my stop, I'm the last one on board. I stand and walk to the stairs.

"Sorry about making you ride the whole route. I should have dropped you off first, but I missed your stop," the bus driver says apologetically. He's an older man with a crew cut and round red cheeks. "It's been a while since your house was on the route."

"That's okay," I tell him and make my way down the stairs.

A dust trail kicks up as the bus pulls away, and I stand with his last sentence repeating in my head. "It's been a while since your house was on the route." If the Frosts have no children, why would this house have been on the school bus route? Did another family live there before? And did the Frosts recently move here?

As I walk up the gravel drive toward the large castle-like house, I have so many questions for the woman I've told Nicole and Jeremy is my aunt.

I look toward the house, the trees swaying along the lane leading to it.

It's all so strange, and now I face the place that seems to be what's causing it all. The stares, the hushed comments—they all started because I'm living at this house.

Before I can decide if I should knock, Mrs. Frost opens the front door. She looks pensive and stressed.

"Welcome home," she says.

I've never considered any place I've lived as my home, but I give her a nod.

She's dressed in a long striped shirt belted at the waist and flared jeans. "I was worried you wouldn't know what bus to take." She directs me inside.

I'm embarrassed to tell her that without Nicole's help, I might still be standing at the school trying to figure it out.

"How did everything go?" she asks.

"Good," I lie. I can tell she will want to fix things if she thinks anything does not go as planned. I found my classes, I had money for lunch, and I didn't get lost on my way to or from the school, so besides the stares, strange murmurs, and Nicole's comments about a kid named Benji, things weren't completely terrible.

She ushers me into the dining room, where a small plate with cookies and a glass of milk is waiting.

"I made you a snack," she says. "Why don't you put your things away first, and then you can have it."

"Okay," I say. I have a small stack of assignments that a few of the teachers gave me stuffed into my notebook.

She follows me to the stairs. "I put some other things for you in your room. Just some clothes you can wear while doing the chores. Jesse will be here around four to help you."

My mood brightens a bit hearing this, and I go quickly up to my room. On the bed are two pairs of jeans, some button-up shirts similar to the ones I saw many of the boys wearing, and thick canvas gloves. There is also a pair of boots. I'm stunned. I lift the jeans and study them. They don't have tags, but they look brand new. The boots don't show even a scuff, and the shirts are crisp. She's giving me work clothes that are in much better shape than my own clothes, and I wonder if I get to keep them.

I also notice that my bed has been made and my black garbage bag is now empty and folded on the bed. Did she throw away my clothes? Before I go downstairs to ask her what she's done with my stuff, I open the closet and find my only other shirt hanging. I take the shirt and smell the sleeve. It's been washed. I find my other pair of jeans folded in the dresser drawer. She's gone through everything and washed it all.

I feel a stab of fear and drop to my knees at the bed, shoving my hand under the mattress. My breath releases when I find the book still safely hidden. I pat the front pocket of my jeans. The solid circle is there. I'm whole. The two things I can't lose are still with me.

Part of me is disturbed that she went through my stuff, but I'm relieved my two treasures are still hidden.

I look again at the new clothes on my bed and think about the plate of cookies waiting for me downstairs. A wave of skepticism goes over me. What does she want from me?

I fold and put away the other jeans in the drawer and hang up the shirts and coat before going back downstairs.

"Thank you," I say. "For the clothes. But are you sure I should wear those to do the chores? They might get dirty."

She nods. "I can wash them."

Again, she wants to do things for me. I have nothing to offer. My hesitations are solid. Don't enjoy this and don't get comfortable. I'll be with my mom soon. I just have to bide my time.

"Did you meet anyone?" she asks, motioning me to the cookies and milk.

I hesitate to mention Jeremy and Nicole, and I don't know why.

"Yes. There were a couple of kids I met on the bus."

She smiles. "Oh, do they live close?"

"Close?" I ask. Does anyone live close out here? "I don't think so. I think they live on a farm, too."

"What are their names?" she asks.

I lick my lips. "Jeremy and Nicole. They're brother and sister."

Her eyes go wide, but she forces a thin smile. I can tell she knows who they are, but there is also something else in her expression.

"What did they say?" she asks.

Do I tell her they asked about the woods and someone named Benji? Will they allow me to find out more about her strange aversion to the grove of trees and why I'm here?

Before I can decide how to answer, she continues.

"Did they ask why you were living here?"

I nod warily. It's as if she was expecting me to receive the odd reactions.

She gives a knowing smile. "I'm sure they were curious. So, what did you tell them?" Her smile remains, but I can tell she's worried.

"I told them you were my aunt and uncle." I have no good lie, so I tell her the truth about my lie.

She blinks and leans back, obviously shocked by my response. "You told them that?"

"I'm sorry, Mrs. Frost," I say, immediately regretting both the lie and telling her, but then her demeanor changes. Her eyes sparkle, and she looks as though she is seeing something for the first time.

"No," she says. "Landis, that's good."

I flinch back, surprised.

She raises her eyebrows and leans closer to me like we're sharing a secret. "And I'm not Mrs. Frost. I'm Aunt Evelyn."

Chapter 11

The tiny cabin was the original house that my great-grandfather, Norman built when he bought the land in 1910. He and my great-grandmother, MaryJane, had seven children, but only three lived past the age of ten. My grandfather, Tom, was the oldest and set to inherit the homestead, and while he helped work the farm, he left to pursue his dream of becoming a doctor when he was nineteen. World War II accelerated that aspiration, and in just three years, he received his medical degree. However, that didn't come without a price. Before his last month of apprenticeship, he was drafted. Tom had just turned twenty-three years old and was sent across the ocean to a hospital in England.

His degree kept him from the combat lines and gave him the title of captain, but that didn't shelter him from the ravages of the war. Most of the injured had been given life-saving measures while on the field by medics, but there was no lack of severe and grotesque wounds that arrived at their door.

It was a large estate that was given over for use as a hospital. The enormous rooms were able to fit the rows of thin metal cots for the sick and wounded. And there was electricity and several places in the home that had running water—luxuries in those old mansions, especially in a time of war.

During a particularly long and grueling day with dozens of new patients in every state of injury, my grandfather met a young nurse named Eugenia. She, like him, never seemed to tire in their work to repair what war did to bodies.

Sometimes, even in the dark, late hours of the night, he would find her alone at the window in one of the corridors, simply staring out into the darkness, deep in thought. In my current state of limbo I can see the roots of her demise were already beginning to grow.

"You should be sleeping," he said, coming to her side.

"We've already sacrificed so many. When will it be enough?"

Her face glowed in the candlelight but looked weary.

"They're out there and will soon make their way in. I feel they're already here watching us. They won't stop until we give them more."

My grandfather was compelled to ask, "Who won't stop?" but felt her fear was the same one they all had—the evil that surrounded them and was making gains with bullets and mortars would soon be at their door.

He felt the urge to comfort her, and before he could reach out, she was nestled in his arms, and in the dim light, he promised to protect her.

In the weeks that followed, he was with her any chance he had. They had worked side by side, and that is when he learned that Eugenia wasn't just a nurse but the youngest daughter of the estate's owners.

Eugenia's parents held the titles of Lord and Lady and were already unhappy with her decision to work, especially in those terrible conditions. The idea of her marrying an American without a title or even money was unthinkable.

Knowing this, the couple married in secret.

Surprisingly, the announcement wasn't met with anger but with a warning—"She will return to us, and you will need to allow it."

My grandfather gave the warning little heed, brushing it off as the emotional extremes of the war.

Just before the war ended, my grandfather was discharged and sent home to the Idaho farm. His younger brother, who was to take over the land, had succumbed to the flu, leaving his elderly father unable to run the farm on his own.

It wasn't my grandfather's plan to be a farmer. He was a doctor. But he felt there was no other choice, and with that, he brought his new bride back to the Idaho homestead, where he did both.

At first, Eugenia did her best to become part of her husband's family, but soon, the distance, the dirt, and the dry Idaho weather began to wear on her.

In a desperate attempt to keep her from returning to her life of prosperity in her homeland, my grandfather planted her a garden and filled it with plants found in the stately gardens at Tyntesfield. And with the birth of the first child, he gave her a ring with an enormous diamond encircled with smaller stones and set in a thick gold band. This was to replace the crudely shaped silver ring he had made from an old coin while sitting up all night watching over a dying soldier. While the ring was created with love, in his eyes, it didn't measure up.

When he presented the new extravagant ring, he expected elation, and while she thanked him for the gift, he rarely saw her wear it and one day found it discarded in the trash.

It must have been a mistake, he thought. A careless misplacement in the daily care of the children and house. Instead of returning it to her or confronting her intentions, he carefully placed it with some other important items in a space he had hidden in a drawer.

There were also other concerns about Eugenia's actions. He would often find her, like he did during their first days together at the estate, standing alone and staring out at the darkness.

The woods seemed to haunt her. Her eyes would be fixed as she stood looking out at the dense, deep groves.

"They're not satisfied. It's not over for them," she whispered into the night.

Tom knew she longed for her life back home, and her fear and obsession with the woods resulted in the large home being placed at the front of the land and away from the river and trees.

With its tall spires, wide staircase, and steep rock fireplace, she would now have some of the lavish life she had lost by becoming his bride.

Two children were born, but when Wesley and Evelyn, my mom, were just five and four years old, they lost their mother, and my grandfather was left to raise them alone.

My mother still grieves the mother she never really knew and feels her life would have been different—happier—if she'd had a mother like everyone else.

The lack of female influence in Evelyn's life often made her feel unsure of what her role in the world should be.

CHAPTER 12

Idaho is called The Gem State, however, the most precious natural resource in Idaho isn't a gem. The shiny, often elusive, and prized commodity is literally the lifeblood of the state. It's water. Vital for the millions of acres of farmland. The lakes and reservoirs help to contain the valuable cache, but with little in the way of yearly rainfall across the Snake River Basin, the farmers and ranchers rely on the mountain snowfall and the subsequent melt that fills the rivers and streams that make their way through the valley.

Some years, the water is so abundant the lakes and rivers swell and overflow, flooding the land and causing dams to breach and ditches to wash out. But more often, it's the lack of water that is the concern. When the drought sets in, riverbeds run dry, leaving growers with dead crops and no income. It's a precise and complex dance that keeps growers always looking to the mountain tops and hoping to see them capped in white.

How high or low the water level is in the Snake comes from the amount of snow in the mountains from the season before. But the tributaries, canals, ditches, and overflows that come off the mighty river are opened, closed, and diverted with numerous gates—like little dams, they hold back the water using large metal plates that are slid in and out to control the flow. They're called head gates and are usually pulled by hand by those who own the water rights or work for those who do.

How many inches of water a farmer is able to take is often what has led to legal battles, property damage, and even violence. The rights to the water were often determined generations before. Many of the farms were homesteaded by pioneers and settlers, making their water rights more valuable than those established more recently. And when the drought of 1945 all but dried up the Snake River, the fight for water turned deadly.

A shovel wasn't intended to be a murder weapon, but in a reversal of sorts, it worked. It turned out it wasn't what actually killed Darrel Jenkins, however, the likelihood he would have fallen into the canal, knocking his head on the concrete head gate and causing him to drown, would have been slim without that deliberate swing.

My grandfather was charged with murder, but a trial with a jury of twelve men found him not guilty. His exoneration wasn't completely accepted within the small community, as there were certainly those, especially those from the other side of the river, who saw the verdict differently.

Bud Harker, Tom's rotund and fiery defense attorney, argued that while there was a verbal exchange and ongoing legal battle regarding the water, it wasn't Tom's intent to cause Darrel physical harm. In fact, it was a matter of self-defense. Darrel's actions against Tom were the reason he met his fate, not the other way around.

It wasn't Tom, but Darrel who swung the shovel in an attempt to keep Tom from stopping the flow of water.

Darrel had been taking the water on that day and had been for years, but when Tom returned from the war and realized what had been happening, he exposed the illegal actions and proved that Darrel Jenkins had no right to the water except the first and third Sunday of the month. It was Monday, and Darrel had already taken the water two weeks before.

Bud Harker argued that it was Darrel who was clearly out of line and became enraged when Tom shut the water off. What ensued was Darrel, while trying to knock Tom away from the head gate with the heavy shovel, missed his intended target and the force of the swing was so fierce that Darrel lost his balance. He fell backward, striking his head on the concrete block of the gate and then falling into the deep water of the canal below. Tom did nothing wrong. He simply ducked.

Tom was still crouched when he heard the splash. He had ducked and was protecting his own head, so he hadn't seen the stumble or the fall. However, the loud splash was enough for him to know Darrel had fallen in. Tom frantically scanned the water and then saw Darrel's lifeless form floating face down, slowly moving with the current.

Tom ran along the edge, thinking he could reach in and pull him to the bank, but it was so steep and the water so strong it wasn't long before the body was down the canal and out of sight.

Darrel Jenkins was eventually found near the diversion where the water fed his crops. There was speculation as to the irony of it. After all, if Tom had been successful in closing the gate, the flow would have been a trickle rather than the strong rush, and maybe then Darrel wouldn't have drowned.

When the circumstances were revealed, some people in the county lifted an eyebrow and simply sighed. Even if it had been Tom's fault, was it murder when Tom was protecting what was rightfully his? Of course, it was a tragedy, but the altercation was about water. Without it, the crops and land would die. Tom was protecting his family's livelihood, and Darrel was robbing him of that. They had already fought the battle out in court, and it proved the water wasn't Darrel's, so what more could Tom have done?

And if things weren't already stacked in Tom's favor, he wore the white hat of town doctor. He was known as the gentle soul who treated their illnesses and came to their aid when babies came into this world, or elders left it. He couldn't possibly have hurt someone on purpose, let alone tried to kill them.

But just a few years later, when Tom's young wife and mother of his two children vanished without explanation, and his tiny daughter was left for dead in the woods, his innocence seemed questionable at best. The mystery surrounding the loss of his wife and a daughter who was now scarred, had the entire town wondering, and those on the other side of the river puffed up with a sense of smug validation. Maybe, just maybe, they were right about him.

The anger and distrust settled into the fabric of those who lived on the other side, smoldering for years, only to ignite when I met Laura.

CHAPTER 13

———————

LANDIS

Jesse pulls around to the back of the house in a large, white truck.

"Hey there, Landis," he says, waving me over.

Mrs. Frost is by the back door and calls to me as I begin to follow him out to the barn. "I'm going to town. If I'm not back when you're finished, the key to the house is under the back door mat, but I shouldn't be long." Then she waves as though I'm going to war.

The way she treats me sometimes makes me wonder if she realizes I'm almost sixteen. Is this how she treats all those who work here?

I think Jesse notices this, too, and gives me a grin.

"I'm not sure why she locks the back door. Most folks around here don't even lock the front door," he says.

He wears weathered jeans, a cowboy hat, and worn work gloves. He walks quickly with legs that are thin and bowed. He looks like a real cowboy, like from a movie.

There are seven horses and about a dozen cows in a small fenced section of the large pasture. They all come our way when they see us in the barn.

"I thought Mr. Frost took the cows with him yesterday," I ask.

"Yep, but these haven't calved," he explains.

I don't ask, even though I don't know what that means.

"They're pregnant," he says, obviously seeing my confusion. "But they should be having the calves real soon, so keep an eye out and call me if there's a problem. Gordon should be back tomorrow night, but they could drop," he stops and corrects himself. "Have their babies at any time."

"What do I do if that happens?"

"Nothing. Mothers know what to do. They'll take care of their babies. Everything should be fine, but if the mothers are lying down and look like they're struggling, call me or Doc Taylor. Evelyn has the numbers."

I take a deep breath and blow it out, still thinking about what I would do if I saw a cow giving birth. "How am I supposed to know if there is a problem?"

Jesse grins. "You haven't been around animals much, have you?"

It's obvious, and I'm not about to try to lie my way through this one. I shake my head. "I've been around dogs and cats a little, and even a parrot, but nothing big like this," I say, pointing toward the horses who are now just feet away. I've always loved animals, and while I'd never admit it, I've dreamed of riding a horse like the cowboys on TV on Sunday morning westerns. Being at this place is almost surreal. It's so different from anywhere I've lived before, and I've never felt so foreign.

The barn is large, with a high loft and a wooden ladder. There are all sorts of ropes, leather straps, and other items hanging from hooks. There are barrels and tarps that are organized and bales of hay stacked four high. He shows me how to use a pitchfork to divide and toss the sections of the hay bales.

Standing so close to the horses, I realize how tall they are and how small I feel next to them. I don't know if they're friendly. I watch and wonder if it would be safe to reach out and pet one.

"Do you ride these horses?" I ask him.

Jesse cocks his head. "No. I ride my own," he answers.

"How many do you have?"

"Four."

"Do you have a farm like this too?"

Jesse gives a small laugh. "No. I have a few acres, is all. I grow grass for the horses, but that's it. My place is about five miles south of here."

I'm not sure if it's a good time or not to ask Jesse about Benji. I feel that I should find out how well Jesse knows the Frosts before I question him about them.

"How long have you worked for Mr. Frost?" I ask. It feels like a good start. It's not too pointed, but it may open the door to more.

Jesse thinks a moment. "Ever since I was in high school. I started out on his place on the other side of town."

"He's got more than one farm?" I ask.

Jesse looks at me like I'm joking. "Yes. There's quite a bit more." He then stops and thinks for a moment. "That reminds me, I have some work to do out there tomorrow and could use your help with the irrigation. I don't want to have to drive all the way back and open the gates. Do you think you could do that for me tomorrow afternoon? It's not hard. I'll show you how."

I nod but ask, "What gates?"

"They're on the far pasture," he says, pointing back toward the woods. "I'll take you out there and show you. I can try to run back and do it tomorrow night, but ..."

"I can do it," I say, even though I have no idea what he is talking about. Anything to keep me outside in this wide open space.

I want to ask him more about the Frosts, but he continues to show me the chores I'll be doing. He explains the best way to use a pitchfork and where I should try to place the sections of hay.

We finish with the horses and cows, and then he shows me where the chickens are and how to feed them and collect the eggs. I'm fascinated when he shows me the nest boxes, and there are actual eggs there. They are large and brown.

"Brown eggs?" I ask, making Jesse laugh.

"You really are a city kid, aren't you," he quips, and I wonder how much he's been told about me and why I'm here. Does he know about my scattered past? I'm not even sure the Frosts know my full story. Do they know I was accused of stealing? If so, why would they agree to take me in? They've given me chores and with no other kids at this home, all I can figure is I must be here to work. It's the only thing that makes sense.

We walk to the shop, and Jesse digs out a pair of dirty rubber boots. "You'll need these tomorrow when the water's in the ditch. I'll leave them out so you can find them," Jesse says. "Come on, and I'll show you what you need to do for tomorrow." He then directs me toward the fields, and he begins to walk toward the back, toward those woods.

As we trudge along, I wonder why we don't drive instead. I don't ask because I don't want to seem lazy, but I look back at how far we've walked, and when I drift out of the channel we're following, he stops and directs me back.

"Stay in the furrows. Don't walk on the fields. We just planted last week," he says, swiping his arm to distinguish the straight, narrow row that we're following. I realize then why driving out here wouldn't work.

I watch the woods as we get nearer. I feel my neck hairs rise as though something out there is watching me, and then I see a small house nestled back in the trees. Tucked amongst the brush, its rustic log exterior has it hidden from view.

"Does someone live there?" I ask.

Jesse looks over. "Yeah, it's Old Tom's place. He's ..." He pauses and thinks for a moment. "He's been here a long time."

It looks like it. The house is old, and there is little about it that makes it look inviting. It's the type of place hermits or trolls live in the books I've read. Is he the reason everyone talks about something happening back there?

We cross a dirt laneway that leads directly back toward the old house.

"Is this his property?" I ask. I'm also wondering why we're going toward the area that Mrs. Frost warned me about and if Jesse knows how she feels about those woods.

"Yes, we have to cross his laneway to irrigate; this is the only way we can get to the head gate," he explains, as though I know what any of that means. I don't ask because I figure he'll show me.

I continue to follow him through the barren fields, still looking over toward the dense mass of trees.

We reach the bank of the canal, and I can see that it snakes its way from around the front of the pasture all the way back and into where I was told not to go.

Jesse jumps down into the dry ditch bed and goes to a large metal plate that separates the ditch. He pulls the plate from its holding.

"In the afternoon, when you get home from school, remove it like this and set it on the bank. It will be a bit harder with the water in the ditch, but it shouldn't be a problem. On Friday, if I'm not back, you'll need to shut it. Just put the gate back in like this," he says. He then reinserts the plate. "Do that at around six and no later than seven."

"Seven in the evening?" I ask.

"Yes. You'll do the same thing with the next two. Just follow the ditch. They each go for twelve hours. There are three sections. Can you handle that?"

"Yes," I answer, but I wonder if I'll be able to find my way when the sun has begun to go down.

He motions for me to follow as he walks along the bank of the ditch. Then I hear a dog barking in the distance. I look up and see a round, rust-colored dog with an odd gait. It's a ways off, and I squint to try and get a better look. "Does that dog only have three legs?" I ask, seeing its strange hobble.

Jesse looks over. He watches for a moment. He sighs and nods.

I continue to watch, and soon, the dog disappears back into the brush behind the house. As we walk along the ditch, we get even closer to the trees, and I find myself staring into them. Then I ask the question that's been haunting me since I was brought to the Frosts. "What's back there?"

"Back where?" Jesse asks as he continues trudging through the soft dirt path.

"Back in the trees."

He stops and looks out into the woods. "It's the river bottoms and then eventually the river."

"The river is right back there?" I ask, remembering the caseworker saying that when we first arrived at the house.

He looks back at me. He can see my curiosity. "Yes. But don't go wandering back there." His friendliness fades.

An odd chill runs through me. "Why?" I ask. I'm hoping he'll explain what's in those woods that seems to have everyone hesitant to even mention it.

"Just stick to irrigating." He stops and measures what he's about to say. "Stay on this side. Don't go back there."

"Old Tom's place?" I ask. "But I thought you said we could be on his land."

He shakes his head. "That's for irrigating, not roaming around by the river."

Again, he starts walking back toward the Frosts, and I follow.

The trees sway, and the breeze encircles me. I hear a whisper in my ear. "Fear. Fear." It's faint and yet urgent.

"Fear?" I ask Jesse.

He stops and looks at me strangely. "What?"

"You said 'Fear.'"

He squints his eyes at me. "I didn't say anything."

There is no one else around but Jesse and me.

"You didn't?" I ask.

"Nope. I think you're hearing things," he says and then keeps walking.

Now I'm questioning my ears. Fear? Was that really a voice, or just the wind?

Jesse trudges on, head down, and I follow, embarrassed.

"Fear," it calls again. The voice is soft but urgent. My heart leaps. I stop and look around, scanning the vast open field for any sign of another person. But there is no one. Nothing. What am I hearing?

"Fear." It calls again.

Am I going crazy? I wonder, still searching the area. And then, a cold breeze coils around me, causing me to shiver and gasp.

"Landis."

I hear my name, and it shakes me from my stupor. Jesse is standing several yards in front of me.

"What are you doing back there?" he asks, obviously annoyed that I'm lagging behind.

What just happened? What was that voice? I take a deep breath and try to shake the odd chill.

"Just looking at what's out there." I can't stop staring out toward the woods. Is that where the whisper came from? Why doesn't Jesse hear the voice?

Seeing my curiosity, he sighs. "Don't rock the boat, kid. It's not worth it. Just do what you're told. Stay away from back there."

I want to ask him why. I want to know about Mrs. Frost's strange comment. "Something terrible happened back there"—but I don't. He already seems annoyed with me, and I know if I push, it won't be good.

"Okay," I say.

He continues to walk, and I continue to follow.

"I know you think there's nothing to do around here but work," he says without turning around.

"I like to work," I say.

Again, he stops and turns around. His face looks as if I'm talking back.

"I like being outside," I say.

His face softens.

"And I don't mind work, especially on a farm."

If what my mother says about the lavender farm is real, then I'll need to know how to take care of it.

Jesse lifts his cowboy hat from his head and wipes his brow. The sun is bright, and I'm surprised by how warm it is after needing a coat this morning.

"Let's keep going," he says. He continues along the bank, and I take another quick glance at the woods, wondering what that voice is and if it will return.

Soon, we're at another gate in the ditch.

"This is the gate to the far pasture," Jesse says, taking hold of a handle on a large metal plate. He slides it out of the dry ditch and then puts it back, showing me again how the gates operate.

"After you release the main gate, you'll need to walk down here and pull this one. Then, just let the water run until the same time the next day. That's when you'll replace all the gates and stop the water. Got it?"

I nod.

"Don't forget, or you'll have everyone on the ditch barking about us taking their water."

I take a wide scan of the area, wondering who he's talking about. "Everyone on the ditch?" I ask. There are no other houses for miles.

"The canal brings water to everyone who lives along this side of the river, clear down almost to Pingree."

Jesse sees my confusion and shakes his head. "There are a lot of different farms and pastures. Everyone gets their turn at the water, and if you don't open and close these gates at the right times, we'll either lose our turn or the people down from us will lose theirs. In other words, don't forget."

"I won't."

He smiles and claps me on the back. "We'll turn you into a farmer yet."

I wonder what he'd think if he knew my plans to be exactly that. Even though I've spent every day waiting for my mom to finally be out of jail and take me to our new life on the lavender farm, I still feel like I'm in a strange dream being here surrounded by dirt and crops. Maybe this is a way for me to learn and get used to what it will be like someday. Is it possible my mom was in on my placement here? I know it's a pipe dream, but I wish it were true. I hope she hasn't given up on our plans. Every time I close my eyes, I see the purple buds of what our future will be. The visions are from books I've studied, as I've never actually seen a lavender plant or smelled its coveted aroma. What a difference it will be from what I'm used to. I wonder if our farm will be similar to the one I'm trudging across now.

These vast fields spread out for miles with no sign of concrete sidewalks or the familiar sound of traffic and bustle feel like a strange dream. Farms were things I'd seen while sitting in the backseat of a car on long drives from one large city to the next. I'd never even witnessed an actual human out in those fields—maybe a cow or a horse—but no people. I've seen corn stalks, but most of the crops that waved as I passed were a sea of green or beige rows, depending on the time of year, and there was nothing I could identify. In all my daydreams of living with my mom on the lavender farm, I've never seen myself actually farming. I'm not planting seeds, digging holes, or letting the water into the fields. I'm just there with her, surrounded by rows of fragrant purple flowers, and away from wherever I'm currently living.

We walk back to the Frost's house, and Jesse goes over what I'm supposed to do one more time. And again, he reminds me what not to do.

"Stay on this side of the ditch. Old Tom keeps a close watch around his house."

Is that what this is all about? Some guy who lives back there? Is he the reason something terrible happened? My thoughts then turn to Benji, and my curiosity takes over.

"Do you know Benji?" I ask.

He turns to me with a look of shock. I immediately wish I had stayed quiet.

"Why? Who told you about him?" he asks.

I shrug, feeling defensive, and a cold shiver hits me. My mind is now racing with questions. "Some kids at school were talking about him."

"What did they say?" he asks.

"They asked if I knew him. They also wanted to know if I went into the woods."

He cocks his head. "Who asked you that?"

I don't want this to get back to Nicole and Jeremy, so I shake my head. "I don't know any of them. It was my first day."

Jesse gives a tired sigh. "Ignore them. They are just being nosy. They're probably just wanting to sneak back into the hollow."

"What's the hollow?" I ask.

"It's like a lagoon back in the woods." He gives me a stern look. "But it's off-limits. No one's allowed back there now."

Off-limits. The same words Mrs. Frost used. And I wonder what Benji has to do with all this? Could he be connected to these woods in some way? I begin to try to conjure what is back there that has them all so afraid.

"Why is it off-limits?" I ask as I try to visualize in my mind what might be lurking in those dark and dense woods. Is there something sinister that lives there?

Jesse rolls his eyes. "It just is. Don't go getting in trouble. Just stay out of there."

"But," I beg him, wanting answers.

"No buts," he says, quickly cutting me off as though he expected I'd protest. "Just stick to irrigating. If you want to swim, go up to the trestle pond. It's not far from here."

That's not why I'm interested. In fact, it's the last thing I'd want to do, seeing as I don't swim, so I nod grudgingly.

My questions are again a source of irritation, and I remind myself I'm here to get by so my mom will be able to find me, and we can leave together. No more slip-ups, no more being moved around, and no more trouble.

I almost blew it by being sent to that group home. It took months before they could figure out that I didn't deserve to be there. Suppose I mess up again; who knows where I'll be sent? As soon as my mom gets out, I'm pretty sure she's planning to move to Washington, and if I'm stuck back in the juvie jail, it could ruin everything.

I shut my mouth and follow him, trying to keep my curiosity at bay, but this is something I can't push aside. I feel something terrible happened back in those trees at that place they call the hollow. And what about Benji? Did something happen to him back there, or was he the cause of the trouble? I stare into the woods and wonder what strange and dangerous presence lives there.

The trees sway. It's like they're calling me and then pushing me away. The green of the leaves is just beginning to emerge, but the grayish brown branches and limbs are so dense, even in the bright sun, it looks like a smoky haze has filled the woods and covered whatever is hiding inside.

I try to ignore the woods and look away, but the cold rush that I've felt seems to surround me. The voice that called to me is now silent, but I still feel something beckoning me back there, and I want to know why.

Chapter 14

Benji

I'm in a rage. There's a presence in the house, and I feel it might be the very one who took my life. Does it feel me lingering and stalking the life signs I've left behind and wanting to remove me altogether from this place? Or is it afraid I will learn the truth and expose what evil they committed? Are they trapped here in this small space of gray like me because of what they did and can't face their terrible fate? It's what keeps me here and away from the light that continues to beckon me. There are so many reasons I need to find the one who robbed me of life, and until I do, I'm stuck.

I rush through the halls and rooms, trying to find the culprit. I swipe and lunge and try to cause a stir, but my rant goes unnoticed.

The world I left was nothing like when I was alive. I can no longer see the colors or feel the temperature of the air. My ability to touch and feel is gone, but I remember those things. What I can do is sense the people I left and the hovering sadness that still lingers around them. The essence of where I am in that house is still strong. I know when I'm going from place to place, and I can tell when my mother or father is there with me.

Their pain is still fresh. My mother is sorrowful. My father is no less hurt, but my mother also harbors a sense of shame. She blames herself for losing me, and since my body is still missing, she continues to aimlessly search and hope that what she told me that day wasn't what caused her to lose me forever.

The source of our conflict was my desire to be with Laura. The angst I felt seems trivial now, but it had taken over my life at that time. My grades had tumbled, my friends faded away, and even my quest for catching the elusive fish I had stalked for over a year, had waned. I didn't care. I just wanted to be with her.

Laura and I knew the conflict when it came to us seeing each other. The feud that began long ago still simmered, but we had no idea the divide between our families was deeper than the river that separated us. But try as they might to keep us apart, it didn't work. We saw each other in between classes at school, and when summer came, I was able to take the path through the hollow and cross the bridge to see her.

"What happens when it snows?" she asked sadly. "You can't cross then. The snow will be too deep."

She was right. The weather would make my journey rough, if not impossible, but I refused to let that come between us, and I knew the real reason for her concern was the other obstacle that kept us apart.

The river may have been the barrier between the two sides of town, but the divide was deeper than just a physical boundary. It was a vast bottomless gorge of ill feelings that no one could physically touch, and yet the weight of that divide was as heavy as the vast amount of water that flowed between.

"I'll be able to drive soon," I told her. "I'll pick you up, and then we can go wherever we want." It seemed so simple, as though driving a few miles away would erase the years of resentment.

I felt that solid divide my entire life, but the burning I felt in my chest wasn't that of hate, but just the opposite. I didn't care where Laura lived or who her family was. We weren't from the same side, but I didn't have the same aversion that others felt for those who lived over there.

As I got to know Laura, I learned that she never knew her father. He died soon after she was born—a war hero, killed in Vietnam. Laura lived with her mother, grandmother, and her brother, Kevin —her twin—the person she was born with, and yet, she rarely spoke of him. It didn't surprise me much. Even though we were all in the same grade and even had classes together, I avoided her brother. Even before I knew Laura, I knew Kevin was trouble. At just fourteen, the police in town knew him well. His crimes were petty, but that didn't stop my mother's already fiery distaste for "those people."

All of them were bad in her mind. It felt as though spending time with Laura meant her family's stigma would rub off on me.

Our attempts to keep our feelings hidden were often in vain. We would see each other at school, and even though we rarely spoke, when we did, my friends would shake their heads.

"She may be pretty, but she's still one of them," Jeremy said as we passed Laura in the hall. Her smile in seeing me spoke volumes, as did my own.

"One of them?" I scoffed. "What's she ever done?"

"It's all of them," he continued. "What about that bridge back there? They built that, and you know it's for trespassing. What if they've been coming over into the hollow? To our fishing hole? We should cut it down."

Jeremy was accusing those who lived on the other side, but I wondered if he realized who else was crossing that bridge.

It was so rickety and narrow that I had to take each step slowly and then wait for the shaking of both the bridge and me to stop before taking the next.

When I made it across and felt the solid ground, I would make my way to a row of thick currant bushes behind her house. There, I'd wait until I was sure no one, especially Kevin, was in sight before knocking lightly on the window of her room. She would sneak out the back door, and then we'd walk to the field down from her house and the birch tree that hid us from view.

We did this for weeks until we were eventually discovered. The man who owned the field saw us and, at church that following Sunday, told Laura's mother.

"Sneaking off with a boy to do what?" she scolded her. "Who is this boy?"

Laura tried to keep from revealing who I was, knowing just as I did the problem that would cause, but the rumor grew, and soon the stories weren't just about meeting each other by the tree, but that we were doing much more. Even though it wasn't true, when Kevin found out, he came after me with a vengeance.

It wasn't just the solid distaste of one side versus the other. Laura's family blamed mine for robbing them of the water, as well as their grandfather.

From where I am now, I can see what really happened between our families all those years ago, so why can't I see what took place just moments before my death?

I want to blame Kevin for my demise. It would be an easy line to follow. We had lashed out at each other before. The hate was there, but as I see what is clear through the veil, I realize he lost almost as much as I did.

It's why Laura is covered in guilt. So many still look at her as the reason I'm gone. It's why I must find the truth about what happened. I see so much that I was blind to before, yet the thing I want to know most is just out of reach and fleeting. Those last moments are what keep me from moving on. Until I can see who did this to me, I have to stay.

The light visits me often now, urging me to follow and leave my quest behind. Its pull is strong, but I feel an urgency to find the culprit and bring my search to a close.

Now, as I chase frantically through the rooms and spaces of my past, I realize the extent of my roaming is limited to the areas where my life still lingers—with the people I love.

It's her scent I still have wafting in my memories. It is a soft and sweet floral that, for just a moment, clears my thoughts and fills me with nothing but her fragrance. But then it all turns dark and cold, and I have to remind myself of what I need to do. I need to help her. I need to shield her from the diatribe that she doesn't deserve. It's that evil that took me that I fear will find those I care about and try to hurt them, too.

My anger boils up as my frustration rises. I want to burst through this shroud, confront this demon, and remove it. That is why I linger and search for the truth.

Chapter 15

It's a rattling, bumping noise that jostles me awake. I look at the soft, glowing face of the alarm clock on my nightstand. It is just after three in the morning.

At first, I think I'm dreaming it, then it sounds like someone knocking on my bedroom door. But as I become more awake, I realize it's not that. There is someone out in the hallway, or at least that's what I think. I sit up and listen, trying to figure out what it is. Is the breeze from an open window making a door rattle? Is Mrs. Frost awake and doing something in the other room? We're the only two in the house, so if it isn't the wind, it must be her.

Moonlight spills into my room through the slats of the window blinds as I lay and listen. What could she possibly be doing at this hour?

The sound isn't rhythmic. It starts and stops irregularly, and the bumps are sometimes fast and loud, other times soft and sporadic. If it isn't Mrs. Frost making the noise, I wonder if she is hearing this too.

After several minutes of contemplating what it could be, I lift the covers, swing my legs to the side, and decide to go investigate.

I pad like a mouse to my door and then wait and listen to see if I can get a better feel for where the noise is coming from. I lean in, and the rumbling stops. But as soon as I step back, it starts again. I wait to see if there are footsteps or any other sounds, but all I hear is the same banging.

I quietly grasp the door knob and slowly turn it, hoping that if it is Mrs. Frost, she doesn't hear me. Again, the noise stops. I pause. My heart pounds as I fear I've been heard. But when the thumping begins again, I continue to turn the knob and then slowly open my door just a crack.

From this small sliver, all I see is the dim darkness of early morning. No forms or shadows moving about. There is no one in the hallway. If Mrs. Frost is the one making the noise, she must be inside the other room—the off-limits area.

The bumping becomes louder. It sounds as though someone is trying to open the "off-limits" door. Is she stuck inside?

I step out into the hall.

"Hello?" I ask softly. I do not want an answer and am relieved when there isn't one. The knocking continues.

As my eyes adjust to the dark, I see the moonlight coming from the thin space under the door. The knocking slows. Again, I listen. There is no other movement or sound but that low rumbling.

I know that Mrs. Frost has banned me from that room, but I'll never be able to sleep if this noise continues; plus I'm now even more curious as to why that area has been deemed off-limits.

I decide that I'll quickly go in, close the window, or move whatever is knocking, and be back in my bed in minutes. Mrs. Frost—even if she's awake—will never know I defied her order.

I tiptoe toward the room. The banging stops. When I reach the door, I hesitate, waiting for the knocking to start again. I'm beginning to doubt where I heard the noise. Was it actually the door or something inside the room? I'm now almost positive my first instinct was right, that a breeze from an open window is what is causing the door to clatter. With the early hour, I think it's simply that—the wind.

As I stand there waiting for it to begin again, a stillness surrounds me. I hear nothing, not even my own breathing. It is complete silence. Looking back toward the stairs to make sure no one is watching me, I reach for the knob. When I turn it, I find that it's locked.

Of course, it is. Mrs. Frost would never leave it open. I saw Mrs. Frost taking the keys when she went to get my jacket from this restricted room. At first, I felt she was worried I'd steal from her, but I now feel it's something else. There are items all over this house that are expensive and yet not sequestered away. What's in this room is different. There is something that she doesn't want me to see, and it's almost as though whatever that something is, its pulling me in and hoping I'll find it.

Still holding the knob, I move it carefully to see if there is play in the door and jam that would cause the banging noise. But there's none. I actually shake it and can't repeat the noise. Then I see the moonlight from the keyhole. The opening is so large that I envision it as being locked using one of those skeleton keys in the old days. This entire house feels like it is out of an old black-and-white movie. The swooping staircase, massive ceilings, and carved wooden furniture are nothing like the linoleum floors and avocado-colored appliances of the homes I'm used to.

I squat down to the level of the keyhole, and closing one eye, I use the other to try and peer into the room.

At first, I see nothing, but I continue to look. It is dark, but with the bright glow of the moon, I begin to make out objects in the room. I see no movement. There is no one inside, but I can see the outline of the window and the solid square edges of furniture.

I kneel on the floor and stare in, trying to see what could be making the noise and also what is so significant about that room that Mrs. Frost deems it as off-limits. There are boxes and other items, but nothing looks anything but ordinary. And as my eyes adjust even more, I can see that the room is similar to mine. It's just a bedroom. So, what is causing the strange bumping noise, and why is the noise now gone? Discouraged, I'm about to look away, and then suddenly, something passes across the keyhole. A cold rush follows. It startles me, and I tumble back. Then, a bang from inside the room. The knocking is back, as though someone is trying to escape. I scramble away from the door. Mrs. Frost must be the one inside. Who else could it be?

Then, the light in the hallway comes on, and Mrs. Frost stands at the top of the stairs.

I gasp and let out a small holler. I look from her back to the door of the room. If she's here, who's in there?

"Landis, what are you doing?" she asks.

I'm startled but also know I've been caught. "There's something in there," I say urgently, pointing to the room. The bumping has again gone silent.

Her brow furrows, and I can tell she doesn't believe me. I clamor up to standing.

She takes a step toward the room and takes hold of the knob as if checking to make sure it's still locked. "There's nothing in there. I told you this area is off-limits. Please listen to me."

"But ..." I don't know what defense I have. "The door was knocking or banging. And I saw something move inside."

"How could you see inside?" she asks. "It's locked."

"I looked through the keyhole."

She takes a deep breath and cocks her head. "It was probably the curtains. I may have left the window open to air things out. Go back to bed. I'll take care of it."

I want to argue. I want to ask her what it is about that room that she wants to keep from me, but her firm stance and my frustration with it all make me relent and go to my room.

She leaves and goes back downstairs but quickly returns. She won't open that door until I'm gone. I step toward my room but look back to see her take a large key from the pocket of her robe. Once I'm out of view, I hear the key turn in the lock and the door creak open. I stand, straining to hear what she's doing. Soon comes the sounds of a window being shut and then the pad of footsteps coming back toward my door.

She looks in as I sit on my bed. "It was only the wind," she whispers. "Go back to sleep. You have school in the morning." Then she pulls my door closed.

There was something in that room, and I know it wasn't the rush of wind or a flutter of curtains. I feel like it's alive, and yet not. I don't know what to think, but whatever is in there feels unsettled and even sinister.

Why else would Mrs. Frost be so adamant that I stay away? I'm convinced she's hiding something in there. Is it connected to the terrible thing that happened in the woods? My mind roils, concocting what horrific things I might find.

Go back to sleep? I scoff at the thought. As though I could simply let it be. The knocking, the movement in that room, and Mrs. Frost's dire comments now have me lying awake and contemplating what terrible secret is harbored there. The cold rush I've felt before hits me like a hovering dread, and again, I wonder why I was brought to this place.

CHAPTER 16

I feel numb from lack of sleep, but when I board the bus that morning, Nicole gives me a half smile. It isn't necessarily welcoming, but when I see that she is seated alone, I decide to slide in next to her. When she doesn't protest, my mood immediately brightens.

Jeremy is sitting in the row behind her and gives me a semi-interested smirk. There are all the other gawking faces like the day before, but I hardly notice or care about anyone else on that bus. Nicole even smells fantastic.

"Hey," I say.

"Hey," she says back.

We both sit in silence as the bus rumbles along.

At the next stop, a guy gets on with a wide smile. I didn't notice him on the bus yesterday. However, I was trying my best to ignore the whispers and stares. Still, I wonder. He would be hard to miss. He's large, both tall and wide, and when he sees me sitting next to Nicole, he cocks his head and takes the seat next to Jeremy.

"So, who's the new guy?" he asks, obviously aware I can hear him.

"Gus, this is Landis," says Jeremy.

I turn back to him. "Hey."

Gus leans forward and puts his elbows on the back of our seat. "I missed the bus one day, and already you're sitting with my girlfriend?"

At first, I don't know what to think, but then Nicole knocks his arms off the seat and rolls her eyes, and I realize he's teasing us both.

Gus laughs. It's infectious—high-pitched and hearty. I can't help but smile, which annoys Nicole even more, but I can also tell she is beginning to lighten up.

"Well, it was good while it lasted," he teases again, then he sits back and begins to talk to Jeremy about a motorcycle he saw for sale.

Nicole sighs. "He's my brother's friend, and he's a dork," she says softly.

"I heard that!" Gus calls up to her.

This time, she laughs.

"I won't be riding the bus home from school today," she says quietly. "Kathy's mom is picking us up and taking us to the mall in Pocatello. Do you remember what bus you need to take to get home?" She asks.

I nod, feeling like a helpless child who needs to be led by the hand. She then covertly hands me a folded piece of paper. "Here's my phone number. We're all going to see Ghostbusters on Sunday. Call me if you want to go with us."

I take the note. I feel like I've been handed a hundred-dollar bill. I carefully slide the paper into the front pocket of my jacket.

"Okay, thanks," I say, trying not to act too excited.

When we reach the school, Gus and Jeremy walk with us up to the main doors.

"Well, look at this," says Gus, motioning to my jacket. "Isn't this ...?" He then stops and looks at his own jacket and then to Jeremy. It's then I notice his jacket is almost the same as mine, and so is Jeremy's. They are the same style but slightly different colors, but what I notice is that they have a patch on their left breast pocket with their names. How did I not notice all this before?

I look down at my jacket. There is no name. "My aunt gave it to me." Inside I'm pleased that I remembered to call her that. I must remember to keep up that lie.

Jeremy's face falls. "She gave you that?"

All eyes are now on my jacket, and an uncomfortable twinge hits me. I nod and suddenly feel like the garment is possessed. What's the big deal? It's just a jacket. Or is it? Is this why I've garnered such strange looks?

Jeremy continues to study me and the coat. I can feel his angst and am confused by it. He didn't seem concerned until he knew where I got it. Why does it matter that Mrs. Frost gave it to me?

"So, where are you from?" Gus asks, and I'm glad he's diverted the attention away from the jacket.

"He's living with the Frosts," Jeremy cuts in. "He's their nephew."

Suddenly, the same odd stare Jeremy gave me comes over Gus. He looks down at my jacket, and his eyes go big.

I, too, look down as though I'm expecting to see that my coat is on fire. "What is it?" I finally ask, confused.

Gus shakes his head. He then straightens and takes a deep breath. "Their nephew?" He asks, but it seems more of a question to himself, as though he's contemplating the validity.

"Yes," I say with emphasis as though that will make it more legitimate. Have I been found out after only a day? No one has ever questioned my lies before.

"Why are you here?" Gus asks. His jovial disposition has turned harsh. He turns to Jeremy. "Did something happen that ...?" His voice trails off.

Jeremy looks at me as though wanting my answer. They must know something that is making them question me.

"What do you mean?" I ask. "Did what happen?"

This scrutiny makes my chest seize. There are usually questions about me being the new kid, but Gus's tone sounds like I've done something wrong, and immediately my walls come up.

I wait for them to call my bluff and expose that I'm nothing but some kid without a home.

Gus shrugs. "Nothing. I didn't mean to ask about ..." Now he's stumbling.

Inside, I cringe because now Jeremy and Nicole are giving me the same odd stares as the other kids at this school. What do they see? I haven't said much at all, and the only lies I've told are much better than having them know I was sent to that jail for stealing, and now I'm in my twelfth foster home. It's all the stuff I learned early on to keep a secret. Even with my status as a foster kid, I keep to myself.

Not only do other kids treat you differently, I've learned that other parents keep their kids away from me. They see me as trouble and fear that I'll somehow rub off on their children.

Only the other foster kids I've lived with know the truth, and since we're all in the same boat—no one usually says anything. Not having other kids at the Frost's house will make things easier when it comes to my lie. It's one I've used before.

The father in house number five told me to call him Uncle Burt. I liked him. He worked as a mortician and told stories about weird facts he had learned about death. He's the one who told me what day of the year most people die—it's January 6th—and that you're fourteen times more likely to die on your birthday.

"You shouldn't tell the children those things," his wife would say.

"Landis isn't a child," he told her, giving me a wink. "He's twelve. That's a young man."

She would roll her eyes and shake her head in disagreement, but I enjoyed his stories, and so did the others who lived there.

There were six of us kids in that three-bedroom house—all boys. Two were their real children and younger than the rest of us. I was the oldest, and I stayed there the longest—almost an entire school year. But like all the other places I've lived, eventually, something happened, and I was sent to another home with another set of so-called parents.

"How long are you staying with the Frosts?" asks Gus.

I shrug. I don't want to let on that it won't be long. I never bring anyone to the houses where I'm living, so the kids I meet at school are unaware that I'm only temporary. I don't ever want to let on that I'm in a foster home, so without thinking it through, I take my lie about my parents being in the military one step further, and it's a big one.

I tell him the lie about my mom being a nurse in the military but then add, "My dad is a doctor. They are both overseas." It's a story I heard while staying at the last foster house. I overheard the father talking about his brother and what a hero he was. A military doctor saving lives overseas. I feel it's a good lie. It not only explains why my parents are gone but also makes them look good. "They'll be coming back soon," I say.

The kids exchange looks, and I worry if I've gone too far, but then Gus pipes up.

"A doctor and a nurse," Gus muses. "Runs in your family?" he asks but then shrugs, not expecting an answer. He seems impressed, and I feel satisfied with my story. Hopefully, I won't have to explain more as this twist of my untruths continues to grow.

CHAPTER 17

The house is empty when I arrive, and a note is left with a plate covered in tin foil. It's from Mrs. Frost telling me she'll be home late and this is my dinner.

I lift the foil and find two pieces of fried chicken, mashed potatoes, and peas. It's early for dinner, but it smells so good, so I decide to eat before starting my chores.

When I finish, I put the plate in the sink and head out back.

The sun is starting to sink, but it's still warm, and I decide to leave my coat in the barn. I take off my shoes and put on the boots Jesse set out for me. They're a little big but will work, so I head off toward the ditch in the far pasture. I follow the same path Jesse used, making sure I stay off of the rows that have been planted.

Without anyone watching me, I find myself staring out at the woods as I walk. The wind that makes the trees sway has the branches seeming to call me over. They wave, and I find myself standing, mesmerized as they beckon me.

"Fear." There it is again. Did I conjure the voice, or will it always emerge when I pass this way? I shake my head as though I'm erasing an Etch A Sketch to clear my thoughts and try to rid myself of the voice so I can continue on with my chores.

I take a deep breath and trudge on, keeping my eyes forward as I follow the furrows of the field.

When I reach the ditch, I'm surprised at the amount of water. It was completely dry just yesterday. I walk the bank until I come to the main gate, brace myself with one foot and grab hold of the handle like I was shown. Just as Jesse said, it is heavy due to the water pushing against it, but I give it a couple of good yanks, and eventually, it begins to slide upward. Soon, the water is pouring through the opening, and I feel a bit like I've pulled the sword from the stone. It feels good to be outside and doing something other than sitting around watching television. I'm also surprised at the solitude. There is nothing but the sound of the water rushing and a few birds, but it doesn't bother me being out here alone.

I'm used to feeling alone, even when I've lived in houses filled with other kids, and yet, being out here without anyone else around, I don't feel lonely.

As I begin to place the gate up on the bank, I see something tumble into the water. It's the paper. The one with the phone number —Nicole's number. It's fallen from my pocket and is now floating off down the ditch.

I toss the gate aside and then begin to run down the bank after it. The little folded bundle floats on the top like the paper sailboats I made when I was little. I would watch them race down the small trickle of water and into the gutters.

"Crap. Crap," I yell as I stumble along, trying to find a way to retrieve it.

The bundle continues down the ditch quickly, and I run farther up, hoping to get past it and then catch it as it floats by. The boots make it hard to run, but I'm able to get past the paper to a spot where I can bend toward the water and try to catch it.

In the glistening of the evening sun, I have to squint to see it coming toward me. I lay on the dirt of the bank and reach into the water rushing by. It's a stark difference against the heat of the sun on my back. As the bundle approaches, I try to gauge where the twists and flow of the water will place it, but I'm wrong. It slips to the side, and I almost fall into the ditch, trying to reach it. I scramble back up and again run clumsily down the bank, hoping to get in front of it and try again, and just as I think I'm positioned perfectly, again, it eludes my capture.

I refuse to give up. Without that note, I would have no way to contact Nicole unless I walked five miles to her house. I don't even know if I have the guts to call her, but she gave me her number, and I can't lose it now. I have to get it back.

The ditch takes a turn and goes into the trees. I keep going, and then as I position myself again, I realize I no longer see the paper. It must have become soaked and is now somewhere at the bottom of the ditch. I walk back along the bank, staring desperately into the water, hoping the white of the paper will stand out against the darkness of the water and dirt.

I trace my steps and then turn and go back. Maybe it passed me, and I didn't notice. I keep walking and searching, and then the sun begins to dip, and I strain to see in the dim light of the evening.

And then I find it. The mess of soggy paper is caught in a grate. I jump down into the water and pull it from the metal bars it's pinned against. The paper is beginning to fall apart, but I'm desperate to save it and I straighten and press it lightly to try and remove as much of the wetness as I can. Even in the dusky light, I'm still able to make out the numbers from the inky smears on the paper. I let out a sigh of relief, but when I look up, I realize where I am, and a chill runs through me. How did I get this far?

A striking orange glow hovers just above the water of an immense river. It spreads out just over a small hill.

Through the trees, it looks black and shiny as it ripples in the last few moments of sunlight. It's like a painting. I stand there in awe. Is this what I was told to stay away from? What terrible evil could there possibly be here?

Darkness begins to creep in around me, and I need to get back. I still haven't opened the other head gate, and now I worry I won't be able to find it.

And then I hear the voice again. "Fear."

I turn quickly but see no one. "Who's there?" I say, even though I know I'm alone.

"Fear," it calls again. I spin, looking in all directions. It's whisper-soft but urgent. It sounds like a boy, but there is no one around, and now I'm not sure if I'm even really hearing a voice. Is it the breeze that is always there? The rustling of the leaves or the water?

I look around, and the massive trees creak and sway above me.

The wind has picked up, and the paper in my hand flaps as it tries to escape. I carefully fold the damp sheet, but this time, I tuck it carefully into the back pocket of my jeans. The pouch holding the ring is secure in my front pocket, and now another precious item will be stored in my pants.

I begin to feel anxious, and as difficult as it is to pull away from the sight of the river, I know it's time for me to leave.

CHAPTER 18

The dusky darkness has started to settle all around me, and I'm worried about finding my way back. The trees are thick and elbow out the little bit of sunshine left in the day, but I've found a thin dirt path. It follows the river, and I believe it's the same trail that led me in.

The voice has now gone silent, but I keep thinking about what I heard, and it makes me alert to every stick breaking or shuffle in my steps.

In the soft glow that hangs above the river, I see a flash and whip of something thin and shiny. It's like a long tail or string, and as I step closer, I see there is a man at the bend of the river, fishing. Was it his voice I heard? Fear.

He's casting the line high above his head in a flying arc. He is unaware I'm there, and I duck back so he doesn't spot me.

From behind one of the massive trees, I peek around and watch him. He's old. I can tell by his weathered face and the way his shoulders stoop. Is this the man they call Old Tom?

He stands knee-deep in the river. One hand holds the line and the other, the pole, and in quick, smooth casts, the line floats and twirls in the air before he directs it gently toward the water. It falls lightly onto the glassy surface. He's focused on where it lands and slowly draws the line in, watching carefully. This repeats several times, like a choreographed dance. I'm mesmerized watching, and yet, I know I need to sneak out of the woods and finish pulling the gates. I've already been gone for too long, and soon, it will be completely dark. I'm going to have enough trouble finding my way back with the small amount of daylight I have left.

Just as I'm about to turn and leave, I see the man jerk the pole up quickly. It arcs under the strain. He's caught something. Even at this distance, I can see his excitement. The line is taut, and the pole straightens and bends as he slowly reels it in. I hear a splash and see a flicker of silver that jumps from the water and plunges back in. My heart is racing as though I'm the one holding the pole and feeling the pull.

I continue to watch until he brings the swirling line to him, and then he reaches for it with one hand behind his back and retrieves a net. With it, he scoops up his shining prize.

He's bent over as the fish tosses in the mesh cradle. He studies it a moment, and then he reaches into the net. His back is now turned from me, and I can't make out what he's doing, but then I see him put the net into the water, and the fish flips and lunges back into the river. The man then stands and watches as ripples fan out away from him.

It's past time that I should go. I'm mesmerized, but then I hear a dog bark. Immediately, I lunge back behind the tree, hoping I'm not spotted. I wait a moment, but the barking continues.

"Rusty," the man calls, and my heart races as the barking gets closer.

In just seconds, I have a scruffy three-legged dog, just a few feet away, barking at me.

"Go on," I say, trying to shoo him away while still trying to hide behind the tree.

"Rusty! Come!" The man continues to call from the river. I don't think he's spotted me, but it won't be long before he is wondering what this dog is after.

"Get out of here!" I try to be stern but still quiet. It isn't working.

I'm cornered. The dog continues to bark and give little whines, but he doesn't act like he's going to bite me. He's even wagging his tail. However, I'm not taking any chances.

The man calls again and then whistles. He's getting closer.

Suddenly, the dog turns and runs back toward the man. This is my chance to get away. I run toward the ditch and away from the river, but the ground is uneven, and I stumble in the oversized boots. I have lost my sense of direction and don't know if I'm going toward the ditch or farther back into the woods. All I know is it's away from the man in the river.

"What are you doing back here?" I hear him call. He's seen me, and I expect I'll soon have the dog yapping at my heels.

"Come back here," the old man yells. He is urgent. Is he the reason Mrs. Frost warned me about this place? Why did Jesse also tell me to stay away and that Old Tom would be watching?

I'm trudging quickly but clumsily with no direction. I glance back, expecting to see the dog on my heels, but it isn't there. I'm relieved but still frantic. I wonder what will happen if he catches me. Will he have me arrested for trespassing? After being told not to come back here, Mrs. Frost will surely have me sent away.

The woods are now dark. Then, through the trees, I see a small, dim light. I run toward it. My breath is hard, and my chest is heaving. I feel like I'm running in sand. I stop and try to get my bearings. Where am I? I stand still and listen. I can't hear the dog or the man. I wonder if I've lost them or if they're still after me. I don't dare move for fear that I'll alert them, but what am I going to do, stay here until morning when the sun comes out? I have to keep going. I know the river is in the opposite direction of where I need to go, so I'll either find my way there or out of the woods and back to the field. I decide to continue toward the light. It looks like a single bulb. I keep going— trotting as fast as I can through the trees and darkness, and then I realize the glow is coming from the back of a house. That house. It's Old Tom's house. At least now I know where I am. The laneway leading to the head gate is right on the other side. I just need to somehow get around that house without being spotted.

If the man on the river is Old Tom, then the house should be empty, and since I saw the three-legged dog at the house yesterday, I'm assuming the man with it today has got to be him. Still, I'm not sure, and I hesitate. Mrs. Frost said it was dangerous back here. Is Old Tom the reason?

The man in the river didn't look like the evil thing I've been warned about, but sometimes people don't look bad when they really are. Jesse said I had the right to be there, so if he catches me, that's what I'll say.

I'm amazed and disheartened at how quickly the dark has taken over. I don't know what time it is, but I haven't been out here that long. My heart sinks when I remember Jesse's warning about opening the gates. If I don't do it right, the water won't get to the fields, and then I'll have to explain why. My eyes try to focus in the dark. How will I find the gates now?

There is a small hill that leads up to the house, and my boots aren't making the trip up easy. I can feel rocks and sticks as I climb with my hands and feet, but soon, I'm at the top, and the light is enough that I can see I'm going in the right direction.

As I rest for a moment against a tree and try to formulate a plan, my eyes focus on the back of the small house. The porch is illuminated, and a small but lush garden spreads out beyond it. Even in the dim light, I can see the straight, well-tended rows and vines loaded with tiny, round, red fruit.

I've got to get back to the ditch and at least try to do the job I was given. The woods are quiet. I don't hear the man or the dog, and I begin to make my way around the house and back to the ditch.

I take a step out away from the cluster of trees I've been standing by, and as I make my way around to the side of the house, a waft of scent envelopes me. It's floral and so familiar that I stop and look around. For a moment, I lose my need to flee and am searching for the origin of what I'm smelling. The scent has my memories flooding back, paralyzing me with a wistful pull. Is it her? It's the one memory I have of my mother. I may not have touched or even seen her for years, but her scent is what I remember, and that is what I smell now. It's her.

I hear the dog bark in the distance, and it snaps me away from my nostalgia. I move away and back toward the ditch.

I run out of the porch light and into the darkness. I know I'm heading in the right direction now. I let out a sigh, but then I hear the crunch of a footstep.

My heart leaps, and I turn to see the barrel of a gun. Then, a light hits my face, and I throw my hands up. "Please don't shoot," I call out.

"Put your hands down," the man says. He lowers a flashlight and he's shaking his head.

It's him. It's Old Tom. Then I see that what I thought was a gun is actually a fishing pole. I feel like a fool.

"You're not allowed back here. You know that." He's stern but not angry. "You're trespassing."

"I swear I didn't mean to be back here," I tell him, my heart still pounding.

"Then why are you? And how did you get across?" he asks.

In the dim glow of the porch light, I see the dog come from behind. He stays next to Old Tom and, balancing on his three legs, wags his entire body.

"I was doing the gates in the ditch, and I lost something in the water. It floated away, and when I finally got it, I was all the way back here," I explain.

He inclines his head. "The gates? On this side?"

"The ditch gates for the water. To water the fields," I try to explain. "I was supposed to pull them out at six."

"I know about the ditch gates," he says, irritated. "Do you mean the gates on this side?"

I shrug, not knowing what he means by "side." "The gates that go with this ditch," I say, pointing to where I wish I hadn't followed.

"So, where's Jesse?" he asks.

"He had to be somewhere else and asked me to do it."

He cocks his head and tries to study me in the dim light. "He asked you. Who are you? Where do you live?"

I hesitate to answer. What if he calls the Frosts and complains? I can't risk being moved again.

His eyebrows furrow in annoyance. I have no good lie, so I blurt out the truth. "My name is Landis, and I live with the Frosts," I say, pointing back in the direction of their house. "They live over there."

His eyes go wide, and he takes a step back. "You live with them?"

I nod.

"What do you mean you live with them?" he asks.

"Um," I search for an answer. "I needed a place to stay and ..." I begin to tell him my lie about them being my aunt and uncle, but he cuts me off.

"You're working for them?" he asks.

"I'm helping out with the chores after school," I explain.

"Do they know you're back here?"

I shake my head. "Please don't tell them. They told me to stay away. I promise I didn't mean to be here. It was an accident."

He raises an eyebrow and looks contemplative and almost sad. My eyes have adjusted to the dark, and he doesn't look nearly as intimidating now.

"I'm sorry I bothered you," I say.

He huffs and then sighs. "You're not bothering me, but you better finish the gates and get back," he says.

I shrug and look out toward the dark field. "I'm not sure I'll be able to find the other gates. I pulled the first one, but then I ..."

"Take this," he says, handing me the small plastic flashlight. "Walk straight this way, and you'll hit the ditch, then just follow it over, and you'll find the gates." He looks at his watch. "You're a little late, but no one should notice."

"Thank you, sir," I say.

"Call me Tom," he says.

I nod, relieved.

Holding the flashlight as I walk off toward the field, I realize I now have an excuse to return. And as I go into the darkness, I wonder why I need an excuse to come back here. What is it about this place that has everyone convinced that I need to stay away?

CHAPTER 19

"Where've you been?"

His voice startles me. It's Mr. Frost. He's back and standing in the barn. I had planned to hide the flashlight there until I found a way to give it back to Old Tom. But now I hide it behind me.

"I pulled the gates in the ditch," I try to explain.

"It doesn't take two hours to pull gates," he says, annoyed. Then he looks confused. "You pulled the gates?"

"Yes. Jesse showed me how ..."

I want to make it clear why I'm late, but I know I can't tell him the truth. "I had some problems pulling one of them out. I've never done it before. Next time should be easier."

"Next time?" he asks. He shakes his head. "No. You shouldn't be up there."

Him too? I think. "Why?" I ask. "If I'm going to be working here, I need to know how."

"Working here?" he says and looks confused. "If you want to help out, we can find you other chores to do. Now get on inside. Evelyn is worried sick about you. She doesn't know you were up there. Tell her you fell asleep in the barn. Don't let her know you were over there." He looks out toward the woods.

I'm tired and annoyed by the rules and the secrets. "What's so bad that I can't go there? I know the way. I'm not going to get lost."

Even in the dim light of the barn, I can see his face turn to stone. He is silent, which is worse than if he were to yell at me.

"I can do this," I say, frustrated. "I'm not a little kid."

His eyebrows furrow, and he gives a frustrated sigh. "We'll talk about it later. But not with Evelyn."

I shake my head, confused, and before I can say anything else, Mr. Frost puts a hand up.

"Please go inside. Let her know you're okay."

I relent and go to where I left the jacket. As I take it and start my walk to the house, he stops me. Looking at the coat, he asks, "Where did you get that?"

I feel awkward, knowing the jacket is his. "Mrs. Frost, let me wear it. I told her I didn't want to take your stuff." I hold it out to him.

He looks back up at me, confused. "It's not mine," he says, but he still takes the coat and studies it. He turns it back and forth as though he's looking for something.

"The pockets were empty," I tell him, worried he thinks I stole whatever he's looking for.

He hands it back to me. "Keep it. No sense of it staying in a closet."

If it's not his, then whose is it? I want to ask, but he motions me toward the house, so I go, leaving him in the dark.

MRS. FROST IS on me as soon as I'm inside.

"What happened? Where were you?" she asks. She looks frantic. I'm not used to anyone worrying about me. The only grilling I get is when they think I've done something wrong, so I'm immediately on defense and unsure what to reveal.

"I fell asleep in the barn." I use the lie Mr. Frost gave me. "I'm sorry."

"You fell asleep?" She stands there, mouth agape, and then she puts a hand to her cheek. "That's right. The wind must have kept you awake last night."

The bumping noise in the off-limits room. Suddenly, I do feel tired.

She also looks exhausted. She's still looking me over like I'm missing something.

"Are you hungry?"

"Hungry?" I ask. "You left me dinner," I remind her.

She smiles. "I'm heating things up for Gordon. If you'd like some more."

Two dinners? I nod, and she sends me upstairs to change. I shove the clothes into the hamper, take a quick shower, and go back downstairs, stomach rumbling.

As I come around the corner into the dining room, I see Mr. and Mrs. Frost together by the table. She has her head on his chest, and his arm is around her shoulder. He's rubbing it, comforting her. Did my being late really cause this? No one has ever cared where I was before.

His kindness toward her is also confusing. After the way he spoke to her on that first day, I find this show of affection odd. I pause and watch a moment, then clear my throat to let them know I'm there. Mr. Frost looks back at me. His face is somber, but he gives me an appreciative nod.

"Let's have dinner," he says.

When Mrs. Frost sees me, she tries to smile, but it's forced.

Mr. Frost waves me over to the table, trying to lighten the mood. "With all the work Landis did around the barn today, I'm sure he's starving."

We're sharing a lie, but it feels more like a good-intentioned secret.

I take my seat, and when Mrs. Frost leaves us to go to the kitchen, Mr. Frost leans over. "If you want to take on the water on the front pastures, we can talk about it."

What's there to talk about, I think, and he can see I'm confused. I've never had anyone worry about me like this, especially when it comes to chores or work.

"She's worried about you being back there, but I'll talk to her."

Before I can ask him what is back in those woods that has her so concerned, she is back and takes a seat, but without a plate. She's just sitting and watching us eat. For a moment, we all sit in silence. It's painful.

"How long have you had this farm?" I ask Mr. Frost, hoping to clear this awkward cloud.

His eyebrows lift, and he looks toward his wife. "Well, ever since we got married, I guess. I also have land up north, but we decided to live here."

"It's a really big house for two people," I say. I'm still wondering why there aren't more like me in this big place, but I see her face turn a bit sad, and then I want to take back my words.

"I didn't mean ..." I stammer.

"It is a big house," she says. "It's where I grew up."

I'm surprised. "You grew up here?"

She nods.

"So you've always lived here?" I ask.

Mrs. Frost gives a small smile. "Almost. There was a short period of time when we were first married, but soon after, we moved in here."

"Why aren't there any other kids here?"

Her face falls, and again, I curse myself for letting my questions get away from me.

"I mean, it's just this house is so big. I've never been in a foster home where it's just me." I try to explain.

Mrs. Frost shakes her head. "Landis, we're not a foster home."

I lean back, realizing I really am here to work on the farm.

She looks to Mr. Frost, who lifts his eyebrows. He seems uncomfortable.

She clears her throat. "We want you here."

Mr. Frost cuts in. "There's a lot that needs to be done around here. I'm hoping you can help with more than just a few chores."

"So, you did bring me here to work on the farm?"

"Gordon?" Mrs. Frost says, obviously uncomfortable.

"It's not work when it's your home. This is your home," he says.

I know they're trying to make it all seem like they're not just using me. I'm actually good with this arrangement. It feels better to be doing something useful while I wait for my mother rather than just take up space.

When we finish the meal, Mr. Frost stands up. "If you're going to be helping out with the chores, Landis, you deserve some type of allowance. Come to my office, and let's talk about it," he says. He then places his napkin on his plate and gives Mrs. Frost a lift of his eyebrow.

Mrs. Frost smiles back at him. She nods and encourages me to follow him, so I do. When we reach his room on the other side of the house, it is filled with books, and several mounted deer heads hang on the walls. The ceiling is high, and their antlers reach up toward it. He takes a seat behind a large, dark wooden desk and takes out a checkbook from a drawer.

I feel awkward having him pay me, but I'll need the money when my mom gets out. "I like doing things like this. I can do more."

He nods, knowing what I'm alluding to. "I appreciate your willingness to help. I did these jobs when I was your age."

"Like pulling the head gates?" I ask. I'm not trying to be belligerent, but I want him to understand I can do it.

He can see I'm trying to make a point.

"I know you're able to do it, Landis. It's just that area is a place you shouldn't ..."

I shake my head, frustrated. "Why?" I interrupt. "I know I had some trouble today, but I can do it. I can handle walking across a pasture and pulling ..."

He puts his hand up and looks behind me. I turn as Mrs. Frost comes into the office, holding two plates with large pieces of chocolate cake.

"I thought you might want this while you're talking," she says, handing us each a plate.

Mr. Frost looks awkward as he takes it from her. We're both silent, and she notices.

"Did I interrupt something?" she asks.

I look to Mr. Frost, who bites his lip.

She stands, waiting for an answer.

Mr. Frost takes a deep breath and sets the plate on the desk.

"Landis wants to help out with the chores," he says.

She smiles. "Yes. That's good."

"He wants to help with the irrigation. He can pull the head gates and help clean ditches in the east pasture and ..."

"What about Jesse," she asks before he can finish.

"Jesse will need the help, especially now that we've taken on the other fields."

She shakes her head. "Why don't you do it now that you're home?"

Mr. Frost gives her an annoyed frown. "Because I have other things I should be doing, and it's a job Landis can do. You know that."

She's becoming agitated. "There are plenty of chores he can do here around the house. He shouldn't be doing all this work. I don't want him up there. It's too close to ..."

I know what she's talking about. It's the woods. The place she has warned me about. The place where I found myself today.

My shoulders sink. It's not so much the work I want, but simply to have something to do. For so many years, I've either been stuck inside a cramped house doing nothing or wandering through some neighborhood or town like a stray dog. I'm finally at a place that has a reason to be out and doing something, and now she won't give me the freedom to do it.

"What is it in those woods that's so bad?" I blurt out.

They both turn to me, stunned that I'm speaking up. It feels odd. I'm arguing to pull gates in a ditch, but I feel compelled to do so. "I'm almost sixteen. You act like I'm going to get lost or something."

Mrs. Frost puts a hand to her chest as though my words have stabbed her.

"He's not going all the way back there. It's just to the head gate," Mr. Frost says.

"It's too much. He's not a farmhand," she pleads.

Mr. Frost closes the checkbook and puts it back on the desk. "No, but it's what families do. They all pitch in, and that is what Landis wants to do."

I look over at him, shocked. Now it's family? Mrs. Frost is also stunned. She looks at me as though wanting my response.

I nod, trying to show that I'm willing and want to help.

She studies me, looking for a crack, but I stand firm.

Then she relents. "If that's what you want. But no going any further than the ditch." Her lip quivers. "Stay away from ..." she hesitates, "... back there."

It's a disturbing command and has me wondering again about what horrible thing has caused her to be so afraid of those woods.

I nod, and inside, I feel I've won, and then I remind myself that my victory is trudging around a pasture and pulling ditch gates.

That night, I look out the window of my room toward that dark and ominous place I stumbled into today—the place I've again been told to stay away from. I watch the shadowy sway of the trees and remember the alluring vision of the river and woods, and I feel the breeze gently tugging.

CHAPTER 20

My mother often finds herself staring out toward the woods. She's always felt the pull of the dark mass of trees, convinced something ominous lies within.

She used to see flashes of memories: darkness, falling snow, and the feeling of icy frost on bare skin. But now those past images and sensations are coupled with an urgent desire to find what might be hidden and lost inside the dark wooded place that has been the constant backdrop of her life.

It's the reason she never ventured out into the space. Unlike her father and Wesley, who found joy in discovering what the woods had to offer, Evelyn preferred to stay away. She wasn't sure what the memories meant or even if they were real, but they were so clear they were hard to dismiss.

It never really made a difference for her until Ramona came into her life.

The year my mother turned twelve, my grandfather had his main farmhand move into the small cabin hidden in the woods of the back pasture. The man was older but worked as hard as the men half his age, and his wife was quiet and spoke almost no English.

Normally, Evelyn had little interest in who lived back there, but when the couple's granddaughter came to live with them a few months later, it changed my mother's world.

All her life, she had never lived close to any girls her age, and while she had friends at school, it was almost impossible to see them during the summer without it being a scheduled and planned event.

Unlike her older brother, my mother wasn't allowed to ride her bike into town or go swimming at the trestle unless Wesley agreed to take her. Working the farm gave Thomas little time to cart his daughter to the mall or even to town, where most of Evelyn's friends lived.

Having a friend she could see every day was a dream come true.

The two girls became inseparable, and although the walk from the big house to the cabin was still long, it was never a burden for Evelyn, and every morning, the girls would meet and spend the entire day together.

Ramona was almost a year older but didn't seem to mind because she, too, was lonely and knew no one in the school. Her mother had died the year before. Evelyn didn't ask how she had died, knowing how awkward that question could be, but Ramona told her one night as they lay in sleeping bags on the floor of the family room watching the show Bewitched.

"Don't you wish that you could make your mother come back just like that?" Ramona mused, referring to the sudden appearance of one of the characters on the show. "That all you'd have to do is wiggle your nose, and she'd reappear."

"I guess so," said Evelyn, softly.

Evelyn had never known her mother, and while she felt the loss, she had no idea what her mother would be like or how it would be if Ramona's fantasy ever happened.

"Don't you miss her?" Ramona asked.

Evelyn nodded.

"My mother died in a car crash. How did yours die?" Ramona asked.

"She was sick," Evelyn answered.

Ramona scrunched her forehead. "Like cancer?"

Evelyn felt a rush of embarrassment. She didn't know. From her earliest memories, she had been told her mother was sick and died. It all happened when she was barely four years old. She had never thought to ask what type of illness took her.

"Yes. Cancer," Evelyn said, not wanting to look foolish.

Ramona sat up and motioned Evelyn to do the same. She stared at her for a moment. "We don't have mothers, and we don't have sisters. We're best friends, but even more than that. It's like we're sisters." She leaned over and gave Evelyn a tight hug. "No matter what happens, let's promise to be sisters. We'll share everything and always be there for each other."

When Evelyn leaned back, she was in tears.

"Why are you crying?" asked Ramona. "You should be happy. We don't have mothers, but now we each have a sister."

Evelyn wiped her nose and smiled. "I'm crying because it's what I've always wanted."

"So, it does work!" Ramona giggled. "You just wiggle your nose and poof, you have a sister!"

Evelyn laughed, and Ramona turned and took a big handful of popcorn from a large bowl. She went back to watching the show as though what had just happened was simply meant to be.

My mother fell asleep that night desperately hoping that Ramona was as ardent about this declaration of sisterhood as she was, and when she awoke the next morning, to find Ramona dressed and in one of Evelyn's favorite tops and sitting at the breakfast table with her father, she felt a twinge of jealousy run through her.

"Good morning," her father said. He stood up and began to take his plate to the kitchen. He paused and put a hand on Ramona's shoulder. "It sounds like you two have a fun day planned. I'll have to check the westside ditch, but I'll be back in time to take you."

Evelyn began to ask where he was taking them but didn't want to feel out of the loop, so she just smiled and let him go to the kitchen.

"Take us where?" she asked Ramona when he was out of earshot.

"The fabric store at the mall." Ramona then motioned to the bright blue peasant top she had obviously taken from Evelyn's closet. "I was just trying it on. Will you make me one? Not exactly the same, but I like it. You have the cutest clothes."

The compliment was genuine, and Evelyn's annoyance faded into pride. Evelyn had been sewing since she was eight years old after finding her mother's old sewing machine in a closet. Her first attempts at even threading it were frustrating enough that she almost gave up, but she eventually learned and was now able to follow patterns and even stitch complex ruffles and sew sleeves, hems, and zippers that looked like they came from a store. But her clothes were different. Every piece was the latest style but with unique touches that had the other girls at school begging to know where she had found them. They had been to all the stores in the mall and seen nothing even similar. Evelyn initially hesitated to tell them she had made them herself, knowing if they looked close enough, they'd be able to see the tiny mistakes and flaws, but when her brother wore one of her shirts during a rodeo competition and announced it was her design, the cat was out of the bag, and to her surprise the requests began to pour in. Her rodeo shirts and jackets became sought after all over the county, and soon, her beloved hobby not only brought her attention among her peers but a small amount of income, which for a young girl was almost unheard of.

She stuck with shirts and tops. Jeans were a staple in their area, and she didn't see anyone giving up their Levi's or Wranglers for homemade jeans; besides, the tough, thick denim was hard to work with. And there was no need. The list of requests for her rodeo shirts alone kept her busy often into the night.

The blouse Ramona wore was from a pattern that Evelyn had altered to look like one she saw in a Seventeen magazine at the dentist's office. She was proud of how it had turned out, and seeing Ramona's obvious desire to own it was intoxicating.

"The same but in a different color, like red or dark pink," Ramona gushed. "We'll look just like sisters," she said, raising her eyebrows for emphasis. Soon, Ramona's closet was filled with as many or more of Evelyn's distinct pieces as Evelyn had for herself.

For years, the two girls were inseparable, but when they entered high school, something changed. What began as a tiny gap in their friendship now felt like a canyon. Her own brother was invading whatever space she was able to cling to.

Until that year, he had all but ignored the girls. Yes, he teased and tormented Evelyn like any older brother, but most of the time, he was either with his friends, helping their father on the farm, or in other parts of the state steer wrestling. But that year was different.

Not only did my mom feel she had to compete with Wesley for her father's attention, but now her brother was honing in on her best friend. Again, Wesley was stealing someone she cared about.

She didn't blame Ramona. It seemed every girl in eastern Idaho wanted to date Wesley, which is why it bothered Evelyn so much. There were so many girls that were falling over themselves for Wesley. Why'd he have to choose her best friend? A part of Evelyn felt he did it just to annoy her.

For months, Evelyn hoped it was only a phase, and soon he'd move on, but even after he graduated, and to Evelyn's irritation, he and Ramona were still a steady couple. And now Wesley had an old truck he bought, enabling him to spend almost every evening with Ramona. This left Evelyn either sitting at home or tagging along and feeling like a tick who was clinging onto them.

Wesley's best friend, Gordon, was often brought along, and while she enjoyed being with him, she also wondered if it wasn't Wesley's ploy to get her out of the way.

Gordon was tall, with smiling green eyes and muscular arms that Evelyn often found herself staring at. He was quiet, and yet he was expressive as he told her of his plans to expand his family's cattle business and bring in a breed called Angus to eastern Idaho.

The two couples double-dated, but Wesley and Ramona always planned where they would go and what they would do. This bothered Evelyn a bit, but when Gordon took Evelyn's hand while walking into a dance at a large barn near town, she caught Wesley giving her a sly and knowing smirk that had her stewing the rest of the night.

When Evelyn began her senior year, she found herself ruminating about what life after school would hold for her. There was little encouragement toward college from her father, and even the teachers at school were directing her toward a life as a wife and mother. She loved her home economics and sewing classes, but did that mean she was destined to be a housewife? What about the clothes she designed? Her ability to imagine and create something of not only use but style. Wasn't that worthy of acknowledgment beyond helping her to find a husband? She was already making money at it. However, a seamstress, even a talented one, was not viewed as a career but rather as a needed skill for a homemaker.

The assumption angered her. It's what everyone expected, and the more she saw her path in life paved by others, the more she became unhappy with the route. It fueled her need for rebellion. She was determined to prove them wrong, but what could she do? No matter how hard she tried to see herself with a different future, the doors in her mind continued to close.

"What do you think about college?" Evelyn asked Ramona one night as they sat at the small table in Ramona's kitchen, painting their nails.

Ramona shrugged. "What about it?"

Evelyn scrunched one side of her mouth. "I don't know," she said. "What are you going to do after graduation?"

"Get a job, I guess," Ramona answered without looking up as she brushed on the bright orange polish.

"A job? Doing what?" asked Evelyn.

"Something in an office. I want my own desk. I don't want to be standing up all day. That's why I took typing this year. My mom was a waitress, and she hated it."

"Don't you want to get married?" Evelyn asked as they contemplated the future. She just assumed she would. Didn't every girl want to get married?

Ramona shrugged. "I don't know, but if I do, I want to marry someone famous."

"Famous?" asked Evelyn, surprised.

"Rich and famous. I want a big house," Ramona said. She then looked up from her toenails at the high ceilings and large spaces of Evelyn's house. "Even bigger than this."

"What about Wesley?" Evelyn wasn't suggesting Ramona marry Wesley—the last thing she wanted was to encourage that, but she knew how her brother felt about Ramona and was surprised when she acted as though he was already just a passing thought.

Ramona sighed. "Wesley?" she gave a stilted laugh. "And live on a farm the rest of my life? No thanks."

Evelyn's heart sank. Not only because it felt like Ramona was demeaning her brother but also because that was the path Evelyn's life was most likely heading.

"We should move to California together," Ramona said with wide, excited eyes. "We could get jobs and rent an apartment and go to the beach. It would be so fun."

"California?" asked Evelyn, having never been there and certainly never considered moving.

Ramona nodded. "Yes. Where I used to live, I have family there."

Evelyn's brow scrunched. "But you said you moved here to be with your grandparents because you didn't have any other family."

Evelyn felt bad about bringing up Ramona's past, knowing her mother's death wasn't that long ago. However, Ramona was almost twelve when her mother died and had at least been able to know her, unlike Evelyn, who wondered if the memories of her mother were even real or just what she wanted them to be. Ramona's stories about her mother were hard for Evelyn to hear, but as sad as it often made her feel, Evelyn also felt fortunate to have something Ramona had never known—a father.

My mother knew my grandfather not only loved her but he also afforded her so many things that Ramona went without. But the money that came with being a Corrigan also brought the sideways glances from some who still lingered in the past.

Most of the kids at school were ignorant of Evelyn's family's troubled past, but some, especially those who lived on the other side of town, were oddly aware, and while they rarely said a word, she saw the disdain in their eyes. But even with the looks and comments, how could she ever fathom the nightmare that night in the hollow would bring?

All my mother could think of at that moment was whether or not Ramona was serious. Was she really planning to leave? And did she expect Evelyn to come with her?

Evelyn had never contemplated moving to a strange state with no family or friends. Why would she consider leaving her life of familiar comfort? It was an intimidating thought. And yet, also a bit exhilarating. The idea of a life in a new place felt freeing. And because Ramona had lived there before, surely she would know her way around. But was that enough?

"I have an aunt," Ramona explained. Her eyes still danced with the idea of it all. "Actually, she was my mom's best friend, but she's just like an aunt. She said I could live with her until I can get my own place." Then Ramona's voice went from confident to unsure. She sat a moment in thought, and when she realized Evelyn was watching her, she sat up straight. "I might go even before I graduate."

Evelyn was shocked. She was used to Ramona's big talk and even bigger ideas, but it sounded as though this was actually being planned. "But it's our senior year."

Ramona shrugged. "The sooner I start working, the faster I can save up for my own place."

The statement seemed forced. Just a few weeks ago, Ramona asked Evelyn if she would make her a dress for their senior prom. Even though Wesley had already graduated, he agreed to take her. Why would she plan ahead like that if she was just going to leave?

Evelyn wanted to ask, but when Ramona's voice became sharp and decisive, she knew it wasn't the time, so she nodded as though she understood and then kept quiet.

CHAPTER 21

I've been at this school for two weeks, and besides Nicole, Jeremy, and a few of their friends, I'm still getting the same odd gawks and whispers as that first day.

You would have thought the new kid stuff would have worn off by now, but it's more than that, and until I can figure out what it is, I get through the day as best I can.

I do most of the homework assignments and take notes in class, but especially in my first period, I find myself drifting off bored, so I've begun bringing my book and propping it up in the textbook so I look like I'm studying.

Just as I begin to flip my bookmark to where I left off, the teacher is interrupted by the office lady who brought me to class on my first day.

A tall, dark-haired, broody-looking boy stands with her, and when the other kids in class see him, I hear a few gasps. I glance around, wondering what they see. Are they going to act strangely about this new kid, too?

His gaze makes a sweep of the room and he seems completely bored already. And while I know I've never met or been around any of the people in this school, there is something oddly familiar about him.

The lady hands the teacher a piece of paper and then leaves the room.

"Take a seat," the teacher says, and the boy goes to the very back of the room and slumps into a desk.

"Someone lend Kevin a pen and some paper," the teacher says, then gives this Kevin an annoyed look. "There may be only two weeks of school left until summer, but you will still be expected to take the final."

He talks to this boy like he already knows him. And with no "new kid" introduction to the class, I figure he has been here before. So, why does he look familiar to me? There's no way I could have met him before.

I glance back at him, but when other students see me staring, I turn back around and start into my novel. I'm halfway through *Treasure Island*, and while I wish I wasn't in possession of this stolen book, my daily escapes into it are keeping my time at this school tolerable. Time passes quickly the minute I am back into the story.

It's the sliding of desks as people stand to leave that alerts me that class is over. I close both books and store my stolen one, hiding it close to me. I doubt anyone would know the book was stolen, except the words "Property of Idaho Boys Home" are stamped on the cover. It could expose both what I stole and where I've been. If that was revealed, who I am, and my whole bag of lies could be exposed.

When Kevin walks by my desk at the front of the room, one of the other boys nudges him and looks at me.

Kevin's eyes go thin, and again, there is something about him that I've seen somewhere before. I look away and gather my things to leave.

As I exit the room, he is just outside the door, talking with two other boys. The look I get from him now isn't one of question but of concern. He looks down as though trying to place me. I have no reason to feel this way, but something about Kevin tells me he's trouble.

When my third hour ends, I head to the cafeteria for lunch. At the entrance, I stand, debating if I should wait or go in, and begin to navigate my way through the line.

The stares and whispers pass by me. It's been a full two weeks, and today it seems worse. At least while I'm in class, the teachers keep things quiet.

I try to ignore them while looking out over the mass of kids in the hall, searching for her brown curls. Now, as I wait, I begin to worry. Even though Nicole gave me her number last week, let me sit with her on the bus, and allowed me to tag along with her and Jeremy and a car full of their friends to the movies on Saturday, I'm still not sure if I'm considered a friend. Do I look pathetic waiting here—the goofy-looking little dork that everyone seems to think is diseased?

Then I see her. She's walking toward me with two other girls. I recognize them from our trip to the theater.

Nicole's curls bounce as she walks, and she smiles when she sees me.

I try to act like I just got there and not like I was desperately waiting.

"Hey," she calls out.

The other girls also smile. I'm relieved and glad to see friendly faces, and I give a small wave.

As they reach me, my mind spins, trying to remember names. Kathy was shorter, and Lisa had really long hair, I sort in my head.

"Do you want to sit with us?" asks Nicole.

"Sure," I say, feeling relieved.

We all go through the lunch line and then carry our trays to an empty table. Just as we're about to start eating, another girl comes to the table and slides in next to Nicole. She whispers to her, and Nicole's eyes go wide.

"Kevin Jenkins is back here?" she says.

Both Lisa and Kathy look stunned.

"They let him out?" Lisa asks.

The girl with the news raises an eyebrow as though there is much more that she isn't telling. It's as cryptic as the mumblings I've heard on the bus and in class for the last two weeks. Again, I'm wondering what's going on.

"How do you know?" asks Nicole.

"He was in my homeroom." She then turns to me. "You were there. You saw him."

I raise my shoulders, confused, but then realize who she is talking about. "Oh yeah," I say. "There was a new guy in class today."

"He's not new, and he shouldn't even be here at all," says Kathy. In a low whisper, she leans toward me and says, "He just got out of juvie."

"Juvie?" I ask, surprised.

Lisa nods and lifts an eyebrow. She enjoys revealing this juicy detail. "Juvie's just like jail," she explains, but I know exactly what it is.

Nicole sighs. "Don't worry about him. He's a jerk. I can't believe they let him back in school after what he did."

Lisa then turns to me. "If he says anything to you, just ignore him. He's nothing but a creep."

I squint at her, wondering what she means. "What would he say?" I ask, but before she can answer, Kathy leans over.

"Here he comes," she whispers. "It's him."

We all turn to see.

"Don't look," she scolds us, but it's too late.

Kevin saunters into the lunchroom, flanked by two other guys. He is tall—much taller than the other two, and his hair is so dark it looks black. It stands out because, besides me, there are almost no other people at this school with dark hair. There are so many shades of blond, light brown, and even red. But dark, almost black, is a rarity.

The deafening chatter of the cafeteria has turned to low murmurs, and Kevin glances around as if looking for a fight. Then my heart sinks. Oh no, this can't be. The realization of who Kevin is and why he's familiar hits me. It isn't just a fluke that I felt I recognized him, and this could ruin everything for me.

Juvie. He was there in that home for boys—that jail. I never met him because we were in different halls, but I remember seeing him in the cafeteria and television room. If he recognizes me, that would be the worst thing ever. He'll not only blow my cover but if anyone finds out I was there, they'll see me as a criminal, too.

His sneer, hunched stance, and dark hair are undeniable. I know he's the same one. Even in this entirely new town and school, Kevin and I have a past. It wasn't a long one, but one incident alone could, unfortunately, have him remembering me.

The Idaho Boys Home. I was one of about a dozen boys staying there. Some were there for petty crimes, but some were just without a place to live—like me, in between foster homes—they were in limbo. However, now that I think about that place, I realize calling it a jail is far more fitting than calling it a home.

It was my second time in a place like that. The first time, I was thirteen, and my mom was supposed to be getting out, but somehow, it got delayed, and there was no plan for me. The older I get, the harder it is for people to take me in. No one wants to hassle with a boy my age, even when I do whatever I can not to be a problem.

Even on my best behavior, I've been accused, suspected, and blamed for things I had no part in. And that is how I ended up at the Idaho Boys Home.

It was Nick, the red-haired boy with big ears from house number eleven, who stole that money from the foster mother, but we both ended up at the "Home" that day.

Because I didn't rat him out, he wanted to chum around as though we were old buddies. I wanted no part of it. I wanted to do whatever I could to be set free for when my mom returned. What good would it do if she got out, but I was still serving time?

While I wasn't guilty of that crime, I had evidence of another theft hidden with me. The one I've carried for years now, and if it was ever discovered, I'd have no defense. I was lucky because I was able to keep my own underwear when I was told to change into the baggy light blue uniforms that we all had to wear.

The entire month I spent there, I hardly spoke to anyone. I stayed in my room or sat reading at a table in a corner and away from the others.

You learn quickly in these places that being private and keeping to yourself is the best way to stay out of trouble. And that's what I did. The first week I was there, I found a book on a small cart called the library, and besides going to the common area for meals, I stayed to myself and read.

The day the new caseworker, picked me up for the drive to the Frosts', I saw Nick's face as one of the men led me out. I was leaving, but he had to stay, and his face looked like someone betrayed.

"Why are you getting out?" he asked, coming to me as the man spoke to the person who controlled the large locked door. "What did you tell them?"

I brushed him off, and then the man blocked him and told him to go back to his room.

"Squealer," he called out, convinced I told on him.

Frustrated with my freedom and his lack of it, he stomped over to where a group of boys stood watching the confrontation. One of them stepped forward. Taller than the others, with slumped shoulders and long dark hair. He joined Nick in his chant. "Squealer. Squealer," they both yelled. And before the door to the common area closed, the entire room had joined in. "Squealer."

It's him. Kevin Jenkins is that boy. I recognize his hunched stance and mass of black hair, but does he really remember me, or am I just imagining it?

As Kevin walks by our table, I put my face down, hoping that because we're away from that place, he won't realize I was the one he called "Squealer."

"One of the ladies?" he says when he sees me surrounded by the girls.

I ignore him and try not to make eye contact. Please don't say anything, I'm begging inwardly. School will be out on summer break in just two weeks. Can I avoid him and what he can expose until then?

"Hey Nicole," he says. "Been back in the hollow lately?" He gives a huff. It isn't a question but rather a poke.

She doesn't answer, and with the silence, I can't help but glance up.

Nicole inclines her head and gives him a look of disgust.

He huffs when he doesn't get the rise he was hoping for.

What does he know about Nicole? I can't help but look up even though I am still worried about Kevin remembering who I am.

Kevin then turns toward the cafeteria entrance. I follow his gaze and see Jeremy.

He scowls and then quickly leaves, saying nothing more.

I feel a collective sigh from the girls and myself.

"He's such a jerk," says Kathy.

"He should be embarrassed to show his face here. At least his sister stays away," says Lisa.

Jeremy sees us from across the room and comes over. He's wearing his jacket, and I feel a bit self-conscious wearing mine, as though I'm trying to be part of a club that I wasn't invited to join.

"Hey," he says, sliding onto the bench across from me.

Nicole is still disturbed, and Jeremy studies her. "What's up with you?" he asks.

She looks up at him, and her face turns even more somber.

"It's Kevin Jenkins," says Kathy. "He's back in school. He came over here and ..."

Jeremy's eyes go wide. He stands up, looking around the cafeteria. His hands are clenched. "What did he do?"

"Nothing," insists Nicole.

Kathy huffs. "He was bugging her."

"It was nothing," says Nicole, but I can see she's still disturbed.

"Who is he?" I ask, wanting to know what it is that has Nicole so upset.

Not seeing any sign of Kevin, Jeremy turns back to me. "He's an idiot. Just ignore him. I'll find him and ..."

"No, don't," Nicole begs. "It will make it worse. Just leave it alone."

Jeremy takes one more scan of the cafeteria and then sits, stewing.

"How could they let him out after what he did?" asks Lisa.

What did he do? I want to ask, but I stay silent and listen.

"They said without a body, they can't prove anything," says Kathy.

Nicole gasps and then turns to me. Her face falls. Then she looks at Kathy and scolds her with her eyes.

"A body?" I ask. My mind reels. What does Kevin have to do with a body? Was he in that home because he killed someone?

Nicole then turns on Kathy.

"What?" asks Kathy defensively, and she then looks at me. "Oh, I forgot. I'm sorry."

"For what?" I ask and wonder what all this has to do with me.

They all turn to Jeremy as though he's the only one who can answer that.

"He destroyed the bridge. He's the one who said he'd kill him, and he probably did. The police say they can't prove it, but I know it was him." Jeremy then takes a deep breath, and the others sit silently and nod in agreement.

I want to ask what this is all about, but they all act like I should know, so I sit in silence with so many questions that my mind is spinning.

"Are you going to eat that?" Jeremy asks, taking half of Nicole's sandwich from her tray.

She sits up and gives him a smirk. I can tell they are both trying to lift the heavy cloud that hangs above us.

For a while, we all eat in silence. I'm relieved when Nicole and the other girls' attention turns to a magazine Kathy has, trying to hide it from view. The cover says "Tiger Beat" and has a collage of photos of Scott Baio, Menudo, and Michael Jackson. The other girls lean in and stare as she flips through the pages.

Kathy runs her finger down the stripes on my jacket. "Purple is Donny Osmond's favorite color."

I look down at my sleeve and shrug. Nicole shakes her head and rolls her eyes.

Again, I find Jeremy staring at my jacket. When he sees me notice, he looks away.

"Donny Osmond? No one listens to him anymore. You only think he's cute because he's Mormon like you," says Lisa.

"No," Kathy protests. "But it doesn't hurt."

I listen to the girls ask Jeremy questions about what he plans to do that summer, and I find myself staring at Nicole and wondering if she's okay. I also wonder what Kevin meant when he said he saw her in the hollow. What is it about that ominous place that makes everyone act like it's haunted?

Kevin has something on her, it seems, and I can tell she's still thinking about what he said. Again, my mind goes to the body. Whose could it be?

She can sense this and glances over to me. I quickly look away.

Whatever Kevin did, I worry about why he's attacking her and also what she'd think if she ever found out that I was also placed in that home for boys. Again, I tell myself that a few months is all I have to keep who I am secret. But with Kevin here now, I'll have to be even more stealthy.

"So, only two more weeks, and then it's summer break," says Jeremy. "Are you taking the cows down with your uncle?"

I look at him, confused. Cows down? My uncle? Then I realize he's talking about Mr. Frost. I need to remember the stories I tell, or I'll be found out.

I shake my head. "No, he wants me to help out around the place while he's gone." It sounds conceivable, and I smile inside.

"I'll be working at our ranch up in Swan Valley for most of the summer," he says. "I'm going this weekend to open the place up."

Kathy pouts, "They're making you work all summer? What about swimming at the trestle and fishing?"

Jeremy rolls his eyes and shrugs.

Kathy laughs uncomfortably, then feigns a whisper. "Do you think the phantom is still back in the hollow?"

Jeremy shoots her a look, and the rest of the group turns silent.

"What?" she whines. Again, she is on the defensive.

"What is it with you?" Nicole snaps. "Stop bringing that up."

Kathy huffs. "I wasn't, besides, Jeremy brought it up."

"Why would I bring that up?" Jeremy says, shaking his head, annoyed. He then pushes his chair out, finished. He stands and straightens his long legs.

Now a phantom? I think. I'm still wondering about what happened back in the woods and whose body they think is back there, and now there's a phantom. This place gets stranger by the minute.

"I'll see you around," says Jeremy as he notices some friends entering the cafeteria. I watch him walk off, and I wish I had his confident stride.

"Do you think he's mad?" Kathy asks Nicole. "I wasn't trying to bring up what happened. I was just asking about fishing in the hollow."

Nicole rolls her eyes. "Then stop talking about it."

Kathy sulks.

As we finish lunch and start to leave for class, Nicole lets her friends walk ahead of us.

"I'm sorry about all that," she says.

"All what?" I ask.

"That stuff Kathy kept bringing up about what happened in the hollow."

"What do you mean?" I ask.

"You know ... It's terrible, and I'm sure it's the last thing you want to think about."

Again, I'm confused, but then the bell rings, and Nicole gives me an apologetic smile. I want to ask what she's talking about—what happened in the place they call the hollow—but will it blow my cover if she finds out I have no idea about any of this? I decide to keep my questions to myself. Bide my time, and hopefully, the truth will come out.

CHAPTER 22

Now that I know Kevin Jenkins was at the home for boys, I walk down the hall dreading my first-period class.

I'm worried after yesterday's confrontation in the lunchroom. It wasn't with me, but I was there, and he looked me right in the eye.

I enter the classroom and quickly take my seat, and as soon as I do, I hear tiny rumblings. I try to ignore them, but when I adjust myself in the chair, I realize there is something stuck to the seat of my pants, and when I reach under to see what it is, I realize a freshly chewed wad of gum is on the chair. I stand up, and a thin, sticky string is clinging to my butt.

I hear their muffled reactions. I immediately look at Kevin, expecting a snide grin, but instead, he gives me nothing but a dark glower.

My new jeans are ruined, but worse, he did this for a reason. He knows who I am, and this is payback. I'm suddenly enraged and want to rip into him, but if I do, I'll be back in that home for boys. I'm also embarrassed and just plain tired of all of this.

Before the teacher enters the room, I'm out the door. I refuse to sit through that class, knowing everyone either finds this funny or feels sorry for me.

I don't know where I'm going, but then I find the restroom and am relieved it's empty. I'm able to turn and see the extent of the gum's damage in the mirror. The spot is not as large as I thought, and I pick at the thick, disgusting clump, trying to remove it. I'm able to scrape much of it away, but the stain is still there and easily visible. I hear the bell ring, and I can either slink back to class or sneak out of the school. I decide on the latter. I'll walk the same route back to the house and hide out until school is over. It will be a long walk, but I figure I have all day.

With my head down, I find my way to the doors and outside. I carefully leave the bathroom. No one is in the hall, and I walk as though I have somewhere to go until I reach the exit, and then I run across the lawn and toward the road. I take a deep breath and then head in the direction I remember the bus traveling. The road is barren of cars, and as I make my way farther from the school, I begin to wonder if Mrs. Frost will get a phone call telling her I've ditched class. I'm so close to finally being with my mom and back to a normal life, and this could ruin it all, but I can't go back now, so I keep walking. I never want to return to that school, but my thoughts turn to Nicole. I then realize the paper with her phone number is in my back pocket. I reach for it, worried the gum has soaked through and damaged it. When I pull it out and see that only a tiny edge of it has been stained, I let out a long breath. The number is still clear. Relieved, I fold it back and place it in the front pocket of my new shirt.

I don't know what I'll tell Mrs. Frost about the jeans. I figure I'll try to wash out the sticky stain tonight and hope the pants can be salvaged. The things I own are few, and being given something that isn't either old or worn out is rare. And what if I'm expected to give these clothes back—just a loan? Destroying them would surely get me kicked out.

I need to get through these next few months without problems. After the last place—being accused of stealing—I'm lucky I was given a second chance. Just make it work for a couple more months, I tell myself. It shouldn't be that hard, and yet it feels like I'm moving through sand.

I see a white horse in a field that I recognize from the bus ride, and I feel confident I'm going the right way. It isn't until I am far enough away from the school so as not to be seen that I slow to a walk, and that is when the anger returns. Most of it is directed at Kevin Jenkins, but the rest is at the tears I can't control.

How do I explain to Mrs. Frost that I'm not on the bus? I've been planning my excuse as I've walked the empty road along the pastures and fields of the route back to the house. I'm grateful that there weren't many turns on the bus ride to the school, and I remember the name of the street—Riverside. Even out in the middle of literally nowhere, there is a street sign where the two paved roads cross. At least I wasn't lost.

During my walk, only two trucks passed by, and neither stopped. I was relieved. Even with this long walk back, I'll still have hours left before the school lets out. I need an excuse. Skipping school is one way I'll surely get sent back to that home for boys.

When I reach the Frost's house, I go around the back and wait in the barn. The horses see me enter and wander from the other side of the corral. I figure they are looking for feed, and since I'm there with nothing else to do but wait, I decide to start my chores now. I can stay out of sight, as there are no windows along the back of the house, except the upstairs that faces this direction.

One of the horses whinnies at me. "Be patient," I tell it as I grab the pitchfork and begin to section the bales like Jesse showed me. The horse paws the ground impatiently. I do everything in the exact order I was shown. I make certain to stay in or around the back of the barn, where I'm out of view. I wish I could use this time to go out and pull the gates of the ditch, but Jesse made it very clear that I wasn't to do that until five.

I don't have a watch, so I have no idea what time it is, but the rumbling in my stomach tells me it's way past lunchtime, and now I'm thinking about the cookies I hope Mrs. Frost has for me like yesterday.

I feed the horses, take grain to the chickens, and shovel out the stalls. When I'm finished, I wonder what else I can do until I hear the bus come down the road.

I'm bored and wish I had the book hidden under my mattress, so instead, I look around the barn at the different tools and what is stored in the barrels and buckets. There are ropes, leather straps, large brushes, and more feed. A door to a small shed is slightly ajar, and I open it. There are rakes, pitchforks, and other tools, and then I see something else. Long and thin, leaned against the back is a fishing pole. I place the other items aside and bring it out. It even has a reel with line and a rusty hook still attached. It must be Mr. Frost's, but it's covered in dust, looking like it hasn't been touched in years. I wonder if he even knows it's still here.

I study it. I turn the reel, and the hook and line retract. It seems to work. Could I really be this lucky?

I look over at the barn door, feeling like I've found a hidden treasure. Looking back into the storage shed, I search some more and find a small box with a handle. I bring it out and place it on one of the hay bales. It has a clip, and I use my thumb to open it. Inside are several tiny colorful pieces of what looks like yarn and feathers. They look like little bugs. I pick one up, and it grabs me with a sharp poke. I reel back, but it's still stuck to my finger. I look closer and see that it's a tiny hook. It's barely embedded, and I'm able to wiggle it loose without any blood.

What are these? I wonder. Carefully, I pick up another. They all have hooks hidden inside them. They must be some sort of bait. I smile to myself. Now I have everything I need. I close the box and store everything back in the shed. I feel excited and also furtive about my find. I begin to scheme how I can sneak back to the river and try them out for myself.

As I sit again, bored and waiting, I see the ladder leading to the loft. From below, it just looks like a place they store more hay, but after stumbling upon the fishing pole, I'm curious about what else is stored in this barn.

I climb the stairs to investigate.

Through the square opening, I poke my head and look around. It's what I thought. Hay. There are stacks everywhere. There is a large, wooden double door at the far end, so I crawl all the way up and onto the floor of the loft. The area isn't completely dark because the light coming from below shows through the slats of the loft's floor, and then I realize how high up I am.

Carefully, I walk to the other end, and when I reach the door, I push it open slightly to see out.

Where I'm standing is directly under the high pitch of the barn's roof. I look over to the house and see that it's almost level with the window to my room, and when I look toward the window of the other room—the off-limits room, I gasp when I see there is someone standing behind the sheer curtains. I take a quick step back into the shadows, hoping I haven't been spotted.

I slowly peek back. It must be Mrs. Frost, but the figure isn't clear. I see no face, just a form. Then I wonder if it really is a person at all. I continue to stare. It just stands there motionless. It looks like a body —a head, shoulders, and then again, maybe not. Then, the form moves to the side and out of view. Again, I startle. It has to be Mrs. Frost. Who else could it be? Then I see Mrs. Frost in the kitchen window downstairs, and my breath catches. It wasn't her in that window. It couldn't be. Is someone else in the house? In that room? I keep watching but see nothing else, and soon, I'm wondering if it isn't just the curtains, the breeze, or something else that is simply playing tricks with my mind.

I hear the bus coming down the road and quickly climb back down from the loft. I sneak around the side of the barn and watch. I'm relieved when the bus doesn't stop at the house. Nicole was going somewhere with friends after school, so she won't notice I am missing, and I'm hoping that my disappearance from school will go unnoticed. I walk around the house to the front door, pretending I just arrived, but find Mrs. Frost standing on the porch. When she sees me, she startles.

"Where'd you come from?" she asks, walking to me and looking around as though I have something to hide.

"I was just getting started on feeding the animals," I say, hoping she'll think I just got there.

She looks confused, "But you weren't on the bus."

"I missed the bus, so I got a ride home."

Mrs. Frost cocks her head. "From who?"

I shrug.

Her face is horrified. "You didn't know them?"

I scramble. "It was the mom of a kid at school. I think his name is Jeff or Greg." My lie is growing and getting worse. "They were real nice."

She blinks and looks like she's trying to clear her head as I ramble. Finally, she relents. She sighs and directs me into the house.

Once inside, I look around for whoever may have been in that window.

"Who else is here?" I ask.

She looks at me strangely. "No one."

I begin to ask about what I saw in that upstairs window but then realize she'd know I was hiding in the loft. I nod and try to brush it off. "I thought I heard something."

"Hmm," she ponders. "I had the radio on in the kitchen. Maybe that's what you heard." Then she smiles and I awkwardly smile back. She wipes her hands on a towel and turns to the kitchen. "I left something on the stove. Dinner is early tonight."

I can smell something warm and savory. My stomach grumbles happily.

"I have to go into town. You can come with me."

"But I need to do the chores," I say.

She looks uneasy. "Are you sure?"

I nod. "Yes. I also have some homework I need to do." This isn't the truth, but I'm feeling smothered. I need space, and unlike when I've been at other places with loads of kids and chaos, there is something about the way she watches me that makes me feel as though I can't breathe.

"All right," she relents. "I won't be very long."

I check the time and realize I have two hours until I can pull the gates on the ditch, so I go back outside and wander around the barn to take up time pretending to do the chores I've already finished.

I look up at the window and try to make out the figure I saw, but I see nothing from this angle, so I decide to climb back up and see if the apparition in the window is still visible, as it was before.

The sun has shifted slightly as I peer across and at the off-limits window. I squint, trying to see if anything or anyone is still there. After several minutes of not finding anything but the glare from the sun in the glass, I quit. But as I turn to go, I look down and there is Mrs. Frost standing on the back porch, looking up at me. Her face is stone, and I feel my stomach lurch. Am I in trouble?

I stand frozen. I begin to make up excuses in my mind as to why I'm in the loft staring over at that window, but then she turns abruptly and goes inside.

I was getting more hay. That's what I'll tell her. I'm feeling as though I've done something wrong and wondering what it could be. Is simply looking at that room breaking the rules? It seems that with every move I make, she is there, hovering and watching me.

I hesitate to go back in, but I'm starving, so I decide to act as though nothing happened. What can she do? Accuse me of being in the loft? Or looking at that window? It all feels so strange.

At the other places I've lived, I've rarely felt anything more than ignored unless I'm doing something wrong, and here I'm watched at every turn.

I walk in the back door and into the kitchen and find her at the sink. The water's running, and she's tying an apron around her waist. Hearing the squeak of the door as I enter, she turns and tries to smile.

"You could have called me, and I would have come and picked you up from school," she says.

Does she know my deception? "I ..." I begin to make up another lie but then realize I have a perfect answer. "I was going to, but I don't know the phone number here."

Her eyes go wide. "Oh," she says, "I guess you wouldn't." She goes to a drawer and pulls out a pen and paper. She writes it down and hands it to me.

"Thank you," I say. I fold the paper, and when I go to put it in my back pocket, I remember the gum and the stain. A dull pain goes through me as I remember the awful scene. I then make an excuse to go upstairs so I can change my jeans before she sees the damage.

At my bedroom door, I hesitate. I look over at the other door. I look back toward the stairs to make sure I'm still alone, and when I hear noises coming from the kitchen, I walk to the other door and lean toward it, trying to listen to what's inside. I stand still, straining to hear, but there is nothing.

Who was that? Or what was that? I know I saw something. And I saw it move. Or did I? I quietly turn the knob. Again, I find it's locked. I'm wary, but I squat down, and again, I peer through that keyhole. In the daylight, I can see more. The edges of what looks like a bed, a table, and some cardboard boxes. Suddenly, a flutter of something comes across the keyhole, and I flinch, almost falling backward like before. But then I realize it's just some cloth. A curtain or drape that is moving in the breeze. Is that what I saw last night?

I think back to what I witnessed in the window. That wasn't just a curtain. I sigh. I try to convince myself that's all it was. I shake it off and decide it's in my head, so I push myself up to standing and go to my room.

I remove the jeans and study the stain where the gum was stuck. I dread having to return to that class. It's only a few weeks until the summer break. I hope that Kevin Jenkins will be tired of bothering me and direct his attention toward some other lowly sucker.

I scrape at the stain on the pocket, and then I remember that Nicole's number is inside. I quickly reach in and am relieved to see it's not ruined. I take it and fold it together with the paper Mrs. Frost gave me and place the bundle into the pocket of my jacket, and then I start trying to scrub the stain on my jeans. I'm relieved when it begins to vanish. When I've removed it all, I press on the damp area with a towel until it is almost dry. Another disaster avoided.

My stomach rumbles. I'm looking forward to another one of Mrs. Frost's amazing meals. That first day, I thought she'd made something special because I was new, but every evening, we sit at the table with a meal that is even better than what we had the day before. If I had been fed like this my entire life, maybe I wouldn't have always been the shortest boy in my class.

———

IT'S JUST the two of us at the table for dinner, but surprisingly, it isn't as awkward as I expected. I'm so curious about what brought me to this place, so I ask her about Gordon and the farm.

"Did Gordon always want to be a farmer?" I ask.

She smiles, amused. "I think he knew that eventually he would be a farmer because that is what his family did, but I think he really wanted to be a rodeo star. He was a steer wrestler. He was very good. He traveled all over the country, and that's how we met."

"You did rodeo?" I ask, surprised.

She gives a surprised laugh and then smiles. "No. It was ..." Her brow furrows, and she grasps for words. She rubs the side of her head, thinks a moment, and then picks her words carefully. "I used to make shirts that they would wear at the rodeo events." She shrugs. "That's all."

I look down at the shirt she gave me. "Did you make this?"

She nods and then looks down.

"Really?" I ask, surprised that she seems embarrassed. "Is this a rodeo shirt?"

She looks up and shakes her head. "No. The shirts I made for the rodeo were a lot more colorful. The cowboys want to stand out."

Then my thoughts turn to the jacket with its purple stripes. Could that be her work, too? But then I think about Jeremy and Gus and their similar coats and wonder why she would be making jackets for them.

"Is the jacket you lent me for the rodeo?"

She lifts an eyebrow and smiles. "It was, and I didn't lend it to you. I gave it to you."

"It looks like the jackets some of the other boys at school have. I think they do rodeo, too."

I again wonder if I'm wearing Mr. Frost's hand-me-downs. I've worn second-hand clothes my entire life, but the thought of wearing something that is his makes me uncomfortable. I can only guess he doesn't need it now that he no longer does rodeo.

"Is that why he doesn't wear it anymore?" I ask.

Her face falls. "Who?" she asks.

Who else? I'm thinking. "Mr. Frost. I mean Gordon. Isn't this his?"

She sits straighter. "Oh," she says, relieved. "Um. No. It's ... it doesn't matter. It's yours now."

She looks at the clock above the table.

"Oh dear," she says as she stands up from the table. "I need to get going."

I stand and collect my dishes to take to the kitchen.

She pauses. "You sure you want to stay here alone?" she asks.

"Yes," I answer too quickly. "I have a lot of homework to catch up on."

It's another lie, but after so many, I feel it's the one thing I'm exceptionally good at.

CHAPTER 23

I finished my chores hours ago, and am pulling the head gates on the northeast field. It takes two hands to hold the metal handle as I prop my foot against the concrete braces and pull. Sometimes, the thin but heavy metal plate slides easily, but most often, I have to yank and jiggle it to get it to move. When it begins to slide, the sucking sound of the water being released is satisfying because I know it's working, and soon it will release. When the plate is free from the brackets, I watch as the rush fills the ditch and makes its way down to the waiting rows of alfalfa.

I begin to walk back to the house, but I'm lured by what is just behind that curtain of trees, back in those woods. What I remember of the glistening ripples of the water and dance of leaves has me being pulled toward it and rationalizing, telling myself I've finished early and what harm would it be to take a quick walk back to the river? It's right here, and I want so badly to explore this place. The sun won't be going down for a few more hours, and if I don't do it now, I know I'll regret it once I'm gone. I've been told not to go back into the woods, but now that I've had a taste of what is back there, I want to see more.

Mrs. Frost doesn't even like to look out toward these trees. She won't see, and I'm not expected for at least another hour. She'll never know, so what could it hurt?

I walk quickly toward the same ditch that I followed when I found myself back there before. I'll need to avoid the old man and his dog and make my way around his place to where the river bends close to the woods.

As I walk, I act like I'm studying the ditch just in case I'm being watched, as though there is a problem that I'm trying to fix and must follow. Once I'm behind the grove of trees, I walk quickly toward the place I stumbled upon in the dark.

Old Tom's house is in view, and I hide from tree to tree until I can see that there is no sign of him or the little dog. I have the small flashlight in my back pocket, so if I am discovered, I can make the excuse that I'm simply returning what he loaned me, but I'm hoping I can avoid him so I can explore the place I only got a glimpse of before.

I make a wide swath as far away from the house as I can, and then once I'm under the cover of the trees and brush, I make my way back toward the ditch. It is what I'll need to follow to get back to the field that leads to the Frost's house. I have a specific amount of time, and I can't waste any of it getting lost.

And then there it is, in the distance, I can see the glistening river framed by afternoon sky and stately trees. I keep walking, but as soon as I'm sure I'm out of sight, I stop and look around. It's even more beautiful in the daylight. I release my breath and go to where I can see the ripples of the water just beyond the bank.

The young limbs of the trees hang like vines. It's as though they are begging me to grab one and swing through the woods like Tarzan of the Jungle. Thick brush keeps me on the thin trail that continues to lead me toward the river.

What an amazing place, and it's right behind the house. It's like a hidden paradise, and I can't believe that Mrs. Frost feels it is a place of dread. What could be back here that has her so afraid?

I walk along, and then I recognize the curve of the path. It's the area where I first saw Old Tom. I look out onto the water where I had seen him standing, casting his fishing line, and I envision myself doing the same.

The thought of luring in a fish, my bait out in the water, and waiting for a bite is so intriguing. I'm lost in the dream of it all, so much so that I don't hear what has come from behind.

A loud snuffle startles me, and I flip around quickly to see a horse and rider. My presence is a surprise to them as well, and the horse jumps back. It's then that I see it's Nicole.

"Are you lost?" she says with a sarcastic lilt.

"No," I shoot back.

She calms the horse and then looks at me with skepticism. "You look lost."

"Well, I'm not," I say, annoyed.

She gives a disbelieving smirk. "I thought you said you didn't come back here."

I shrug. "I don't." I feel like I've been caught. I take a step back. The horse looms over me, and with that, Nicole stares down with furrowed brows. "Then what are you doing back here?"

Suddenly, I'm searching for an excuse. "I had to open the head gate, so I came back to check the river."

Her brows dip even lower. "Check it for what? The head gate is clear over on the far side of the pasture."

I scramble for an answer. "I'm thinking about doing some fishing." Then I turn my attention to her. "What are you doing back here?"

"I'm riding," she says, motioning to the large animal as though I didn't notice it. "I'm allowed back here from a trail that is on our land, so you don't need to tell anyone."

"Why would I tell?" I ask, curious about why she doesn't want me to tell.

She shrugs.

"Are you not supposed to be back here?" I ask.

"I just told you I'm allowed." She gives a huff. "Does your aunt know you're here?"

Now I'm defensive. How does she know that Mrs. Frost doesn't want me back here? "Yes." I lie. "I have to do the water. I'm allowed back here because of the head gates," I say, feeling smug that I was able to parrot what Jesse had told me.

She rolls her eyes. "Well, no, duh. Of course, you're allowed." She inclines her chin and studies me. "So, you came from all the way over there, through Old Tom's place, to get to the hollow?"

"The hollow?" I ask.

"Yes, I thought you said you were looking to go fishing. Isn't that where you were looking to go?"

"I don't know, I guess," I say.

"I thought you weren't lost."

"I'm not."

She lifts one shoulder. "Then why did you go the long way?"

"What do you mean?" I ask.

She feigns frustration. "The path that's right behind your house is a shortcut. It's a lot quicker to get to the hollow than going all the way around from over there." She scrutinizes me again. "Are you sure Mrs. Frost knows you're back here?"

"Yes," I say. "I've only been here a couple of weeks; how am I supposed to know about all these paths?"

She sits up tall in the saddle and studies me. "She told you that you could come back here?"

"Yes. Why wouldn't she?" I ask, this time really hoping she gives me some clue to Mrs. Frost's aversion to this place.

She leans back as though I've thrown something at her. For a moment, she sits stunned, and then she cocks her head. "It just seems strange."

Before I can ask why, she looks out into the trees. "Do you want me to show you how to get to the shortcut?"

I do, but I worry about how long it will take and where I'll end up. "How far is it? I have to be back at the house before seven to finish my work."

She lifts an eyebrow. "It's a shortcut. That means it will take a shorter ..."

"I know what a shortcut means," I snap back. She's pretty but often talks with a bite.

She begins to turn the horse. "Follow me."

"Now?" I ask.

She pulls back on the reins, and the horse shuffles as though it's annoyed by the lack of decision. "Why not? It's a lot quicker than going all the way back the way you came. You already closed the ditch, right?"

I nod.

"Then, let's go. Hop on."

I step back and shake my head. "That's okay. I'll just walk."

"You sure? It'll be faster if you ride."

I'm sure. I've never been on a horse, and I'm still getting used to being near them. "Yes, I'll just walk."

She shrugs and then leans back in the saddle. "Are you sure she knows you're back here?"

Now I feel she's taunting me. Somehow, she knows about Mrs. Frost's aversion to the woods and her demands that I stay away. I huff, trying to act like she is sorely mistaken.

"Yes. So, show me," I say.

Along with my annoyance, my curiosity is piqued, and yet, I'm a bit nervous about where this trail leads and whether it will reveal to Mrs. Frost that I went against her warnings to stay away from the woods. I'm hoping that even if she is watching for me, she won't expect me to come from that direction. Oh, please let her not be watching.

The horse lumbers forward, and I am unsure how close I should follow the large animal. Even with my limited time around horses, I know you should never walk behind one.

"So, do you ride back here a lot?" I ask. I have to practically yell it up to her.

She turns back and laughs. "Why are you all the way back there?" She stops the horse and waits for me to catch up.

I make a wide berth around to the side of the horse.

"Are you sure you don't want to ride?"

"Yes."

"Don't you like horses?" she asks, obviously seeing my discomfort.

I nod and give a shrug. "I'm just not used to them."

Even after a week of feeding them in the corral, I'm still uneasy with their size and strength.

"Have you ever ridden a horse?" she asks.

"No."

"Really?" She says it as though she's asked me if I've ever had ice cream.

"I'm from Sacramento. There weren't any horses there."

She cocks her head. "What about here? You've visited here before, haven't you?"

I pause, unsure what to say.

I see the shock on her face. "You've never visited your aunt and uncle until now?"

I shake my head. It does seem far-fetched if, in fact, I was their actual nephew.

"What about ..." she begins to ask a question but then stops.

I wait, and when she looks away uncomfortably, I push. "What about what?" I ask.

She takes a deep breath and ponders what she is going to ask; then she lifts her shoulders in resolve. "It's nothing." She looks up ahead. "Come on," she says and moves the horse forward, evading my look of query.

I can tell she's keeping something from me. Does everyone have secrets here?

I follow along, and as I watch her rock side to side on the back of the horse, I see up ahead the clouds turning gray against the intense blue sky. It looks like rain, and I wonder how much longer it will be before we reach the path to the house.

The horse follows the trail as if it knows the way, and soon, I see a river come into view. It surprises me. I had no idea which way we were heading.

The river is so much bigger than I expected. Thin gravel islands and giant logs create curves and dips in the flow. I'm in awe. I find myself breathing so deeply that my chest expands and releases, allowing my breath and my normal clutter of thoughts to escape.

"I love this trail," she says. "Sometimes there are deer. I even saw a moose a couple of months ago."

I look around, wondering what other critters could be hiding in the brush. Up ahead, I see trees. A large grove rises up from the river. It looks like the woodsy area behind the Frosts' home, and I begin to worry that Mrs. Frost will find out that I'm in the very place I was told not to go.

As the mass of trees gets nearer, my mind drifts to what I saw that night while trying to escape from that dark and obscure place. It isn't either of those things in the daylight—nothing ominous or threatening, just a thick grove of trees.

A duck quacks and flies up from the river. The horse flinches, giving me a start as I'm shaken from my stupor. I'm letting Mrs. Frost's dire warnings make me crazy. I remind myself that there's nothing back here that's going to get me. If Old Tom didn't kill me when he had the chance, what other terrible demon could there be?

Nicole giggles as the duck races above us. "That scares me every time!"

She turns back to me, and I try to act like my heart isn't beating out of my chest.

Her smile is as bright as the sun on the water. Her curls dance in the light wind. The birds chirp, and the breeze that seems to follow me everywhere is now warm. I could stay right here all day. But then my reverie is broken.

I hear a voice. That voice. It's back.

"Here." I feel it must be Nicole since it's just the two of us, but it's not her voice, and she's looking right at me. She smiles again, obviously not hearing it, and then she turns back toward the trail, and the voice comes again.

"Here." It's louder this time, and I look around, expecting to see someone in the trees.

The enormous cottonwoods bend, making a natural tunnel over the path. They are so immense that only a few peeks of sunlight flow through. It's like they're channeling me to go further in.

"Here." The voice whispers again. It sounds like a demand.

"Did you hear that?" I call up to her.

"Hear what?" she says, turning back to me.

A bird twitters.

Her eyes follow up on a tree limb. "That's a chickadee," she says.

"No," I say. And then the voice calls out again.

"Here. Here. Here." Each time, it grows louder.

"That!" I say. "That voice."

She stops her horse and looks at me oddly. "Voice?"

"Didn't you hear it?" I ask.

She looks around. In the silence of the woods, it seemed so obvious. The voice was clear and urgent. It filled the empty space like an echo, and yet now the voice is still.

She shakes her head and then leans back and peers up to the tops of the towering trees. "I think you're hearing them creaking in the wind. My grandpa says the cottonwoods moan. It can sound like someone talking."

I shake my head. Just like before, when the voice called, and Jesse didn't hear it, it's here again, and Nicole is also unaware. I listen and watch the craggy trunks as they sway. Something like a groan emanates from them, and now, I question what I heard.

Nicole's eyebrows are raised as she studies me.

I'm so awkward in this unfamiliar place, and now I feel foolish hearing murmurs in the woods. But it's not just that. Something more has me unnerved. The breeze that follows and surrounds me, even when the wind is still, has now become more intense. It's as though it's pushing me, directing me toward something.

"It's just the wind," she says again, trying to relieve my unease. She moves the horse forward, and I follow, scanning the woods, expecting to see eyes peering back at me.

I swallow hard, and then the voice calls again. "Here." I shoot Nicole a look as though maybe this time she's heard it. But she is unmoved and unaware. How can this be? I shiver. The trees begin to close in on me, and my heart begins to pound. "Where are we?" I ask.

"We're getting close. The overflow is just ahead," she calls back.

I look up ahead. There is a large dip and bowl that the path has spread into, a deep, wide channel filled with sandy gravel. It isn't the same packed dirt and grass of the trail we've been on, but I can see it clearly continuing in the distance. It's as though something has cut out a chunk from the path—a wide swath of the earth. It's not so steep or big that we can't cross, but it looks odd how it separates the trail. The trees are thick along the path on both sides, but where this swath of sand and gravel snakes through the woods is open to the sky.

As quickly as it came, the wind turns still, and the voice is silent, but I feel something is there with us. The noises of the woods are still there, but as though I'm hearing them from underwater. I shake my head, trying to clear my ears.

"This is the overflow," Nicole says, pointing at the wide sandy dip in the trail.

I snap out of my stupor, and the woods come alive again as though they've awakened from slow motion.

"If it's full of water, don't try to cross it. Go back the other way, but that shouldn't matter since you're the one who is shutting the gates. But sometimes when it rains hard, it can flood then too."

I try to clear what feels like a fuzz in my brain. Again, she's staring at me like I have horns, and I nod, trying to act normal and letting her know I heard her.

She gives the horse a nudge with her boots, and it walks down and into the sandy drift. When I step off the bank, I slide a bit, and some of the sand fills my boots I try to shake it out as I walk across and climb up the other side.

At the top, Nicole is waiting for me, and we walk a short distance. With each step, I feel the pressure of the woods' release, as though I've been underwater and have now surfaced.

Nicole turns the horse and urges it through a small break in the woods, and I take a deep breath as we emerge from the trees. She stops the horse and then points to a field.

"That's your house. See this little trail. It's what the deer use. They're all over, but that path is how you get to this trail." She then points to a trail that leads in the opposite direction, back into the woods. "And over there is the trail that leads back to my place. Jeremy used to use it to get here. He thought no one knew," she says.

"Jeremy comes back here too?" I ask.

Her face turns cold. "He used to. But not anymore."

"Why not?"

She cocks her head, and her face looks pained. She begins to answer but stops. Again, I know she's keeping something from me.

"He just doesn't. And don't tell anyone about this trail. Like I said, it's secret." She lifts her eyebrows for emphasis.

"Then why did you show me?" I ask her.

I can see I've stumped her with my question. She sits up straighter in the saddle and thinks for a moment. She then seems to soften.

"If you live here, you should know. It's the way it's always been, I guess. If you don't live here, you don't need to be back here anyway. So, that's why."

Then she smiles, and it's genuine. I can't help but smile back.

"But I still wouldn't tell anyone, even your aunt and uncle, that you know about it, okay?"

Of course, I'm okay with them not knowing. So, I nod, then I look toward the field and am relieved when I see that the barn almost completely blocks the view from the house. I can make my way back without being seen.

"Do you think you can find your way back now?" she asks. "I told you it was a lot shorter from your house, that is, unless you're going all the way back by Old Tom's. But you only need to go that way when you're opening the head gates."

I'm surprised she knows about the water and gates. "Thank you," I say.

"I'll see you around," she says. "And if you ever want to go riding, I'll teach you. It's super easy. They do all the work. You live with all those horses. You should learn how to ride them."

I'm hesitant to agree, but I've always wanted to ride a horse, and having her ask means she actually does want to be with me again. Maybe giving me her number wasn't just an act of sympathy after all.

CHAPTER 24

Again, I've been shaken from my sleep. I dread that the noises have returned. Is it the same bumping and knocking from the other room or something else? I lay there motionless, listening, and then realize the sound is coming from outside.

The time on the clock is just after five. I push the bedcovers aside and walk to the window. There are two trucks at the barn; one is Jesse's, and the other I don't recognize, especially in the dim morning light.

A glow is visible through the slats of the barn. I see Jesse come around and get something from the back of his truck. He looks urgent. I want to know what's happening, so I quickly throw on my clothes and go downstairs. In the dark, I walk across the dining room and through the kitchen. When I open the back door of the house and the morning air hits me, I wished I had brought my coat.

I can hear voices in the barn and the sound of movement. Mr. Frost sounds angry, so I wait by the door, unsure what to do. I lean in and try to listen. It's an unfamiliar voice, and I'm curious, hearing the sharp tones.

My breath freezes as I exhale, and I contemplate whether to go back for the jacket. However, I stay, straining to hear what they're saying. It's then I hear the low moan of an animal, and then the voices turn low and somber.

I want to go inside. From just the sounds, I can tell something bad has happened. Soon, I can't hear anything but mumbles. I wait and wonder if they'll tell me to go back to bed. I figure that's all they can do, so I push the door open slightly.

Mr. Frost, Jesse, and another man are standing together, looking at something on the ground. A large cow stands, drooped and panting nearby. Mr. Frost looks up and sees me. I freeze, expecting him to shoo me away, but instead, he gives me a sullen lift of his eyebrows and continues the discussion. I step inside and close the door. It's much warmer now that I'm out of the breeze.

Jesse looks over. He lifts his head in greeting, but his usual smile is gone. "Starting early this morning?" he asks, walking toward me. "Gordon said you'll be irrigating for me now, so you must be doing things right around here."

I nod, feeling relieved that the job I wanted has been confirmed, but I'm anxious to know what's happened.

"What's going on?" I ask, motioning to where the other men are standing.

"Nothing good. We lost a calf."

"Oh no," I say and wonder if I should have been watching better. "When? I didn't see anything yesterday."

"Who knows how long it's been going on? I saw the cow struggling when I got here this morning. The vet was lucky to save the mother."

I peek around Jesse, but I'm not sure I want to see. "The baby died? Is Mr. Frost mad?" I ask, still worried I may be to blame.

"He's not happy, but it happens. Fortunately, not too often."

We walk over together, and there in the dirt, covered in blood and muck, is the lifeless calf. I assume the other man is the vet Jesse spoke of, and he seems surprised to see me. He looks to be the same age as Mr. Frost. He's dressed in similar clothes and boots, but he's covered in mud and blood.

"Landis, this is Doc Taylor," Mr. Frost says.

By habit, I extend my hand. The vet smiles and holds up his hands. "I don't think you want this all over you, but it's nice to meet you. So, you're working for Gordon?" he asks.

"Um," I give a half nod, and I'm relieved when Mr. Frost cuts in.

"Landis is staying with us and helping out."

The vet gives a nod. "Here for the summer?" he says, and I wonder how he knows I'll be leaving in a few months.

"I have a son at school, but his semester doesn't end for a couple of weeks. Are you in school around here or in Utah?" he asks.

"Um," I begin to answer, not completely sure why he thinks I would be in school in another state.

Mr. Frost laughs. "Landis is still in high school."

"Oh!" says Doc Taylor surprised. "I thought you were on break from college."

Mr. Frost gives me a nod. "He's got another year or so until that."

College? It sounds strange being directed at me. First off, I've never considered being able to go to college, and second, I can't remember ever being mistaken for being older than I am, let alone college-aged.

Mr. Frost's smile fades, but he gives me a nod as he and the vet leave me and go back to discussing what to do with the mother cow. The animal seems like it's going to survive, so I'm wondering why they are questioning what to do with her. I go to Jesse.

"What's going to happen to the mother cow? Is she okay?"

"She'll be fine," says Jesse.

I continue to listen to their discussion. "Why are they talking about keeping her or not?" I ask.

Jesse sighs. "Without a calf to raise, she isn't worth much. Her job is to produce calves."

"Are they going to kill her?" I ask.

I can tell that Jesse is tired of my questions. "These are beef cattle. They are raised for beef. It's a business, Landis. If a cow isn't raising a calf, then it costs money to feed it and with no return."

He's trying to be patient, but I'm not making it easy. I look at the cow and feel sorry for it.

Mr. Frost calls to Jesse, saving him from my questions. "Doc says he thinks the Hoskins have a bum we can graft onto her. Will you take care of it?"

"Sure," Jesse says. He then turns to me. "She may have just got her free pass."

I follow him. "What do you mean?"

"There's a bum calf—a baby without a mom," he explains. "We'll try to put it on her."

It's just a cow, and yet I'm relieved, but when I look at the small, lifeless body of the calf that didn't make it, it's hard to feel completely good.

Jesse stops and talks quietly. "There's a lot of this stuff on a farm. I know you're not used to it, but it's what happens. Sometimes, it's not so pretty." He then pulls out a pocket knife and walks off toward the dead calf.

"What are you going to do?" I ask.

He stops. "You may want to go do the other chores. I have to skin the calf."

I begin to ask why, but Jesse has already figured that question is coming.

"The cow won't accept the other calf unless she thinks it's hers. We tie the hide of the dead calf onto the other, and then she smells it and, hopefully, thinks it's her baby," he explains.

I contemplate this, and when he kneels down and lifts the dead body, I decide to leave the barn. I've seen some terrible and gross things in my life, but I know this will be worse.

I've seen other kids crash on bikes, get in fights, and fall off all sorts of things. They end up bloodied and bruised, and I've even watched them get stitched up, but when it comes to animals, I can't watch. There is something about them that is different for me.

When a stray dog was hanging around one of the schools I went to, some of the other kids were harassing it, throwing things, and laughing as it looked at us with confused eyes. They tried to draw me into their heckles, and when I punched one of them to get him to stop, I was suspended; that's when I moved to home number eight.

I've always been that way with animals. They remind me of the little kids I've lived with. They have no idea what's happening to them and have no control over any of it. They don't understand or see how awful life can be. Maybe that is why I can't watch what's about to take place, so I leave and try to focus on my chores.

·   ·   ·

It's late in the afternoon, and I'm home from school. When I open the door to the barn, I'm hoping the evidence of the dead calf is gone. I step inside and see the cow standing in a corral that's been sectioned off from the other animals. At her side is a tiny calf with the still-bloody hide of the one who died wrapped around it. The mother seems uninterested, or maybe she's still tired after the travail of that morning. I walk closer to get a better look as the new calf huddles close to its adoptive mom. This seems to disturb the cow, so she tries to move away. I step back, not wanting to cause her stress, but watch the small calf as it longs for the comfort of a mother.

Jesse told me that sometimes the mother still rejects the new calf, even with the scent of the lost one covering it. I'm intrigued that the cow uses that sense to identify her baby and wonder why the calf doesn't have a similar issue bonding to another mom.

The tiny calf seems unaffected by its lot in life—unaware it's an orphan. It has simply moved on to another mother. It doesn't care that it's not its own. It just wants a mom. I worry that the cow won't accept the baby—and then what? Hearing the men talk, it sounded as though the cow would have been killed if it hadn't had a calf. I wonder if both will die if the bond doesn't happen. Neither has any idea how much their life relies on the other.

I go to the barrel, fill some buckets with chicken feed, and get to my chores. Mr. Frost and Jesse have gone to the other fields across town for the day, and I'll be pulling the head gates later.

I give the orphaned calf another look before I leave the barn. Its new mother leans down and brushes its head with her chin. It makes me think about my mother. I still remember when she would tousle my hair. I then think about Mrs. Frost, who has no children, and wonder why.

I've lived with so many other kids whose parents didn't seem to want them. My mom doesn't have a choice, but it seems like so many others do and just don't want to take care of their children. And then there are people like Mrs. Frost, who I think would have made a real good mother, and she doesn't have any children.

This thought follows me throughout my chores as I collect eggs, sprinkle feed, and pitch hay. When the horses come in again, I stand and try to imagine myself sitting on top of one. They eat as though

I'm not there. I wish I was as unaffected by their presence as they are by mine. Nicole offered to teach me how to ride and I want to take her up on that. I do want to learn, but I want to be with her even more. I have her number. It's now folded neatly in my front pocket after I dried the paper by spreading it out on the bathroom counter. But I still don't have the nerve to make the call.

"Landis?"

Her voice startles me. Mrs. Frost is at the barn door.

"Sorry," she says, seeing me jump. "I was calling you from the house, but you didn't answer. You have a phone call."

"I do?" I say. Who could be calling me? I still have to shovel out the stalls, and I look over at them.

I hear Mrs. Frost sigh. "Don't keep her waiting," she says.

Her? My heart leaps. It's Nicole. It has to be. There is no other girl who knows where I live, and even if they did, they wouldn't call. I drop the pitchfork and hurry out of the barn.

"You can take the call in Gordon's office. It's more private than the phone in the kitchen," Mrs. Frost says as I come into the house.

She leads me to Mr. Frost's den and motions for me to sit in a cushioned chair next to the desk. Handing me the phone, she smiles, but it looks forced, and then she pats my shoulder.

"I've already accepted the charges," she says.

My breath catches. I look up at her, and she's aware I'm just realizing who it is. Her lips press into a thin line, and her brow creases. She looks as if this pains her, and now I feel that way, too. My excitement in contemplating Nicole on the other end of the line has fallen into a mixture of disappointment and fear.

She leaves the room and pulls the door closed. I'm now alone with the phone. I take a deep breath, preparing myself for what I'm about to learn. It's never good.

"Hello?" I ask as if I'm unsure it's really her, and part of me is hoping it isn't.

"Landis?"

It's her. It's my mother, and it's the first time I've heard her voice in years.

CHAPTER 25

I easily recognize her voice. Part of me is angry and wants to demand she tell me why it's been so long, but then I remember that day at the prison. It was the last time I saw her in person, and that was over three years ago. Desperate to know when she would be able to come and get me, I peppered her with questions.

"I'm not wasting my visits if this is how you're going to be," she scolded me.

I backed off, and then, after we both sat in silence for a moment, she suddenly became happy again and wanted to talk about lavender farms and how someday she was going to make millions from growing and drying the herbs she had been reading about.

She talked about moving to Washington or somewhere with a farm. I can't remember exactly, but it was strange to see her so excited, and I listened intently for what role I would play in her grand plan. I pictured us both in a large field covered with fragrant purple flowers. The sun is bright, and she is happy, almost floating in the joy of our freedom.

I was eleven years old, and just a few weeks later, I was moved even farther from the prison to a home on the other side of the state. I'm not sure why. I hadn't gotten into trouble and couldn't see any reason for the change, but I'd already been moved so many times I'd stopped asking.

"Mom," I say.

I hear her huff. "Landis, I've told you before to call me by my name. Yes, I'm your mother, but I'm also a person with a name. Okay?"

I'm not sure why she feels this way, but at the risk of upsetting her, I acquiesce. "Okay."

"So, do you like the place you're at?" she asks.

"Yes," I answer. "It's a farm, and I'm learning a lot. It will help us with our plan."

"What plan?" she asks. Then there's silence.

"You know, the lavender farm," I remind her, hoping her situation hasn't changed again. "I've been learning how to irrigate, and I take care of a lot of the chores, so I can help you run it."

I hear her sigh, and my stomach drops.

"You're still getting out in September, right?" I hear my voice crack.

Another stretch of silence, then—"I don't know when," she says softly.

"But the judge said September 9th." My voice cracks, and I cringe.

September 9th is the day of the year most people are born. When I learned this from Uncle Bert at foster home number five, it felt fitting. Like her release day was a sign of birth, of a new life.

I try not to sound desperate. I know she hates it when I push her, but I've been counting down the months, weeks, and days to her release. It's a date etched into my mind. It's what I've grasped onto with every move, every uncertain or awful situation, but every time I bring it up with my caseworkers, I'm told the same thing—it's up to the judge. This one man, sitting high, dressed in a long, dark robe, and looking down at my mother. He will decide when she'll get out and when I, too, will be free.

"Don't worry about it," she says. But how can I not worry? I've lived every second of my life with her release like a carrot dangling out in front of me. Doesn't she want to get out? Have they completely beaten her down to where she doesn't even try?

I hate them all. Every one of them had a role in putting my mom away and keeping her there—the people who came to the apartment with their money, the police who didn't believe her, the judges who keep her in prison, and me. I hate myself for starting that fire. I was the one who caused it, but because I was hurt when she was at work, the judge added more time to her sentence—our sentence.

"Maybe I can get a job and help pay for stuff," I tell her. She's obviously worried about how we'll make it once she's out.

I hear her give a huff. "You're a kid. No one will hire you."

I feel slighted and need to defend my abilities. "I'm already kind of working, and I know I could do more."

I feel like I'm grasping at loose ends, trying to keep her on track for our plan. It's as though she has lost hope that it will work.

I'm desperate and want to remind her I still have the treasure she gave me, however, she's made it clear I'm never supposed to talk about it over the phone. They record everything, and if they find out I have it, they would think we stole it, and then neither of us would be free.

"We'll have money. Remember, I have the ..." I lower my voice to a whisper. "The ring."

She gives a huff, and I worry that what I've been clinging to all these years won't be enough.

"You said it would give us a home. We can sell it and use the money to ..."

"I didn't say that," she snaps. "I said it reminded me of home."

It's not what I heard all those years. I know that. I've put all my dreams into that tiny treasure, knowing it would eventually pave the way for our new life.

"But we ..."

"Landis." She shuts me down. It's just like before. I've pestered her to the point that she is now frustrated. But I'm frustrated, too. We're so close, and I feel her pulling away like before.

"You should give it to Evelyn." Her voice is now low, resolved.

"What?" I ask, stunned. "Why would I give it to her?"

"Because she deserves to have it."

"No," I say, trying not to let her give up on our plan. "They don't need the money. I can run the farm. That's why I'm here, isn't it? So, I can learn and take care of us?"

"Stop!" she says. Then her voice turns shaky, and I can tell she has had enough. "You're just a kid. You shouldn't have to take care of anyone."

Just a kid? I can hear defeat in her voice. She's got to know things will be better when she's out. I can tell she's tired of my questions, but I'm desperate to keep her hopeful and on the line.

"I'm almost sixteen," I blurt out, hoping she'll see that I'm not just a kid.

I hear her sigh. "Yes, and happy birthday. I'll always love you, Landis."

My heart drops. It's how she ends every call because every call is on the same day each year. My birthday call. I'm not almost sixteen. I am sixteen. It's late in the day, and I just now realize it's my birthday. This call wasn't to plan for what we would do when she was released, and it was no different than every year on this day. Her birthday gift to me—a phone call.

My desperation kicks in even stronger as I hear her trying to go, trying to wrap up another year of me. But this year was supposed to be the last of these calls. She'll be free in just a couple of months. I need something to hold on to, to keep my plan and my future in place.

"At least tell me you're getting out," I beg.

"Be a good boy, and it will all work out. Goodbye, Landis." And then all I hear is the dial tone.

I sit enveloped in the cushioned chair as my eyes sting and my throat tightens. If I'm good, it will all work out? Does that mean she'll be here? Goodbye Landis. It sounded final, but I refuse to believe that. She can't just desert me. Even if she wasn't coming, I still have a year before I'm legally on my own. At seventeen, I can leave and join the Army or get a job, but until then, I'm stuck in this revolving door of nightmares. I push those thoughts aside. She'll be here. In two months, things will work out. It will be just like before. Before it all came crashing down. I rub my hand and wonder if what I did will ever stop haunting me. I may have been young, but I knew what I was doing was wrong. I started the fire, and I have the scars to prove it, and while she's told me it wasn't my fault that she was taken away, I know it is. Why else would she always tell me to be good? And why don't I listen? She knows how many places I've been moved and she probably knows why. Be a good boy, she keeps telling me, but do I listen?

I want to fling the phone across the room, but I know that would only get me moved again. This time, I'd be back in that jail for sure and probably for good. Part of me actually wants that. I'm tired of trying. At least if I was put away, I could relax and quit feeling like I'm walking on eggshells.

I want to run, go somewhere I can scream out to the sky, and let my anger release, but if I leave the room now, my red and swollen eyes will make Mrs. Frost wonder what the problem is now.

So I sit, staring at the phone in my lap, and for no good reason, reach into my back pocket and remove the crumpled and ink-smeared paper.

Nicole's number stares back at me. She didn't have to give it to me, but she did, and she didn't have to offer to teach me to ride, but she did. I have an overwhelming need to talk to her, and for no good reason I can fathom, I make the call.

———

I ASKED for it and I have no one to blame but myself. My fearless burst of confidence now has me full of regret. I didn't expect Nicole to invite me over right away. I swallow hard, our conversation replaying in my mind.

"I still have to shovel out the stalls," I'd told her, trying to find an excuse to push this back. I really just wanted to talk to her, and learning to ride was my excuse.

She didn't take the hint, saying, "That's okay. I'll get the horses saddled and be ready when you get here."

After I hung up, I left Mr. Frost's den stunned at what I had agreed to. I'm not only on my way to Nicole's house but onto the back of a horse.

It's been less than an hour since I hung up with Nicole. I'm sitting in the car, and Mrs. Frost smiles at me as she gets into the driver's seat.

I asked Mrs. Frost if it was okay for me to go to Nicole's to study. I'm not sure why I didn't tell her the truth about what we planned to do. Maybe I was hoping it wouldn't happen.

She agreed far too quickly, as part of me was hoping she'd say no, and when she said she could drop me off on her way into town, I felt the entire world was against me.

She sticks the key into the ignition, but before she turns it and starts the car, she looks over. "How did the talk go with your mother?"

Could this get any worse? I not only feel odd but somewhat defensive. No one's ever asked about my phone calls from the prison, and I've never wanted to discuss those conversations.

"Fine," I answer quickly.

"Did she say anything about you living here?"

I flinch back. Is she trying to figure out when I'll be out of her hair? I know it has been a long time, but I've been to other places much longer. I'm helping out with the chores and staying out of trouble. I know it upset her when I was late coming in the other night, but that shouldn't be enough to get me kicked out already.

"She'll be here to get me in September," I answer.

Mrs. Frost's face turns to dismay as though my words have slapped her. I'm sure the caseworker told her when I'd be gone. Why does she act like she's unaware of this?

"Okay," she says, trying to regain her smile. "But I want you to know we want you here. After all, I'm your aunt, remember, so now we're your family." She lifts her eyebrows.

It's not my home or my family. She's taking this further than she needs to, and now I'm regretting saying anything. I just hope she doesn't think I am one of those kids who's desperate for a home and family. I'm not. I just need a place to stay for a few more months. Nothing more.

I squirm in my seat, wishing she'd just start the car. When she does, I lean back, glad to be on our way. And now the anxiety of what awaits me begins to set in. What if I can't get on the horse, or it bucks me off? What if I look like a complete fool in front of Nicole?

The drive is shorter than I expected, and when I reach for the door handle, she stops me.

"Be careful," she says.

This startles me. Not only because I was deep in thought about my impending horse ride but also because of her tone. I throw her a look, wondering how she can possibly see danger in a study session. My stomach clenches, wondering if she knows what I'm really planning to do.

I nod, wanting to ask her what she means by being careful, but I don't. It will just add to her array of looming, ambiguous threats. I want to avoid any other discussion. I don't like the lies, and I know if I'm caught doing anything wrong, it could mean being thrown out and having to move yet again, but Mrs. Frost's constant fear of everything has me keeping the riding lesson to myself.

"I will," I answer her.

Before I open the door, I look out to the long gravel driveway of Nicole's large white house. I'm nervous. I don't usually get invited over to other people's houses, and Nicole isn't just other people. But Mrs. Frost seems anxious as well.

"They painted their door red," she says with a sigh. "It looks nice." She continues to stare out, deep in thought. It's as though she sees something here that I should, but I don't.

I'm relieved when she shows no intention of leaving the car and will simply drop me off without speaking to anyone. I thank her for the ride and open the car door.

"Call me when you need a ride home," she says. "I have my errands to run, but it won't take me long. I'll hold dinner until you get back." She seems to be deep in her own thoughts as I close the car door.

I start to walk up the path to the house as she backs the car out and onto the road. Before I reach the door, I stop and watch as Aunt Evelyn drives away.

Chapter 26

I begin to walk up the stairs of Nicole's house when I hear her call to me from the side.

Her brown curls are tied back, and she is holding some long leather straps. She waves me over.

"I've got everything out back," she says. I follow her around to a corral, where two horses are standing. They barely look up as we approach, looking almost bored.

"Have you really never ridden before?" she asks.

I shake my head.

"Why haven't you ridden at your place?" Nicole asks. "The Frosts have a bunch of horses."

"I don't know," I reply, knowing the answer. It's taken me several weeks just to get used to standing next to them as I dole out their feed. I haven't had the desire to climb up on one. "I've been busy with the chores, and Mr. Frost has been gone, so I don't see Mrs. Frost showing me how."

She looks at me strangely. "Why don't you call them aunt and uncle?"

I cringe inside, worried I may have blown my cover.

"I haven't been around them much. Sometimes I forget."

She smiles and nods, and I feel confident that my lie is still solid.

I look around the place. They have a barn, corral, and fields stretching toward the woods.

"Is your brother at home?" I ask, hoping for more time to rally my courage.

"Nope. He went with my dad up north. They'll be gone until Sunday."

"Do you have other brothers and sisters besides Jeremy?"

"Just us," she answers and starts putting a metal bar connected to the straps into the horse's mouth. I realize they are the reins.

I should be glad to have this time alone with her, but seeing the horses with saddles on and ready to go, I'm regretting that I agreed to do this.

"You just sit and guide them with the reins," she explains. She can see I'm terrified, and I immediately try to wipe the look of fear from my face.

"This is Mischief," she says, patting the neck of the tall, black horse. "I was going to put you on Sheila because she's shorter, but Mischief will be better for someone who's never ridden before."

I stand silently, staring at the horse; Nicole can sense my fear.

"She's sound-minded, so don't worry."

"What does sound mean?" I ask, noticing the horse's name doesn't fit with being safe.

Nicole smiles and tosses her curls away from her face. "It means she's not going to buck or go running off. She's older, and even little kids ride her." Telling me that doesn't make me feel any better about this. I feel even more out of place.

She explains how to put my foot into the stirrup and then swing my leg around to get into the saddle. She stands at the horse's side, holding the reins, and waits for me to climb up. Feeling my heart pounding in my head, I try to do as she says, but just trying to put my foot up into the stirrup is a challenge, and she has to help me up so I can grab the saddle and then pull myself high enough to swing my leg up and over. Suddenly, I'm sitting up higher than what it seemed from the ground and grabbing onto a stumpy handle on the front of the saddle with both hands. My scars ache with the intensity of my grip. I notice her looking at the red and raised scars, but I'm in no place to be able to hide them.

"That's called the horn, and you can hold onto it," she says, putting the attention on the saddle and not my scars. I'm relieved. She either doesn't want to embarrass me or doesn't notice, but how could she not?

"You also need to use the reins," she says, continuing on with her instructions. She then demonstrates and explains how to tell the horse what to do by gently pulling back or to the sides with the long leather straps.

The horse takes a step back and then forward again, and I tense.

Nicole smiles. "You'll get the hang of it," she says and then easily climbs into the saddle on the other horse.

She seems so tiny against the massive animal, and yet she makes it look effortless. "Hold the reins, and Mischief will follow my horse. Ready?" she asks.

I'm not at all ready, but I nod anyway. She gives her horse a nudge with her heels, and it starts to lumber off. My horse follows. Each step jostles me from side to side.

At first, I'm convinced the saddle is going to slide, and I'll slip off and onto the ground, but after several minutes, I begin to relax, and soon I'm getting used to the motion of the horse and looking out at where we're going.

The sky is so blue and immense. There are no buildings or power lines to obstruct the view. And the thing I notice is the noise—or actually, the complete lack of it. Only the solid clomp of hooves on dirt as the horses make their way along the trail.

"Do you want to race?" Nicole asks, turning back.

"No!" I quickly answer, and then she laughs, and I realize how stiff I must look.

"Very funny," I call up to her.

From behind, I admire her curls and the shape of her back and hips. I then start to wonder how I got so lucky. I've only been here three weeks, and I'm now riding a horse out in the woods with one of the prettiest girls I've ever seen. Worry sets in. If Kevin Jenkins tells her who I really am and that I've lied to her, all of this would end. It's the reason I rarely talk to anyone outside of the kids I live with. I've never had anyone, especially a girl like Nicole, to talk to me or even give me a second look.

The trail follows small dips and bends, and the flutter of tiny leaves on tall, thick trees dance in the sun. The birds chirp overhead, and the air feels warm and smells clean. I'm still awkward on the horse. This animal is so large, and I can feel its bulk and strength under me, but I'm beginning to settle and watch what is all around me. Is this what it was like for cowboys in the old days? I wonder. I begin to daydream about a book I read years ago, *The Black Stallion,* about a boy and his horse who were on a deserted island. I think about reading it again now as I find myself atop a black horse.

We ride through the woods on well-traveled paths and also on tiny, almost invisible trails. I've been back in these woods, and yet I'm surprised that with each turn, the view is different and even more stunning. I'm amazed she knows exactly where to turn and what route to take.

We ride up a short but steep embankment and then down into a sandy channel. I cling on, worried I'll fall off, but soon we're both in the middle, and she stops her horse. I pull back on the reins like she showed me, and my horse also comes to a stop. I smile to myself.

Nicole points up ahead and off to the side. "Does this look familiar here?"

A breeze comes from that direction and encircles me, and then the voice from my last venture into these woods returns.

"Fear," it whispers.

Why is this happening again?

"See that big log and that hill. The path to your house is just across here."

"Fear," the voice is not only in my ear but also in my head. I try to ignore it. The breeze is cool, and yet no leaves rustle, and the air is quiet.

"Are you okay?" she asks.

I shake my head. I'm trying to focus. "I'm just confused. Where are we?" I want to go back, but the rush of air wants to pull me in.

"Here, follow me." She moves the horse forward, and I nudge mine to do the same.

We walk the horses up further toward the log and hill, but I'm still looking around, waiting for the voice to return.

Then she points to a tiny sliver carved into the tall grass that breaks off from the path we've been riding. It's barely visible.

She smiles. "Right there. Now, do you know where we are?"

I take a breath and sit up in the saddle. I hear only the rustle of the brush and leaves. The breeze has eased up, and my nerves begin to follow.

I try to sit tall so I can see over the hill. "Is this the trail that goes to my house?"

She nods. "Yes, it's the path I showed you the other day when we were out here."

I then look back to where we came from. "And it also goes back to your place?"

She smiles. "I told you Jeremy used to take this path all the time before he could drive. It's a bit shorter than following the road, and they'd take the shortcut that leads to the hollow."

I lift my shoulders. "What's the hollow?" I've heard talk about it. Mrs. Frost told me to stay away from "back there," and the kids at school spoke of a phantom in that place. Is that why she doesn't want me back there?

"It's where the secret fishing hole is. It's all Jeremy used to think about." Then, her face turns sad. She sighs and is deep in thought.

Fishing. It makes me think about when I stumbled into the back woods and saw the man they call Old Tom standing thigh-deep in the river, the early evening glow spreading across the water and the silvery flash of his line being cast back and forth. The idea of Jeremy and Old Tom together fishing is surprising, but I shrug and ask, "Jeremy goes fishing back here? I'd love to go with him sometime."

She looks at me with a face full of pain. She shakes her head slowly, and her words are labored. "He won't go back there anymore."

"Why not?" I ask.

When I stumbled into the woods while chasing for her phone number on that note, it felt dark and eerie, but was that because of what I'd been told, or is there really something ominous back here besides an old man and his three-legged dog? Staring at the area now, it looks like nothing more than a thick grove of trees. I wonder what lies beyond it.

Nicole sighs and looks uneasy. "It's where they think it happened. Jeremy hasn't been back there since."

"Where what happened?" I ask.

She swallows and looks even more uncomfortable. Her horse

moves forward as though it's impatient and wants to keep going, but Nicole uses the reins to turn it back the way we came from. She guides the horse up along the side of mine so we're facing. "Where Benji went missing. They think it happened back in the hollow."

Benji. It's the name I heard whispered on the bus and in the halls. And now I see clearly the letters that were crudely carved into the trunk of that enormous tree.

She says his name as though I should know who he is. I have to find out more, if only to gain some knowledge of what I'm supposed to already know.

I'm bewildered and filled with so many questions. Not only who is Benji, but what happened to him? Was he killed in that hollow? It has to be the reason Mrs. Frost is so afraid of these woods. A boy killed back there would definitely do that. And now my thoughts turn to the other name I've heard—the phantom. Is some creature living back in those woods to blame? But then my mind flashes back to the discussion in the cafeteria at school.

"Is this about the body they were talking about?" I ask.

Nicole nods sadly. "It's where they think he might be. They searched for weeks, but they never found anything. Now it's like the hollow is haunted." She looks down, sad.

"Why do they think Kevin did it?"

She gives a huff. "Because he hated him. He even said he was going to kill him."

"Why?"

Nicole shakes her head. "A girl. It was all over a stupid girl."

Chapter 27

Jeremy wasn't at the fork in the trail, so I waited until I knew it was long past our two o'clock meeting time and then went on without him. He didn't miss very often, but like me, sometimes chores were added, or something unexpected came up, and we both knew that anything more than fifteen minutes meant we were to go on without the other.

I was disappointed because it felt as though the stars had aligned. The water was low, and when I pulled the gates earlier that day, I saw sunlight flicker off of newly hatched flies. Flies that were exactly like the ones I had tied earlier that week with my grandfather. The conditions were perfect for a chance to land the one fish I had stalked all last year.

I wanted Jeremy there as a witness and to celebrate if I was successful. Yes, it was possible that Jeremy would be the one to land the elusive monster we had hunted all year, but I had the advantage. I had crafted flies I knew were the closest thing to the insects I now saw floating around me.

It was my grandfather's skill that was passed down to me, and it was evident in what I had created. My grandfather was a master, and that spring, I had sat patiently watching him spin, pluck, snip, and knot. I followed his pattern and tied so many of the tiny rust-colored bugs I would have enough to last the entire season. But it only takes one, and it's as much in the timing, and now was that time.

Stone flies live in the water, and at the beginning of summer, they emerge, crawl onto the rocks of the river, and then molt. It happens quickly, but if you're lucky enough to be in the hatch, it is magic. It is the newly winged bugs that the fish are after, and in my tackle box were the replicas I planned to cast and gently place on the surface of the water.

My grandfather was also often there with me, waders to our thighs in the slowly swirling shimmer of the hollow, but that week, he had gone up north with my father to help with the cattle, a job I would take over once school was finished. But for now, I was able to relish my time doing what I loved, in the place I could have stayed forever.

When I emerged from the woods and out to where the hollow's wide bowl spread, the soft haze of the hatch was unmistakable. I had been privileged to witness it before, but this time, I felt on the verge of something new.

I checked my line, clipped my net to the back of my suspenders, and then waded down into the cool, clear water. I caught my breath when a loud splash came from my right side. I caught just a glimpse of its crest and jump, the flash of reflection off its silvery scales, and yet, the one I was there for had yet to be seen. In fact, it hadn't been seen all season.

My grandfather was the first to talk about the giant fish.

"He's a lunker. One of the biggest I've seen in my sixty years back here," he told me as we waded back to the shore after an early evening trip to the hollow. I had watched from a distance as his rod bowed, and the line was taut and quivering. It was a massive fish.

That was years ago, and while I've never had him on my line, my grandfather's been able to claim that honor twice. I've seen Old Tom hook him, strain as he reeled and released, reeled and released, and then, as he was about to bring the fish in, have it break away and be gone in a flash of shimmery defiance.

"So sly," he said after one of the failed catches. "You begin to wonder if he's real or just your imagination."

As I began to cast, the sun was high, and I turned to block the light so I could see the fly on my line. My first cast was heavy, so I pulled it back in and dried the fly, lifting it up into the air, back and forth above my head, before letting it out and placing it back again on the surface. It was a good cast, with the fly in perfect view. Then I watched, my eyes glued to the blip of fuzz dancing on the ripples and silently willing the fish to take it. Nothing. I continued to wait. Still nothing.

I reeled it back and repeated, drying the fly, and again let it soar out before it lightly landed on the roiling waters. Then I saw the snap, and I jerked the rod upward. Did the hook set? Was the fish on the line? When the rod bent and the line pulled, my heart leaped. Fish on.

I reeled and released—not too hard, but just enough pressure to keep the fish on without it breaking the line. I could feel that it was good-sized—not the phantom, but a fighter. For several minutes, I ran out my line as I continued to reel and draw him in. Soon, I could see the lightening shimmer under the water. It was getting closer. I pulled up, bringing the rod high, in the hopes of getting the fish near enough to use my non-reeling hand to reach behind me for my net.

As I straightened to retrieve it, movement from the far bank caught my eye. Rusty began to bark. He'd seen it too. Was it a deer or a moose?

"Quiet, Rusty," I said, calling him back; I then looked to the water and the fish that was still fighting.

Maybe Jeremy was able to break away and make it after all, I thought as I tried to keep my attention on the fish. I pulled the rod to bring the fish in closer but took another glance back up. What I saw was now watching me. A person, but too far away for me to really see who it was. It had to be Jeremy, as I've never seen anyone back here except him and Old Tom. This was our own private place, our hidden cove that no others even have access to.

I strained and wondered why he was so far over there. The fish pulled. I had it right there, and as I reached down to dip the net in and retrieve it, the line snapped. I sprang back just in time to watch the flash of silver disappear.

"Shit," I said. Then I sighed and look up, annoyed. Why didn't Jeremy go the normal route, I thought, cursing him for distracting me and blaming him for my loss. But it wasn't Jeremy. The figure I saw across the pool was a girl, and when she saw me staring, she stepped back into the trees and into the cover of the woods.

I stood and continued to watch and see if she would reappear. Who was she, and how'd she get back here? After several minutes of watching and waiting, I went back to my fishing, but was distracted, wondering who was back there with me in the hollow.

I continued to cast and reel in several times, trying to go back to what I came to do, but my interest had waned, and finally, I gave up and walked back to the bank, determined to see what and who may be over there.

I left the rod and tackle box under a tree near the path back to my house and then followed the rim of the hollow over to where the girl had been. Rusty trotted along beside me, excited about the adventure.

As I trudged along without a trail, but just the border of the large pool to follow, I realized that in all the years I'd spent at the hollow, I'd never been on that side. The river flows in from the east, swirls into the large bowl that creates the pool, and then flows out again on that far side.

When I reached the area where I saw the girl, there was no sign of her. The woods were thick, just as they are along the trail I take to get to the hollow. And the view, even from all the way over on that side, showed the thin path back to my grandfather's house, along with the trail that leads back to mine. On that side is where I'd been from the time I can remember, but from over here, looking across, I saw it as though it was brand new.

I heard the crunch of a footstep on dried leaves, and when I peered back into the brush, I saw her. She was trying to get away.

Rusty took off after her, and I followed.

"Hey, who are you?" I yelled out to her.

She didn't respond or even slow down. I followed, running from tree to tree, still calling out to her. "Wait! I just want to talk to you."

When she finally slowed down, she was at the base of a small hill, and I realized it was the canal that carries the water out to the main river. Rusty's tail was wagging as he gave little yips of excitement. There was nowhere to go, and she looked like an animal that had been cornered and was looking for a way to bolt.

I slowly came toward her. "How did you get back here?" I asked, and then when I was about ten steps away, I realized who she was. It was her. The girl at the trestle. The girl with the raven hair that had smiled at me and told me her name.

"I remember you. You're Laura."

She stared back at me with big, dark eyes.

I couldn't help but smile at my good fortune. It had been months since the day I first saw her, and I had begun to wonder if she was an apparition.

"I'm Benji," I said, and she nodded as though she already knew.

"How did you get back here?" I asked her again, wondering how she could have walked so far. The nearest house to Jeremy's was the Nebeker's, a good two miles from his. I already knew they didn't have any daughters our age.

She shrugged, not wanting to tell me, but then motioned back toward the hill. "I came over the bridge."

I inclined my chin, surprised. "A bridge?"

"I wasn't doing anything but walking around," she said defensively.

"Wait," I said. "There's a bridge across the river, here?" That couldn't be, I thought. The only crossings over the water are the railroad trestle and a large highway bridge all the way back in town. If you have to get from one side to the other, that is the only option.

Her face turned to fear.

"Where?" I asked.

She pointed to the top of the hill. "Over there."

Then, what that meant settled in. "You live over there?" I asked.

Cautiously, she nodded.

She was from the other side. It hit me strangely. When I saw her at the trestle that day, I just assumed I'd never seen her because she was from a different school. I never thought she might be from over there. I had never given much thought about anything from the other side, except that I would soon be in the same school with the kids from across the river. People I've never met, and for some reason, my family seems adamant about avoiding.

"Are you going to Snake River High next year?" I asked.

She nodded, and I smiled. Seeing her at school each day would be wonderful, but that's an entire summer away. I began to scheme how I could see her again.

"Do you come over here a lot?"

"No. And I don't think I'm supposed to," she admitted with a small smile. "I didn't know the bridge was even here. I was riding my horse back there when I saw it. I was curious where it went."

Her dark hair was windblown and tousled, her shirt had flakes of hay on it, and there were scuff marks on her jeans. Yet, she was still the prettiest girl I'd ever seen.

She tentatively took me to the hidden access across the river.

From atop the hill, I saw the narrow section and realized it was barely a bridge at all. There were several strands of rope tied to boards that were strung across and anchored to large trees on each side. It looked precarious and unstable, and I was surprised she even attempted to cross.

I could see the water line on the far bank and realized that the only way the bridge could be used was because the water is so low this year. If the water was at its normal level, it would flood the narrow passage and would cover the bridge completely, hiding it from view.

"You came across this?" I asked her, surprised. I wondered if I would dare to traverse that steep and treacherous span.

She nodded. "My horse is tied just behind those bushes, so I better go back."

My heart dropped. "Meet me here tomorrow?" I blurted out, not wanting her to leave.

Laura looked unsure.

"Or I can go across and meet you over there," I offered.

"What for?" she asked.

I shrugged. I had no idea; I just wanted to.

She thought a moment, then smiled. "What time?"

My heart leapt. "I finish my work at two, and then I'll come over."

She took a contemplative breath. "Okay. But stay in the trees so no one will see you."

I agreed, and I wondered if she was aware of the aversion my family and friends had toward those who lived on her side of the river.

As I walked back toward the hollow, I thought about the reasons the two sides of the same town were at war. Why did they seem to hate people they didn't even know? I wanted to ask my parents what it was, but I also didn't want them to know about my plans to go over there.

This was the beginning of my end. And all those involved, both on their side and ours, are now left without answers but also with the guilt of the role they think they played.

Chapter 28

LANDIS

I know summer break is just a week away, but it's the only good excuse for me to be gone for an extended amount of time.

"Nicole is helping me with some assignments in English. We have finals next week, and this will help, so I won't have to repeat it next year." It's what I told Mrs. Frost. I'm not happy about these lies I tell her, but it's the only way I can be away for hours without question.

Mrs. Frost is thrilled that I'm so interested in my school work, and when I tell her I can walk to Nicole's, she contemplates this for a moment and then agrees to let me.

I leave out the front, but when I'm down the lane and out of sight, I go around to the barn and to my hidden gear.

The sun is dampened by clouds gathering and turning dark. I hope it is only a threat and won't end in cutting my plans short.

The tall grasses and thin willows sway in the wind, and I'm relieved when I find my fishing pole and tackle box exactly where I put them. I take a deep breath and smile at what awaits me.

The path leads back into the brush and toward the thick grove of the woods. At first, I walk quickly, and then I begin to jog, knowing my time will go quickly. This trail behind the fields and pastures is a much shorter trip than the paved road around the front of this swath of land, but it's still a hike, and I'm winded and sweating when I finally reach the area where I've seen Old Tom casting his line. I stare out over the river, looking for him as though he never leaves that spot. I don't see him, so I continue up the path.

As I come up the bank and around to where the river curves into a slowly rotating swell, that's where I find him. He's farther out into the flow. His tall rubber waders are secured by wide suspenders, and he's wearing a vest covered in small tools that rock and sway with his movements. Again, I'm mesmerized by the swish and swoop of his casts and the line hanging in the air until he gently lets it fall onto the water's surface. The fly is barely visible in the glimmer of the water, and I hold my breath, waiting to see what happens.

Then I hear a bark. Old Tom hears it, too, and looks up. I'm spotted. My instinct is to back away and leave, but instead, I hold my ground, my fishing pole in hand. For a moment, he just studies me, and when the dog is at my feet, he calls out to it, and the dog reluctantly runs back into the trees.

I go to the river's edge and set my gear on the ground. He's far enough away that he can't see just how inept I am, and I'm grateful. I pull out what gear I've pilfered and then loop the knot through the tiny metal eye of the lure.

Even though I have the knee-high boots I was given, I have no desire to venture out into the water, so I'm anchored to the bank, which is fine. Have no idea how deep the water is, but seeing the swiftness of the current, I'm not about to test my inability to swim.

Still ignoring Old Tom's glare, I position myself in the stance that most resembles his. I hold the rod and the line, and then with as much confidence as I can pretend to have, I whip the rod up, and the line, with the hook and lure at the end, follows. I watch it soar back, and then I bring the pole forward, just like I've seen him do, and the line follows. I'm doing it, I think. However, instead of the lure landing far out onto the river, it drops into the shallows right in front of me. It wasn't a complete failure, but it will never catch a fish.

I pull out more line, leaving a long loop that I hope will shoot the lure out further. Again, I try to emulate Old Tom and wave the pole high up, back and forth several times, and then cast it forward. I'm sure the lure will reach the deep water this time, but when I look to see where it landed, it is gone. So is my line. I follow the pole up and see that the line is still behind me, and caught in the spindly branches of a willow tree is the lure.

"Ugh," I say under my breath. I pull on the pole, and the line tightens and wiggles the branches. I still hope Old Tom hasn't realized my failure or my acknowledgment of it.

I take a quick look over and see that he has, in fact, witnessed what happened and is now turning and moving farther away.

I spend the next several minutes trying to untangle the line and retrieve the hook so I can start over. I swing the pole forward and back. I try to pull the line tight and then release it quickly, but nothing helps. Soon, I'm frustrated and end up cutting the line. And then, as if even God is watching and against me, I feel a drop of rain hit my face. Within minutes, the entire sky has opened up, and the whole bank is turning to mud. I gather my gear and move closer under the cover of a tree. I look up and see Old Tom is gone. I don't know when he left, but I'm sure it was while I was struggling to release the hook. Now I sit wondering why I ever thought this would work and how I'm going to get home without getting soaked and without an excuse.

"Come with me." The voice startles me and I turn to see Old Tom standing on the bank behind me. He is now wearing a long, thin jacket with a hood that blocks the rain. The three-legged dog stands beside him with a panting smile.

"You can wait at my house for the storm to pass."

"That's okay," I say and look back toward the trail that brought me there. My hesitation to go with him is obvious.

"You'll get covered in mud going through the field now," he says, as drops splatter on the ground around me. "Come to my place and wait till it passes."

My shoes and pant legs are already wet and dripping. I can't go back through the secret trail, and his house is on the way, on the other path to where we are now. If I don't take him up on his offer, the walk back to the farm is at least a mile. I have no idea how I'll walk through the water and mud without ruining my shoes and the new clothes I've been given.

He loses patience, turns, and starts toward his house.

I'm not sure what to do, and then the dog barks as though calling me to go with them. I relent, gather up my gear and follow. I can wait until the rain stops and then hopefully make it home without raising suspicions.

Old Tom is a good distance ahead of me and hasn't turned back. I wonder if he knows I've decided to follow. For an old man, he's formidable. His strides are long, and his shoulders are wide. The night he found me in the woods, he was intimidating, but I figured it was because he startled me. Now I know that he's just as large as I thought he looked that night.

As we get farther back into the thick grove of trees, I begin to tense, knowing it's where I'm not supposed to be—none of this is— but as the shadows overtake me and the willowy branches stretch and bend above, I see how the trail winds back and around to an enormous cove. This is where I saw him fishing as I stumbled upon him in my quest to retrieve the paper note. The sun had begun to set that day, and the sky was already dusky, so I wasn't able to see all that was back here.

Even with the rain, the sunlight stretches through the canopy of trees and dances on the slowly rotating flow of the diverted river. It's as though the water comes in for a rest, swirling through the calm and quiet channel before making its way back out to the rush of the open current.

I continue to follow as the path bends and leads to Old Tom's house. It's such a completely different route than the one that I take to the front of his place when I release the water at the ditch. Had I not followed that note as it floated away in the canal, I would have had no idea what lies back here.

When we reach the back of his house, I see the large garden. There are rows of neatly mounded dirt and tiny sprouts in perfect lines. The dog barks as if asking me to pay attention.

Old Tom climbs three stairs to the back porch and then opens the door, and motions me inside. Every bell and whistle in my mind is blaring, telling me I shouldn't be doing this. What if he's a deranged killer, a hermit living back here with bodies buried in the yard? I've seen movies, and this is exactly the type of place where they live.

"Take your shoes off on the tile," he says, and then he reaches into a cupboard behind the door and hands me a towel.

He removes the long jacket and tall rubber boots, and his clothes are completely dry underneath.

The house is warm, and I can feel the frigid cling of my wet clothes. He gestures for me to sit on a wooden chair near a stone fireplace. An orange glow radiates from it. I do as he says and set my fishing pole and gear nearby.

I glance around the room. There is log furniture and chairs covered in cow hides. A deer head hangs above the fireplace, and a large fish is on the other wall. Tiny needlepoint pictures and ceramic cows and chickens sit on tables and shelves. It looks like what would be inside a little cabin, or at least what I think a cabin would look like.

The dog trots in like he owns the place and goes to a small cushion on the floor. He curls his three legs under himself and snuggles into it.

"You can hang your clothes on the back of that chair. Pull it up next to the fire," he says, walking toward a room. "I'll find something for you to wear until they're dry."

He wants me to take off my clothes? I take a deep breath and contemplate if I should just leave and take my chances with Mrs. Frost, knowing she'll be more upset if she knows I'm here.

Old Tom comes back out with a flannel bathrobe and hands it to me. I take it and stand there awkwardly, not knowing what to do.

"I don't have a dressing room if that's what you're waiting for." He then walks toward the kitchen, giving me some privacy.

"Right," I say, and then quickly strip off my shoes, pants, and shirt, leaving my underwear on, thankful they are still somewhat dry. I look back, making sure he isn't watching as I take the treasure from my pants pocket and hide it in my underwear. I then wrap the towel around my waist, hoping to hide it even more, and then pull on the robe.

"How old are you?" he asks as he fills a tea kettle and sets it on the stove next to a long counter with two metal bar stools.

"I'll be ..." I stop and correct myself. "I'm sixteen."

"Sixteen?" he says, then gives a small huff.

Like most, he is surprised. I'm much older than I look.

"Well, from the looks of your feet, you haven't stopped growing yet. You may want to dry those socks as well."

I look down at my feet. My socks are soaked, so I strip them off.

My feet are red and puckered from the cold water. I drape my jeans, socks, and shirt over the back of the chair and then wonder if I should sit on the edge or just stand and wait until my clothes are dry.

"Take a seat here," he says, pointing me toward a barstool. "Do you want some tea?"

Tea? "Um. Okay," I answer. I've never had tea, but the idea of something hot sounds good as I shiver. Even standing here half naked, with the whispers I've heard about this place, my hesitations about Old Tom feel unwarranted.

When the kettle starts to squeal, he removes it from the stove, pours the hot water into two mugs, and then plops tea bags into each. He hands me one that is red with the words "Farmall" across the middle. He takes the one that is faded yellow with the word "Grandpa." It strikes me as strange, but then I think, why couldn't he be someone's grandpa?

I see two framed photos on a side table. One shows three people sitting around a campfire. It's a man, a tall young man, and a girl with long blonde hair. Even though the image isn't very clear, I can see that the man is Old Tom. It must be an old photo, as his hair is brown, not gray. The other photo is of a boy that looks to be about my age. Could that be his grandson? And if it is, I wonder where he is now. I've never seen any sign of anyone that would fit the age of a grandson.

"Do they know where you are?" he asks, and I feel my shoulders twinge.

I give a non-nonchalant shrug. They think they know. Isn't that good enough? No one's ever cared where I went as long as I wasn't causing trouble. I may have lied to Mrs. Frost, but am I really doing something wrong? Am I supposed to sit in that house and do nothing when there is all this to see and do? Besides, I'll only be here for a little while.

"They have me helping out, and when I'm not doing work, they don't care what I do." Why should they care? Being the only kid in the house has me unable to fade into the background and just do my own thing.

His eyebrows lower, and before he can continue to question me, I take a gulp of the tea and start to look around the room.

Along another wall is a carved wooden rack holding several fishing poles and a glass display case. I stand and walk to it. Inside are dozens of tiny, colorful, bug-like objects. I study them. "What are these?" I ask, hoping to divert the unconvinced stare boring a hole through the back of my head.

"Those are flies."

I squint at them and then look at him perplexed. They don't look like real flies. They're fuzzy and look like small pieces of lint. "Flies?" I ask him.

He sighs and decides to let up on his scrutiny.

"For fly fishing."

I shake my head, having never heard the term.

"It's a type of fishing," he explains. "You use these instead of bait. And the rod is longer, and you cast differently."

I look at the rods in the rack and then over to the one I found in the barn.

"Different, how?"

He smiles at me as though he's suddenly humored. "Is that what you were trying to do out there?" he asks.

There is no point trying to fool him, so I sigh. "I don't know what I was trying to do. I saw you fishing and wanted to do it. But it was terrible."

Old Tom laughs. "Yes, it was."

I look at him, wondering if the indigence I feel is warranted, but when I see him taking down one of the rods from the rack, I'm more interested than insulted.

"This was one of my first rods. It's called a South Bend model 359. It's old, but it will still catch whatever's out there." He hands it to me.

"This is a lot longer than my fishing pole," I say, again looking back at my pole and gear by the fireplace.

He huffs. "That's a hook and bait pole. That isn't fishing. It's sitting around hoping you'll get lucky. There's no strategy to that."

My face scrunches in confusion.

"It's different. Impossible for me to explain. But once you've caught a fish on the fly, you'll know. It's nirvana."

His words seem far-fetched, but I'm intrigued. I study the rod and look at the long willowy shaft and large reel. "Nirvana?" I ask. "What do you mean?"

He smiles. "Until you do it, it's hard to explain."

"It's still throwing the hook out into the water, isn't it?"

He takes a deep breath, and then he lifts his shoulders. "I've been doing this since before I was your age, and I still don't know exactly what it is. There is definitely technique and practice, but some days the fish are just hungrier than others."

Hearing the word hungry makes my stomach growl. I know I should be getting back to the house, but I'm intrigued. "Is it hard to learn?"

"It takes some time to get into the motion. And I don't think you ever really master it. That's why I love it. The water, the weather, the bugs, the way you cast, everything works together, and when even one thing isn't right, then no matter what you do, the fish won't bite."

It sounds like a lot of effort without much reward, but I want to try.

I admire the tiny, fuzzy, colorful flies. "Where do you get these?"

Old Tom smiles. The lines on the sides of his eyes stretch back. "I make them. It's called tying."

I raise my eyebrows, impressed. "You made these? All of them?"

Again, he smiles. "Yes. With string, fur, feathers, and other things."

"You must eat a lot of fish."

He chuckles. "I eat some, but not that many. I prefer to catch them, admire them, thank them, and then release them back so I can catch them some other time."

"You let them go?" I ask, surprised.

He gives a laugh. "The bigger they get, the smarter they are. It's a game of strategy."

I cock my head. "A game with a fish?"

He nods and gives another chuckle.

I like him and wonder how anyone could be afraid or have reservations about being near him.

"Will you teach me?"

Suddenly, his face turns reserved. "Well ..."

"I'm a quick learner. Even Mr. Frost says so."

Old Tom looks at the ground sadly. "We'll see."

Now I'm kicking myself and hoping he doesn't tell the Frosts where I've been. "You don't have to. I can just figure it out."

"After what I saw today, that could take years."

I throw him a look.

"Tomorrow's Saturday. I plan to go out in the morning. Come by after you set the head gates if you want." He then walks to the fireplace and lifts one of the pant legs draped on the chair. "Your clothes are dry."

And it sounds like it's time for me to leave.

Chapter 29

"Looks like the irrigation went well," Jesse says as we walk from the barn. He returned with Mr. Frost yesterday with a large trailer filled with cattle they gathered from somewhere in the hills outside of town. "Any troubles?" he asks.

I shake my head.

A small pickup truck is parked just outside, and he hands me the keys.

"Back it up to the bales," he says, pointing at the tall stack.

I look at the keys and he sees my hesitation.

"What is it?" he asks.

"I don't have a license. I'm not old enough to drive."

For a moment, he looks stunned, and then he chuckles. "If you can reach the pedals, you can drive here on the farm."

I give an unconvincing shrug.

"Have you ever driven anything?"

I shake my head.

He smiles. "Don't worry. You'll learn. There's a lot of room out here to practice." He takes the keys and motions for me to follow. "I'll go with you today, and you can practice later, and then you can feed on your own."

Hearing that I'll get to drive, even if it's just around the farm, has my head spinning with anticipation. I slide into the passenger seat, and I'm relieved to see that it isn't a stick shift. I've been in cars with those, and they look difficult and confusing.

He starts the truck and then backs it up to where the hay bales are stacked in the barn. We both get out and heave the heavy bales into the truck bed. When it's full, I jump from the tailgate.

"I can drive. Just tell me where to go," I say with confidence. Being given the chance, I'm now eager to try.

He cocks his head and smiles. "You sure? I thought you said you'd never driven anything."

"I've watched, and I can do it."

He nods toward the truck, and I slide into the driver's seat. I turn the key, and the engine starts without issue. I release my breath, relieved. The radio comes on, and Jesse reaches over and turns it up.

"You always turn up Waylon," he says.

It's not a song or a name I know, but I raise my eyebrows.

"You've never listened to Waylon Jennings?" he asks.

I grin and shake my head.

He rolls his eyes. "I've got my work cut out for me with this one," he says up to the sky.

I reach over and turn the radio up even louder, and he laughs. Then I sit back and wait for him to tell me what to do next.

"Put it in drive and go slow so we don't lose anything off the back," Jesse says. "The pasture can be pretty bumpy. Go to the far end of the pasture, turn around, and then we'll make our way back."

I nod and do as he says, and the truck moves forward with the radio crackling and blaring as Waylon sings, "Everything we had is gone. If you can't see, that's what you get for lovin' me."

Jesse sings along as he directs me toward the south pasture. As we enter the field, the cows see us and begin to move in our direction. The truck rumbles and bobs as we roll along.

When I get to the far fence, he puts up a hand. "Start right here and then just slowly drive a straight line. Stop about every ten feet and put it in park. Leave the engine running."

With hands gripping the wheel, I do as he says. At the first stop, we both get out and go to the back. He climbs up on the tailgate, pulls out a pocketknife, and cuts the twine on a bale. He then tosses a large section of hay onto the ground where the waiting cows have gathered.

"Only open one bale at a time, or you'll have a mess back here," he explains.

We both get back in, and I put the truck in drive and move it forward another ten feet. Each time we stop, the crowd of cows is smaller, spreading out just as we have done with the hay.

On the next pass, Jesse stays in the back of the truck. I creep it along, and he tosses the hay as we go. We repeat this process until we've covered the entire length of the pasture. As we finish, he looks at me and smiles. "That's all there is to it. Any questions?"

"No."

"Okay, well, no joy riding, but if you're okay doing this on your own, I'll have you fill in when I need it," he says.

I nod. "I could do it every night on my own," I say. It's more of a plea than a statement. The idea of being out there on my own and driving doesn't feel like a chore.

He laughs. "Trying to take my job? How will I feed my family?"

I laugh with him but then realize I had no idea he had a family.

"You have a family?" I ask, surprised.

He then laughs even harder. "You act surprised that anyone would have me."

I realize my blunder and try to reel it back. "No, it's just I ..."

He laughs again. "Yes, I have a family. I'm married, and I have a little boy. His name is Zane."

"Zane?" I ask, having never heard that name before.

"Yep, like Zane Grey. You know?" he answers, assuming I know who that is.

Again, I look stumped.

He turns the music down a bit so I can hear. "First, it's Waylon, and now, you've never heard of Zane Grey? He's an author."

I lift my shoulders. I have no idea.

"Don't you read?" he asks.

I scrunch my forehead, wondering how I should take that. "Yes, I read."

"No, what I mean is, do you like to read," he clarifies.

"Yes," I answer hesitantly. I've been teased before about how much I love to read. I've learned to keep it to myself. When I'm into a book, it is often the only time I don't feel I'm alone. I have two books.

One is mine, and the other came with me. I've had the book, *Island of the Blue Dolphins*, ever since I was ten. My fourth-grade teacher gave it to me. Her name was Mrs. Funk. The other kids made fun of her name, saying she was anything but funky. All I remember was that she told me I was smart. She told me that even though the main character in the book is a girl, she reminded her of me.

"Smart and resilient. And a survivor," she told me. I already loved the book, but that made me love it that much more.

When I don't have access to a library, I read that book over again. I've read it so many times; the pages are now soft, and the book is thick from being pressed open.

The other book I have is one I'm still reading. I started it in the place before coming here, but when I was forced to leave quickly, I shoved my things into the plastic bag I was given and forgot that it was something I was supposed to return. I don't need to be accused of stealing again, so having it could sink me if they discovered it. Along with my other treasure, I do everything in my power to keep it hidden. I've almost finished it, and I've been dreading what I'll do when I need a new book to read.

"Zane Grey is one of the best authors to have ever lived," explains Jesse. "He writes westerns. I've read them all. I have a bookshelf full of them."

"They sound good," I say.

"I can lend you some if you'd like."

I nod enthusiastically. "Sure."

"Okay. I think I even have one in my truck. You can start with that and then let me know what you think. I'll turn you into a cowboy yet." He smiles.

As I drive us back to the house, I'm feeling high. Me, a cowboy. The more I'm with Jesse, the less my time here feels like a sentence. Until my mother is out, I hope this will last.

I pull the truck around to the front side of the barn, and in the glow of the back porch light, Mrs. Frost is standing, arms folded, and face aghast.

"Hmm," Jesse ponders. "That doesn't look good. I wonder what's wrong with her."

I put the truck in park, turn it off, and the music goes silent, making the creak of the truck doors as we open them, even more pronounced.

"What are you doing?" she yells as she comes off the porch and toward us. Her eyes are wide and frantic.

"We were feeding. I took Landis to show him ..." Jesse tries to explain, but she cuts him off.

"Why is Landis driving?" she demands.

Jesse shrugs. "If he's going to do the feeding, he'll need to use the truck."

She shakes her head and gives an exasperated gasp. "Then he's not doing the feeding. He is not to be driving."

"Why not?" Jesse looks apologetic but also perplexed. "He did fine."

Mrs. Frost is unconvinced. "He shouldn't be driving."

Jesse nods. "But it's in the pasture. The kids around here do it all the time. I started driving when I was ..."

"I don't care," she says, cutting him off. "I don't want him driving." She then looks at me with eyes that are panicked. "Do you understand?"

"It was my fault," I say, trying to help Jesse. "I told him I knew how."

"Not again," she says.

"But I ..." I try to object.

"Not. Again." She repeats the words deliberately, but then her voice cracks. She takes a deep breath like a solid exclamation point, puts a hand to the base of her neck, and then turns and goes into the house.

If I was brought here to work, then why does she care if I drive the truck?

Jesse and I stand there looking at the closed door, and then I turn to him in bewilderment. He, too, is wide-eyed. Neither one of us knows how to respond.

"I'm sorry," he says.

I shake my head, still dumbfounded. "What did I do?"

"Nothing. I should have asked if it was okay first. I know she has a lot going on and ..."

"Am I supposed to just sit in the house?" I ask him, not really expecting an answer. "She doesn't want me going anywhere. I have to sneak back there to go fishing."

He gives me a sour look. "I told you not to go back there. If she finds out, you really will be stuck in the house."

I roll my eyes. "What's so bad about being back there?"

He takes a deep breath and blows it out loudly. "I think she's worried something will happen to you."

I scoff. "Why? Mr. Frost had to talk to her because she wasn't going to let me do the gates for the water. She says I can't go back near the woods. She acts like something terrible is back there and is going to grab me."

He raises his eyebrows and bites his bottom lip. He's keeping something from me, just like everyone else.

"I have to go," he says, walking to his truck.

I follow, peppering him with questions. "What is it? Tell me what's going on. Why doesn't she want me back there?"

He stops and turns to me. "It isn't my place, Landis. I'm sorry, but she's already upset with me."

He opens the door of his truck, reaches under the seat, and then hands me a book.

"This is a good one," he says, and I can see that he isn't going to answer any of my questions.

I sigh and look at the cover. A cowboy and a woman, both on horseback. The title is *Riders of the Purple Sage*.

"Let me know if you like it, and I'll let you borrow some others."

I nod, defeated, and then I stand and watch him drive away, leaving me alone, with the moths and the lowing of the cows in the distance.

I turn toward the back door of the house and wonder if I should go inside and face her or steer clear. I decide on the latter and go out to the barn instead.

The calf is already looking bigger and stronger, and it isn't as skittish as before. I grab a handful of grain from the barrel and go to the corral. I offer it to the mother in hopes she'll bring the calf along with her, and she does. It no longer wears the coat of its dead predecessor, and its spindly legs have now straightened out and grown.

I squat down and try to coax it to me.

"Come here, little guy," I say, extending my hand.

It is curious and takes a step closer; it stretches its neck and takes a quick sniff of my hand, only to leap back, practically crashing into its mother. The cow chews the grain without noticing. I stay still with my hand extended, and the calf does this step, sniffing and leaping several times, making me laugh.

"I'm going to call you Rontu," I tell the calf. It's the name of the dog in one of my favorite books, *Island of the Blue Dolphins*. Rontu, the dog, was also orphaned and then saved.

After a while, my stomach urges me to go inside. Even in the pungent air of the barn, I can smell the aroma of Mrs. Frost's cooking wafting from the house.

I sigh and wonder what to say or how she'll be after what happened. Will she revoke my chores and keep me from doing the water now? I have to make things right. Not being able to be on the river would be the worst thing I could imagine.

Stepping out of the barn, it's already dark. The moon is full, and a wisp of clouds laces around it. I begin my walk toward the back door, knowing it leads directly into the kitchen, but then I see her standing there on the porch.

She is looking out toward the woods, her apron in her hands, and when I come out of the shadows and into the light of the porch, she releases what looks like a year-long sigh of relief.

CHAPTER 30

I pull the head gates as early as possible and the strong gush of water bursts forward. I lay the large metal plates on the bank and then make my way to Old Tom's. Mrs. Frost said she'd be gone most of the day, so I didn't even have to make up an excuse for my planned venture.

When I arrive at his house, he's in the back garden. There are dozens of rows and mounds with tiny sprouts. There are tubes at the ends of the rows, and a small stream of water is making its way down, turning the dirt dark as it begins to soak into the ground.

"You look ready," he says, at my obvious eagerness.

There are two fishing rods leaning against the back of the house.

"You can use this one today," Old Tom says, handing it to me with both hands, like a king presenting a sword to a knight. It's the fly rod he showed me before. It's his old one, but for me, it's as though he's given me something as precious as the treasure I've hidden all these years.

I was so overwhelmed by his offer that I almost turned it down. I'm so glad I didn't.

With the loaned rod in hand, I'm eager to get on the water, and when he directs me to the gravel laneway at the front of his house, I'm confused.

"You need to learn a couple of things before we get on the water. Stand here and hold the rod like this," he says, demonstrating. "You lift the fly and take the line back and forth, letting a bit out each time, and then when you feel it's right, you release it and let the fly land on the water." I watch as he makes it look easy.

When it's my turn to try, I immediately realize how *uneasy* it is. My rod is too high, the line is loose, and I can't find the fly while I'm trying to do what he told me.

"Try it again, and this time, think of your arm as the hand of a clock. You whip the rod at ten and two. Ten and two," he repeats while showing me.

I try again, and after several more dismal attempts, I have one that garners a "that was close."

I keep at it, and after I've made at least six attempts that weren't terrible, he decides I can try it on the water, but only if I promise to continue also practicing on land.

I agree.

We take our gear and walk the path back to the place where I saw Old Tom that first time.

"I'm going out just past that gravel bar. You stay right in the area. Don't go past that outcropping. That's where the water gets deep," he explains.

I didn't have any plans to even get in the water at all, so I had no problem with his directions.

For most of the morning, I find myself watching him and then trying to emulate what he does. I have to keep reminding myself that he's been doing this longer than I've been alive, and by the time he wades back over to where I am and exclaims they "just aren't biting today," I am wondering if I'll ever be able to learn this weird dance of rod, line, and hook.

"Keep practicing, and you'll get it," he says, seeing my frustration.

For a moment, we stand on the bank and talk about what he thinks is going on with the water, the bugs, and the effect it all has on our success with the fish, and then he gathers up his gear, and I do the same.

"I'll most likely be out here at the same time tomorrow if you want to join me, but don't be skipping out on your chores to do so." He then laughs. "My grandson was an expert at that."

I smile at the invitation and then hand him the rod he allowed me to use.

He waves it away. "It's yours to use while you're here."

"Really?" I ask, stunned. "Thanks."

"You can leave the other one behind."

I nod and begin to follow him back to his house when I realize the shorter route is behind me. The sun has already begun to fade, and if I go that way, I'll be able to hide the rod in the barn.

"I'm going to go back this way. I'll see you tomorrow," I tell him and then wave as I begin my walk back into the woods, back to the hidden trail.

At first, Old Tom gives me a questioning look, but then he nods and waves back. Rusty barks his goodbye.

"I'll see you tomorrow too, Rusty," I call back to him.

The sky to the west is turning dark red as I walk and think about my day on the river. Even without a single fish biting, I'm in awe of this place and my luck at being here.

My chores are finished, and I begin to dream about what delicious meal will be waiting. The deep breath I take of the early evening air makes me feel as though I'm floating.

Birds twitter around me as I walk, and I can see that the sun is much lower than I had thought. It must be later than I planned, so I pick up my pace.

When I reach the hill that leads up to the channel, I hear a rush of water, and by the time I get to the top, I see that it's full.

"Oh no," I moan. The water doesn't look really deep, but its pace makes me wonder if I'll be able to make it across. My work boots are waterproof and to my knees, but what if the current knocks me down?

I turn and look, contemplating if I should go back and take the long route around Old Tom's and across the far field.

Again, I look at the sunset. I'm already late. What if Mrs. Frost is already home?

I sigh and look back at the water. It can't be that bad. I grip both fishing rods in one hand and the tackle box in the other and decide to test the depths of the water.

I carefully make my way down the bank, and when I reach the

edge, I can only see the muddy flow. I can't see to the bottom, so I have no idea how deep it is.

I take a small step near the edge and see that the water barely covers my foot. It can't be too deep even in the middle, I think, so I decide to press forward.

I now have both feet in the water, and when I try to walk forward, the force of the flow makes my steps difficult. I'm trying to shuffle across, but I soon realize it's easier if I lift and step.

My grip on my gear tightens as I reach the middle. The water is now lapping near the top of my boot, and my heart is racing. If I lose my balance, I will not only fall in, but I might also lose the precious fishing rod.

I curse myself for losing track of time, but I'm soon near the other side, and with just a few more strained steps, I'm able to make it to the bank.

I release my breath with a relieved "Woah," and now I'm hoping my luck holds out so I can make it stealthily to the field that stretches back behind the barn.

The low sun makes my walk back to the barn easier, and once I get inside, I grin with satisfaction.

I return the old fishing pole and tackle box back to where I found them and store my new rod next to it in the shed. It's safe there, and I'll be able to keep it and my escapades to the river hidden.

Being able to sneak out from behind the barn to the trail that leads to the river without anyone in the house seeing me has been the one reason I've been able to roam and explore without issue.

I'm still in an airy reverie when I come out of the barn.

"Where were you?" It's Mrs. Frost, and her voice is sharp.

My contemplation turns to panic as I grapple for an explanation.

"I was in the back with the hay truck," I say with as much confidence as possible.

She's at the back door, eyes wide and wringing her hands.

"Was there a problem?" she asks.

"No, it just takes me longer now that I'm doing it on my own."

She strains, looking over and around me toward where I told her I had been, and then she sighs.

"I can't see anything behind that barn. I was looking everywhere for you. Didn't you hear me calling?"

I give her an apologetic shrug.

Another big sigh, but she relents. She looks so relieved.

Why does she worry so much about me? I'm still not used to anyone being so concerned about where I am and what I'm doing. Staying out of the way and not causing problems has been what I've tried to do up to this point. Even that, however, hasn't always worked. But this time, it has to. My mom knows where I am, and I need to be here and ready when she is free.

It's been almost a month now. The time has gone by surprisingly fast, but it seems as though Mrs. Frost only gets worse with worry. I have to be stealthy just to be able to go out of the house for anything other than chores or when I tell her I'm going to Nicole's.

I'm not sure why, but Mrs. Frost doesn't seem to mind the time I spend with Nicole, so I use that excuse often.

I tell Mrs. Frost I'm going to Nicole's house for our "study sessions" almost daily. She beams at my intense interest in my grades. I have gone to Nicole's a number of times. We've even taken the horses along the same trail we took that first day, and I'm becoming more comfortable and even able to get on and off without help.

I now let the horse follow along and am able to watch as we go. The trail is the same one we always take, but the views seem different with every ride. With every trip I take back into those woods, there is something that has me wanting to return even more.

I do feel guilty lying to Mrs. Frost about being where she has deemed off-limits, but when I come around to the barn, back across the field, and then into the trees, the guilt vanishes, and any cares I have are swept away, carried downstream with the river.

CHAPTER 31

Mr. Frost left again, and this time, Jesse went with him. I'm now not only doing the irrigation and my other chores, but I'm also feeding the cows.

After Mrs. Frost's fit at seeing me in the truck, I thought I'd never be allowed to drive again, and yet the very next day, Jesse threw me the keys.

"Gordon spoke to her. She said it was fine as long as you don't take it out of the pasture or second gear," he said with a scoff.

"But how will I know what gear I'm in? It's not a stick shift," I asked, confused.

He scrunched his shoulders and rolled his head. "I guess she doesn't know that, so just don't be doing any drag racing." Then he laughs.

I'm thrilled to be back behind the wheel—even if it's just driving around in the pasture. It's good that I'm learning these things, which will help me when I'm eventually back with my mom and we're on our own farm. My last call with her wasn't what I'd hoped. I wanted the assurance that our plan was still in place, but she's always been so adamant that the farm was where we'd be. It's the stress of everything coming to a head. But I know it will work out, and when she sees I have the treasure, she'll know we have everything we need.

I start the truck and begin my slow drive down the row. Even with Mrs. Frost's orders to stay in low gear, I kick up some dirt when I've reached the end of the hay line and am making my way back to the barn. She can't see me in this area, so I press my luck. It must be working because now, after almost two weeks of nightly feedings, Mrs. Frost doesn't even blink at what I'm doing. Things have settled down with her. She doesn't ask where I'm going or question where I've been. She is still doting and convinced I don't eat enough, but I no longer feel her hovering like I did before. I wonder what has changed, but don't question it. However, even with my new freedoms, I still keep my treks to the river and fishing with Old Tom a secret. I don't think her ideas on those things have changed.

She spends her days visiting the older people in her church. It's like a job, but she doesn't get paid. She cooks large meals for the three of us and takes the extra portions to them several times a week.

Leaving in the late morning, she is rarely home before five in the evening. This has given me plenty of time to finish my chores and still be able to make my way through the fields to explore the woods and the river.

Every waking moment has me wanting to stand, pole in hand, in pursuit of what lives in that water. I plot my evenings after school and chores to have even an hour of fishing before sunset. And on weekends, I wake up before the sun rises to get things done and then head for the trail.

The feel of the long and willowy rod Old Tom has loaned me is unbelievable, and with some practice, I'm now starting to make arching casts similar to the ones that I've admired while watching Old Tom.

We haven't set a specific time, but Old Tom's there when I make my way through the back pasture and to the hidden path. He meets me each afternoon at the third bend of the back trail, and then we decide what part of the river looks best for the day. And Rusty is there, too. He wags his entire body when he sees me, follows us to where we plan to fish, and then finds a shaded place on the shore to nap until we're done.

So much of the time I spend with Old Tom is like being in class, and I'm enthralled with what I'm learning.

He doesn't say much when he's teaching—"Pole down when you're reeling." "Let the line hang before letting it fall." "Let the fly follow the current."—in fact, until a fish is on the line, he says nothing at all. When I ask him questions or comment on the river or the weather, he puts a finger to his lips.

"Do the fish hear us if we talk?" I asked him when we were back at his house one day.

"I believe they do," he said. "But it's more than that. It's what you hear that matters, and if you're talking, you can't listen."

I think for a moment about what sounds the fish make that I could possibly hear. "What do the fish sound like?"

He laughs. "It's not the fish. It's everything around you. You need to see it, hear it, and feel it."

"How does that help you catch them?"

Old Tom smiles. "Catching fish is the goal, and it's good and fun, but it's everything else that goes into it. That's what makes it nirvana."

I lift my eyebrows and nod, having heard him describe it like that before. That first time, I had to look up the word in the dictionary, but the definition couldn't be more accurate.

"It means being in the perfect place—like being in heaven," I say.

And it is. This massive stretch of blue sky and the rolling rush of the river. The green flutter of leaves in the sun and the random sightings of deer along the banks or an eagle perched high in a tree. And even with all that, what I find myself thinking about, even when I'm not here standing in the midst of it, is the thrill of the catch.

It's not just the hooked fish but the plotting, choosing the perfect tiny lure of tied feathers and fur, testing the direction of the wind, the whip of the rod and throw of the line, and the anticipation as the fly touches down lightly on the glassy surface. It all comes together, and then you wait and wonder. Did I place the fly correctly? Am I standing upwind? Is this swell in the river where they're hiding today? Was that a nibble or just the ripple of the water bumping the fly and teasing me?

Take it! I want to plead to what lurks in those dark crevices beneath. I stand unmoving and silent, barely breathing as I wait. Even the breeze that I've now come to accept is still. And when it happens, my heart leaps, and I gasp. That tiny but distinct nudge of a fish taking your fly. The tug of the line between your finger and the rod and knowing what's at the end. When the hook is set, it's a gentle but steady reel, watching for that iridescent flash.

In my visits with Old Tom, I've learned so much. He knows this river, these woods, but his skill with the rod and fly is what I revere.

It's the same wide and swooping casts that mesmerized me on the first day I saw him. It's what I try to emulate, and while I'm nowhere near as agile as he is, even at his age, I'm becoming effective.

I've caught eight fish in the four days he's allowed me to spend with him. He stands close, and when I reel them in, I take just enough time to admire my catch, and then I carefully remove the hook, just as he's shown me, and softly place the fish back in the water. They flip and shoot away, and I wonder if I'll ever catch that specific one again. Do they learn and become more aware of what is waiting for them above the surface?

As soon as I see the fish has fled, I check the fly and am ready to cast it out again. To see it all come together, not luck but a true strategic effort, is breathtaking, and I think Old Tom enjoys my successes as much as I do.

Today, as I round the bend, I see him holding a pair of tall rubber boots.

"These will get you out into the river," he says, handing them to me. "They might be a little big, but they should work."

Out into the river? I take the boots hesitantly but thank him. I've relished my time casting the willowy rod and watching the tiny puff on the end of the line settle onto the water, but the idea of stepping out into the flow, even just a couple of feet, makes my heart race. The water isn't deep near the shore, but the current is swift.

I'm hesitant to let him see my fear, so I take a seat on the ground, push my feet into the boots, and then stand and pull the rubbery material up to my thighs—the tops of the boots are at my crotch. My legs are over three feet long. I have no intention of going into water that deep. Hoping he doesn't see my fear, I take a settling breath and swing the suspenders connected to the boots onto my shoulders.

"Those will keep the boots up and in place," he says, pulling on his own for emphasis. "You don't want the waders sliding down and the water getting in and dragging you down."

The idea of being drug into that river makes my neck hairs stiffen.

"How far out do I need to be?"

He looks at the river and then back to me. "The river is low today, so we may be able to find places closer in. It isn't about how far you go out into the water, but finding the holes."

Hearing the word holes, I begin to worry about falling into one.

Again, I take a deep breath and try to keep my terror in check. I decide to find a place where I can step into the water but keep as close to the bank as possible.

I gather my rod and gear. Old Tom nods his approval and then heads off, and I follow him. The waders feel clunky and awkward, but it's what Old Tom is wearing, so I'm hoping they will help my chances, even if I don't use them as intended.

Instead of stopping near the gravel bar or where the huge fallen tree has created a swell, we continue walking back into the woods. I soon realize we're heading straight into the hollow.

I've fished on the edge of this elusive and forbidding place. I've been close enough to try and peer into the dense mass of trees and attempt to envision what evil beast haunts it, but I've never been where we're headed. Why is he taking me here?

A curved berm borders the area, and the trail narrows as the trees become denser the farther we walk. I hear creaking and twittering. Is it the hollow or the tales of this place that make me feel anxious and leery the closer we get? The breeze that follows me is now stronger than it's ever been. What is it hidden within the trees and hills that conjure this ominous feeling? I have to push branches away as I walk. In the brush, I see eyes upon me, or am I imagining it all? Do I actually think some creature—a phantom inhabits this place?

"Where are we going?" I ask, trying not to sound anxious.

He smiles. "You asked about the hollow, and I think this is the perfect time to show it to you."

I continue to follow even though I feel my stomach clench with every step.

"Show me what?" I ask.

"It's the hatch," he announces it as though it's an event.

"What does that mean?"

His eyes are wide and animated. "You'll see," he says as he motions me forward.

I'm reluctant to follow, even though I've seen nothing that makes me distrust this old man.

The trees are so thick that the trail is only wide enough for one of us at a time to follow along. I'm directly behind Old Tom and can't see where we're heading except for the dark canopy of trees closing in overhead. No one knows where I am or who I'm with. The only sounds I hear are the crunching of dead leaves and sticks underfoot. My mind is now racing with an ominous feeling of dread. Should I stop and go back? Should I run like hell, or do I push my reservations aside and follow?

"It's time," he says. "Look at it."

The path opens up, exposing a large and lush cove. The sound of birds chirping, leaves fluttering, and the river's rush has returned. The water is a slowly churning immense pool of glistening blues and greens. A large gravel bar extends beyond the diverted bowl, and as I stare out over it, I see it. The hatch.

At first, it's only tiny flickering dots dancing just above and on the water. Then I see that they are actually bugs. They are so small, and yet, as a swarm, they are immense. They are like glistening fairies so light and small that they skim the glassy sheen as though teasing the fish beneath.

"They're called Caddis," he whispers as though the fish can hear us. He begins to assemble his gear, and I quickly do the same. He opens his box of flies. "This is what you need," he says, handing me a tiny, sheer, but shiny fly. I take it and, using the knot he taught me, attach it to the end of my line.

It looks exactly like what is landing in droves out on the river. Old Tom has created the perfect replica of what the fish are now after, and we'll be sneaking in like Trojan horses to outwit them.

"Here's another," he says, carefully handing me a second fly. He looks me over and his brow crinkles. "We'll need to get you a vest, but for now, hook it on your shirt just in case."

I take it. It is the size of a pea, but the hook is sharp, and I gingerly snag it safely on my shirt. I haven't lost a fly yet, and now, seeing the hours of work that go into these tiny lures, I'm not about to fumble and lose it to the current.

Slowly, Old Tom eases into the pool. It's shallow, so my fear of the water subsides, and I do the same. It's an odd feeling stepping into the cold water of the river and yet not feeling the soaking wetness seeping into my shoes. The soles of the boots are unfamiliar and feel thick and spongy, but they cling to the rocks, unlike my sneakers. Old Tom looks over and gives me a smile when he sees me in the water with my new waders.

"Go around to the edge of the gravel bar, and I'll go to the other side," he says softly.

I nod and head off to my spot, relieved that getting there puts me closer to the bank.

The overhang of the trees allows just enough sunlight to illuminate the entire cove. I can see out to the main flow of the river, and as I walk to the gravel bar, I see a huge bird with a long bill and tall legs spread its wings and fly. I look back toward Old Tom, amazed at the sight, and he calls over to me, "A Great Blue Heron. They know when the fishing is good, too."

It's a slow walk, but I make my way in the shallow current to the spot Old Tom suggested. I check the area for trees or anything else that could snag me. There's nothing. I'm out in the middle of the river, surrounded by the woods, and the only thing I can hear is the familiar breeze that is always with me.

I can see Old Tom in the distance. He, too, is surveying his surroundings, but he soon releases his line and then begins his graceful back-and-forth casting—the fly reaching higher and farther with each whip of the rod.

For a moment, I just stand and watch as he lays the fly out gently onto the water. I want to emulate that same easy motion. It has to land with just the lightest touch for the fish to believe it's real.

I turn back and find an area of the water that is calm and has a slow, back-circle flow.

I let the fly release and then pull out a large length of the line.

Just as I've been taught, I lift the rod with quick up and back motions, letting the line whip and fall forward, whip and fall forward. Then I cast it back and let the line hang just enough for the fly to hesitate and then land on the surface. I watch as the tiny white dot dances with the movement of the river. The cast was good, so I feel hopeful it will work. I squint in the sun as the fly bobs and sails, and when there is no hit, I reel it back and try again.

The breeze is behind me now, and I feel a light spray of water as I raise the line off the water and high into the air. Back and forth. Back and forth. I'm drying the fly, just as Old Tom has taught me, and when I feel the line is out and hanging, I let it shoot forward and drop it out again. This time, I can see the fly just above a glassy pool. It hovers slightly, and then I feel it. A quick tug of the line, and I yank back. And then, with even more strength, the line goes taut, and a big pull tells me I have something. My heart is pounding, and I see the line cutting a dizzying path into the water's surface. I try to reel, but the line keeps going out.

I shoot a quick look over to where Old Tom is fishing, hoping he has noticed, and he has.

The fish is pulling and fighting, and I'm trying to keep the rod up and let him run just enough to keep from breaking my line.

I reel in a small amount of the line and then wait. He continues to flee. I've never felt anything pull so hard. And then I see the flicker of silver as he launches out of the water. He's huge. His tell-tell rainbow blazes in the sunlight, and it's all I can do to keep from frantically trying to reel him in. Stay calm. Don't let him break the line. Don't let him spit the hook.

I'm now reeling slowly, and again, the fish leaps from the water in a twisting flash.

I quickly look over to Old Tom, who is now wading toward me.

"Rod up," he calls over. "You're doing great. Keep the line steady but not too tight."

I'm beaming and panting as I see the large fish being drawn closer. I keep the rod and line just as Old Tom has told me, and when the fish is just a few feet away, I reach behind my back, where my net is hooked to my back, and pull it forward. Lifting the rod even higher with one hand, I use the other to reach the net down and into the water to scoop up the most beautiful rainbow trout I've ever seen.

I can't hardly speak when I see how large the fish is.

"Incredible!" says Old Tom.

I lift the net, and we both shake our heads at the size of the fish cradled within. I then reach in and take hold of the fish just under the mouth, and just as Old Tom has taught me, I steady my grasp and begin to slide the hook from the fish's bony jaw. It flips, and I almost lose my grasp. I try again, and am able to slide the hook free. I then lift the fish from the net, carefully holding it with one hand near the gills and the other just below the fins. I turn it toward Old Tom with a smile. I'm both proud and amazed. The fish gives a sturdy wriggle to try and break free, but I hold on and admire its beauty and its size. Its mouth gasps, and its eyes stare out, and now it's time to release him. I lean down and gently place the fish into the water. At first, it seems stunned, but then, with a quick whip of its tail, it shoots off back into the current.

The warm wind wraps around me as I stand and watch my incredible catch swim away.

"I'll bet that was at least twenty inches," says Old Tom.

I nod and smile.

He directs me toward the shore. "That was a monster. And you brought it in perfectly. There was a time when ..." he then drifts off.

I look over as he stares off into the hollow.

He takes a deep contemplative breath and then continues his thought. "It was a day just like this that we first saw the phantom."

My eyes grow wide at the mention of it.

Seeing my reaction, his face spreads into a satisfied and animated smile.

"A phantom?" I ask, wanting to know more.

He lifts his eyebrows, and he looks reminiscent. Nodding, Old Tom is deep in thought as he talks. "We started calling him the phantom because just when you thought you had him, he'd vanish."

I'm stunned. I look out at the dense woods. "Is it still out here?"

He shrugs. "It's been years, but I've hooked him several times. He's a fighter. I'll bet he's over thirty inches and weighs twenty pounds. But every time I'd get him close, somehow he'd spit the hook and be gone."

I feel my breath release, and my shoulders sink. "A fish? The phantom is a fish?" I ask. I'm feeling both duped and foolish.

He looks at me, humored, and then laughs. "Well, of course. What did you think it was?"

I raise my shoulders, feeling chagrined.

"I heard the kids at school talking about a phantom and saying to stay away from the hollow because of something back here, and I just ..."

The smile fades from his face.

I've never seen Old Tom look this distant and disturbed, and again, I find myself wondering what terrible thing happened in these woods.

I stay quiet, wishing I hadn't said anything and hoping the gray cloud hanging over us will pass. I have an entire summer to wait, and the thought of losing the ability to do these things I've come to enjoy fills me with dread. It's not just fishing. It's this river, these woods, and Old Tom. I worry he'll decide I'm a bother. I'll be stuck in that big, empty house alone and bored.

We both sit on the bank, our rods lying in the grass beside us. He looks out over the water as the sun bounces off the surface like a mirror. The tiny bugs still dance about but are beginning to wane.

"How long will the hatch last?" I ask, hoping to direct things away from the awkward silence.

He takes a deep breath and comes out of his stupor. "It's not something you can predict."

"Then how did you know it would happen?"

He shakes his head. "You wait and watch, and if you catch it like we did today, it's magic."

"Nirvana," I say.

He shoots me a look as though he's surprised I remembered what he told me. How could I not? It's what I feel every time I'm here in these woods and along the river.

The sunshine and wide spaces and Old Tom's company are beginning to feel fleeting. Instead of eagerly waiting for the days to pass, I now want to tighten my grip to keep the sand from slipping through my fingers.

We sit for a moment, looking out over the babbling ripples, and then he retrieves his rod and pushes himself up to standing. "You ready to head back?" he asks.

I'm not, but then I realize how long we've been out here and know I have just a short window of time to stash my gear before I have to make excuses for where I've been. I take a deep breath and soak in as much of this as I can before I relent and agree to leave.

As we walk back toward the path, I relive my catch. "I thought my rod would break. It was so big."

"There've been plenty of huge fish pulled out of this river. Lunkers, we call them, and that one was definitely a lunker." He says with a smile.

Again, I think about the phantom and shake my head, thinking I believed it was some sort of monster lurking back here. But then again, in some ways, that's what the phantom is—a monstrous fish.

I'm hesitant to bring it up again, but I'm curious, so I ask. "Do you think the phantom is still out there?"

"Possibly. But he's sly and a bit evil."

"Evil?" I ask skeptically.

He nods. "How do you think Rusty ended up with three legs?"

I gasp and shoot a look over at Rusty, who's now following a small white butterfly along the bank.

Old Tom laughs so hard that I feel even more foolish than before. He bends over, unable to speak, and when he finally catches his breath, he claps me on the back. "And that's what you call a big fish story."

CHAPTER 32

I've made it. I've survived this school without issues, and now I just have to get through this final day. I'm sitting in my first-period class, deep in the last chapter of my book.

The teacher is droning on, and I'm settled back into my story—the book hidden by my binder—propped up at just the right angle for it to look as though I am diligently listening and taking notes.

The story has me buried in the happenings of Jim, the young cabin boy who finds himself searching for treasure and having to escape the pirates who are part of the ship's crew. He managed to make his way to the ship and cut the anchor to try to get away while the pirates were on the island.

I begin to drift off into my own escapades on the river, slyly making my way back to meet Old Tom and eventually hunting the phantom. I take a deep breath as I feel the coolness of the water swirl around my waders and smell the warm breeze in my nose and lungs. I can even hear the twerp of the birds above and the soothing rush of the river surrounding me.

Suddenly, I'm jolted from my daydream as the book is ripped from my hands.

"Class is over, book nerd. Didn't you hear the bell?" It's Kevin.

I didn't realize anything. The time passed so quickly.

I lunge at him, trying to grab the book back. "Give me that," I say.

I don't yell it because I don't want to draw more attention to myself or the stolen book.

"Geez, the way you were drooling over this, I would have thought it was Playboy, not ..." He then looks at the cover. "Treasure Island." He starts to laugh, but then his face turns cold as he takes a closer look.

I realize if I continue to reach for it, he'll only try to provoke me further, so I sit back and act unaffected. "I'm surprised you can read at all," I say, unable to control my vitriol.

He smirks at my sarcasm, and then he sees the black lettering stamped onto the front and spine of the book.

"Idaho Home for ..." he reads but stops short of the entire name. He squints at it and then looks over.

My heart drops, and a sickening wash comes over me as my secret begins to unravel.

"Why do you have a book from there?" he asks.

I want to tell him it's none of his business and try to divert his attention away, but I know it will only bring more scrutiny, so instead, I ignore his question, slide from the desk, and stand as tall as I can as though asking for a fight. I'd rather be punched or kicked out of school for fighting than have my secret out. Either way, I'm facing a terrible outcome.

"From where?" one of the other boys asks, confused.

Kevin shoots him a look as though he's forgotten they were there with him. "Go on," he barks at them. "I'll meet you after."

The two boys give me the once over and then reluctantly leave the room. When we're alone, Kevin looks back at me. "I thought you moved here from California?"

"I did," I say, reaching for the book and wondering how he knows this.

I'm surprised when he allows me to take it back.

He stares at me for a moment. I can see his mind racing. "Why did you come here? Why are you living with them?"

"They're my aunt and uncle," I say, repeating my lie. "What's it to you?"

He huffs. "They lose one and replace him with another?"

I flinch back. "What?"

Kevin doesn't answer. He's studying me, and it's making me worry that he'll realize who I am.

"What did they tell you?" he asks.

"Who?"

The door of the classroom opens, and the teacher walks in. He sees us and smirks. "I know it's the last day, but you still have class, and you're late."

I use this to get away, stepping aside and toward the door, but Kevin pushes by me, and before he leaves the room, he looks back with a face that clearly questions—who are you?

———

When the final bell rings, I'm at the bus, and my relief must be evident.

"Someone's happy about summer break," Gus says, giving my shoulder a bump.

We board the bus, and Nicole and I sit together. The strange murmurs from the others have ceased, or at least I don't notice them any longer.

"I know you'll be working all summer," she says, "but maybe we can go riding again?"

It's what I've told her—that I'm working for the Frosts, and it's true. What I haven't said is that I'd be gone at summer's end, and what surprises me is the pit in my stomach at the thought of it.

"Sure," I say, and she smiles.

"Where do you ride?" Gus asks Nicole, obviously eavesdropping.

She looks back at him, and I can see her uneasiness.

"Just around the back," she says. She looks at me, and her face tells me to keep our hidden path a secret.

"You ride back there? How far back?" Gus asks.

"Not there," Jeremy cuts in.

Gus then relents, gives a nod, and sits back.

Nicole stares straight ahead, and while I know what's been said about the dead boy in the woods, it's hard to believe that Gus and Jeremy are so averse to going near the place called the hollow.

We sit in silence the rest of the ride, but when we reach my stop, she gives me a smile and waves as I go down the stairs.

———

THERE IS no one at the house when I get home, so I do my chores and pull the first two headgates, then make my way to the headgate on the northeast field. I pull the plate and watch as the water diverts from the ditch and begins to fill the smaller channels. Then, I continue on to Old Tom's.

"You spend a lot of time taking care of this garden," I say as we walk through the rows. I'm ready to go fishing, but I'm impatient because he has to water and weed.

"Yes, but if I don't take care of it, what will I eat?"

I shrug. "Can't you just go to the store and buy all these things."

Old Tom's eyebrows knit over what I said, and again, I wish I had thought before I talked. But then his face shifts. "I could, but it's more than that. It feels good to grow something from a seed and see it go from a sprout to a bloom and eventually a vegetable or fruit. And it tastes a whole lot better."

I look at him skeptically, wondering how it could taste any different. He continues through the rows of green, plucking a weed here and there and thinking. When we reach the end of the row, he steps toward the tomato plants. Their limbs are bursting from the wire cages that are holding them upright. Small, red fruit dot them. Old Tom plucks a few and then pops one in his mouth. He holds the others out to me, and I step closer, taking one.

When it bursts in my mouth, the flavor is so sweet I wonder if it isn't a berry. I bend toward the little red globes, studying them.

"These are tomatoes, but they don't taste like regular tomatoes," I say, realizing what he said is true. They do taste better.

I reach out to pick another but hesitate, and I look up at him for approval. He nods.

"They aren't regular tomatoes," he says. "You're probably used to what comes from the grocery store. When you have your own garden, the fruit can ripen on the vine. You can smell the flavor as well as taste it."

He's right. The sweet, earthy smell of the plants and the fruits they bear are all throughout the garden. I walk the dirt paths, admiring the rich green leaves, flowering vines, and budding bushes. I quiz him on what he expects from the plants in each of the individual rows. He lists off carrots, green beans, peas, turnips, corn, beets, squash, and, of course, tomatoes.

As I study the different stalks, leaves, and colors, I look over to see him staring out over a large patch of bushes at the side of the house.

Feathery grayish-green bushes dot the area in even rows. Each is large—over four feet around and almost three feet high. If not for their symmetry, I would have thought they were just natural brush or weeds. And although bushy and wild, it is apparent they have been planted and carefully tended.

"What grows on them?" I ask.

He scans the large shrubs, almost as though he is seeing them for the first time. I wait, expecting him to tell me a type of berry.

After a long silence, he turns to me, almost as if he forgot I was there. His eyes shimmer, and with a deep breath, he smiles and then looks back to the willowy bushes. "No fruit. These bushes are grown for their flowers."

"You planted a crop of flowers?" I ask, surprised. He had just said that everything he grows is what he eats.

His smile fades. "It was for my wife. She was from England, and she missed her home, so I planted these to remind her of what used to grow there."

I look out over the muted and straggly bushes and wonder why he didn't plant something prettier, like roses, but I shrug and say nothing.

"They take up a lot of space, and I don't have much need for them. I'm surprised they're still growing. We moved, and then my wife died, and I forgot about them; somehow, they survived."

"You moved from here?" I ask, surprised.

He nods. "For a time, but this has always felt like my home."

I wonder what that feels like.

He sees me ponder this. "Do you miss being home?" he asks.

I look up, surprised. I'm not sure I've ever known what being home feels like. "When my mom comes to get me, then we'll go home," I say with as much confidence as I can muster, but I'm beginning to doubt my own words.

"Where is your mother?" he asks.

I take a breath and immediately begin to rattle off my story about her being in the military, but there's something in the eyes of this old man that forces me to face what is real and tell him the truth.

"She's in prison." I look down when I say it but try to keep from making it as glum as it sounds. "But she gets out soon, and she's coming to get me." I hear the words and realize I can't remember ever saying them out loud.

I can see the shock in his face. He thinks for a moment and then lifts an eyebrow. "And Evelyn and Gordon know this?" he asks.

I nod. "The harvest will be done right before I leave. They won't need me after that."

"They brought you here to help with the harvest?" he asks, surprised.

I lift my shoulders. "Most of the places I've stayed were just foster homes. But I like being here helping on the farm. I like being outside working. And fishing." I give him a smile.

"Yes, that makes the work worth it," he says. But his angst remains. "I'm sorry to hear you're going to be leaving soon. It doesn't give us much time to land the phantom. We better get busy."

I sigh. I've never felt this way about any place I've stayed, and I, too, am feeling a heavy sadness about leaving this place and leaving him. "Maybe I can come back and visit," I say. "I'll be on a farm in Washington, but maybe in the winter when it isn't busy. Washington isn't that far away."

Old Tom tries to smile, but his attempt is weak. He lifts the small basket full of tomatoes. "I'm going to put this in the house, and then we'll go to the hollow."

He walks inside, and I look back at the rows of willowy bushes.

A stepping stone is at the beginning of each row. They are made of cement and are similar sizes but in different shapes—an octagon, a diamond, or a heart. On the heart-shaped stone, something is written on the concrete. I bend down and dust the dirt away. In crude, crooked letters are the words "Tom and Eugenia" with a small heart underneath. I smile, realizing it must be Old Tom and his wife who planted these bushes.

"You ready?" he says, standing on the porch behind me.

I turn and smile when I see him with all our gear in hand. He hands me my rod and small tackle box.

As we hike along the trail leading back to the river, Rusty runs over toward the secret trail Nicole showed me and begins to bark.

Old Tom calls him back. "Every time we go this route, he does that. He must sense something back in those trees."

"Like what?" I ask. I glance at the opening of the trail, but not enough to let on that there is anything there.

"A deer or raccoon, probably," says Old Tom with a shrug. "There are critters all over these woods, but for some reason, he is convinced there is something in that particular spot."

I nod but say nothing. Nicole made me swear I'd keep the thin, hidden trail our secret. I look at Rusty, who is still sniffing and meandering back into the area. I wonder if he knows of that hidden path. Is he trying to alert Old Tom to it? He's a dog, I have to remind myself. But what if he does know something and is trying to expose what lies back there in those woods?

Chapter 33

BENJI

It was a typical fall day when I found him. I was burning the ditch near the road to remove the weeds and clean it up for the next season when I heard him whimper. I searched through the tall grass and dried brush until I came upon the dirty and bloodied mass of fur.

The reddish brown streaks and long tail had me thinking it was a fox or young coyote, but then I saw his snout. Short and square. I was never sure what breed of dog he was, but his sad eyes and pitiful cries had me convinced I was not only going to help him live but that he'd be mine.

I wrapped him in my denim coat, and he yelped when I lifted him from the embankment, but he didn't fight me. I took him back to the house, knowing what response I would get and preparing for my argument.

In the barn was an empty grain tub that I lined with some straw and then placed him inside. I found an old pie plate in the kitchen cupboards and offered him water and some stale bread and cheese.

He lifted his head just enough to take a few licks of the water but ignored the other. He laid back and gave me an exhausted look that broke my heart.

When my dad got home, I hesitantly showed him my hapless find.

"It's a stray someone dumped out here. He's badly injured and suffering, and you'd be doing him a favor to just put it out of its misery," my father said.

I shook my head. "No. I won't kill him. Can't we please call Doc Taylor?"

My father was frustrated and not about to pay good money to save a vagrant mutt. The vet was for the livestock and working animals that were needed on the farm, not for a dog that had no job or purpose.

"I'm not paying money to save some stray."

I knew what he would say, and I was prepared. "I have money. I'll pay for it."

He sighed, already exhausted and knowing my mind was set. "I thought you were saving up for a truck."

I rolled my eyes. It was true, even if it felt futile.

My mother was actively trying to discourage me from driving at all. I knew why she was so afraid, but I still felt she was being unfair, and regardless of how well I argued my point, she was adamant. Raising the money and buying a vehicle myself was my only option. Even my father was tight-lipped about the beat-up old farm truck I secretly drove in the fields.

"I won't shoot him, and I can't just let him die. Please drive me over to Doc Taylor's," I begged him.

My father wasn't cold-hearted. He just wasn't raised with animals that were pets. It's the way many of the people in the area felt. Any emotion for animals was limited to how it affected the business of the farm. That is why I was so relieved when he relented and agreed to take me to the vet clinic.

As I held the scruffy and mangled dog on the way over, I found myself worrying I'd spend my two years of savings on a dog that would probably die anyway.

"He'll need X-rays, but I already can tell his leg is badly broken," said Doc Taylor, speaking to my father as though I wasn't there. He obviously figured my dad would be the one having to pay for it all.

"I can work around broken legs, but if his back is broken, there's nothing I can do," he said again, speaking to my father rather than to me.

"How long will the X-rays take?" I asked, unwilling to give up.

"They don't take long, but ..." The vet said, still speaking to my father. "Do you want to do the X-rays?" he asked, as though he figured we wouldn't.

My father then turned to me. "We don't even know whose dog this is. I think it's a lost cause."

He could see my determination and sighed. "It's your decision. It's your money."

I looked down at the dog. Its eyes stayed with me as though begging me to give him a chance, or at least that's what I saw. The blood was now dried and dark on its coarse, red fur, and I realized just how badly injured he was.

"Yes," I spoke directly to the vet. "I want you to try and save him."

The vet cocked his head and gave me a skeptical smile. "Well, first, let's see if there is anything left to save."

A woman came in and took the dog out of the room, leaving me and my dad sitting in stiff metal chairs to wait.

I felt awkward having him sit there with me when I knew he had other things he needed to be working on. I also knew he thought I was being silly for using my hard-earned money on a stray dog.

I looked at the floor and studied the chipped tiles as the gap of silence between us widened.

He must have felt it, too. He cleared his throat.

"You and Jeremy had quite the time last weekend. I thought you were going to top everyone," he said.

I tried to smile at his attempt to talk to me.

Jeremy and I had just started competing in team roping. I was the header, who roped the calf's head or horns, and Jeremy was the heeler and lassoed the calf's back legs. It was our first year on the high school team, and while we were the youngest members, our times were as good or better than the boys who were years ahead of us.

"You keep those times up, and you won't need the money. You'll be bringing home trucks as prizes."

I looked at my dad, surprised. It wasn't often he doled out praise. It wasn't that I felt he didn't care or love me—I knew he did—but the only emotion I ever really saw from him was in the form of disappointed grumbles directed toward low beef prices or harvest yields. My mom was the one who felt the need to tell me she loved me every night, hugged me when I wandered into the kitchen in the morning or cried when she saw me in the rodeo jacket she had made. And yet, it was my dad I found myself trying to impress and win his approval. That is why seeing him shake his head when I told the vet I wanted to save the dog made my insides ache.

"I doubt that will happen anytime soon," I said. "I'll probably be pulling the horse trailer with the hay truck all next season."

He laughed. I wasn't trying to be funny, but seeing him smile at what he perceived as a joke made my mood lighten.

"We'll figure it out. And maybe this new dog can learn to herd," he said and then laughed again.

I sat up a bit straighter. Had he really come around to the idea of me keeping this dog? I was feeling relieved, but when Doc Taylor came back into the room, my mood fell when I saw his face.

My dad and I both stood, waiting to hear the bad news.

"The leg is completely crushed, but his back and pelvis aren't broken," he said.

"So, he'll live?" I asked, hopeful.

The vet tipped his head. "He can survive this, but the leg will have to be removed."

I gasped. "Amputated? Can't you put it in a cast or something?"

The vet shook his head. "It would take the type of surgery I don't do, plus even then, it may not work. The leg is too badly damaged."

My dad cut in. "Only three legs? Will he be able to move around?"

The vet shrugged. "It's actually not as bad as it sounds. I've had to do this with many dogs, and they adapt just fine—as if they've always just had three legs."

"He'll still be able to walk?" I asked, surprised.

The vet nodded. "Most dogs are up and walking in a couple of days. It doesn't affect them much at all, but a lot of people don't want a three-legged dog."

The vet smiled. "I just want you to know I'm not trying to convince you to do anything. It's your dog."

My dad gave an amused huff and turned to me. "You heard the vet. It's your decision. It's your dog."

I smiled at him and nodded.

Doc Taylor walked us back to where the dog was wrapped in an old towel and lying in a kennel. He looked tired and even scruffier than when I found him. He opened his eyes when I looked through the metal bars of the cage.

The doctor explained the procedure and when he would be ready to go home. As he wrote some information on a card that was attached to the kennel, he paused a moment and then asked, "Does he have a name?"

My father looked to me.

I raised my eyebrows, unsure what to say. I had only had the dog for a couple of hours, and all I knew about him was that he was a boy and he looked like the thick rust-colored grass that he was lying in when I found him.

"Rusty?" I said, but it sounded like a question.

"Rusty it is," said the vet as he wrote it out in large black letters.

I took another look at the sorry and solemn dog and wondered if I was really doing what was right for him or if I just wasn't strong enough to see him be put out of his misery.

As we left the clinic, my dad and I sat in silence until we arrived home.

"Hmm." He said as he stared out at our house as we sat in the driveway.

"What is it?" I asked.

He raised his eyebrows and shook his head. "I'm not sure how your mother's going to react to a dog. I guess I should have thought of that before I agreed to all this."

I had never heard my father discussing much of anything with my mother. They had their roles. His involved what went on outside, and hers encompassed what went on inside, with the exception of her small flock of chickens.

"I'll make sure he isn't a problem," I said. "I promise I'll take care of him and make sure everything else gets done, too."

He sighed. "It's not just the dog. I know it's still about a year until you start driving, but I know how your mother feels about that."

I sighed. "I've been driving the trucks in the fields for over a year now."

"That's different than on the roads. And for your mother, it's a lot different."

I was surprised to hear that it was such an issue. "Why?" I asked, but I already knew. From the time I could remember, I had heard the stories of my uncle Wesley and how he died, but it wasn't until I was on the verge of becoming an adult that I realized how it would affect me.

His death continued to haunt my mother with guilt, convinced she would someday pay for what she felt was her role in his demise. But it also left me with something that, had he lived, I most likely wouldn't be facing. I would inherit the land and farm.

It wasn't my father but my mother who owned the massive acreage that had been acquired decades before. She was given all this, but only because Wesley was gone. It was he who stood to take over, to live in that house and work those pastures and fields. And only when he died did my grandfather give it all to my mother.

My dad toiled and tilled and grew the farm into one of the largest and most successful farming operations in the county, if not the state. It was Gordon Frost whose cattle and beef were known for their quality, and a job at Frost Farms was highly paid and sought after. And while he expanded the operation and had brought his own land into the mix, he could never really feel that it was his.

He married into the land. It was my mother whose name was still on the deed and the precious water rights that came with it all.

It wasn't a role she particularly wanted or planned for, but just as Wesley's death came without warning, so did my life, and with that, she felt she had no choice.

This was her home, but also her connection to the family she always felt she was clinging to. And with a new life soon to come. She buried a secret and did the only thing she felt would help her survive.

Chapter 34

There is no one home, but I'm not alone in this house. I can feel something watching me or following me, and it's not just the breeze that is there.

"Hello? Is anyone here?" I call out. There is no answer, but I know someone is here. The presence, I feel, isn't new. It's the same odd and eerie sense that struck me that first night, but now it feels even more pronounced. It surrounds me and follows me as I go from room to room.

I don't believe in ghosts, but after hearing the odd noises in the other room, the breeze that follows me, the voice that only I hear, and the looks, comments, and assumptions of others about the strange happenings that surround this place, I'm starting to question everything.

It's early evening. Why isn't anyone here? Mrs. Frost is usually in the kitchen at this time, and now that Mr. Frost is home, I usually find him somewhere outside fixing fences or checking the herd—but not today. Where could they be?

Mrs. Frost's ominous talk about the woods and the off-limits part of the house has stuck with me, and while I've begun to get used to her odd, hovering ways, I know this sensation is somehow related to her. I feel it stronger when she's around. But she's not here now, and the presence is almost suffocating.

Did Mrs. Frost figure out my lie and go to Nicole's to see if I was there? It's been weeks now that I've been able to get my chores done and sneak around the back and to the hidden path.

Every time I go, I make sure I return with plenty of time to hide my rod and gear and make sure there is no evidence of my ventures back to the river.

I pad through the living room and peek inside the kitchen to be sure. Then I go down the hall toward Mr. Frost's office, where again I find nothing. Then I peer up at the stairs. The room calls to me. Its door is always closed and locked, which only piques my interest. I hear the warnings and threats about going in there, and yet, I want nothing else but to see inside. There are so many mysteries in this place, and this may be my chance to solve one of them.

I don't know how much time I have, so before I lose my nerve, I go to the kitchen cupboard where I saw her store the key, and then I quickly take the stairs, two at a time, and go to the door.

Looking back toward the stairs, I slip the key into the lock. I feel the release of the knob, and my heart pounds as I turn it. I wonder if I might actually find the lost boy sitting there inside. Were they the ones who had him hidden? I shake the ridiculous notion from my mind.

Slowly, I open the door. The first thing I see is a wooden table with several bolts of fabric, a sewing machine, and a tall padded form with a drape of sheer material standing near the window. It's a headless upper body, similar to the ones in the women's clothing departments at stores. It makes sense now. It must be what I saw that day when I looked out from the loft of the barn. It's shaped like a woman's body—curved and draped in fabric. I stand for a moment, wondering why Mrs. Frost was so adamant about keeping this room locked.

I'm a bit disappointed that I'm not finding anything but ordinary items, so I search deeper. I go to the closet, hoping there will be something more. Inside, I find clothes. Most are shirts. At first, I'm uninterested, but then I realize what kind of clothes. They're similar to the ones Mrs. Frost has given me. I look down at the shirt I'm wearing, and as I sort through them, I see that they look like my size.

Is she hiding them here with plans to give them to me eventually? Is that why I was banned from this room? Was it so that she could surprise me with these clothes?

On the floor of the closet, I find boxes. Several short stacks of different sizes are neatly placed. Then I see something peeking out from behind, and I push the boxes and hanging shirts aside. It's a fishing rod—a fly rod. It's leaning against the wall. It seems out of place and alone in the back, as though someone has hidden it.

"Wow," I whisper to myself as I admire it. It looks almost brand new. Then my stomach sinks. Does Mrs. Frost somehow know of my travels to the river to fish? No one knows about that except Nicole and Old Tom. Why would they tell?

I pull it out and study it and get my hopes up that, along with the clothes, the rod will be mine, too. All these objects in the closet are for a boy my age. Is all this what she plans to give to me?

After a quick peek down the hall to make sure I'm still alone, I go to the boxes. There are no labels or identification, so I pry open the closed edges of the box on top and unfold the flaps. Inside, I find small flat boxes, what look like scrapbooks, and a carved wooden box with a golden latch. I open one of the flat boxes, and inside is a large carved metal belt buckle. The inscription reads, "War Bonnet Rodeo." I open another, and there is a similar buckle with the words "Stanley Rodeo." These aren't items for me. These are someone's memories. A chill rushes over me, and for a moment, I feel like I'm not alone. I shake it off, pull one of the larger boxes away from the wall, and take a seat. I lift the carved wooden box onto my lap and open the latch. Inside is a lock of hair tied with a blue string, a purple patch with the letter "B," and some tiny white, shiny rocks. Using my finger, I turn one of the stones over, exposing a craggy, dark pit.

They're all odd, random items that make no sense, so I set them aside.

I flip through the scrapbooks. The pages are filled with crayon drawings, photos of a baby, and then others of a little boy. In one, he's at a birthday party; in others, he's petting a kitten, riding a horse, and proudly holding a fish. Mrs. Frost said there were no other kids who live here. So, who could he be, and why does Mrs. Frost have his things?

A single photo slips from one of the back pages. I pick it up and gasp when I see what looks like the same boy but now older. In this photo, he looks to be around my age, and he's standing with the Frosts. He's arm in arm with Mrs. Frost, and Mr. Frost has a hand on his shoulder. All three are smiling widely. It looks like he's their son. But if that's so, why would she lie to me? And where is he now? In the bottom corner of the photo, a date—1980—is written in pen. That's just a few years ago. So, why isn't he here in this house? Then I notice the jacket he's wearing. It's the same as mine—similar to the ones Jeremy and some of the other boys wear. I squint to see that on his left chest is a purple patch. I can't see it clearly, but there is no doubt in my mind it is a "B." I go back to the wooden box and open it again. I lift out the patch. I look down at my own jacket where there is no patch, and now I know why. This jacket belongs to the boy in the photo. And that boy is their son.

I turn the photo over and in pencil is written, "Mom, Dad, and Benji."

My entire body goes numb. Benji, the missing boy. It's their son. He's most likely dead, and I'm wearing his clothes.

Suddenly, my mind goes to the orphaned calf and the dead hide it had worn. "We graft the skin of the dead calf onto the live one so the mother thinks it's her own."

Is that what this is? Am I wearing the jacket of a dead boy? Is she trying to replace her dead son with me? I suddenly feel sick and stand to remove the coat. The box falls to the floor, and the white rocks scatter. As I begin to pick them up, I realize they aren't rocks at all. The white, shiny stones with dark crevices are teeth.

I let out a horrified yell.

"Landis? Is that you? Are you upstairs?"

It's Mrs. Frost. I didn't hear her come home. I can't let her see me in this room.

I gather the box and its contents together and quickly put it all back in the closet.

"I'm in my room. I'll be down in a minute," I yell out, hoping to keep her from coming up and catching me in that forbidden place.

"I have groceries in the car. Can you help me bring them in?" she calls back.

"Yes. Be right there." Then I listen and am relieved when I hear her footsteps fade away. I peek around the corner and slink out into the hallway, close the door, and use the key to lock it. I hurry downstairs, put the key back into the cupboard, and then run out to the car. There, Mrs. Frost is lifting stuffed brown bags from the trunk.

"Here, let me take them," I say.

She hands me the bags. "When did you get home?" she asks.

"Right before you," I answer. It's not a complete lie.

She nods and seems unworried. I hope that it's a sign that she is unaware of my intrusion into the off-limits area.

We walk back to the house. I have bags in both arms, and it isn't until we're inside the house that the breeze that was absent outside swirls around me. I look over to her. What is going on, and why am I here?

CHAPTER 35

I want to ask Mrs. Frost about Benji and why I'm being kept in the dark about it all, but I know that the only way I could do that would expose going into the forbidden room. How else would I explain how I knew? And with her strong warnings, it could be my ticket out of there for disobeying her.

I have to bide my time with her, and that means no trouble. I decide to wait and ask Old Tom during one of our fishing trips.

We have a plan to meet in the morning, as he can't meet me today. I'll be on my own with the river today, and I smile to myself just thinking about it.

Regardless of what I'm doing, whether it's feeding the chickens, tossing hay, or even sitting in the loft reading my book, I'm drawn toward the woods. It's as if the voice I hear follows me home and nudges me to return.

I would be there from the time I woke up if I could pull it off, but I'm still under the watch of Mrs. Frost, and while she's become far less hovering, she's still interested in knowing what I have planned each day.

Mr. Frost was home for a week and seemed pleased with what I've been doing. The barn is in order, the animals are doing well, and even Rontu is no different than the other calves. Jesse removed the dead calf's hide after a week, and now Rontu is gaining weight and is no longer sequestered with his new mother. They seem no different than the other cows and calves. It's as though he has no memory of his rough start. I shiver as my thoughts return to the dead boy and the jacket that was his.

"Jesse may be out of a job if you keep this up," Mr. Frost said one evening, clapping me on the back.

"We need to get you up on a horse. You need to learn to ride if you're going to be bringing in the cows this fall."

I nod and smile, wishing I could tell him I've already started to learn, and while I'm happy that he wants me to be a part of what he does, I know I won't be here, and I wonder why he doesn't already know that.

There is so much about this place that I will miss. The wide open spaces, the animals, even my chores, but it's my time on the river that I wish I could bring with me.

The subtle sounds of the morning when the sun is soft and the river is like glass are what I long for each day.

Now that school is out, I have a lot more time, but Nicole has gone with her family to their land up north, and even if she was home, my excuse of studying with her is no longer a good one, so I have to wait until Mrs. Frost goes into town for errands before I can steal away back to the river.

I know the trail well now and have no problem navigating my way back toward the hidden path, and as always, the voice calls when I reach it.

It's become softer—more of a whisper in my mind—but it's there nonetheless. It doesn't disturb me as it used to, but a tug of anxiousness always follows when I begin to hear it.

I was able to be on the river early this morning, but the time has passed quickly, as it always does, and I will need to get back and hide my gear before Mrs. Frost wonders where I've gone.

I take the shortcut path that Nicole showed me, and when I don't see any sign of Mrs. Frost, I slink into the barn, holding the rod and tackle box. I'm feeling pleased by my ability to use the trail leading back and relieved that the large barn keeps me hidden from the view of the house. I'm able to walk the entire length of the pasture from the river without being spotted.

I go to the shed in the barn where I hide the gear Old Tom has lent me, but just as I reach to open the shed's door, I hear Jesse's voice.

"What do you have there?" he asks.

I turn, startled. He's carrying two buckets, and when he sees what's in my hands, his face falls.

"Don't tell me you've been going where you were told not to."

I shake my head.

He sets the buckets down and cocks his head to the side, unconvinced. "So, I suppose you're dropping your line in the horse trough?"

"I didn't go all the way back there, just to the river."

I can see in Jesse's face that he knows I'm rationalizing. I become defensive because I feel caught. "It's just fishing. I can get to the river right back there. It's not a big deal," I explain.

"If it's not a big deal, then why are you hiding this stuff?" Before I can answer, he shakes his head and puts his hands up. "You're not my kid, so I'm not going to get on you about it. But don't say I didn't warn you."

He's not my parent, and neither are the Frosts, but I feel like everyone acts like they are.

"Warn me about what?"

Jesse sighs. "I just don't think the Frosts want you back there."

I lift my shoulders, still frustrated with his avoidance. "Why? Because of what happened to Benji?"

He looks at me, obviously surprised, and then sighs.

"What is it? Why won't you tell me?" I ask.

"Because it's not my place to talk about what happened."

"Well, I wish somebody would. Whatever did happen has nothing to do with me, but it's making my life a nightmare," I huff.

He cocks his head as though I'm being overly dramatic.

My shoulders drop. I'm so tired of being in the dark. "Please tell me what happened. Is Benji their son?"

Jesse sighs and nods his head in defeat. Then he finds one of the log stools and takes a seat. His head is low, and I can feel the weight of what he's about to tell me.

He motions for me to sit as well.

I put the fishing pole and box in the shed and then drag a stool over to him.

"It happened about a year ago," Jesse begins. "Benji, the Frost's son ..."

I knew this was true, but I'm stunned to hear it confirmed. The Frost's son is Benji, and he's the boy I've been hearing about—the boy who is missing and the one Kevin went to jail for.

"And he's the one that was killed?"

Jesse shakes his head. "Killed? Who knows? Supposedly, he was last seen back in the hollow. There was a bridge, and he may have fallen in the river. They searched for weeks but never found anything. They blamed it on a kid from the other side, but it was his word against ..." he stops and sighs.

"Kevin Jenkins," I say, and Jesse flinches back.

"So, you already know about this?" he asks.

I shake my head. "I've heard about a missing kid, and at school, they said that Kevin Jenkins went to jail because of it, but I didn't know he was their son until recently. They haven't said anything."

Jesse ponders this a moment.

"Why's it such a big secret?" I ask.

He takes a deep breath as though it's hard to continue. "I don't think they know what to say. They still don't know what happened. There were so many other things that came up and everybody was pointing fingers."

I'm curious. "What other things?"

He shrugs. "Like, where he was supposed to be and who was with him. There are all kinds of stories about what might have happened back in those woods. Some people started making up stories about what they saw and thought happened. And then they started blaming people."

"Like Kevin Jenkins," I say.

"And others," he says softly.

"Like who?"

He shakes his head but looks out toward the back fields, toward the old cabin. I feel my neck tingle.

"Old Tom?" I ask. "No way," I say, thinking about the man I've watched fishing in the river. The man who tends his garden and is so kind to the three-legged dog. "Is that why I've been told to stay away from back there? Do they think he had something to do with it?"

Jesse begins to gather his tools and other gear he had come for. He shakes his head.

"It's not Old Tom. It's just that place, the whole area back there. I think they don't want you to go back there because it's where some bad things have happened, and they worry about you."

"Things?" I ask. "More than just their son missing?"

I can tell he's getting uncomfortable with all he's telling me, even though it doesn't seem like much.

"There are all kinds of stories about stuff that happened in those woods. And the people around here make it worse by spreading rumors and making up ghost stories."

A cold chill hits me as I think about what I've heard about the missing boy and what might have happened in the hollow.

"What else happened back there?"

He shrugs and let's my question slide. "Like I said, it's a bunch of rumors. It goes back years. Having Benji go missing just added to it all."

I think about Mrs. Frost. "That's why she is so scared of the woods." I say it out loud when I'm really just thinking it to myself.

Jesse sighs and lowers his head. "Can't say I blame her. It would feel like your family is cursed. And now her only kid—gone. There was no funeral, no grave. For a long time, she didn't even leave the house. I heard she just sat in his room—hoping he'd come home."

His room. I shiver when I realize what room that is. His bed, his clothes, his stuff. It's why I'm banned from that area. I then begin to wonder why I'm here at all. What reason could the Frosts have for wanting me here after suffering such a terrible loss?

"What did they tell you about me?" I ask.

He scrunches his mouth to the side in thought. I can see he is struggling with what to say, so I offer.

"That they needed help around the farm?"

This makes him grin. "I'm sure you are a big help, but Gordon has plenty of that. He told me you were someone they used to know and that you'd be living with them now. That's all," says Jesse, ending our talk.

Someone they used to know? How could that be?

"I'd never met them before. How could they know me?" I ask, hoping to keep him talking.

Jesse's already gathered what he came for and is making his way toward the door. "I don't know. I've worked for Gordon for a long time, but it's not like we talk much outside of that. I've told you all I know. They must have wanted you here."

But for what reason? I ponder. Their son, who is around my age, goes missing, and now I'm here? It feels like I've dropped into the life of someone else.

I begin to wonder if that is why the Frosts never speak of their son. I've never heard them even say his name. And to think he may still be back in those woods.

Mrs. Frost's strange ways, her ominous talk of forbidden places, and her constant worry start to make more sense.

She'll be calling me soon for dinner, so I walk outside with Jesse and watch him leave. I begin to go toward the house, but then I stop and look out toward the trees that encircle the place called the hollow. I've been in those dark and dense woods. I've heard the breeze call to me like a warning. Fear.

Could there actually be something back there with malicious intent lying in wait, or are the only things ready to torment me the thoughts I create in my own mind?

Chapter 36

After hearing about the Frost's missing son, I'm now a bit hesitant about what's back in those woods.

Did someone take him, kill him, or did he run away? Is there some sort of animal, a cougar or a bear, maybe? How could a boy my age just vanish? And even with the terrible scenarios of what might have happened in those woods, I'm still drawn to them.

All my life, I've only been surrounded by concrete crowds and the chaos of the city. Being in those woods with no noise or even people, I feel free and strangely comforted.

The idea of being beside that river—fishing rod in my hand as I cast that tiny fly out into the wide stretch of water, is what settles into my thoughts every time I allow myself to drift off. The sounds of the birds, the flutter of leaves, and the rush of the river are like steady hands on my shoulders.

My quest to lure the fish, tempting it in, is my focus. I have something precious that will draw it to me. A bauble that mesmerizes and fools the fish into thinking it is something that it can't live without. Its fierce determination to attain it is what gives me the edge in this game of wills.

I anticipate the nibble, the pull of the line. My heart leaps as the flash of silvery scales breaks the surface. It's the hunt, the thrill of finding something elusive and alive.

An odd sensation hits me, and I say the word aloud—alive. I

know it's nearly impossible, but I wonder if the Frost's son could really still be out there.

Jesse said there was no proof that he was dead or alive. There doesn't seem to be any evidence at all of where he could be.

From the first day I arrived, Mrs. Frost has shown nothing but dread toward the woods. She must be convinced that whatever happened to her son happened back there. She still hovers, worrying about what I do each day while she is at work, and this is why I continue to keep my excursions to the hollow and my fishing trips to myself.

Since school let out, I've been fishing with Old Tom any chance that I get. I make my way through the field, to the hidden trail, and to the sandy bank along the water that has become my spot. I can't help but smile when I see him standing in the river, rod in hand and the line arching above him.

Old Tom is closer to the edge today and smiles when he sees me.

"I've seen several feeding on the surface," he says quietly as I quickly make my way into the shallows.

A large splash startles me from behind. It's what Old Tom calls a jumping rise, and I feel they are all around me. I begin to speak, but he puts up a hand to silence me.

"Listen. Can you hear it?" he asks in a whisper.

I can barely make out what he's saying above the wind in the leaves and the slow swirl of the pool. I stand still for a moment and wonder if the voice has returned and if he now hears it, too.

I listen intently, but there is nothing but the water, wind, and moan of trees.

I begin to shake my head, but then it's there. It's like a pebble dropping into the water— Glup. I hear it again. Glup. Glup. It's the fish. They are rising, their mouths open and grasping at the tiny bugs that are landing on the surface. Glup. Glup.

Old Tom watches and smiles when he sees the awareness of what's happening around me.

I release the line of my rod and begin to gingerly place it out above the water, letting it reach further with each arcing cast.

Still enthralled with the sounds that I would have missed without taking the time to listen for them, I'm overwhelmed by the glimmer of the water, the sigh of the wind, and the swell in my chest.

The afternoon has passed, and I'm watching my fly on the water's surface when movement from the side catches my attention. Old Tom has reeled in and begins to walk toward the bank. The sun is starting to fade, and I realize the day is done, and I need to pack up and head back home.

"That was a good day. I caught almost a dozen," I tell him when he reaches me on the shore.

"Any day fishing is a good day," he says, and I agree.

I sit on the bank and carefully place my fly back into the small handled box Old Tom has loaned me.

"You can't catch the phantom from the bank," he says. "That's what the waders are for. Wednesday we'll get you out into the swell."

I'm still nervous about the thought of being out in the water of the hollow, but the idea of Old Tom wanting me out there with him in pursuit of that elusive fish makes me smile.

But then my heart sinks a bit as I realize where I'll be in just a few weeks, or rather where I won't be. Will I be able to find this peace and enjoyment in my new place? The idea of not having Old Tom and the contentment of the hollow somehow makes the day turn cloudy. It will be okay, I tell myself. But I'm not so sure it will. What used to feel like comfort, knowing I'd be leaving, now has me feeling uncertain and anxious. Being back with my mother is what I've planned for and wanted for all these years, and now I'm wondering what that will really mean. Are the daydreams and expectations I've had real? I try to push my thoughts away, knowing I have no choice. Besides, it's what I want. It's what I've always wanted.

When I leave Old Tom and head toward the trail home, instead of quickly walking back and finding my path, I make my way into the cover of trees and then stop and turn back, watching him amble toward his home. Will he be okay? Will he miss me? I wonder if I should tell him that I only have a few weeks until I'm gone. But what good would that do?

I continue to watch as Rusty follows him, making side trips into the grass, sniffing here and there, and then sprinting back to the man who cares for him.

The breeze comes, and this time, I welcome it. It's expected, and I've come to embrace its cool, consistent tug. I breathe it in as I watch Old Tom and Rusty disappear into the darkness of the grove, and I do the same, going in the opposite direction.

The air directs me like a hand on my shoulder, and when I reach the overflow, the voice is more urgent than before. There is no water. It is safe to cross, but the voice is so loud it rings in my head and makes me squint.

I know that once I cross, it will ease and soon diminish, so I take the step down into the trench and trudge through the sand and gravel toward the other side.

I make the ascent up, and just as I'm about to take the last step out of the overflow and up onto the other side, a flicker of light catches my eye, making me pause and study where it came from.

Behind a long, thin root of a tree, sticking out from the bank, I see a shiny, red object. The setting sun peeks through the flutter of the leaves, making it shine when the beams of light hit it. I go back into the trough, and when I reach it, I use the root to pull myself up to where it is. Sticking halfway out of the gravel, I lift the object out of the sand and dirt and then, using my shirt, wipe away the grime. I'm amazed when I see it's a small pocket knife.

I make my way up to the top of the overflow and study it closer. I pull at the metal sections and see that there are not only two types of blades but a tiny set of scissors that all fold neatly into the hard casing. What a find! There is an inscription of three letters carved in the red metal that read W.B.C.

I shrug and place my new prize into the front pocket of my jeans along with my other treasure. It will be the perfect addition to the tools I use for tying my flies. I can even bring it with me out onto the water to use when I'm replacing a line or clipping a knot. I'll no longer have to borrow the one Old Tom uses.

When I reach the back pasture and see the glow of the lights from the house, a feeling that is strange and new washes over me. I feel somehow tied to this place. Instead of the usual dread I feel about being forced to live somewhere and constantly wanting to leave, now I find my dread is because I know I can't stay.

CHAPTER 37

It's already getting dark, and the cows are lowing as I load the hay bales into the bed of the truck. The radio kicks on when I start the engine, and I'm surprised when the song is one I know. I smile to myself, thinking Jesse would be proud of my newfound appreciation of Country music.

I've been doing the feeding for several weeks now, and most days, I've been able to complete all my chores, including the days I have to open the head gates, and still have plenty of time for fishing the river with Old Tom.

I always want to stay at the water longer, but I know exactly how much time I'll need to make my way back and finish my chores before Mrs. Frost returns home. I usually take the shortcut that Nicole showed me, but if the irrigation has been diverted to the overflow, I have to allow myself at least an extra half hour to go back around Old Tom's place and through the other field.

Rusty often follows me to the overflow and then watches from his vantage point along the bank, barking his goodbye until I'm out of view. If I go the other way, he will stay with Old Tom at the river. It is rare to have Old Tom come back to the shore before I have to leave. I wave, and the sun gives him a dusky silhouette as it begins to sink over the tops of the trees.

Pulling the truck around toward the corral, I follow the same route toward the far fence, and the cows begin to gather and follow.

When I stop the truck to begin the feeding, I realize that if I keep the truck in drive, it moves slowly on its own, and I grin at what I've just discovered. If I point the truck and keep it in the tracks I've made, it will roll along without the need for me to stop it. I can climb into the back and push the hay out without ever stopping. It would cut my feeding time in half. And the truck is going so slowly, even if it got off course, I could quickly jump in and steer it back.

I turn and point the truck directly toward the corral and then start it on its way. I easily jump into the bed. I smile, satisfied, when I use my newly found knife to cut the twine to release the hay and begin tossing sections in an even row as the cows fall into line.

It's working perfectly, and the truck is making a slow creep straight to the back of the barn, where I'll be able to reload and begin my trek again on the other pasture. I'm elated and wondering how this stroke of genius hasn't been figured out before.

I'm almost to the end of the last bale and am excitedly anticipating telling Jesse of my brilliant new way to do this chore when the truck hits a dip and then comes to a stop.

I give a disappointed huff, swing myself over the side of the bed, and go to the cab. I'm almost to the barn, so I get in and realize what it needs is simply something to brace and keep the gas pedal engaged in order to keep the truck moving forward.

I turn off the engine and look through the glove compartment and on the floor, and then see my borrowed copy of Zane Grey on the seat. I grin and wedge it above the gas pedal to see if it will give just enough pressure to keep the truck at a steady and slow pace. The book is thin, but I feel it should be the perfect width to sustain the slow speed needed.

I remove the book and then start the engine. With the book in hand, I bend under the steering wheel and shove it in place to test my design. The truck moves forward. It's working. I begin to come up, looking forward to watching my creation in action, but then the truck tips as it rolls over a dip in the ground and then lurches, sending me forward onto the gas pedal. A loud rev hurdles the truck forward so fast I can hear and feel the bumps under the tires as I squirm frantically to release myself and then free the pedal. This only braces me harder against the floor of the truck and on the gas.

My arms are pinned, and when I roll to my side to release them, that puts even more pressure on the pedal, and I hear the truck rev and speed forward. When I'm able to roll up and back into the seat, it's too late. The barn is coming toward me at a dizzying speed, and before I can step on the brakes, the truck pummels into its side. The force of the impact slams me into the dashboard, my forehead hits the windshield, and my neck whips back, throwing me back into the seat. A heavy beam comes down and lands on the hood of the truck, and then everything comes to a stop. A slight hiss can be heard, but what is deafening is the stillness.

God no! I scream out in my head. My neck is throbbing, and I can't tell if I'm hurt or just stunned and sore. I try to straighten myself, and a sharp fire of pain hits my side. I slump back into the seat and continue to try and look around at the mess I've made. Even in the dark, the light from that lone bulb shows I've slammed through part of the corral fence and into the side of the barn. It's then I hear the high pitch of her scream, and I know everything I've worked so hard for is now gone.

I hear her long before I see her, but soon, she's at the truck's side, and in the faint light, I see her at the window. She's pulling on the handle, trying to open the door, but it's stuck. Then she's gone.

I try to sit up again, and I release a loud groan.

"Don't move!" she yells, now at the other window.

This startles me, and even that small amount of movement makes me cringe in pain.

"Landis!" It's Mr. Frost, and he's now trying to force the door open.

"It's jammed," she calls over to him.

"Are you hurt?" he asks me through the glass of the window.

I begin to shake my head, but when he sees me hesitate, he yells over to Mrs. Frost. "Call your dad."

"What?" she asks.

"He needs a doctor. Hurry," he says, sensing her reluctance.

Dad? Doctor? Did I hear that right, or am I delusional from the pain?

Mr. Frost is now at the other window, and I no longer see Mrs. Frost.

"A doctor?" I ask. "I don't need a doctor." I've already caused too much trouble, and now they're having to call a doctor.

Mr. Frost ignores my pleas, opens the passenger door, and leans in. "Can you sit up and move this way?"

I try, but the pain in my side keeps me from being able to move much at all. When he sees me wince, he tells me to stay where I am, and so I do.

I lean back and close my eyes as what I've done begins to sink in.

"I'm so sorry." My voice is weak and cracks. "I've wrecked the truck and ruined the barn."

I wait to hear him reprimand or at least agree, but instead, I feel his hand on my shoulder.

"We can fix the barn and replace the truck. Be still," he says.

I open my eyes. I'm shocked and overwhelmed, but I know if I don't make it right, I'll end up back at the place I was before.

"If you let me stay, I'll do the work, and I'll pay you back. I promise," I plead with him. "Please don't make me leave."

I'm so ashamed that I can't meet his eyes, and when I hear nothing in response, I know I'll be sent away. My eyes begin to well, and when I begin to cry, the pain in my side shoots with every sob.

"Landis, you're not leaving. We're going to get you out of this, and you'll be fine. Now tell me where you're hurt. Your legs? Your head?"

I take a breath and do a quick evaluation of what I can move and what is in pain. "My side, in my ribs. And my neck. But mostly my ribs."

He reaches in and takes hold of my arm with one hand and puts the other under my other arm. "Try to scoot this way," he says as he tries to guide me.

With just a small movement, I wince at the pain on my side, but now I'm over far enough that he can grasp me tighter, pulling me across the long bench seat. When I'm on the other side, he lets me rest a moment.

"Do you think you can walk?" he asks. "With my help?"

I nod, but I'm not sure, and yet I'm still so horrified at what I've done I wish I could run.

Gritting my teeth, he helps me slide from the cab of the truck to standing. He puts my arm around his shoulder, but when he reaches around my waist, I yelp. He quickly releases his grip.

"That's not going to work," he says. "Here, lean against me, and we'll go slow."

I nod and take a deep breath. Together, we take short steps, stopping after each as he waits for me to recover and take the next. As we make our way around the barn and toward the back door of the house, Mrs. Frost comes out. She startles, surprised when she sees us.

"He shouldn't be walking," she says.

"Is your dad coming?" asks Mr. Frost.

"Yes, he should be here any minute."

Her dad is a doctor. I did hear that right.

She comes to my other side, and I lean away from her when she tries to help brace me.

"I'm pretty sure he's got broken ribs, but I think that's it," he explains. "Open the door for us," he directs her.

She quickly goes up the steps of the porch and leads us in. Mr. Frost takes me to the long sofa in the front room and helps me ease down slowly.

Mrs. Frost grabs the colorful pillows from the two large upholstered chairs and uses them to prop me up.

When I'm settled on the sofa, they both stand, assessing me. Again, all I can think is how stupid I was and the disaster I've caused. Before I can apologize again, there is a loud knock at the door, and then before either of the Frosts can answer it, Old Tom makes his way in carrying a small, black, rounded case. His face is full of worry.

My body tenses, shocked to see him.

"I was able to get him inside," says Mr. Frost, motioning toward me.

I look at Old Tom as he comes to my side, and I'm confused as to why they've called him to be here. Do they know about my covert fishing trips with this old man?

He shakes his head and furrows his brows. "What happened?"

I sigh and shake my head. "I crashed the truck into the barn."

"I think he has some broken ribs," says Mr. Frost.

Old Tom takes a deep breath and blows it out slowly. "Not much we can do about broken ribs, but let's see what else we have."

He sets the black case on the table by the sofa and unlatches the top. The two sides open out, and he removes an instrument with an eyeglass on top. When he clicks the bottom, a light turns on.

"Look straight ahead," he says, and he leans down and points the light toward my eye.

I lean back. "What's going on? What are you doing?" I ask.

"I'm checking to see if you have a concussion. Stay still and look at the wall over there," he says, moving the light this way and that.

Mr. Frost steps toward me. "Listen to Doc." He says.

"Doc? You're a doctor?" I ask.

He stands up straight and looks over to where Mr. and Mrs. Frost are standing. He then looks back at me. "I am, or I was."

"But I thought ..." My mind is spinning with questions, and yet I can't seem to form a complete one.

"That I fish for a living?" he says with a chuckle.

When I see Mrs. Frost's eyes go wide with awareness, I know I'm in even more trouble than crashing into the barn. Then I realize the man I call Old Tom, is who Mrs. Frost calls Dad.

<h1 style="text-align:center">CHAPTER 38</h1>

I'm stuck inside the house, and what's worse is the weather continues to tempt me. From my window, all I see is the blue sky. How I wish I could make my way to the river.

I've spent days now doing nothing but watching television or reading. Normally, this would be something I'd dream of, especially being able to choose whatever program I want. But now all I can think about is to be free of this stuffy room and out on the water.

"Patience and rest, or you'll make it worse," said Old Tom the last time he checked in on me. "The river isn't going anywhere," he whispered, reading my mind.

Broken ribs and a sore neck, but nothing that won't take more than time to heal. I can barely turn my head, and coughing or even a deep breath makes me cringe in pain, but none of this hurts as much as knowing what I did and the consequences that I'm sure will follow.

The Frosts haven't said anything, but I can feel their disappointment. It's as though they are waiting just long enough for me to heal so I can pack up. Even with Mr. Frost telling me that wasn't their plan, which was before they knew I had been lying to them and stealing off into the woods to fish with Old Tom.

Old Tom—I'm still trying to reconcile that he is Mrs. Frost's father and a doctor. I was stunned to learn all this. And yet, I never did ask him much about who he was or what he did. I assumed he lived there alone like a hermit and fished all day.

He's come to check on me every morning following the crash, but I haven't seen him this morning. Why didn't anyone tell me who he was? Old Tom knew I was living with the Frosts and never said a word.

He's Mrs. Frost's father, and yet, they barely talk when he comes here. During his visits, he checks my eyes, asks me how I feel, and then leaves. I want so badly to ask him about the river and whether or not he's been back in the hollow, but Mrs. Frost hovers close by, so I usually stay quiet.

As I lay around trying not to take big breaths, I wonder if I'll ever see Old Tom again. I'll be watched like a hawk now, with little chance to steal away into the woods and onto the water.

The thought of never being back there again is worse than having to go back to that home for boys, and I'm sure that's where I'm headed. The thought is so crushing that I try to push it from my mind by trying to drum up ways to make things right, but how?

I just can't go back there. It will ruin any chance I have of being able to go with my mom. She won't be able to wait for me, and I'll be stuck in that jail for who knows how long.

Just a day after the crash, I heard the sound of hammers and could see Jesse from my window carrying posts around to the back of the barn.

He can fix the corral easily enough, but the barn will be a much bigger project. They may have to tear it down and replace the entire thing. I don't really know the extent of the damage that I did, but even in the dim light the night it happened, I could tell the entire corner had been destroyed.

I wait until Mrs. Frost is leaving for the day.

"I made you a sandwich. It's in the fridge. Watch television or read. You have to rest," she says as she gathers her purse and keys.

I nod, but the idea of sitting around doing nothing while the damage I had caused is being fixed is too much to bear.

Making my way out to the barn has me wincing, but if I simply walk, the pain in my side is tolerable. Maybe I can still do my chores after all, I think. That idea is quickly dashed when the act of sliding the barn door makes me bark out in pain.

"What are you doing out here?" I expected to possibly see Jesse, but instead, it's Mr. Frost.

Before I can answer, my attention goes to the side of the barn that I destroyed. There is a large hole, and there is a pile of broken wooden beams next to a stack of newly honed boards to replace them. The extent of what I did, even knowing it was bad, still shocks me.

"Tom says you shouldn't be up for at least several days," he says.

I nod and want to apologize again for what I've done, but the more I do, the less genuine it sounds.

For a moment, we stand in awkward silence, and like usual, any tension or stress has me rubbing the scars on my hands. He notices, and I stop and sink them into my pockets, trying to hide the evidence of another of my transgressions. At least the injuries from this most recent debacle won't leave physical scarring. The feel of the satin pouch that holds my treasure makes me sigh, and I want to return to the house before he can make me feel worse about what I've done.

"I'll head back," I say, but when I turn to leave, I notice Rontu and his mother standing in their pen. I then realize how close I came to hurting or possibly killing them with my stupid actions.

"Are they okay?" I ask, and then take a sweep of all the animals in the corral. "Did any of them get hurt?"

"No. You only damaged yourself," he says.

I close my eyes in relief.

"It's about time for these two to join the others out in the field, which will make it a lot easier for things to get fixed in here."

I look at Rontu. "If they're with the others, will he still be able to find his mother?" I ask. "Will she stay with him?"

Mr. Frost sets down the tools he's holding and walks toward me. "Yes. We don't wean for another seven months."

After his rough start in life and the attempts to bond him to his new mother, I'm worried all of it will be lost when they are mixed with the others.

Mr. Frost sees my hesitation. "What we did worked," he tries to assure me. "They have no idea they aren't related. They are mom and baby, just like any of the others. It's just like humans. Blood may make you related, but it's not what makes you family."

Surprised at his statement, I take a deep breath, and the pain in my ribs bites, making me gasp. It's the most I've heard him speak since I arrived, and while I've only been here with the Frosts for a short while, I feel he's been mulling this observation over for a very long time.

CHAPTER 39

———————

In my state of limbo, behind the veil, I can see what has shaped those who were with me when I was alive. Both significant and trivial experiences come to me from their past and I wonder if this is what will help me learn how I got to this space and why I can't move on.

It's my mother's story that comes to me most often. I think her pain is what drives me to understand the life she lived before I became a part of it. Her life as simply Evelyn before she became my mom.

There is no order to what I see and often the visions are blurred and confusing, but I know I'm seeing them for a reason. I just wish I knew how it all plays into my demise.

———

It felt like a world away, but several young men in their town had been drafted and already sent to Vietnam. Evelyn wasn't sure what the war was about, but she had heard the discussions at the dinner table between her father and Wesley and could feel the fear in her father's voice.

Her brother seemed unfazed, even flippant about what he might face, making Evelyn wonder if his sense of invincibility was real or just posturing.

"I wouldn't be happy about it," said Wesley as Evelyn began to clear the table. "But I'm no draft dodger like some of those hippies in California."

"I'm not suggesting you do that, but if you were in college, then you could possibly avoid it," my grandfather said, trying to reason with him.

"And do what?" Wesley asked. "I don't want to be a doctor like you. You know that. I want to farm. I want to raise beef. That's what I've always planned to do."

My grandfather knew it was fruitless to try and convince him, but he had seen the ravages of war, had tried to mend the shredded bodies, and wanted his son to avoid it.

Wesley pushed the chair back and stood tall. He put a hand on his father's shoulder. "Stop worrying. There's a good chance I won't get called up, and even if I did, I'll do my service and come back. I can take down a five-hundred-pound steer. I'm not letting some little gook scare me."

My grandfather wanted to protest and explain his concerns, but he had never told the truth about what he faced during his own war, so why would Wesley heed his warnings now?

He gave a pain-filled sigh, knowing that the scars these young men would bring home would be deeper and last far longer than anything they could imagine.

For Evelyn, the idea of Wesley being drafted was less about the danger of combat and more about having her friend and her life back. Some time apart from him, and Ramona would surely lose interest. Wesley spent more time with Ramona than Evelyn did, and she found herself annoyed with him and his never-ending presence. She often wished he wasn't always there, but being sent to war? A twinge of guilt hit her.

It was late spring, and the breeze was steady as it came down from the hills and filled the valley.

"He's going to be nineteen in April. He might be drafted," Evelyn said as she and Ramona walked along the ditch bank. They both carried cloth bags and searched for asparagus amongst the tall grass. It was early May and the perfect time to find the tall, tender stalks.

Ramona continued to pick, not looking up. "There's nothing I can do about it, so why think about it."

Evelyn sniffed. "If he has to go, he may be gone for over a year or even longer." She then cringed. She hated how obvious she sounded about wanting Wesley out of the picture.

Ramona shrugged. "Want a cigarette?" she asked, hoping to change the subject.

Evelyn put out her hand. "I can't believe your grandma still doesn't know you steal them."

"She hasn't noticed anything since my grandpa died; she just smokes and watches soap operas. She buys them in those big cartons. I know she doesn't count them. She hasn't even missed the big bottle of vodka I took last week."

Then Evelyn gasped. "Does Wesley know?" She was sure Ramona already shared too much with him, and if he knew about Evelyn smoking, he would somehow hold it against her.

Ramona flinched back. "He doesn't own me. I'll do whatever I want. He tried to tell me I couldn't go to the bonfire."

Evelyn blew out the smoke quickly. "He knows about that?"

Ramona shrugged. "Who doesn't? He was threatening to show up. Like that would scare me into not going."

"I bet he was pissed off," said Evelyn, and she was surprised that this actually gave her some small satisfaction.

Ramona scoffed. "So, what? He can be such a square. He's supposed to be my boyfriend, not act like he's my dad."

Evelyn took a long drag from the cigarette and blew it out slowly. Wesley had always been overprotective, but she thought that was reserved for her—his little sister. She found it odd that she was jealous to have to share even his traits that annoyed her. And then her frustration turned to Ramona. She wasn't thrilled that her best friend was dating her brother, but having Ramona act as though she didn't care about Wesley was equally upsetting.

"We don't have to go to the bonfire," said Evelyn. "We can watch movies and stay at my house."

Ramona rolled her eyes. "Because it's on the other side?"

"No," said Evelyn quickly, but in fact, that was the reason. She didn't know the people from over there, and what she'd been told made her leery.

"Listen, if you don't want to go, don't, but I'm not spending my summer inside watching movies," Ramona scoffed.

Evelyn stayed quiet as they continued to hike along the ditch, snapping off the heads of the fresh green stalks.

"I didn't say I didn't want to go," Evelyn eventually grumbled. "I just wasn't sure you wanted to."

Ramona stopped and put her hands on her hips. "Of course I want to. Don't be weird. We're supposed to be having fun. It's summer!"

Evelyn forced a smile, but a gnawing dread began to fill her. Something didn't feel right, but she had no idea why. She had heard the stories about the "keggers" that were held on the other side of the river. Tales of drunken escapades and legendary rebellions from those who lived on the other side only enforced her ideas of what those people were like.

Why Ramona wanted to go to the bonfire was a mystery to Evelyn, but the rise it got from her older brother made her wonder if the reason wasn't simply to get at him.

She knew of his disdain for the boys from the other side of the river, and if Wesley were to show up and find her there, she would probably never be allowed out of the house again. She couldn't allow that to happen, so she made a plan to make sure it wouldn't.

———

IT WAS JUST STARTING to get dark as Evelyn made her way across the pasture and to the small house on the back of their land. She had waited for her father to go to bed, then she sneaked out the back door.

Even at night, she knew her way, having walked it hundreds of times, but tonight, she followed the path as though she were floating. It was the high of anticipation of what the night would bring.

Ramona's grandmother went to bed early, never checking or caring what went on in that house. It would be the first time in months that she would have her best friend to herself, even if it was for one night.

She'd be free of Wesley, she mused as she reached Ramona's porch and saw no sign of his red truck. She patted her pocket and lifted a sly eyebrow. She had made certain he wouldn't be able to show up and ruin their plans.

The girls locked themselves in Ramona's room, and when Ramona started pulling clothes from her closet and eying them against Evelyn, that she stepped back and gave a confused laugh.

"What are you doing?" she asked.

Ramona gave a sly smile and lifted an eyebrow. "You can't go to the bonfire looking like that."

"Why not?" Evelyn asked. For years, she had heard about the raucous party that those on the other side held at the end of each school year, but she had never considered attending. But when Ramona suggested they go, just the two of them, Evelyn quickly agreed.

Even with her reservations about those from the other side, the idea of a night without her brother in the middle was something she couldn't pass up.

"My friends can't see you like this," Ramona said flippantly.

Evelyn felt her stomach drop. She knew that Ramona had lived over there before moving to the small house at the back of the fields, but that was years ago, and she had never referred to anyone over there as her friend.

"What friends?" Evelyn asked.

Ramona lifted her shoulders and gave a sigh. "Just some of the people that I know. It will be so fun."

"Have you gone to the bonfire before?" Evelyn was not only surprised but confused.

Ramona huffed. "Of course. Don't be a square. You'll be fine. But you can't wear this." She motioned toward Evelyn's baggy jeans.

"Does Wesley know?" Evelyn wondered if he was aware of Ramona's connection to those across the river.

Ramona scoffed. "No! He'd throw a fit if he knew where we were going. I told you this was going to be the best night ever, so stop asking questions, and let's get ready." She lifted a skirt that was far shorter than anything Evelyn owned and tossed it toward her. "This will be so cute on you."

Evelyn picked up the garment but was still unsure about Ramona's plans. Yes, she had agreed to go but hadn't really considered what she was going to face once they arrived.

"How are we getting there?"

Even though Ramona was old enough to drive, she didn't have her license, and Wesley seemed to take her wherever she wanted to go. She certainly wasn't expecting him to drive them, and even if she was, with what Evelyn had taken, he wouldn't be able to use his truck anyway.

Again, she patted her pocket, and then a wave of guilt washed over her.

Ramona rolled her eyes. "We're walking. It's across on the other side, but I have a shortcut. Just get dressed so we can go."

The other side? But how? Evelyn knew there was no way to get across without going all the way into town and across the large bridge. And there wasn't much reason to go there. The people over there stayed on their side, and they did the same.

"You can't go looking like you're wearing handmade clothes. You'll look great in this," said Ramona, handing her a top.

The comment stung. Evelyn had always thought Ramona loved her hand-sewn creations. She'd never seen her in these skirts and tops that were now strewn across her bed.

My mother grudgingly tried on the skirt and tight-fitting tube top but shook her head when she saw herself in the mirror.

"Foxy Mama," Ramona said, lifting an eyebrow when she saw Evelyn in her new outfit.

Evelyn scrunched her face. She stared into the long mirror Ramona had propped on the bed and turned from side to side. "I can't wear this. I look like a dork," she said.

"Not at all!" Ramona said, going and standing next to her. She looked at the two of them in the mirror and then sighed. "I'm getting fat."

"No, you're not," said Evelyn, almost too quickly. She had, in fact, noticed something was different about her friend. She had passed it off as part of her lack of seeing her, but whatever it was, Evelyn wasn't about to say anything for fear of Ramona lashing out. My mom knew well that sometimes even the smallest things could set Ramona off, and that was the last thing she wanted, especially that night.

It had been weeks since they were able to be alone together, and while Evelyn wasn't excited about going to a place with people she didn't know, she was grateful to have this time with her.

Ramona locked her bedroom door. She gave an evil smile and then went to her bed and pulled a large paper bag from beneath, making Evelyn cock her head in question.

When Ramona lifted out a big jug of vodka, Evelyn's eyes went wide. "Where did you get that?"

Ramona motioned toward the closed door. "She has no clue," she then burst into laughter. "This party is going to be crazy." She then began dancing around with the bottle. "Want some now?" she whispered, even though both girls knew her grandmother couldn't hear her.

Evelyn didn't want to disappoint her. She lifted her shoulders tentatively. "I guess."

My mom had tried drinking, but it was little more than beer, and it was usually the last couple of swallows from the cans my grandfather left on the kitchen counter. She was never all that curious about alcohol, and hard liquor was never in the house, so Evelyn was both anxious and a bit worried about this new experience.

Ramona pulled two tiny glasses from under her bed. She set the glasses on her dresser and used both hands to pour the large jug. When she had filled them both, she handed one to Evelyn, took the other, and raised it high.

"Here's to the best summer ever!" she said.

Evelyn smiled. She worried that Ramona was growing out of her and would soon find older friends like Wesley. He had already taken so much of her attention. Her brother hadn't even been dating Ramona for that long. However, Evelyn felt those months had chiseled an immense chasm between them.

They clinked glasses, but before they could take a sip, the phone rang out in the kitchen. With eyes wide, Ramona turned toward the door. She then motioned for Evelyn to hide the glasses and bottle under the bed.

As they pulled the bedspread down over their stash, a knock came at the bedroom door.

"Ramona. Phone." It was her grandmother's muffled voice.

"Okay," yelled Ramona at the closed door. "I'll be right there." She shook her head, annoyed, and scanned the room for anything that would expose their plans before she opened the door. She slowly swung it open, and the coast was clear. She walked the short distance to where the phone receiver lay waiting on the kitchen counter.

"Hello," she answered.

Evelyn strained to listen in, almost certain it was Wesley, and worried now that he would ruin their plans.

"I can't tonight. I need to help my grandma with some things." She turned to Evelyn and gave a sly smile. It was obvious then who was on the other end of that phone line.

Ramona sighed and rolled her eyes. "No, she isn't here. I haven't seen Evie all day." She paused a moment, listening, then huffed. "I am not. Why would I lie?" Again, she rolled her eyes as she listened. "Fine!" she then hung up the phone and stomped back to the room.

"God, why can't I have one night to go have fun without him? I know he's going to try and show up and ruin everything." Her shoulders slumped.

"I thought you said he didn't know about it."

Ramona shook her head, annoyed. "Everyone knows about it. God, he'll probably show up and make a big scene. Maybe I should call him back. We can just hang out with him at your house." She then sat on the bed, looking defeated.

"No," Evelyn said with resolve. She wasn't about to have her night ruined once again by her brother.

"So, what if he knows? He can't go anywhere without these." She reached into the pocket of her jeans that were lying on the bed and pulled out a set of keys. They dangled from a key chain made of red leather in the shape of a horseshoe. Wesley's keys.

Ramona's eyes went wide. "You took his keys?"

Evelyn nodded. Evelyn just knew her brother would try to upend the night.

Ramona giggled. "How'd you get them?" she asked.

Evelyn shrugged with a devious grin. "If nothing else, he'll be looking for them for hours."

Ramona smiled, and Evelyn was buoyed. Her night of fun with her best friend had been saved. But the excitement that Evelyn felt was short-lived. She was happy that it was just the two of them again, but as she tucked the keys into the pocket of the tight skirt, she also felt a pang of guilt for her deception against Wesley. But why? Ramona was her friend first, so why couldn't she have a night without sharing her with her brother?

Ramona laughed and reached under the bed and produced the two glasses filled with vodka. She handed one to Evelyn, and they clinked them in exaggerated conquest.

Each took a sip.

Evelyn flinched back, and her entire body shuddered. Her face pinched, making Ramona laugh.

"Don't worry. It'll get better."

Evelyn tried again, and with the same effect, but eventually, she finished the tiny cup.

A warmth rose through her and eased its way into her shoulders and into her mind. Suddenly, the nerves she felt about the bonfire had lessened, and when both girls were finished touching up their hair and make-up, they hid the bottle of vodka in a blanket and sneaked out the back door.

Chapter 40

Being stealthy really wasn't an issue, as Ramona's grandmother was hard of hearing and had been worn down by the exhaustive challenges of raising a teenage girl when you were almost eighty years old.

As they made their way across the kitchen and to the door, Ramona stopped. She went to the phone, quietly removed the receiver, and laid it on the counter. She put her finger to her lips and then whispered, "Now he won't keep calling and wake her up."

Evelyn nodded in agreement.

With a single flashlight, their giddy buzz followed them out and around to the backside of the small home.

But when Evelyn saw the dense wall of trees, she stopped. Even though her family owned all this land, she had never gone past the back porch of the old house. Even during daylight, the woods drew her back to a dark winter night that left her with a chill so cold her skin felt like it was being touched by fire.

Realizing Evelyn was no longer with her, Ramona stopped and turned back. "What are you doing?" she whispered loudly.

"Where are you taking me?" Evelyn asked.

"I told you. The bonfire is just on the other side."

The warm buzz had faded, and Evelyn could feel the trees closing around her. "The other side? How?"

Ramona walked back to her. "I have a shortcut. It's not that far. Come on," she urged.

Evelyn watched her friend set off again as her heart began to pound. The hollow is where she had wandered off as a child. Something had called her back into the darkness, and in those frozen woods, she was found close to death. The remnants of that night were the scars she bore. They reminded her of the dangers that lurked in the depths of those woods. And while she stayed away, she always felt its gaze. It was watching her as if summoning her to return.

She took a deep breath and tried to convince herself that she was no longer a little girl and that the childish fears she fostered were foolish.

She exhaled and took a step forward. Her bare shoulders tingled in the summer night air as she followed Ramona into the brush and to a thin trail leading to the hollow.

The chirp of crickets and the shimmer of the moon on the river is what guided them.

"Where are we?" Evelyn asked as Ramona veered off the path and around the tall banks of the hollow.

"We're almost to the backside. You'll see," Ramona answered.

The backside? Evelyn thought, surprised that she never knew of a backside or that Ramona seemed so familiar with it.

There was no path, and Evelyn winced with each step as her exposed legs were scratched by downed branches and sharp grass.

The glow of a fire was faint as they made their way around the curve of the hollow's large bowl. A gravel rim went all the way around to the back. The hidden side. That is where the kids from the other side of town were gathered. But how would they get there? Evelyn thought. The river was divided in two by the outcropping of the gravel and sand that made up the hollow, but the water was still deep enough to require some sort of passage.

Ramona and Evelyn walked the rim of the massive natural pool that was formed by the backflow of the river, the encircling trees, and the canopy that all created the hollow. When they reached the top of the ridge where the water was deep and flowed from the main river Evelyn gasped.

"How are we going to get over there?" Evelyn whispered, knowing the large swath of water was not something they could cross.

"There's a bridge," Ramona answered.

"A bridge? Where?"

Ramona motioned off toward the glow of the fire. "It's over that little hill."

Evelyn stared off, and Ramona nudged her. "Don't say anything."

"What do you mean?" Evelyn asked.

"If you tell, they might come and find it and take it down," Ramona said with a scoff.

"Who would?"

"Wesley, for one. He'd be mad if he knew they could get over here."

Evelyn thought about Wesley and knew that what Ramona said was true. "But they aren't supposed to be ..." Evelyn began to protest.

Ramona huffed. "Why do you hate them?"

Evelyn flinched back as though she'd been slapped. "I don't hate them," she said.

"Then promise you won't say anything."

Evelyn wished she'd never agreed to go with Ramona. This was not the night she had planned and looked forward to. But she swallowed and straightened her shoulders. "I won't tell," she said softly.

Ramona nodded and then nudged Evelyn forward. "It's not that much further."

They continued through the trees and then up a sandy hill. When they reached the top, in the glow of the moon, Evelyn saw it—a bridge. It was narrow and swung slightly from the rope that was attached on both sides. Long pieces of mismatched lengths of boards were strung together, making a thin deck that spanned the entire length.

Evelyn and Ramona paused a moment as they stood looking down into the dark chasm below.

They could barely see the shimmer of the water but knew it was there from the noise of its powerful rush.

"Come on," Ramona ordered, stepping out onto the bridge.

"Are you sure this is safe?" Evelyn asked. Any remnant of courage from the alcohol they drank earlier was now gone.

"Yes, but wait until I'm across before you start," Ramona said as the bridge heaved and swayed.

She held onto the ropes tied up on each side. The flashlight was on and held in her mouth, and somehow, the vodka jug was wrapped in the blanket and secured under her arm. Slowly, she inched her way across. When she was safely on the other side, she waved for Evelyn to start.

"This is bad," Evelyn whispered to herself, but she took that step and held on, never letting go as she shuffled and slid forward. When she hit the center, she paused, wanting to turn around, but there was no going back. She had no choice but to get to the other side.

She pressed on, and when her foot stepped onto the solid dirt, she released her breath.

Ramona gave her a clumsy hug. "Wasn't that crazy?"

Evelyn was still paralyzed with fear, so all she could do was nod.

Ramona grabbed her by the arm, and they walked up a slight incline.

In the crackling glow of the bonfire below, they saw the faces of those who had gathered. Some were familiar. Evelyn had seen them at school, but most were not.

Would they recognize her? And did she want them to?

Seeing her reservations, Ramona playfully bumped her shoulder to Evelyn's. "Don't act so sappy. We're here to have fun." She gave her a goofy look and wouldn't stop until Evelyn smiled back.

Ramona giggled, and someone at the fire below yelled, "Hey! It's Ramona!"

They knew her. These were the kids from across the river. They were strangers and from "the other side." It was the reason Evelyn was so nervous about going. Her entire life, she had avoided them. She knew some of their names from school, but that was all. Part of her was curious and intrigued, but she also wondered how they knew Ramona. She thought she knew everything about her best friend. How often had Ramona been over the bridge and to this place before?

Before Evelyn could ask, Ramona smiled down at the group, their fire-lit faces looking up. She lifted the large jug from the blanket like a warrior holding the decapitated head of a fallen foe.

For a moment, there was silence, and then the crowd cheered and laughed and motioned for the two to join them.

Evelyn followed Ramona down the hill, and while the others seemed friendly and accepting, she still felt as though she was a sheep being led into the wolf's den.

They were bumped about as they walked through the giddy and gabbing crowd, and within seconds, Evelyn was sloppily handed a plastic cup filled with something that sloshed out and covered her shoes.

A boy with thick, dark hair watched her from the other side of the fire. He appeared older and stared so intently that she pulled at the short skirt and wished she hadn't agreed to wear the outfit Ramona gave her.

"Hey, aren't you a Corrigan?" he asked over the crowd. "Don't you live in the castle house?"

The chatter of the group went from loud and laughing to soft murmurs. They were waiting for her reply.

Evelyn felt on display. "It's not a castle. It's just a house," she said.

"Just a house?" he chided her.

"Knock it off, Mark," said Ramona. "You're just jealous."

He threw his head back and laughed. "Jealous of what? Getting away with murder because I have a bunch of money?"

Evelyn turned to Ramona. What did he mean?

Ramona scoffed. "Leave her alone. You don't know what you're talking about."

He shrugged, but as he turned and began to walk off, he made sure Evelyn could hear his parting words. "If I lived there, I'd be wondering how many more bodies are buried back in those woods?"

Before Evelyn could rebuff his ridiculous claim, she was pulled to the side and into the shadowed area away from the fire.

"Don't listen to him," said Ramona.

"What was he talking about? Murder and bodies?" Evelyn had been told about her father's dispute with a man from the other side. She knew the man died, but her father was innocent. That had been proved in court. It happened years ago before she was even born. It was impossible for anyone to know about that and bring it up now.

"He's teasing you," said Ramona. "It's just a joke."

Evelyn flinched back. It didn't feel like a joke. She was regretting her decision to come. She wanted her time with Ramona, and this was not what she had envisioned.

"Let's go," she said.

Ramona leaned back and moaned. "No. Don't let him get to you. We just got here. Drink your drink. I promise they're cool. Come on back to the fire. You'll see."

Evelyn stood her ground, and when Ramona could see she wasn't budging, she sighed. "Fine, but let me at least say hi and goodbye to a couple of people first." She then shoved the cup she was holding into Evelyn's hand. "Drink this, and I'll be back in a minute, then we'll go."

Evelyn took the cup. Now, she had one in each hand. She reluctantly nodded, and Ramona made her way back into the circle of bodies.

As she stood just outside the glow, she took a sip and then reeled back. She dumped the rest.

She continued to wait but soon became impatient and walked closer to the crowd, scanning the group for Ramona.

She wanted to leave, to get away from the horrible things they were saying about her and her family. Why did Ramona bring her here? Didn't she know how they felt about her?

"Hey, rich girl," she heard a voice call out. It was him again, and that was when she decided, with or without Ramona, that she was leaving.

She stepped back out of the crowded circle and away from the glow of the fire. Into the darkness and toward the bridge she went, hoping her exit was unnoticed. She hesitated, wondering if she should go back or at least hide in the shadows and wait for Ramona, but when she heard the same boy still calling out, looking for her, she decided she had to go alone.

At the bridge, her stomach clenched. At the top of the fill where the base of the bridge was set, she could barely make out where the ropes were tied. The faint light of the moon and remnants of the bonfire were just enough for her to see where the bridge began. At least in the dark, she wouldn't be able to see how high up she was as she struggled across.

A loud roar of laughter boomed from the party and pushed Evelyn forward. It didn't sound like fun but like a war party ready to pounce.

She held her breath when she took the first step out. The bridge swayed, and she gasped. The ropes were rough, but she gripped them tightly as she took each step.

When she felt she was at the halfway point, a gust of wind came through, lifting the short skirt. Her instinct was to pull it back down, but she wasn't about to release her hold.

"Nice ass." It was him. He had followed her.

She tried to look back but knew if she did, the bridge would rock.

"Where are you going?" he asked.

The bridge then bowed deeply, and she realized he was on the bridge behind her.

"My brother is waiting for me," she lied, hoping this would dissuade him from continuing after her. She pulled herself forward, each step closer to solid ground and away from him.

"But we were just getting to know each other," he said.

In the dim light, she could see the other side, and this gave her the push she needed to stand straighter and move quickly. When she saw the base, she leaped and landed on the bank, but as she began to feel relieved that she was safe on the other side, he too was right there, and before she could get away, he had her by the wrist.

Her first reaction was to yank it away, but then she felt the strength of his grip and relented.

"Leave me alone," she said. She tempered her voice. She wanted to sound stern but also didn't want to let him know she was scared.

"What's wrong?" he asked. "I just want to talk some more. I didn't mean to make you feel bad."

He tried to sound sincere, but she could hear the smirk in his voice.

He nudged her. "We can sit over here, and they won't even know we're gone."

Her heart was racing. She licked her lips nervously, wondering if she could break free and run into the woods to hide.

"I'm sorry about what I said. I was kidding with you. Okay?"

She gave him a slight nod, but his grip on her didn't change.

"I told my brother I'd only be an hour, and then I'd meet him back here."

"In the woods? In the dark?" he asked.

"Yes," she said.

He gave an unconvinced humph. "Okay, if that's what you want, I'll walk you back. I can't have you being back here in the dark all by yourself."

Her breath caught. Now what?

"That's okay, I'll be fine. You don't need to ..."

"Oh, I don't mind. Come on," he said, directing her down the embankment and into the dark woods.

CHAPTER 41

With little more than the light of the moon through the trees, she tried to make her way toward the trail, still in his grip. With each step, she planned her break, but until she knew where she was going, she knew it would be futile to try and run.

"Let's stop here," he said. "If we go much further, I won't be able to see you at all."

She looked around, searching for a break in the grass, but saw nothing.

He pulled her arm, turning her toward him. He was tall and so much bigger than her. The only chance she had of getting away was if she could run enough to find a place to hide in the dark.

"Why do you look scared?" he asked. "I'm not going to hurt you. I just want to talk." With the hand not holding hers, he lifted the edge of her skirt.

She jerked back, batting it away. Any possibility of him just wanting to talk left her mind, and she knew she would have to fight.

He laughed. "Why'd you wear a skirt like this if you didn't want to show off your ass?"

"Leave me alone," she begged. She cringed at how terrified her voice sounded, feeling if she appeared scared, that it would only embolden him.

He yanked her to him, and she reached up and tried to push him away, but the more she resisted, the tighter he held her.

She could barely breathe, but with her free hand, she thrust it up and onto his face, grasping his cheek and, with the nub of her finger, gouged at his eye.

He shrieked and shoved her back so hard she landed on her back on the brush-covered ground. Dried branches and rocks dug into her, and the air slammed from her lungs with its force.

She was stunned, and soon, he was on her, wrestling her arms to the ground and pinning her underneath him. She tried to scream, even though she knew her cries would only fade out into the vast cover of night.

With an arm pressed across her chest, he reached under her skirt and grabbed at her panties. His intent to pull them down was done with such force they tore, giving him the access he desired.

Now, the fear of what he planned to do came rushing along with tears.

"Please stop," she pleaded. "Please don't."

Again, she tried to yell, and as she drew breath to give her voice any bit of strength she could muster, she felt him enter her. The stab of pain made her knees draw up, and her scream came out as nothing but a guttural yelp.

Her mind began to numb, and her body turned slack in defeat. She turned her head away from what was happening and sobbed into the dirt.

Her head spun in and out of the realization of what was happening as she began to fear what he planned to do next. Would he leave her alone and allow her to run through the woods and back home, or because of what he had done, would he silence her completely? Would he cover his tracks by making sure she never spoke again?

She felt a sharpness at her hip and reached down to find the point of Wesley's keys poking from her pocket. Evelyn slid them out and secured one between her fingers. With all the force she could muster, she shoved her hand up toward what she thought was his face. She felt the key strike something solid, and she ripped it down into what felt like flesh.

He let out a wail and jolted up, but his weight was still on her. She was still pinned.

"You stupid bitch!" he screamed, and Evelyn knew then she had only made it worse.

Even in the moonlight, she couldn't make out his face, just his form, and she braced herself for what other horrors he had planned. She tried to cover her face, convinced he would strike her, and when she heard a solid whack, she wondered what it was he had hit.

She heard him moan and then slump over to the side of her. Something had hit him hard. His weight was still pinning her legs, and she screamed and struggled to free herself.

Then, she heard footsteps in the dried leaves and wondered who else was there and if they planned to hurt her, too.

"Evie?" A voice called out from the darkness. It was Ramona.

Evelyn tried to answer but could only cry instead. She pushed the leg that was still on her, and it slid off with a thud. She scrambled to stand and was ready to bolt back into the woods. She had no idea what direction but didn't care. She just wanted to get away.

The light of the small flashlight clicked on, and when Ramona saw the disheveled and terrified face of Evelyn, she gasped in horror and reached for her.

"Oh, Evie," she cried. "Please tell me you're okay."

Evelyn wasn't okay; she was frantic and resisted Ramona's embrace.

"I should have never taken you there," Ramona continued.

Evelyn had no reply. Her only thought was to run, but when she stepped away from Ramona's tight clutch, the flashlight's beam fell onto the shoe of her attacker.

Ramona gasped. "Did I kill him?"

Still wanting to bolt, Evelyn scanned the area for an escape.

"What do we do?" asked Ramona.

"We need to leave."

"But what about him?"

Evelyn's first reaction was disdain. "Who cares? I just want to go."

"But they'll find him and ... if he's dead ..." Ramona's voice trailed.

"You were trying to save me."

Ramona took a halting breath and let the flashlight scan the lifeless form. "They won't believe me. We went there and ..." she put her hand to her mouth. "They'll say we asked for it."

Evelyn's heart sank. "They'll say I asked for it," she clarified.

"No, this is my fault," said Ramona. "I did this."

Pulling at the skirt and brushing the twig-entwined and sweat-matted hair from her face, Evelyn let out a whimper. "Are you sure he's dead?"

Ramona used her foot to nudge the body. She shivered and then nodded.

"What do we do?" asked Evelyn. "Should we hide him? Bury him under something?"

Scratching her head anxiously, Ramona looked around the dark woods with the narrow beam of the flashlight. "How? Where?"

The light hovered on the body as they pondered what to do.

"What about the canal?" Evelyn answered. "It's deep now. The current will take it out to the river, or it will sink, and the water will freeze soon."

"Drag it there? But they'll see us."

"Not at the bridge. If we go down further, the trees will hide us."

Ramona turned to Evelyn. "Drag him?"

Evelyn nodded. "Yes."

Both girls' hearts were racing, and their breathing was fast and loud.

"Take a leg," directed Ramona. "Even if they do find him, they'll think he fell in and drowned or something." She then placed the flashlight into her mouth to illuminate their way.

Evelyn cringed at the thought of touching a dead body but also having to touch him again. The horror of what took place fell over her, and she put her hand over her eyes.

Seeing her friend's hesitation, Ramona took the flashlight from her mouth and pointed at the other leg. "Come on," she directed. "We have to do this. If we leave him here, they'll find him, and they'll figure it out."

She waited as Evelyn tried to compose herself. "Come on, Evie. We have to do this."

Evelyn looked at her friend. She was shivering and nauseous, with a wet slick still covering her legs.

She wanted to melt down and cry, fall asleep, and let it all turn out to be nothing more than a horrific nightmare, but seeing the body and feeling the breeze on her sweat-covered face, she knew it was all real.

Taking a deep, determined breath, she bent down and took a leg. She swallowed hard and then nodded to Ramona.

"You ready?" Ramona asked.

"Yes," said Evelyn. But was she? What if he wasn't dead and woke up to realize what they were doing? Shoving the thoughts aside, she gripped harder and steeled her resolve. It had to be done.

Ramona placed the flashlight back in her mouth, and the two girls braced their stance, anticipating the weight they'd be pulling.

The first tug had them both worried they wouldn't be able to move him at all, but once they began to pull in unison, the dried leaves and grass of the woods helped slide the body along.

They pulled for a distance and then stopped to rest, and then pulled again, slowly making their way toward the watery grave.

As they approached the area near the bridge, they could hear the music and laughter of the party still booming above the rush of the water. Ramona stopped and dropped his leg, and Evelyn wondered why she had quit moving.

"Why are you stopping?" she whispered loudly.

Ramona reached up, took the flashlight from her mouth, and clicked it off, giving Evelyn her answer. She then picked up his leg, and they resumed their trek in the dark. They would need to get away from the bridge and down as far as possible to stay out of view.

The embankment would be their biggest challenge, but when they reached a point where they could be at the top without being seen, they took the steep hill at a long angle and heaved the body until they reached the landing.

The moon's glimmer on the water made the girls pause and then look at each other. They were going to dispose of a body.

A big burst of laughter from the bonfire made them duck down, but it also shook them from their stupor and made them focus on the chore at hand.

"Pull it to the side, and then we'll roll it down," whispered

Ramona. What they were doing was so unimaginable she could no longer see a person but a thing. The body was an "it."

From their crouched position, they pushed and pulled until the body was teetering on the edge of the steep bank.

"What if they hear a splash?" asked Evelyn.

Ramona shook her head. "They can't hear anything."

Evelyn thought about her earlier screams for help. They didn't hear that either. Her mind flashed back, and again, she felt the pain and terror of the attack. She moved toward the back of the body, bracing herself, and then used her foot to push the body. She gave a single shove to send it rolling down the embankment.

Ramona stood up, surprised. Then, the two girls waited, trying to hear the splash, but there was none.

"Is he in the water?" Evelyn asked.

Ramona peered down at the water, trying to make out the form in the darkness, but could see nothing. She pulled the flashlight from her pocket and pointed the beam toward the water. The flow showed small waves and ripples as the light darted back and forth, searching frantically.

Then, near the edge, the light fell on a solid form. The legs were barely visible along the shallow part of the bank, keeping the body from drifting into the main flow, and as the light followed the form, the face of the corpse lifted up and out of the water.

Evelyn gasped, and Ramona screamed, dropping the flashlight. It clicked off, leaving them in the dark.

"He's still alive," Evelyn cried. "He moved. I saw him move."

Ramona dropped to the ground, searching for the flashlight.

"What are you doing?" asked Evelyn. She was swaying back and forth, debating whether to run.

When Ramona found the flashlight, she clicked it on again and pointed it back toward where the body had been. She flicked the beam from side to side and all over the canal.

"Do you see him? Is he still there?" Evelyn asked frantically.

"No. He must be in the water. He's dead. He's dead."

"But he looked up. You saw it. He's still alive." Evelyn said in a frenzy.

Still trying to scan the water, Ramona put her other hand to her forehead. "No! It was just the waves in the water that made it look that way. He's dead. I hit him hard. He can't be alive."

Then, in the distance, just above the noise of drunken laughter, the squeal of a siren broke through. Ramona stood straight and shot a look at where it was coming from. "Police," she whispered.

She turned back and again tried to locate the body. What if he was alive and now trying to climb out? The light bounced off the sides of the ditch, but she could see nothing.

The scream of the siren was getting louder and closer.

Evelyn gasped. "Police? Do they know?"

Ramona turned to her. "No. How could they?"

"What if somebody saw?" Evelyn whispered hysterically. She turned back toward the water. "Where'd he go?"

"I don't know. I can't see ..." Ramona flashed the light again and again but saw nothing.

Soon, the loud, raucous chatter of the bonfire turned quiet, replaced by the sounds of engines revving.

"What's going on?" asked Evelyn.

"I don't know, but we need to go," said Ramona. "Come on."

"But," Evelyn hesitated, still not knowing if the body they had shoved down into the ravine was dead or alive, but Ramona grabbed her by the arm, and the two girls slid down the embankment and into the woods.

Using the flashlight to direct them, they ran back through the trees and over the uneven brush-covered path toward the little cabin.

The crunching of each step made Evelyn want to look back, feeling like she was being chased. Would she always be looking over her shoulder, expecting him to be after her?

They continued to run, still hearing the sirens, but as they got closer to Ramona's home, the sirens began to fade, and the sounds of the water and woods near the cabin filled the night air.

When the porch light came into view, Evelyn felt a weight release. She didn't feel completely in the clear but a bit closer to safety. They paused at the steps and then quietly sneaked into the back door and to Ramona's room.

Ramona released her breath when she closed the door, but when she flipped on the light and saw the ratted hair, dirt-covered skin, and blood on the legs of her friend, her adrenaline drive shattered, and she burst into tears.

Her best friend, the one she had committed to as a sister, stood there bruised and broken, and all because of her.

CHAPTER 42

Ramona helped Evelyn into the shower, but no amount of soap and hot water seemed to be enough to wash away the horror that covered her.

She dried off and got dressed in the clothes she had worn to Ramona's house. She hadn't put much thought into the jeans and simple green sweater, considering she had no idea what was awaiting her.

She looked at her brother's keys before placing them in her pocket. They were stained with blood, even on the leather horseshoe, and she worried what Wesley would say because surely he would notice. What lie could she tell him?

The girls hardly said a word. The events of that night crowded their heads and had them both unable to fathom what had happened.

The sirens had ceased long ago, and now they were both wondering if they had really heard them at all.

But there were cops, and there were sirens. However, they weren't coming for two girls hiding a body or even a bonfire with a crowd of drunken kids.

It wasn't until several hours later that the flashlight beams fell on the body. There was no chance of resuscitation even if they had found him sooner.

Early the following day, as Evelyn sneaked back into the house, she found her father still in his nightclothes, standing in the kitchen. His tear-stained face surprised her. She knew he'd be mad at her for sneaking out, but crying? Did he know what had happened to her? She wanted to run into his arms, but when he asked her where she'd been all night, she knew his tone wasn't compassion but anger.

"I was at Ramona's," she said, trying to dampen what she was sure would be an angry lecture. She needed comfort and to feel safe again. His lip quivered as his eyes met hers, and she saw an awareness sink into his face.

"No, you weren't," he said as his eyes turned cold. "He went there. He was trying to find you."

Evelyn was confused. "Who?" she asked.

Her father bit his lip and then answered. "Wesley, he went looking for you."

"He's lying." It was a defensive response, but fear set in as she wondered what Wesley knew about the night before.

Her father huffed, and he wiped the wetness from his cheeks. "Where do you think Wesley is?" he asked.

Evelyn took a quick glance around. She figured, like most mornings, he was already out in the fields. She raised her shoulders in question, still trying to form her excuses.

When he told her what happened, it came out like blame. Wesley had gone to find them, but after searching for his keys without luck, he took the old farm truck.

The curve of the road was sharp, and a combination of impatience, anger, and faulty brakes had Wesley fighting for control and losing. The truck veered and rolled into a ravine, and now her brother would never come home.

It wasn't true. It couldn't be, Evelyn thought as she sat stunned and alone in her room. But her father's grief-stricken face kept surfacing in her mind, reminding her that it was, in fact, real.

Did he know the part she played in her brother's demise?

Evelyn then felt the hard bundle in her pocket, and the tears that were already covering her cheeks poured down onto her lap when she reached in and pulled out Wesley's keys.

The finality of her loss was so severe, and the pain so great, even the horror of what she had endured and done that night was closed away.

For days, she waited and wondered if news of another death would surface, but she heard nothing.

———

Just over a week after the crash, Wesley was laid to rest. Evelyn stood at his casket and, through a blur of tears, quietly begged him to wake up. It couldn't be, she thought. His body was there. He had to be somewhere still inside.

"Please, don't leave me here alone," she whispered.

So final and abrupt. How could he be gone?

She often wondered how she would have felt had she been older when her mother died. Was this the pain she never experienced with that first tragedy in her life? Every time the realization of Wesley's death came over her, her eyes would spill over, and her throat would sting. He teased her, bossed her around, and made her mad, but he was also the one she always knew would be there for her. And the last words she said to him—I hate you.

She knew that he didn't take her seriously, but those words continued to hover every time the woeful jolt of realization washed over her.

It was Gordon who now stood by her side. Wesley's best friend was there the day after it happened and never left. He did the chores that Wesley had always done and drove with the family to the funeral.

He spent evenings filling the void and keeping Evelyn and her father from being alone with just each other. For this, she was grateful. The guilt she felt seemed to scream out whenever she even looked at her father.

The events of that night continued to play over and over, like a movie, looping relentlessly, reminding her of the horror. And the days that followed only elevated her pain.

Her father's sorrowful sobs, the forlorn faces of people stopping by the house, bringing flowers and food as though that would soothe their loss, and the hundreds of kids from school, all claiming him as their best friend, filling the large church for the funeral.

So many faces covered in sympathy and sadness. It seemed like the entire town was gathered for the ceremony. Everyone was there. Everyone except for Ramona.

The day after Wesley's funeral, my mom marched across the fields and through the trees to the small house. Still wracked with grief and stunned over the loss, she was both sad and angry at her friend's avoidance.

No calls? No visit? Evelyn was certain Ramona knew what had happened—everyone did. Was she avoiding Evelyn because of what they had done that night? But what about Wesley?

Was Ramona so devastated by the loss that she hid herself away? Even that was no excuse for not showing any sadness or acknowledgment of his death. And what about her? Ramona couldn't be there for the person she called her best friend—her sister. Especially after what they had both gone through?

Evelyn climbed the stairs to the porch and knocked twice. Her heart was racing in anticipation of telling Ramona exactly what she thought of her disrespect and thoughtlessness.

The door opened, and to her surprise, it was Ramona's grandmother. In all the years Evelyn had been making the trek to see her friend at the small house, she never remembered anyone answering that door except for Ramona.

"I need to see Ramona?" she said.

The old woman sniffed and straightened. "She's not here."

"When will she be back?"

"She's not coming back," she said, her voice gruff and pointed. "She's gone. She moved."

Evelyn felt her heart and stomach drop. "She moved?"

"Yes." The old woman snapped and then stepped back, ready to shut the door.

"Wait," Evelyn called. "Where did she go?"

The woman shook her head, continued to step back into the house, and then pulled the door closed.

For several minutes, Evelyn stood on the porch staring at the peeling paint on the door. Gone? She thought. But where? How could that be? She blinked back to the empty porch. Should she knock again? Demand that the old woman tell her where Ramona went? She was confused, upset, and alone with her heartache.

Her thoughts raced but then came to a halt as a breeze encircled her. It was cold and intense, making her turn into it and to the direction it had come. She realized then she was looking out toward the woods.

It was there, past the trees and over the hill, that it happened—where it all happened. The bonfire, the attack, the killing, and the body that seemed to come back to life. She had heard nothing of a body being found or of anything from that night, but until then, she had never heard or cared about what went on over there. And now it was also the place that took her brother. That is where Wesley, in a frantic frenzy to find them, lost his way along with his life.

The tears came again. Why did she go to that bonfire, to that evil place on the other side of the hollow? It was like a tempting flame drawing the weak and misguided moths to their demise.

If Ramona hadn't convinced her to go, if she hadn't taken his keys, none of it would have happened. No attack, no hiding a body, and Wesley would still be alive.

A burning and boiling rage stirred. The promise she made to Ramona dissolved, and an intense hate rose within her.

Chapter 43

It was Wesley's prized possession that found its way into that special box in her father's drawer. He had carried it with him always. It wasn't expensive but held value in how it was used and who gave it to him. The precise cuts of the small but sharp knife and tiny scissors that folded back neatly when he was done were used to cleanly finish the knots in the thin line tied to his flies. He used it for other tasks as well—cutting twine from hay bales, slicing an apple, removing a splinter. He never left the house without it.

Placing it in his pocket each morning was habitual, like putting on underwear or brushing his teeth. And with its bright red color and engraved initials, this gift from his father was distinctively his. Now, it sat cherished by the one who had gifted it as a reminder of what was lost. It had taken its place in the sorrowful box of memories.

Evelyn felt tears rise when she saw it there. She picked it up and rubbed her thumb over the "W" carved into the red metal. It felt out of place, like it should have been buried with him. Did her father purposelessly keep it as a remembrance, or did he forget to place it in the coffin?

At the funeral, the minister spoke of the new journey Wesley was now on, and Evelyn found herself wondering if he would miss not having his trusty tool where he was now. She closed her eyes and scoffed. It was nonsense to think he needed anything anymore. Wherever he was now, he certainly didn't need anything he had left behind, including her. But at that moment, the overwhelming loss drove home just how much she needed him.

He was really gone. He wasn't out in the fields. He wasn't in the hollow fishing. He wasn't on an overnight trip for a rodeo. He was never coming home, and she had never felt more alone. She no longer had a brother. Her entire life, she had felt the empty space left by her mother, but this loss felt like a cavern in her soul.

Was her mother with Wesley now? Is that what heaven would bring? She looked at the box of trinkets and thought that must be why her father kept them. It was a reminder that they weren't gone forever, just gone for now.

Maybe that is why she had always found comfort in his box of treasures. Her mother's ring was what she had always sought out when she needed to find solace. That is why she was there now. She hadn't expected to see Wesley's knife amongst them. It was the ring she had come to see.

She opened the little black box, expecting to see the satin pouch and shiny string, but as the lid popped up with its familiar crack, it was empty.

She squinted down as though it might suddenly come into focus, but, of course, nothing materialized. Evelyn turned the box over and then searched the corner of the larger box for any sign that it had fallen out. Had she forgotten to put it back into the tiny box? Of course not. She always left it exactly how her father expected it to be. He never knew about her escapades into his secret place, and she was determined to keep it that way.

Everything was exactly where it was supposed to be, including the little black box. For all those years, it was still in its place in that box of sorrowful treasures in the corner of her father's top drawer, as were the gold bracelet, emerald earrings, dozens of stock certificates and letters. Items that should have been in a safe or in a locked box at the bank but instead lay exposed in a dresser drawer. Everything was just as she had always left it, but the one item my mother was drawn to was missing.

Again, she worried that she had forgotten to put the ring back into the box the last time she had been there. It had been a while since she had looked at it. With all the horrifying things that had taken place, the attack, the crash, and the funeral, she hadn't had much time to do anything but try to wrap her head around the grief and the realization that her brother was gone. And to add to it, the worry and wonder if her attacker was dead or alive now haunted her.

They had heard nothing in the week since it happened, and her mind went back and forth between the horror of that night and the devastating loss of her brother.

She found herself in her father's room that day, not only looking for the ring but for the comfort it had always given her. She needed it so badly at that moment, and now her emotions turned to fear.

Then she wondered if her father had moved it, put it under some of the velvet fabric that held numerous other pieces of jewelry, or had he inadvertently knocked it further back in the drawer. Even closing the drawer too hard could do that. But why would the box still be there? She opened the square black container again as though the ring would magically appear.

Her shoulders sank. "No, no, no," she whispered as she lifted and pushed aside the other tiny pieces of her mother's life, silently praying that she would find it.

Now, her heart was racing as her careful examination of the drawer turned into a frantic search. Where could it possibly be?

She dropped down to the floor and ran her fingers over the thick shag carpet, worried she may have dropped it. She reached under and all around the dresser, but there was nothing in the dense mat. Defeated, she stood up and again reached in and around the open drawer.

She had sneaked into that room and stealthily sorted through those special items dozens of times. She knew her father's routine and was able to enter his private domain, admire the ring, daydream about the woman who had worn it, and place it back in the box, all with him being none the wiser.

For years, this had gone on. It wasn't daily or even weekly, but it was with some regularity. She used it often as a comfort, and as a teenage girl, there was enough going on in her life, whether real or imagined, that needed the small relief of holding something solid and filled with tiny glimpses of the person who once wore it.

Had she become lackadaisical and disturbed things enough for her father to notice? Had he figured out her secret scavenging into his hidden treasure and then decided to move it somewhere else? But just the ring? And for what reason? She often wondered why she felt it necessary to hide her stealthy visits in that drawer at all. Why would he care if she looked at what would someday be hers anyway? She was the only daughter. She was all that was left. Who else would be given those trinkets that held the memories of his past life? A life with the mother she wanted so badly to remember.

"What are you doing?" It was her father. He wasn't angry, but he was surprised to find her in his room, and the drawer, filled with what he held precious, opened.

Startled, she leaped back from the dresser, eyes wide. The hand that had been in the drawer was now behind her back. When had he come home? She was so enthralled with her desperate search that she hadn't heard him enter the house.

"I was just ..." she stumbled over the words. There was no good excuse, so she became defensive. It was what she had learned to use whenever they were at odds. "Where did you put the ring?" she asked.

His forehead creased, the bushy brows coming together in question.

"What?" He was already stepping toward the open drawer. He peered over it, scanning the objects.

She hoped her question had diverted his attention away from her being caught going through his things. Besides, were they really just his?

"My mother's ring," she said. "Where did you put it?"

He inclined his chin, confused about whether he should confront her about being in the drawer or defend himself against the accusation. He reached for the black box.

"It's not in there," she said before he could open it and see for himself.

He ignored her and popped the lid, and as she had said, it was empty.

He looked at her and then back to the drawer. He began to push the other items around, searching.

"It's not in here. I've already looked," she explained.

He stopped and then, still deep in thought, turned to her.

"Why were you in here?" Again, his tone wasn't anger but rather confusion.

She refused to accept that. "I didn't take it," she snapped.

"Well, how did you know it was in here?" he asked her. This time, his tone had changed.

Slowly, she pushed her shoulders back and lifted her chin in defiance. Caught and confronted, she felt a hot rush of anger. Without coming right out and saying it, he was again blaming her for the terrible things that were happening in their lives. It was her fault that Wesley tried to follow them out to the bonfire. He'd still be alive if she hadn't sneaked out and gone to the hollow. And now the large diamond ring—the prized possession and one of the only things left of her mother was missing, and there she stood, the only other person in that house. Again, the transgressor.

Her armor began to dissolve. The pain of so much loss was overwhelming—first her mother, then Wesley, then Ramona, and now one of the only things that gave her connection to what she'd lost. She began to feel as though her heart had been taken along with the precious ring. She didn't even know her mother, couldn't remember her face or her touch, but the ring gave her some sense of certainty. Her mother had been real and had left the ring as a symbol of her love. The engraving may have been done before Evelyn was born, but it spoke to her. "To E. Forever yours." Yes, the E was for Eugenia, not Evelyn, but deep within herself, she felt it was a message from the grave that said otherwise.

"I said I didn't take it!" she screamed at him.

"But there's no one else in this house!"

They both stood stunned with the realization of how true that statement was. It was just the two of them, and even with each other, they both felt alone.

She began to continue her rage against his accusation, but then her thoughts turned to the only person to whom she had ever shown that hidden treasure—Ramona.

CHAPTER 44

LANDIS

We sit side by side at the work table. I now have my own vise, pliers, and magnifying glass. He had extras, he told me, but these look new.

It's been two weeks since the crash, and my ribs still ache at times, but I'm now back to doing some of my chores; however, irrigation isn't one of them.

I'm allowed to walk the distance to Old Tom's because he says I need to start getting up and moving around. This came as wonderful news, and I've used this as an excuse to make my way back to his house. I'm pretty sure Mrs. Frost isn't completely happy with this, but surprisingly, she hasn't forbidden it.

When Mrs. Frost learned that I'd been spending time with Old Tom, I could see her disappointment, but what surprised me was how she was with her father.

The odd and awkward way they acted together was nothing like what I'd expect from a family, and I wondered why they seemed so distant. He lived right behind her, and until I was hurt and learned about their connection, I would have never guessed they were even related.

I had never had a father, but I always dreamed of how it would be if I did. Didn't they see how lucky they were?

Watching them interact was uncomfortable, and when I saw Mrs. Frost anxiously rubbing her fingers, I saw my own nervous habit and wondered if she, too, felt she was to blame for her scars. Since that first day I arrived, I've wanted to ask her about them, but like me, I'm sure it isn't something that she wants to remember.

Being in this little house, I feel an odd sense of calm, like I've been here years before. I know that's impossible, but there is something that makes me feel content in this space.

"This is a cool old house," I say.

He turns to me with a grin. "I don't know about cool, but it's definitely old." He takes a reflective breath. "I was born in this house."

"Really?" I ask, surprised.

He nods.

"You've lived here since you were born?"

"Not exactly. I moved away for a while. However, it's not so much the house but this entire place I call home."

A cold chill hits me. I've lived in so many different places, but they've never felt like home. Even in Sacramento with my mother, the only things I remember about that place are the things I wish I could forget.

He notices my quiet contemplation.

"Sorry, I bet you miss your home back in California."

I shrug. How do I miss something I hardly remember? I tell people that's where I'm from, but my only sense of home has been my mother, and I haven't lived with her in over ten years.

"I don't remember much about it," I admit. For years, I've told big stories about my time in California. I act like my current situation is simply a blip in what was an amazing life and one that I'd soon go back to. *Don't pity me. I'll soon be heading back and leaving all this behind.* My lies were my armor. But I don't feel the need to shield myself from Old Tom.

"I've hardly lived anywhere for more than a year, and none of it ever felt like home."

He looks at me, surprised at my candor.

"You haven't been here long, but maybe someday this place will feel that way." He smiles and then turns back to his work.

I feel a tug so strong I have to steady myself on the stool. For the first time in my life, I want it. I could stay in this place with these people, and this has my heart torn. The tug is the guilt I feel for wanting it. The pull is so intense I feel my eyes begin to sting, and I bite my bottom lip to keep them from leaking out.

"Tea?" Tom asks as he pushes back from the table and goes to the kitchen.

"Sure." My voice sounds croaky, and I clear it. "Thank you."

As he pours the water, I bring myself back. *Don't get your hopes up. This isn't going to last, and you know that. Someday, you'll leave, and it will all be just a memory.*

September seems to be rushing closer. The ticking of the clock on the wall is a reminder that my time is running out. I used to count down the months and weeks, but now I'm grasping at the hours and minutes I have left.

I push the thoughts from my brain and return to the fly I've started.

I have my hook in the vise, and I'm wrapping thread and then a fuzzy type of yarn Old Tom calls dubbing to make the body of the fly. The hooks are so tiny, and the thread so thin that with one small twist or bobble, the fly ends up looking contorted and botched.

Tom returns with the mugs and sets one on the bench at my side. I thank him again, and he settles back into his seat.

He takes a deep breath and stretches his arms and hands as though he's preparing to conduct an orchestra.

I try to watch without him noticing me studying him.

Old Tom's hands move quickly, and the thread goes onto the hook precisely. He makes it all seem so easy.

I look back and forth between his work and mine, and while I'm not unhappy with the way my fly is coming together, his has the sleek and perfect lines of a master.

This isn't a new fly, but one we've been working on. There are only two types he has taught me so far, and this is one I'm feeling good about. The thread is going on evenly, and the hair I'm tying to the top is flared just right.

I reach for the clippers to remove an extra piece of string and find that he is already using them. I then remember the pocket knife in my jeans has a tiny set of scissors, so I pull it out. Snipping off the excess thread, I smile to myself. I then feel him watching me. I hope he can see my work. My fly is feathered in just the right places, the string tied precisely and out of sight, and the colors are almost an identical match to the bug that I'm trying to duplicate.

I take a deep and satisfying breath and glance over at him. I expect to see him admiring my exquisitely tied fly, but instead, he's staring at my knife.

"Where'd you get that?" he asks. His eyes are wide.

It's more accusatory than curious, and I become defensive, knowing it isn't really mine. Can I really be in possession of yet another of Old Tom's missing items?

"I found it," I say. It isn't a lie.

He puts his hand out. "Can I see it?" he asks, and without hesitation, I give it to him.

He studies it and looks up at me with eyes that are confused and sad. I can see by the way he's holding it that it means something. He turns it over and rubs the crudely carved letters— WBF.

"I gave this knife as a gift to someone years ago."

"This knife?" I ask.

He nods, still studying it. "I had it engraved with those initials. It was a gift to my son, and when he died, I gave it to my grandson."

I look at the photos on his workbench. "Is that your son?" I ask, pointing to the photo of what looks like him and his two children around a campfire.

"Yes," he says sadly. "That's one of the last photos I have of him."

"How'd he die?" I ask, then cringe, feeling as though I've poked at his sadness.

Old Tom stares off as if seeing something from the past.

"It was a crash. It was a long time ago, but I still miss him very much."

"And this is your grandson?" I ask, motioning to the other photo. He's never mentioned a grandson. He's never mentioned any family. If I hadn't seen the photos on his workbench, I would have thought it was just him and Rusty.

I look back at the knife in his hand. "I found it. I swear," I blurt it out, convinced I'll be accused of stealing yet again.

He gives me a reassuring smile and hands the knife back to me.

I hold up a hand. "Keep it," I say. "You can give it back to him."

His eyes shoot up at me, and then his eyebrows furrow. He sits up straighter and takes a deep breath. "I can't. He's gone."

A twinge hits me. "He died?" I ask.

He stares straight ahead in thought and lets a long breath escape him.

"I'm sorry," I say, realizing he has lost both a son and a grandson.

He pushes the knife toward me. "I want you to have it."

"But," I begin to protest.

"Please take it," he says.

I pick up the knife and study it. I look at the initials engraved into the red metal. W.B.C. "Are W.B.C. your son's initials?"

He nods. "Yes."

"What does it stand for?"

"Wesley Benjamin Corrigan," he answers.

I flinch back. "Wesley?" I say, surprised. "That's my name."

Old Tom cocks, his head confused.

"My real name is Wesley," I explain. "But I go by my middle name."

He lifts his bushy brows and nods. "Is that so? My grandson also went by his middle name. He was named Gordon Benjamin, but he went by Benji," he says, still staring at the knife.

I'm stunned. It's Benji. The Frost's son who went missing. I shouldn't be surprised. When I learned that Old Tom was Mrs. Frost's father, I should have realized that Benji was his grandson. I look at the knife in my hand, and suddenly, it feels like I'm holding a ghost. A chill rushes up me.

He sees my realization, and his face turns sad. "Did they tell you about Benji?"

I shake my head. "Not really. But I did hear some stories about how he was missing. I didn't realize until now that he was your grandson."

He lifts an eyebrow and sighs. "That doesn't surprise me."

I sit speechless. I think about how Mrs. Frost tried to keep me away from Old Tom's place and how, even now, they seem more like strangers than father and daughter. I'm still surprised she's allowed me to spend any time back here after learning about our secret fishing trips. It makes no sense. There is a wall between them that I can only imagine must have been built long ago.

I look up at him. He's stirring his tea and looking sad and tired. I've spent weeks with Old Tom. He's been so good to me—patiently teaching me to cast, generously giving me his time. I've watched him tend his garden, point out the birds that frequent the hollow, and care for Rusty, the crippled old dog he saved. After all the years of waiting for my mother to return, I see the distance between them as such a waste. What I wouldn't do to be able to call someone like Old Tom "family."

I've never had a father, and whatever it is that is keeping Mrs. Frost from hers is something I'm sure I'll never understand.

CHAPTER 45

It was long before I came to be with the living, and yet the scene plays out as though I'm standing there now, watching it unfold.

Something called to her. Disturbing voices in Eugenia's mind had been growing for years. A combination of the trauma she still harbored from the loud blasts that shook the land and killed so many, coupled with the illness that festered, allowed the demon to easily enter her mind. It told her lies, gave her promises, and threatened her if she didn't do as it said.

My grandfather witnessed her troubling rants and distant stares into the nothingness of the dark nights. But often during the days, she was lucid and spoke as though nothing was wrong. The normality of life, caring for the house and children, was what he usually came home to, so when those dark episodes took place, he calmed her and let her rest for the day, alone in her room, until the cloud passed.

When she came back to herself, she often apologized, even cried for what she made him endure, and then weeks, even months, would pass without incident.

It was a typical winter in 1956. January brought thirteen inches of snow, and the temperatures regularly dipped below freezing. My grandfather knew she was struggling, having found her on the back porch staring out and telling the wind she was tired. Later, he would regret leaving, but he was desperately needed across town. A midwife had tried for hours to deliver a baby only to realize a cesarean section would be needed as the baby was breech.

"I'll be no later than ten," he assured Eugenia. He then turned to his young son. Wesley had just turned six. "Be a good boy and go to bed early tonight. Play with Evie in your room and let Mommy rest."

The little girl had been sick with a cold and slight fever, so he gave her some aspirin to help with the lingering headache and kissed her forehead, noticing it was still a bit warm, as he left the house.

Wesley had been watching over his younger sister for what seemed like years, so he took her by the hand and walked her upstairs, where they pushed toy cars through the carpet until both fell asleep on the floor.

He awoke to Evie's muffled whimpers and watched as his mother carried the girl, wrapped in a blanket, out of his room. He assumed she was taking her to her own room and putting her to bed, but soon, he heard the back door of the house open and close, so he went to his window and watched as his mother stepped into the deep snow and began to trudge while carrying his sister, out into the field and back toward the woods.

———

EVIE WAS STILL sleepy and unaware when the rush of cold wind hit her face. She startled and gasped but clung to her mother and tried her best to hide herself against the frigid wind.

She had no idea where they were going and soon found herself nodding off, lulled by her mother's rhythmic steps and soft murmurs.

"We're coming." She heard her mother call out through the whisper of frost, and she wondered if they were on their way to meet her father.

Her mother's march through the field kept going, and soon, Evie was deep asleep. Even the breeze couldn't keep her awake.

When the footsteps stopped, Evie's eyes fluttered open to see just the sprinkle of stars above her. The wind had ceased, and everything around them was still. Her mother's labored breaths were the only thing she heard.

"Where's Daddy?" Evie asked sleepily.

She got no reply.

Her mother took a deep breath and then stepped into the curtain of darkness.

"I've done what you asked. She's what I promised you. I'm begging you to keep yours."

Eugenia then sat Evie on the snow-covered ground.

"Who are you talking to?" Evie asked.

In the cover of the woods, she could see nothing, not even her mother's form, but she soon heard the crunch of snow as her mother's footsteps became faint.

Stunned, Evie came fully awake and called out to her. "Where are you?"

But there was nothing; even the sound of her mother's trek back was gone.

Evie tried to stand up, but the snow was deep, and when she used her hand to push herself up, she sank into it. Soon, she was cold and wet, and the realization of being alone sank in.

"Mommy?" she called. At first, it was thin and pleading, but soon, she was screaming out into the night, tears covering her face. When her desperate calls went unanswered, she sank defeated into the blanket and cried quietly, wondering who or what might be out there with her in those dark woods.

———

EVELYN DIDN'T WANT to move back to her childhood home. Not only would she feel obligated to her father for what he had given her, but she felt this secured her future by doing what he had planned for her all along.

She was already on that path, now pregnant and married to Gordon. Their growing family would need the room, is what her father told her, but she knew it was more than that. Any life she saw away from that stretch of pasture was now gone.

The homestead and land were Gordon's dream, not hers, but the pregnancy changed that, and Evelyn acquiesced to the fact that her life would now be that of a farmer's wife.

Gordon was thrilled with the idea of moving into that house and onto that land. His family owned several large plots on the other side of the county, but his father still owned the land, and with two older brothers, the likelihood of it becoming his was slim. Being given land, even if it was his wife's, would give them a huge leg up in their young lives.

It was when Evelyn was moving into her father's old bedroom that she found the truth about her mother.

While Evelyn was cleaning out her father's closet, she found an old shoe box on a shelf above and behind the door. It was something you wouldn't see just standing in that space, but only if you had a stool and were up above the high shelves. She opened it, looking behind her, fearful her father would catch her like he had done when she was a teenager, rifling through his secret drawer.

The newspaper clipping of Wesley's obituary was the first thing she saw, followed by some property deeds and water rights certificates. She ran a finger over the clipping, outlining her brother's smiling face. He was so young. The older she got, the more that sank in. She quickly sifted through the other papers in the box, seeing nothing of real interest, until her mother's name—Eugenia—caught her attention. It was a telegraph from England. Evelyn stepped down from the footstool with the box and dropped into the plush recliner draped with her father's clothes, still on hangars and ready to be moved to the little cabin.

A tingle went up her neck, but then her body went numb as she read the printed teletype giving the details of her mother's departure. The telegraph was to her father, telling him what ship would take Eugenia back to England to "recuperate."

Her mother returned home. That was what Evelyn heard, but what her childhood memories held onto was that her mother had gone to heaven. She hadn't left her but was taken. Evelyn now stared at the telegraph as the reality set in. Her mother didn't die. She had literally returned home.

Her mother had been sick. Evelyn knew that, but why did she have to go all the way to England for treatment? Weren't there doctors back then who could treat her here? After all, her husband was a doctor. They had two young children. Why would her father send her away?

Her childhood self had envisioned her mother lying in bed, fighting to hang on and eventually losing her battle. Evelyn was so young when it happened; she didn't remember much of anything, and she had almost no recollection of what really happened that night or any of the other smaller incidents. Even though she had been in the house, her father was able to shield her and remove the evidence before it could turn into a memory. Even the injury that left Evelyn permanently scarred was something she didn't relate to her mother. Secretly blaming it instead on an unknown and ominous threat lying in wait back in the woods.

Her father's grief-induced silence and her delusions of the mother she never knew but missed kept the truth shoved away and hidden like that shoe box.

The note explained that money would be wired and Eugenia's return to Tyntesfield would be in the best interest of all parties.

The wording was stiff and sounded more like a legal agreement rather than a plan to help her mother. The date on the letter was April 25, 1957. Evelyn was just four years old, and Wesley would have been six. She had no recollection of any of that. She had almost no memories of her mother except for what Wesley had told her, and he was so young, she wasn't sure if he really did remember their mother or if he had made up what he hoped she had been.

Even without knowing her mother, Evelyn always felt the hole she had left. It was there when she watched her friend Catherine's mother stroke a lock of hair behind her daughter's ear. It was there when she went alone to the small department store to buy her first bra. And it was there when she sat at the vanity trying to pin her own wedding veil to the top of her head. So many times, she pined for her mother, and yet, all she had were the memories told to her by her brother who'd only been six years old when she disappeared.

Her father rarely spoke of her mother, and when she did ask questions, his answers were short if she got anything from him at all. She was very sick and had gone home. She thought it was her father's gentle way of explaining death. Eventually, Evelyn stopped asking about her. She was gone, and her father never corrected her assumption that she had died.

As she sat with the brittle and yellowed telegraph, she wondered if anything she thought or had been told about her mother was real. Her father lied to her. Could it be possible that she was still alive? That question made Evelyn sit up straight. But if she wasn't dead, why had she never returned?

With the papers in hand, she set out across the large field to the small house tucked away in the cottonwoods near the river. It was a path she had taken hundreds of times as a young girl, but now it seemed so far away as her heart raced and her anger grew.

The uneven rows of dirt and dried remains of the winter wheat in the field made her stumble as she stomped toward where her father was unpacking.

As she reached the front door of the house, all of this came together in a chaotic rage.

"You sent her away," she accused, flinging the door open and finding him putting things away in the kitchen.

His expression went from surprise at her entrance to confusion.

"Why?" Evelyn continued.

He sat the stack of plates he was holding down on the counter and cocked his head. "What are you talking about?" he asked.

"I know that you sent her away, and I want to know why." Evelyn wanted to push the telegram at him but kept her fist clenched at her side. Let him lie to her first before calling him out with the proof.

He began to speak but then stopped and began again, but then his shoulders sank. He knew he'd been caught. "I didn't send her away. I thought it was odd that she didn't come around when Wesley was killed. I called and got no answer, so I went back there, and she was gone. She had left."

He took a deep and somber breath.

"Ramona?" Evelyn asked, confused. "You're talking about Ramona?"

He nodded. "Who are you talking about?"

Evelyn closed her eyes and sighed. "This isn't about Ramona. It's about my mother." She raised the hand with the telegraph. "I found this in your closet. My mother was sick, and you sent her back to England. She didn't die!"

He held up a hand. "She did die."

Evelyn held up the telegram. "No, she didn't. She was sent back to England."

"Yes. She went back to England," he tried to make her listen. "But then she died."

"Was it cancer? Why didn't you take care of her here?"

Thomas shook his head. "I wanted to, but it wasn't that easy. It wasn't cancer. It was something else."

"What was it then?"

Thomas looked down.

"Why won't you tell me? When did she die? When?" Evelyn screamed.

Thomas sighed. "Two years ago."

Evelyn took a step back as though she'd been slapped. "Two years ago," she said, the words barely able to escape her mouth. "She was alive all that time, and you didn't tell me?"

Tears welled in her eyes. "Why?"

Her father straightened and gave a resolute breath out. He took her hand, but instead of taking the telegraph, he turned her hand over, exposing the fingers with missing joints and digits. "This is why."

———

It was in the depths of those woods that she would take her child and give the persistent phantom who lived there what it wanted. Her offering would be what would finally give her peace.

The constant beckoning of that dark monster would be satisfied and then allow her to hear the voice no more.

The walk was slow and long. The snow was high with a thick crust that broke through and made a hole with every step.

"I want to go home," the little girl cried, but Eugenia marched on.

Her young daughter's cries were halted briefly because the wind made her startle and gasp. She was four years old, and while Eugenia was not a small woman, the child was difficult to carry in the deep snow.

Though wrapped in a pink crocheted blanket Eugenia had made herself, the cold was able to easily slice through and prick at the tiny legs and arms underneath. Eugenia made no attempt to comfort or silence her daughter. The only sound she could hear was the crunching of each step she took her closer to the thick line of trees that held the demon she was hoping to appease.

It would be a relief to them all. For so long, it had tormented her and, in turn, brought grief to those she cared for and loved.

When she reached the border of the woods, she paused and gazed deep into it. So often, she felt its pull and resisted. Now that she was there, it seemed far less angry, and when she took that first step in, she felt the wind cease and a calm surround her.

———

THE SURGERY THOMAS had gone to perform went quickly, and when he returned home, he found Eugenia in the rocker by the fireplace. The flames were low, and the glow illuminated her face. She didn't turn when he entered. She sat, unmoving, staring into the fire.

"Eugenia?" he asked, hoping to rouse her from her stupor, but there was no response.

"Daddy?" a small voice called, startling Thomas. He spun around to see his young son. The boy's cheeks were red and wet, and upon seeing his father's stunned face, he began sobbing.

"What's happened?" Thomas begged him, but the boy could only cry.

Thomas picked him up and went to Eugenia, standing in front of her and blocking her view of the fire.

"Look at me," he demanded.

She slowly raised her head to him but said nothing.

As he stared down at her, he saw the floor around her feet was a puddle of water. She had on her tall boots, and they were shiny and wet.

"What's going on? Where did you go?"

She blinked twice and then smiled absently. Softly, she said, "It's over now. It's gone."

"What's gone?" he asked.

She didn't answer and looked past him. Thomas, horrified at her strange demeanor, suddenly feared for his daughter.

"Evie. Where is she?" he asked, not expecting a clear answer.

His heart seized, knowing something was amiss. He set his boy down, bounded up the stairs, and threw open the door to her room. He ran to the bed and found it empty.

"Where is she?" he screamed down from the top of the tall stairs, but there was no answer.

Again, his son began to wail.

Frantically, Thomas called out his daughter's name. He went to each room and opened the doors, quickly scanning the area and calling out. Without luck, he ran back down to where his wife sat, placed his hands on her shoulders, and shook her, demanding her to tell him where the girl was.

"She saved us all. The sweet dear saved us all," Eugenia calmly answered.

"Where is she?" Thomas yelled again.

His son continued to cry, and between sobs, he pointed toward the woods. "She took Evie out there."

Thomas turned to his son. "Where? Where did she take her?"

Again, his boy simply pointed toward the wide expanse at the back of the house. "She took her out there and didn't bring her back."

Without thought, Thomas ran toward the back door. He flipped on the porch light, and in the crystal white blanket that reached all the way back to the woods, he saw the path of boot prints in the snow. He ran to the tall pantry doors and pulled out a large metal flashlight. He clicked it on, and with both fear and dread, he leaped from the porch and began to tread the deep snow, following the prints toward the dark haze of the frost-covered grove.

When Tom found his daughter frozen, with snot covering her face and barely breathing, he rushed her to the hospital, and all that he had tried to cover up for years came spilling out. It was his young son who divulged the gruesome scene, and as Tom watched the raised brows and wide eyes of the nurses and other doctors, he began to reel back his story in the hopes of retracting the horror his son had just released.

He tried to claim the boy was half asleep and that his little girl must have wandered away from the house, but how does a four-year-old walk in two feet of snow for over a quarter of a mile? And what about that wife of his? She had already been known to yell at the trees and stare out from the top-floor window of the large castle house. The little boy's story of his mother taking his sister to the woods didn't seem far-fetched.

He gave up the excuses as he watched helplessly, while they frantically tried to revive her. The truth of what happened hung like a dark haze in the room. His heart broke again as his daughter began to scream from the sensation coming back into her little body as her blood warmed. And while they were able to save his daughter's life, they were unable to save her fingers. He wept at the horror, knowing the bitter cold was too much for her tiny hands.

The dark cloud followed them home and stayed even after Eugenia was gone, and the guilt of what happened every time he looked at his little girl was often too much for him to bear.

He was a doctor. Trusted with the lives of those who lived in the county, and yet he hadn't been able to save his own child from the woman he knew was sick.

Retreating away from what he perceived as the whispers and stares of condemnation, the broken family holed up in the house he built for the woman who had caused it all.

"I don't know how long you were out there," my grandfather tried to explain to her. "If you hadn't been crying, I may never have found you. I was so grateful you were alive, but ..." He took both of her hands and rubbed the stubs where her fingers had once been. Instinctively, she pulled her hands back.

"We tried to save your fingers, but they had been exposed for too long. I've never forgiven myself for leaving you alone with her. I knew she was sick, but I never thought she'd hurt you."

Evelyn swallowed and shook her head slowly. "She left me to die in the woods?"

Thomas lifted his forehead, taking a deep breath. "She was sick. She didn't know what she was doing. I tried to get her help. I put her in the hospital, but her father wouldn't have it. He thought I was making it all up, so he convinced me to let her return to England. He said he would find her the best doctors, but I knew that meant she would never return. He never wanted her to come here in the first place."

"You told me she died when I was a four. She didn't die until I was in high school. Why did you lie to me?" she asked.

Thomas sighed, and with weary eyes, he looked down at her. "I thought it would be better if you thought she was dead instead of knowing the truth. I didn't want to lie to you, but how do you tell a child their mother left her for dead, caused her to lose her fingers, and that even though she is alive, she can't be with you ever again?"

"Did she ever try to come home?" Evelyn asked sadly.

He lowered his head and looked at the floor. "I don't think she ever got well enough to remember any of her life here. She was never the same." He then looked up pleadingly. "I'm sorry, Evie. I tried to take care of her, but when this happened, I knew I couldn't keep you safe. Her father told me they could get her help. I stayed in contact with her family, hoping she might get well, but he put her in a hospital. She was never going to be well enough to come back. I thought it was best that you didn't know any of it. You wouldn't have understood. I didn't want the only thoughts you had about your mother to be ..."

He couldn't say the words.

"That she tried to kill me," Evelyn said, completing his sentence.

"She didn't know what she was doing. I thought I was being kind by letting you think she had died," he said. "I thought I was protecting you and Wesley."

Evelyn's thoughts turned to her brother. It was less than a year since he had died. And yet, at that moment, all she could think about was that their mother had spared him. It wasn't Wesley who was left alone in the freezing woods. He didn't bear the scars of a mother gone mad. Why was she the one her mother didn't want?

Evelyn looked at her hands and placed them on her protruding belly. Her baby wasn't due for several months, and yet she already felt a fierce desire to protect the growing life inside her. What could possibly drive a mother to want to kill her own child?

Thomas saw her mind turning. "Evie, I thought I was doing what was best for you. I never wanted to hurt you."

But he had. All those years, she was led to believe that she wandered away and got lost in those frigid woods.

In his attempts to keep the truth about her mother swept away, her father had pushed her aside as well, and allowed her to believe she shouldered the blame for the loss of her fingers.

As Evelyn made her way back through the dusty fields to the house she had always known as home, she paused and turned toward the woods. The sway of the trees in the wind made the trunks moan and the leaves whisper.

All her life, every time Evelyn found herself glancing at that grove, she saw flashes of blowing snow, heard the howling cold, and felt frozen tears on her face. The cold and bitter sensation of being lost and alone is what kept her from venturing back there.

Along with blaming herself, she felt it was something back there that was responsible for the loss of her fingers. Ever since she could remember, she had looked at the woods and felt something waiting to take even more. And on the one night she faced her fears and stepped deep into those woods, she lost almost everything.

Something about entering into the dense and dark place brought evil and heartache. She had so many reasons for staying away. So she never went into those woods again—until the day they lost me.

Chapter 46

It was a source of comfort to sneak into her father's room, pull open the top left drawer of his bureau, and lift the lid of that wooden box. Inside were treasures. A dried flower with a pin, an 1878 silver dollar, a small grainy photo of her mother and father, a thick envelope, and a small black box that held a tiny satin pouch tied with a ribbon. Inside that cloth pocket was a ring. It was gold with delicate little leaves swooping up to where a large brilliant single diamond was set. It was the most beautiful thing she'd ever seen. The large center stone sparkled so brightly that it often made shimmering lights reflect on the walls of the room.

Evelyn felt her breath seize every time she pulled it from the cloth and let it dance in the sun. It was as though she was waking it from a deep sleep, and this was its way of thanking her with its glittery glow. It was her mother's ring.

It was something her father wished he could have given her mother when he proposed. However, at that time, he was a young doctor from a small farm town in America and not a wealthy English aristocrat like the men who came to call on her.

The courtship and marriage came about largely because of her insistence on working as a nurse while the estate her family owned was being used as a war hospital.

Instead of following her sisters and marrying men with large mansions, titles, and wealth, she balked at her family's traditions and rules and, with a thin band of tin, secretly wed the lowly American. She left her family and her place in society for a plot of farmland along Idaho's Snake River.

She never complained, but there was something in her eyes that had him convinced she regretted her decision, and he worried she resented him for it.

He became bent on making her happy by trying to create some small parts of the life she had left behind. Instead of the small farmhouse, he built her a large home with stone spires, a dark mahogany staircase, and an enormous fireplace. The people in town called it "the castle" and rolled their eyes at its pretentious opulence.

Above the intricately carved mantle of the fireplace hung a portrait of her posed and dressed in the same manner as the paintings he had seen hung in her family's England estate. It was a gift for the birth of their son. And when their daughter was born, he gave her a diamond ring to replace the crude tin band she wore. He had to travel to Salt Lake City to find something with a stone that large and flawless. Inside, he had it engraved with "To E. Forever yours."

"Is the E for me or Evelyn?" she asked him one day when he found her staring at the inscription.

"It's for Eugenia, of course," he countered, but she seemed unconvinced.

Was she jealous of her own child? Did he cause this by his gifts and expressions of love when the children were born? He fretted, and inside, he prayed she would be happy with the life he had given her. But as the months passed once his daughter was born, he saw her fall deeper into sorrow, and he blamed it on the life she had given up.

———

EVELYN WAS SO young when she lost her mother. Try as she might, she couldn't remember her. Not her face, her voice, her smell—nothing.

She felt like she remembered something because of the photos she had stared at since she was young, but she knew that was more wishful thinking than real memories. However, it did feel good to hold that ring and know it had once touched the woman who gave her life.

When she placed it on her finger, she wanted to imagine it on her mother's hand, but as usual, Evelyn cringed at the sight of her disfigured and missing fingers. She had become an expert at hiding them—never using her hands to talk and keeping her other fingers bent so as to keep the missing digits undetectable.

That is how she would admire the ring on her hand. All fingers bent, keeping the missing ones hidden, as she held it up to the light.

Her father never suspected she was looking through that box, and even though she felt he was planning to give her the ring eventually, Evelyn never discussed it, knowing it would only give away the fact that she was going through his things.

———

It was like any other day, so Evelyn wasn't sure why she decided to show Ramona the treasured box. For so many years, it was her own little secret. Her own ritual for tamping down her loss.

Ramona's eyes went wide when Evelyn revealed the ring.

"Is that real?" she asked.

Evelyn nodded. Even though she had never specifically asked, somehow, she just knew.

"If it's yours, why is it hidden in here?"

Evelyn shrugged. "He hasn't given it to me yet. He doesn't know that I know it's here. It's even engraved. To E. Forever yours." She didn't reveal that her mother's name was Eugenia, and the ring and inscription were actually hers. "I think he's waiting for when I get married."

"Married. Why?" asked Ramona. "It's the guy you marry who gives you a ring, not your father. Are you sure he's planning to give it to you?"

Evelyn felt her heart drop. What if he wasn't planning to give it to her? Who else would possibly be the recipient?

"It would be a gift from him, not my wedding ring," Evelyn tried to clarify. "Besides, I wouldn't wear it now. It might get lost."

Ramona was still studying the ring but lifted an eyebrow in response. "It's probably worth a lot of money. Why doesn't he keep it in a safe or something?" She handed it back to Evelyn and reached for the envelope. It made Evelyn flinch at her brashness. She didn't even feel that comfortable looking through those tiny bits of her father's memories.

"What's this?" she asked, pulling out and unfolding the papers. She squinted, reading the first few lines of the typed document, and then her eyes shot open, and she dropped it all as though it was on fire.

Evelyn gasped. "What's wrong?" she asked, gathering the papers from the drawer.

"It's your dad's will," she said, with a quiver. "It's like reading about someone planning to die."

Evelyn felt a chill go over her, but she straightened the papers and studied them. She had never looked or even wondered about the contents of that envelope before.

The meticulously typed document was full of long and complicated sentences that Evelyn didn't understand, but as she stood with Ramona reading over her shoulder, the words and their intent were clear. The entire farm, ranch, and land that her father owned, including the houses and even the items inside, would be left to Wesley.

"He is the oldest son. It's not like you'd live here after you're married anyway. You'd live somewhere else with your husband," said Ramona, knowing what Evelyn must be thinking. "The sons always get everything," she said, rolling her eyes. "And if you are like me, even if you don't have brothers, there's nothing to give you anyway." She then laughed. "I plan to get everything on my own."

Evelyn pretended to listen but was intent on finding her name somewhere in that will. She quickly poured over the papers, scanning every paragraph, but her name was nowhere. She gave a huff and shook her head as she folded the papers and stuffed them back into the envelope.

"I don't care. It's not like I was planning to stay here anyway. So what if Wesley gets it all? He can have it. I hate living here." And at that moment, it was true. The stabbing pain of betrayal was so deep that if she didn't let the hate fill her, the other would have been too much to bear. Knowing her father had overlooked her again and had chosen Wesley made the smoldering burn of resentment ignite a new fire.

Evelyn slammed the lid back on the box and closed the drawer. "Let's go to your house."

Ramona sighed. "But we were going to watch Bandstand."

With no television at Ramona's, it was about the only reason they spent time at Evelyn's.

At Ramona's, there was no one watching what they did or when they came in at night. They could smoke on the back porch or steal beer from the fridge, and Ramona's grandmother either didn't notice, didn't care, or simply didn't have the energy to confront them. It was different at Evelyn's. Her father was eager to ask about their plans. He tried to joke with them, but it was even worse when Wesley was at home.

For years, he paid them no attention and avoided their giddy silliness, but that year things changed. Ramona was no longer the skinny and awkward friend of his little sister but a strikingly pretty girl who listened to his stories and laughed at his jokes.

Instead of going with his friends on Friday night, Wesley found reasons to stay at the house when she was there. And Ramona made excuses to be downstairs instead of sequestered away with Evelyn in her room. Several times, Evelyn found Ramona on the couch with Wesley watching television, as though she had forgotten that Evelyn was upstairs waiting for her to return. Soon, neither Wesley nor Ramona were at the house at all, but in his truck at the drive-in movie or on a hidden lane somewhere near the river. At night, alone in her room, Evelyn would lay awake stewing and dreaming about Wesley going away forever.

———

THAT SPRING, eastern Idaho was covered in green and tiny dots of yellow and pink—some of the color that was to come. Most of the young people were feeling light and eager for the warmth to return, but Evelyn only felt the isolation of the rural farm and the loss of her only close friend to her brother.

"Show him that vest thing you made," Wesley said to Evelyn as he and my grandfather sat at the dining table.

My mother had just finished eating and was taking her plate to the kitchen. She rolled her eyes, knowing neither of them was really interested.

Her father saw the gesture. "What did you make, Evie?"

"It's nothing," she grumbled.

"I think it's pretty cool," said Wesley. He then turned to his father. "She wore it to school today. I heard her sewing machine going last night in her room. She made the whole thing herself."

Evelyn was skeptical of her brother's compliment, and his tone made it feel like he was ratting her out.

Her father turned back to her. "I didn't get to see it. I was out in the barn when you left for school this morning. Go get it. It must be special if you wore it on the last day of school."

Begrudgingly, she went upstairs to her room to retrieve the vest. She had hung it up carefully after school before her chores. It was a deep forest green with a satin trim. She turned it back and forth on the hanger, admiring it. Evelyn didn't just sew the vest; she designed it. There was no pattern or instructions. It was her creation completely. As she brought it back downstairs and to the table, her father smiled.

"This looks like something you'd see in the store. Sewing like this will serve you well. It's like cooking. Those are important things a girl will need to know."

He said it with all good intentions, but for Evelyn, her love of sewing wasn't something she did in some determined pursuit of becoming a wife, and this made his statement feel damp and condescending. Regardless of her talent, it was a skill of little value outside the realm of a housewife.

She knew that was what her future held, and while she wasn't against getting married and having children someday, the expected eventuality was disheartening.

"I think it's kind of ugly, actually," she said, tossing it over the back of a chair. "That's why I took it off when I got home."

Wesley scoffed. "Then why did you offer to make one like it for Ramona?"

Evelyn's chest seized. She had offered, but why did Ramona have to tell him? Now, her brother was mocking her, knowing her pride in the vest, and making it worse by revealing that he and Ramona were obviously talking about her.

Ramona. Her best friend. The one person she was able to talk to. The one who promised to keep her deepest secrets. Evelyn was not only crushed and horrified that Ramona was so tight with Wesley but also wondered what else her brother might know.

"Gordon sure likes that shirt you made him," Wesley said with a smile.

His best friend had been sweet on Evelyn for a while, but his shyness almost equaled hers, so most of their conversations were short and left both of them feeling awkward.

"You may need to make him some others. I think he's going to wear that one out he wears it so much."

Evelyn rolled her eyes and gave him an annoyed sneer.

"You should be proud of your work, sweetheart," her father said. He went to the chair and held the vest up. "I'm sure there are quite a few girls who wish they could make something this fine. It's no less than a work of art."

She sighed, but inside, she couldn't help but enjoy his praise.

Wesley came over and took the vest from his father. "If you don't want it, you should give it to Ramona."

Evelyn whirled around and snatched the vest from his hands. There was a loud rip, and both their eyes went wide. The seam was torn, and the threads of the delicate satin were exposed.

"Why'd you do that?" asked Wesley.

The sting of tears from the mindless act hit Evelyn like a wave. Her prized creation was now a tattered ruin, and she had no one to blame but herself.

"I hate you!" she seethed. Then she ran up the stairs and to her room.

CHAPTER 47

LANDIS

The sky is a dusky shade of blue, and the storm-filled clouds have smothered the sun and turned everything dark.

Even the river is murky and thick as I wade in. When did the breeze turn cold? The air is crisp and feels nothing like the dry heat that has been with us for weeks now.

My waders tighten against my legs with the weight of the water. My nerves tingle every time I feel the power of the river surrounding me.

I find a place just beyond the large pool where I've found success in the past and shore up my footing before taking my rod from its holder on the back of my vest.

I'm anxious to find what's out there, and instead of my normal wind-up of back-and-forth motion to release the line and extend the reach, I am quick to get the fly out and onto the water.

My cast is strong, and the fly lands, and while only a speck, it is bright against the black mirror of the water. It's one I tied myself. It's as though I've thrown part of me out there in the hopes that my hard work makes a difference.

For weeks, I've watched and emulated Old Tom arduously twist and fasten the tiny pieces of feather, foam, and fur with precise amounts of string and glue.

"To catch a fish on a fly is a thrill, but to catch a fish with a fly you've tied is like giving the river a piece of your soul," he says while looking through his large magnifying glass, tweezers, and thread in hand. "You'll get back what you put into it."

It's another skill he's teaching me simply by observation and patience. It's like watching an artist paint or a sculptor carve. The delicate weaves and knots eventually come together into a tiny replica of what the fish are searching for. The creations are both beautiful and functional.

Now, my creation is dancing on the water, and I'm hoping my focus on the details will pay off.

I can hear my breath and wonder why the roll of the current isn't filling my ears as it normally does. It's a hush. A whisper-like summons that I not only hear but feel, unlike the voice that calls to me when I'm near this place. Here. Here. This rustle in the wind is a constant nudging, and I look over to where Old Tom usually stands, but today, I'm alone. It's not the first day I've fished on my own. To come back to this place brings me a calm I've never felt. It buoys me, and even if I don't get a nibble, I always leave feeling intact and light.

It's the sound of the river, the chirp of birds, and the rustle of leaves. It's a melody that fills my soul—something I've never felt I had until now.

Drifting without a home, I've never felt part of anything, but being with this river, the woods, and the life that resides here, I feel at one with this place.

The line in my hand then jerks with a shot. I pull back, and with a stronger, even more powerful tug, the rod is almost yanked from my hands. I tighten my grip and reel back, but the strength of the fish is unlike anything I've hooked before. I reel and pull, reel and pull, just as Old Tom has taught me.

The rocks beneath my boots are sturdy, and I feel grateful as the pull of the fish has me, at times, off-balance.

"Keep the rod up, but keep it steady," I hear Old Tom say as I continue the fight, but the fish is so determined to flee I'm worried the rod will snap in two.

"Stay with me. Come on. Please just stay." I'm now begging the fish to relent. I see the line being pulled around in fast, large circles with no indication of the fish tiring. How can it possibly keep up this battle, and how long am I willing to hang on?

Then, the rod and line go slack. I fall back from the release of the tension. My heart drops. Have I lost it? Has the fish broken free?

But then, a massive dark form comes into view under the surface. It seems to grow and is now coming toward me. Its large body slithers forward, and I want to retreat, but I'm frozen. My feet can't move—it's as though they are glued to the riverbed below.

The dark form is just a few feet away, and as my heart races, I see a face in the water. Not the face of a fish but of a woman. Her dark eyes peer up at me, and a tousle of black curls floats around her face. This isn't real. It can't be real. Her expression is of torment and sorrow, and when she swims up to the surface, I see my hook in her lip. Instead of a fly, the ring I've carried all these years is what has lured her in. The face is my mother.

My breath sucks back into my body, and I yell out, "What's going on? Why are you here?"

With a quick flash, she dives back into the dark water and away. My line is then pulled, and I grab the rod to try to keep her there. Where is she going?

The rod is bent with the strength of her flight, and even though I keep reeling and pulling, the line just keeps spilling out as she gets further and further away.

I want to know how she got there and why she's trying to flee.

"Mom!" I try to call out to her. "Why are you leaving me? Mom, please come back!"

I pull and reel and pull and reel. The line comes in. It's working. I continue until my fingers turn white from my grip, but now I can see her shape in the bubbling roil of the water, and with everything I can muster, I yell, "Mom, please!"

For just a blink, her face emerges from the blur of the water, but I can see the resolve in her face. She can't stay, and I can't go with her. And with a quick flip of her head, the hook is released, and the weight of the pull on my rod is gone, and so is she.

I reel frantically until the ring is back in my hand. "No! Please stay. I have the ring. I have the ring." I yell, reaching out to her. I wipe the tears from my eyes, trying to see through the blur of where she has gone. But it's no use, and I stand back and watch the ripple of where she has swam away.

The wind becomes strong and surrounds me like a cape, as though trying to comfort me. It calls to me. "Landis." It's a voice I know, and I look frantically, trying to find who it is.

"I'll give you the ring," I call out, still hoping that will make her return.

"Landis." It's not the voice that calls to me in the hollow. This is a woman's voice. Not my mother's, but the voice is familiar, and again, the tears fill my eyes.

"Landis!" She calls again, even louder.

I try to go toward the voice, but my body is wrapped so tightly in the wind that I can barely move. And now I feel as though I'm being pushed from my place there in the river.

"Landis, wake up."

And when I do, I find Mrs. Frost leaning over me, her face wracked with worry lit by the dim moonlight shining through my bedroom window.

Chapter 48

I step away from the window and go to my bed. I push my hand in between the mattress and find the money I've been pilfering from what I didn't use for lunch. I know it's a pittance, but I have to try and pay for what I've done.

I count the bills. Fifteen dollars. That isn't enough to build a doghouse, let alone a barn. I have no idea what it would really take, but I know it's a lot, and I reach into my front pants pocket and pull the treasure from its hiding place.

It's what I've counted on to help us build our new life, and yet, if I'm stuck in jail, what good will that do? Maybe if I give it to Mr. Frost, he'll give me whatever is left after the barn is fixed. It might work. Or maybe they'll think I stole it and see even more reason for me to go to jail.

I have no choice but to try. I'll beg them to allow me to stay. It's only a few more weeks.

Making my way slowly down the stairs, I can hear her in the kitchen. The ring is clenched in my hand tightly. I don't remember ever carrying it outside of its satin pouch.

When I come through the swinging doors of the kitchen, she is standing at the sink. She sees me and startles a bit.

"Landis," she says. She then looks me up and down. "Is everything okay?"

I nod.

"You should be resting. If you need something, I'll bring it up to you. Now, go lay down."

"No," I say and walk closer to her. "I don't know what it will cost to fix the barn, but I want to pay for what I did."

She nods and takes a deep breath as though it's only words.

"I don't have money, but I have this, and I know it's worth a lot," I open my hand and show her the ring. "You can sell it."

She looks at the ring, and her forehead creases as she studies it. Then she reaches and carefully lifts the ring from my hand. My heart clenches. It's the only time anyone has ever seen it, let alone touched my precious treasure.

For a moment, she stares at it, stunned. She obviously sees the huge diamond and knows its value.

"I didn't steal it," I say.

She looks up at me as though she forgot I was there.

"Where did you find this?" she asks.

Surprisingly, she doesn't sound accusatory, just curious.

"My dad gave it to my ..." I begin to tell her but stop short. What if the story she told about my dad giving it to her was a lie? What if my mom stole it? Will she get even more prison time if that's true? Then my heart sinks. What if all this time, I've been carrying around and counting on something that really isn't hers? She said my father gave her the ring, but?

"Your mom had this, and she gave it to you," Mrs. Frost says.

Images of smoke, flames, and my frantic search for treasure fill my head. My mom didn't give it to me; I scavenged it and saved it from the fire I caused. The fire that sent my mom to prison, and with that, me having to go from one house after another. The scars on my hands begin to throb, and I rub them together to take the terrible images out of my head.

I swallow hard. How do I make up a lie now? I avoid her question. "I'm sure it's worth something and can help pay for what I wrecked."

She squeezes the ring in her palm and closes her eyes. She looks pleased. Maybe she won't kick me out after all.

When she opens her eyes, she sighs and looks at the ring again.

"I know this ring," she says.

I flinch back. How could that be?

She sees my disbelief and nods. "My dad used to have it hidden in his drawer, and I sneaked in and looked at it. I thought it was lost forever."

"Old Tom had this ring?" I ask.

She smiles and then lifts the ring and points to the tiny engraving inside the band. "To E. Forever yours."

I shrug, but then it hits me. The E must stand for Evelyn.

"I swear I didn't steal it," I blurt out, realizing what she must think.

She lifts her eyebrows and sighs. "I know you didn't. I'm just surprised to see it. For all these years, I thought it was lost."

I had wondered about the engraving. If my father gave it to my mother, why would it say "To E" That isn't my mom's initial. But I realize now that it is Aunt Evelyn's.

"The E is for you," I say.

Mrs. Frost gives a genuine smile. "No. I used to pretend it was when I was a child, but it isn't. The E is for Eugenia. That's my mother's name. My father gave it to her."

She has the ring on her finger. It's the one that isn't damaged, but she has it bent with the others that are missing the tips. She's still admiring the ring. "I used to sneak into my father's room and look at it. One day, it was gone." Her face turns sad.

"I'm sorry," I apologize. I didn't steal it, and yet, somehow, I feel I'm to blame.

She looks up. "Landis, you didn't know, and you didn't do anything wrong."

I can't help but feel strange about having this precious piece of Mrs. Frost for all those years. This ring that once belonged to Old Tom's wife. And again, all I can think is—how did this happen?

"Are you going to tell Old Tom?" I ask, worried about what he might think when he finds out I have it.

She lowers her brows in thought and then sighs. "Someday, but right now, we need to talk about you."

The pain in my side increases as I lean back against the kitchen counter, weary with what she's about to say. Here it comes, I think. She's going to tell me that I need to leave. For a moment, she just looks at me, but then she directs me out of the kitchen and to the table. She pulls out a chair.

"Wait here," she says, and she quickly goes upstairs, leaving me confused and unsettled.

I hear doors opening and things being moved, and then a few moments later, she comes back to the table holding two frames. They are turned toward her, not ready yet to reveal. She takes a seat and then gives me a small and somewhat sad smile.

Inside, I want to beg her not to make me leave, but I'm also curious what the purpose of the frames could be.

She looks at me, gives a long sigh, and then turns it towards me. I'm surprised to see it's identical to the photo Old Tom has propped up on his table. It's the family photo of Old Tom and his daughter, who I now know is Mrs. Frost, and his son, who died.

"That's the same photo that Old Tom has," I say.

She smiles. "It's my dad, me, and Wesley," she says.

I nod because I already know this. "Your brother that died," I say. "Old Tom told me about him before I knew about you."

"Did he?" she asks.

"Yes. He told me he was killed in a crash when he was nineteen years old."

Her face turns somber, and her brows knit. "Yes. It's not a very good picture, but it's the last one we had of us all together."

She then turns the other frame. It's a boy about my age. He's wearing a shirt that looks like the shirts Mrs. Frost makes, and he has a big smile with a gap in the middle.

I find myself using my tongue to feel the space between my own teeth.

I cock my head and study it. "Is this your brother?" I ask. He looks like a younger version of the blurry photo of the family.

"It is," she says with a smile, but then she turns serious. "Landis, I think my brother is your father."

My eyes go wide as I look from the photo up at Mrs. Frost. "What?" I ask, stunned. "Why would you think that?"

"Because your mother used to live here when she was young. She lived in the house that my father lives in now."

"The old cabin?"

She nods. "She was my best friend, and she and Wesley were ..." she pauses, searching for words, "they were together. Last year, I got a letter from her that said she had a son, that Wesley was the father, and that she wanted you to come and live here."

I shake my head, completely baffled by what she is saying. "She lived here? That can't be. She told me that when she was young, she lived on a lavender farm. She said my dad was in the army." I hand the frame back to her as though it's on fire. "This isn't my dad."

"Wesley was supposed to leave for the army but then he died."

Mrs. Frost takes the picture and places it with the other on the table. She leans forward and meets my eyes. "I'm not positive that he's your father, but when I look at you ..." she sighs. "Ramona lived here and was with Wesley. She disappeared right after he was killed, and I never knew where she went. All I know is she wanted you to come here, and when I saw that your birthday was seven months after she left ..." She lifts the ring. "It was soon after she left that we realized the ring was missing too."

"You think she stole it?"

She shrugs. "At the time, I did. But now I think that maybe Wesley gave it to her. Maybe he knew about you."

Maybe he knew about me. I sit for a moment, thinking. It's so much to contemplate. Too much. I keep thinking about what my mother has told me over the years, and I want to call her and demand that she tell me what's real.

"I need to talk to my mom," I say, pushing the chair back and standing. Then I wince at the pain in my side. "Why didn't she say anything about this? She never told me about you or Old Tom or this place. She never said she lived in Idaho. She said it was a lavender farm, not potatoes and cows. They grow lavender in places like Washington and Oregon and England." A hard twinge hits me. England. Now I'm rambling. I'm not just confused but angry. If this is all real, why didn't my mother tell me I had family? For years, I was shuttled from one strange place to the next while being told I had no one but her.

"She lived back there?" I ask.

Mrs. Frost nods.

"For how long?"

"Not long. Maybe five or six years. We were around twelve when she got here. I believe she had just turned eighteen when she left."

I think about Old Tom and, if what she says is true, what this would mean for both of us. My grandpa. It's something I never fathomed I'd ever have, and now I wonder what he thinks. Or if he is even aware. I look in the direction of the little house in the woods.

"Does he know?"

She bites her bottom lip. "I haven't said anything to him."

"Why not?" I ask. And then the doubts begin to grow. If I truly am her brother's son, why would that be kept from the man who is my grandfather?

She looks down, searching for words, and then takes a deep breath.

"When I got Ramona's letter, it was a shock. I hadn't heard from her in so many years. I didn't know what to think, and before I could even start arranging to get you, Benji went missing and ..."

She puts her hand to her mouth.

I allow the skepticism to take over my mind. This can't be real. Why wouldn't my mother tell me anything about this place and instead fill my head with lies about a lavender farm?

Lavender. It hits me so hard that I have to hold onto the counter.

Mrs. Frost tries to keep me from leaving, but I have to get away. And before she can stop me, I'm out the door and headed back toward the woods.

My ribs ache with every step, but I continue toward the place that summons me.

Chapter 49

When I reach his house, I find him in the garden. He's bent over, digging at something, and when he notices me, he stands upright, his brow knitted.

"What is it?" he asks, obviously seeing my distress.

I don't know how to answer. What do I tell him?

"I wasn't expecting you until tomorrow." He walks toward me, removing his dirt-covered gloves. "I hope you aren't thinking about going fishing. Your ribs aren't quite up for casting." He smiles, but when he sees I'm not smiling back, he stops, and his face pinches with worry.

"What's is it, Landis?" he asks.

I hear the phone inside his house begin to ring and know it must be Mrs. Frost trying frantically to find me or warn him of what I've learned.

He hears it, too, and turns toward the door but stops and decides to ignore it.

"I just needed to get out of that house for a little while," I tell him.

His eyes are still draped with concern, but he nods. "I know it's hard to stay put, but you need the rest." He begins to direct me inside, but I hesitate.

Something has called me to that place, and I find myself moving toward the side of the house. The closer I get, the faster my heart begins to beat.

"Come in and sit down for a while," he urges, but a fragrant breeze pulls me until I'm standing at the edge of the field, dotted with large bushes. I feel my breath catch. The normally muted limbs are swaying and covered in deep purple blossoms.

The hot sting of tears fills my eyes. I wipe them away, and when I turn to him, he's watching me.

"What's wrong?" he asks.

"They're lavender bushes," I say.

He looks confused but nods. "Yes. English lavender," he says. "I told you my wife was from England. I planted them for her. Why? What is it?"

I feel my eyes begin to fill again, and I swallow, trying to keep them at bay.

"My mother used to talk about living on a lavender farm and how someday she wanted me to live there too." My voice cracks, and I clear my throat.

Through the blur, I look over to him. "Did a girl used to live here?"

Without pause, he nods.

"What was her name?" I ask. I'm sure I already know, but I want to hear from him.

He cocks his head at me, confused, and then a veil of understanding passes over him, and his face turns to shock. Now he knows, too, and he says her name. "Ramona."

The validation releases my greatest fear. My mother's not coming for me. I've been dumped here. It may have been her plan to come for me in the beginning, but now I see that for years, she has been grooming me for an eventual life on my own. She played upon the emotions of Mrs. Frost by presenting me as the child of her dead brother and, in the face of losing her own son, Mrs. Frost agreed to take me in. She didn't even believe it was true at first. I was just some boy without a home. It's been the story of every place I've lived in. It isn't my home. I'm a visitor who eventually wears out their welcome and needs to move on. Even if I am their real nephew, what do I offer that would make them want me to stay?

I can't bring back her brother or son. I can't take their place. All my plans now lay in ruins.

The sounds of tires on gravel shake me from the whirlwind in my mind. I hear her before I turn to see Mrs. Frost standing on the back porch. She's gone through the house and out the back door and found us here. She's wringing her hands, rubbing them the way she does when she's worried or scared.

"Evie," says Old Tom when he sees her. His daughter, and yet he looks so surprised to see her.

She looks from him to me.

Old Tom clears his throat. "He's Ramona's …"

"Yes," she says, turning back to him.

I watch as his eyes search her face for answers.

She tries to look away, but then Old Tom drops the bucket he's holding, and little red tomatoes spill out. His face pinches, and he whispers, "Wesley?"

Her nod is small but giant in what it confirms.

Now they both just stand, staring at me like they've seen the ghost of the man they say is my father. I still don't know if it's really true, but they obviously feel they do.

I am now feeling like I've run a mile. I want to argue because they can't be certain, but for now, I relent and just sigh.

Old Tom walks toward me and motions for us all to go inside. I hesitate, not knowing what to expect or do. Will they want to interrogate me on what I know and what my role was in being there? Do they think I had a part in my mother's scheme to find me a place to live? Although I've suspected for years, the chances of her actually coming to get me now feel slim to none. I've been on my own, and now even her last-ditch efforts to pawn me off will be fruitless.

The three of us sit awkwardly on the sofa and two cushioned chairs in Old Tom's tiny front room.

"Look what Landis found," says Mrs. Frost, reaching into her pocket and pulling out the ring.

I close my eyes and sigh. Now Old Tom is sure to think I'm a thief. I've ended up with both his dead wife's ring and his dead son's knife.

I hear him gasp. "Is that really it? I thought it was lost forever."

I open my eyes to see him holding it, admiring the ring like he's greeting an old friend.

He looks at me. "Where ...?" he then holds up a hand. "It doesn't matter. I'm just so glad it's been found."

He's smiling, but then it turns to whimsy, and he looks at Mrs. Frost. He holds the ring out to his daughter.

She is surprised and shakes her head, but he insists. "It's yours," he says. "It was always supposed to be yours."

She looks hesitant, as though she's not sure of what he's saying. I feel a mixture of happiness that Mrs. Frost has been given back the lost relic of her mother, but I'm also sad knowing that if it was always supposed to be hers, then my mother did, in fact, steal it.

Before accepting it, she turns to me. "Thank you, Landis."

I feel compelled to apologize, but before I can say a word, Old Tom lets out a chuckle.

"I'd say Landis is good luck. Show Evie what else you have," he says, and I cringe inside again. I begin to act like I'm unsure what he's talking about, but it's futile, and I pull out the knife and hold it up for her to see.

Her eyes go wide. "Wesley's knife," she says. "He used to have that with him all the time." Her demeanor then goes dark. "Benji," she whispers. I can see her mind spinning.

"How did you get this?" she asks.

"I found it." I begin to tell her where, but then I'd be giving away my secret path into the woods and to the river.

Old Tom sees my hesitation. "Where exactly?" he prods.

After all that has been revealed today, I have no energy to keep up my lies. Mrs. Frost already knows I've been sneaking back here just to fish with him. What difference does it make in how I get here?

"I found it at the overflow."

Old Tom cocks his head. "The overflow?" he asks.

Mrs. Frost looks from him to me and back again. "What overflow? Where?"

Old Tom stands up. "Find Gordon," he says to her.

She shakes her head, confused. "What is it?" she asks.

"I'm not certain, but I want you to find him and also call the sheriff. Tell them both to meet me here."

She's not willing to leave without some explanation. Old Tom sees this and puts his hands on her shoulders.

"I'm not sure what this might mean, but Benji didn't go anywhere without this knife either."

The dismay of what this could mean is evident in her eyes, but she complies, leaving me alone with Old Tom.

"Why were you back at the overflow?" he asks.

I bite my lip and reveal my secret route. "There's a trail that leads to the back of the house. It's a shortcut."

"Is that how you get to the hollow?"

"Yes."

I wait as he processes what I've told him.

"I want you to take me there."

I nod, and he walks toward the back.

"Now?" I ask.

"Yes."

We're out the door, and I realize rain has started. Tiny drops hit the ground and the young leaves of the plants in the garden. Seeing he has no intention of letting it stop him, I lead him in the direction of my covert path. I feel like I'm revealing a secret I've promised to keep —but to who?

He looks out over the river as we walk. The flow is high, and the water is white where the crests break, making the rush even louder.

A crack of light and a thunderous boom make us both pause a moment, but he gestures me forward. I still wonder if he believes me and why he is determined to see the spot. I offered to give the knife back, but he declined, and now it feels heavy in my pocket.

The thunder rumbles again, and then I hear the voice. "Fear." I look up and around. Even after all this time, I still expect to see someone.

"What is it?" Old Tom asks, but I just shake my head and keep walking. I see the area up ahead, and I point it out, but water has risen to where I can't clearly see where it is. I cross, and now I'm wondering how I'll get back to the house. There was but a trickle when I crossed just an hour ago. It has come up so quickly, and being unable to swim, I would never be able to cross or even try.

We walk up to the tip of the trail, which takes a steep dive down. At this point, even the path is covered, and more is beginning to pour in. The trees along the banks thrash wildly as the water reaches up and pulls at their willowy arms.

"It's full of water," I say.

Old Tom looks at me oddly. "It's where the water is diverted when the river is high. Is this where you found the knife?"

"Yes," I say and try to point out the area, but there is nothing but several feet of dark, muddy, churning water.

"There's usually a big dip in the path. There is never this much water. I found it stuck in the gravel up against the bank," I tell him.

A cold wind bursts from the trees. "Fear!" It calls out so loudly that I take a step back.

When I look over at Old Tom, he is standing, stunned, with an expression that tells me he had to have heard it, too.

We're both silent as the breeze picks up leaves, dances in circles, and snakes around us.

Then the wind stops, and in a still small voice, "Here," is what the voice calls.

Here?

"Here," it calls again. Is that what I've been hearing this entire time? Was it always telling me that? I listen closely, ignoring Old Tom's stare as the rain comes down in sheets.

Old Tom shakes his head and then looks out toward the woods. His voice is low and grave. "All this time, I've been in fear of what I might find if I looked."

"Here." The voice is now calm. It is now clearer than ever. It wasn't fear that I heard calling me but the nudging of what needed to be found.

I feel an overwhelming rush of relief. I'm not sure why or how, but the breeze has now buoyed me to where I feel it could lift me off the ground.

"It was here," I say. "This is where I found it."

Old Tom takes a faltering breath, looks at the swelling channel, and then, with red eyes, wet from both tears and rain, puts a hand on my shoulder. I'm not sure if it's to reassure me or to steady himself.

"Come back to the house," he says over the pounding of the storm. He begins to direct me toward where we came from, but then he stops and looks back. I follow his gaze and see Rusty sitting at the side of a tree, rain pelting his already dripping fur. He looks out at exactly the area I pointed to earlier.

And that is where they found Benji.

CHAPTER 50

"Where do you think you're going?" she asks.

I thought she was in her sewing room and wouldn't see me leaving.

"I'm going to Jeremy's," I lie.

She twists her head skeptically. "Jeremy is in Salmon with his father."

I stop and throw my hands out, frustrated. "I need to get out of this house," I say with venom so she knows that I want to be away from her.

She grabs a yellow and green sponge and begins to wipe the counter with vigor. "Grounded means grounded. You stay in this house until I say you can leave."

"You can't keep me locked up like a prisoner. I'm not a child."

She stands straight and glares at me. "You're my child, and until you're old enough to be on your own, you will do what I say."

"I can't wait for the day I can get out of here." I'm feeling emboldened and angry, so I push past her and head for the back door.

"Benji, I told you, you are grounded!"

"I'm just going for a walk," I say. I want to lash out, throw something, or just run until I can't breathe. Why is she doing this to me?

"I know exactly where you're going, and I told you, I don't want you near her."

I roll my eyes, give a huff, and continue walking toward the back door. "How can I go near her when you took my keys? She lives all the way over there, remember? I'm just going for a walk back in the woods."

"You're lying," my mother says calmly.

I feel a pulse of uncertainty hit me. Could she possibly know? She never wants to go anywhere near the woods or the river, but has she somehow found out about the bridge?

I try to act like her ability to see through me isn't working. "You don't know anything," I say, and I step toward the door.

She looks at me like I've grown horns. "Don't you dare leave this house."

My hand is now on the doorknob, and my heart is pounding.

I turn and stomp. "This is stupid. You can't keep me locked up inside."

"Benji, I'm not going to argue with you. I don't want you over there."

I'm frustrated and can feel my anger begin to boil over. "Why?" And yet, I know exactly why. My mother has held on to a grudge for almost two decades, and it has nothing to do with Laura. My mother has never even met her. But what runs along Laura's house and in her veins is why my mother can't accept the fact that I love her.

"Because her last name is Jenkins?" I spit out at her.

She says nothing, but I see her bristle.

"You don't even know her. This has nothing to do with Laura. You don't like anyone who lives on that side of town. Why?" I'm now yelling.

This only shuts her down. Her eyes are red and becoming wet. Is she angry? Or is she sad? I'm confused and perturbed that she's so adamantly against me being with Laura that it's bringing her to tears.

"What'd they do to you that makes you hate them all so much?" I demand.

She takes a sharp, shuddering breath in. Shaking and with fists clenched, she yells back at me, "I mean it, Benji. I don't want you over there."

I give an amused huff and stomp off. "I'm going. I don't care what happened before. It's not her fault."

She whips around, hand gripping the sponge so tightly that water drips onto the floor. "If you leave this house, that's it!"

I pause and shake my head at her threat. "What's it?" I ask.

"If you leave this house—you're not coming back."

The words that would haunt her—because it's exactly what happened. I left, and I never came back.

Of course, she said it, never believing it would end like this, and even then, during that heated and fiery exchange, I knew she didn't mean it. But now she feels she had a hand in my demise. That somehow, those words are why I am lost. How I wish I could erase it all, but I know as I linger here watching, the past is the one thing that always remains.

I gave my mother a disgusted humph when she leveled her ultimatum. I then grabbed the doorknob, stepped out of the house, and slammed the door behind me.

My face was hot, and my head was pounding as I stormed out. Rusty followed along, his happy pants a direct contrast to my angry grumble.

I stomped through the field; the ground was uneven, and large clumps of tilled soil impeded me, making my intentional and angry steps uneven and awkward. This only added to my anger, and I reached down, grabbed one of the large dirt clods, and hurled it across the pasture.

My mind was reeling, and I could think of nothing but going against what my mother demanded. I was already late for our meeting, but I hoped Laura would wait. Daylight was beginning to wane, but I needed to see her more at that moment than any other time I had made that trip back to our meeting place.

Rusty followed along as he always did, but as we got closer, he let out a little whine and stared off into the trees as though something was there watching us.

The noises of the woods are intensified as the sun begins to fade. The chirp of crickets, the rustle of dry leaves, and the constant rush of the river that borders it are all sounds I know. And while I've been alone back in the trees and brush many times before, this time, my breathing is quicker, and my heart jumps with every snap of a branch as I make my way back to Laura.

Kevin threatened to kill me if I went across that bridge to see her again, and my mother told me that if I left, I was not to come back. I ignored both of these threats. I saw Kevin's as empty and my mother's as emotional. It didn't matter either way because when I got to the top of the canal bank, Laura wasn't there, and the bridge, my only avenue across, was gone.

The ropes and boards hung in tatters. I quickly scanned the area for any sign of Laura, but I was alone on the banks and saw no one in the fields on their side.

Again, I studied the remains of the bridge. It laid against the steep concrete bank of the canal so long it almost touched the water. My mind quickly went to Kevin, sure that he was behind it all, but then I realized that made no sense. Someone had severed the ropes that secured it to the cement anchor on the bank. The frayed strands still clung to the base, but the bridge was still tied to the other side. The bridge had been cut by someone standing where I was at that moment.

If the reason for destroying the bridge was to keep me from seeing Laura, then it couldn't have been Kevin. Even if he had come across and cut the ropes, he would have been stuck. It had to be someone from over here.

My mother wanted to keep me away, but she didn't know about the bridge. My entire life, I had never seen my mother take a step back into the woods. She thought I had been driving over, which is why she took my keys. My grandfather was the one who taught me to fish and who loved the river, but I had even kept that hidden trail and bridge a secret from him. The only person from our side who knew about that bridge was Jeremy.

Jeremy? Was he that upset about me and Laura that he would risk being caught destroying the bridge? It made no sense, but who else would want to keep me from going over?

I then heard the crunch of footsteps. I turned quickly toward it but saw no movement. Am I being followed back here in the woods? I began to conjure up who it could be. Did Kevin sneak back here and cut the bridge to make it look like it was one of us? Was he waiting for me to come, and is he stalking me now?

I held my breath and listened. After a moment, I began to question my own ears, but then, in the distance, the footsteps were there again. Were they coming toward me or going away? The moonlight illuminated the space between the trees and I see a dark form dart from one tree to another. It isn't a deer or other animal, but a person. But is it Kevin? Rusty barks, sensing it, too. I hush him, and he comes to my side and pants as he looks in the direction of this thing in the shadows.

A loud crack of a branch breaks the silence, and Rusty lunges toward the noise.

"Who's there?" I yell out.

There is no answer, but again, I see a form moving away from me. It's someone small, so I know it's not Kevin. Someone else is hiding back within the trees. They are trying to flee. What has them running from me? Is this who cut the bridge? I try to run toward them, but Rusty follows. I keep my arms out in front to block the hanging limbs as I try to run in the low light of the moon. Rusty leaps over the fallen branches and is now gaining on them. I tried to call him back, but he ignored me, intent on the chase.

Soon, he is out of sight, and I am scanning the woods frantic to find him, worried whoever he's chasing might hurt him. I then hear a crash of brush and a small scream. It's a girl. Could it be Laura? What other girl would be here in these dark woods? Did she somehow make it across the bridge? But if it is her, why would she run from me?

"Stop running! It's me! It's Benji!" I call out, hoping she'll hear me and stop, but she doesn't.

I follow the sounds of Rusty's barks, and soon, I'm upon them. Rusty's tail is wagging, and he's panting with excitement.

Dressed in a black jacket with a hood over her head, she's turned toward the tree and is struggling to stand.

"Laura," I say. "Why are you running away from me?" I ask.

She doesn't answer but uses the tree as a brace and pulls herself up. Then, without acknowledging me, she again tried to run. She seems to know what direction she is taking as she begins to head east —the exact opposite direction of the bridge. Before she can clear the branches that tripped her, I lunge forward and grab her jacket. She tries to pull free, but I hang on, and as the moonlight glows around us, I yank her toward me, and the hood of her jacket falls back.

"Leave me alone," she begs, and then I see it isn't Laura.

I'm so shocked that I release the jacket, and she runs off, leaving me standing stunned and Rusty wondering if he should chase after her.

Chapter 51

She followed me back. Ever since she was a little girl, she has been there—not really with us, but in the background. Nicole was less than two years younger, but she was always Jeremy's little sister, and while we were never mean to her, as much as she tried, we did our best to keep her from tagging along.

Things changed a bit when we entered junior high. Nicole and her friends began to hang out with us as a group, going to the trestle to swim or sledding on the foothills in the winter, but when it came to fishing, that was Jeremy's and mine alone.

The pursuit of the phantom was something we didn't share with her or with anyone. Our friends were aware of our adventures from the stories we told about our epic quests, but no one knew how to find our hidden spot. It was only my grandfather who knew the route to the hollow because he was the one who gave me that elusive and precious gift.

I had just turned twelve the summer my grandfather took me back to the hollow. It wasn't until the following year that I hesitantly but excitedly took Jeremy and showed him the mecca where we would spend every waking hour of early spring through late fall that the following year.

He was my best friend—like the brother I never had, and I could tell he felt our bond was even stronger with my sharing of this secret spot.

We both had our chores on our family farms, and now that we were older, we were also expected to take part in the roundups, brandings, harvests, and other events that would mold us for what our future held. But the moment those things were done, we would steal back to where our paths met in the woods and make our way to that wondrous, swirling cove we called the hollow.

The summer I met Laura all that changed. The hollow became something more. For Laura and me, that wide and magical place seemed to pull us in, embrace us, and protect us from whatever was outside of it. The hollow was a place we both independently discovered and where we found each other. I was convinced it was a sure sign of what was meant to be.

We were so young, but I didn't see it that way. If what we had wasn't real, how could I possibly feel so strongly? I'd never been more certain about anything.

I was excited to talk about her, but found little interest in return.

"She's okay," said Jeremy with a shrug. "But it's not like you're going to marry her."

I shrugged at his comment, not letting him see that I had every intention of doing just that.

It's why I was so careful to keep our meetings in the hollow a secret, telling my friends I'd met Laura at school. I didn't want Jeremy to know I had broken my promise and given our secret away, even if Laura had found it on her own.

My parents saw us as something that would ultimately fade. "Puppy Love" my mother called it before knowing where Laura was from, and when they found out, a battle brewed. But when Laura's brother learned about us, the battle became an all-out war.

I felt interrogated at the dinner table, and at school, Kevin sought me out to accost and threaten me, making my friends question my devotion to Laura even more. Of course, none of this worked to diminish my feelings. The more they all tried, the fiercer I became.

Even as Laura began to back away, I found myself clinging on and begging her not to give up. This made the fight with my mother and my furious stomp back to the bridge even angrier. Was I the only one who felt this way?

———

When I had been at the bridge and found it cut and hanging, there had already been several visitors before me that day.

All I could do was stand there defeated. There was part of me that wondered if Laura herself hadn't destroyed my path and I know now that wasn't the case. It also wasn't Kevin.

He had gone to the bridge, planning to wait for me to cross, but when he arrived, the bridge was already gone.

He stood on the high bank, looking down at the water below and wondering who had done what he had wanted to do himself. And then something caught his eye on the edge of the bank, sticking out of the brush.

He bent down and lifted a hatchet. Looking at the bridge again, he knew this must be what was used, but how could that be when it was cut from the other side? As he studied it, he saw movement just past the bank, and before she could duck out of view, he saw her. She darted back into the shadow of the trees, but it was too late, she had been spotted.

Her instincts to flee took her back deep into the woods and toward the path that would lead her home. As the evening sun began to dip and shadows filled the woods, she heard the sound of someone else in those trees. Had Kevin somehow been able to get across and followed her?

She had seen him with the hatchet. She caught him, and now he was after her, but there was no way he could have come over. She hesitated, listening to where the steps were coming. The crunch and crack of dried leaves and brush, was close. She tried to hide in the trees but was spotted.

The footsteps she heard were mine.

———

"I saw what happened in the hollow," Nicole said softly.

Jeremy stood behind his sister as she told my parents what she had witnessed that day.

"I went to the bridge, and I saw Kevin Jenkins there. The bridge was cut, and he was holding a hatchet."

She hadn't wanted to reveal that she had secretly spied on our treks to the hollow, but after I'd been missing for two days, Nicole told Jeremy in a tearful confession that she not only knew about our hidden path but also my bridge crossings to see Laura.

"What bridge?" my father asked.

My mother stood beside him and closed her eyes, convinced now more than ever that the loss of her son was her fault alone. In an attempt to keep me from seeing Laura, she had most likely caused my demise.

"Where did you see Benji?" my mother asked Nicole.

"I saw him in the woods. He was with his dog," she told them.

Nicole hadn't seen me at the bridge, but because she knew that's where I always went, she told my parents she was sure that's where I was going.

Nicole stood on the stoop of my house and told my parents what she had witnessed, as my mother's heart continued to drop.

The bridge—that crossing that changed everything. She had hoped she could keep it solidly in the past, but now she was in fear that to learn my fate, all she had fought to keep hidden would be exposed.

She bit her bottom lip and kept what she knew inside.

"Did you know about this bridge," my father asked her.

My mother shrugged. "Ramona said something about it years ago."

My father was shocked. "It's been there all this time?" he asked. "Why didn't you ever tell me?"

Evelyn's face was pinched with pain. She knew why and now the reason was even more pressing.

"I don't go back there. I never thought about it until now." This of course was a lie. She had thought about that bridge and what had happened back in the hollow almost every day since that horrible night, and now what she feared most was coming true. The choices she made years ago that caused so much heartache, were now coming back to haunt her.

The regrets began to crowd her mind. Why had she agreed to go to that bonfire? Why had she stolen her brother's keys? The terrible choices that changed her life were now bubbling at the surface taunting her with the fear of the other secret she still hid.

CHAPTER 52

Evelyn stood at the edge of the woods, the wind biting at her cheeks, much like it had all those years ago. Her fingers throbbed, the old scars aching with a memory that never fully faded. The trees whispered around her, their voices mingling with the distant cries of a child. She took a deep breath and stepped forward, her heart pounding as she grasped the hatchet and took that step in.

The dim of early morning had the woods feeling dark and ominous, but something deep within her pulled her toward a hidden path—one she hadn't trod in years.

As she pushed through the thick underbrush, a wave of dizziness hit her, a sensation that had her wondering what terrible memory would hit her first.

It was there at the brim of those woods that her first brush with loss and pain occurred. What had previously been quick flashes of the past, the tingle of a frigid night, the sense of abandonment, and the sound of a child's cries, were now as vivid as though she had never left. The moonlit glow of her mother's expressionless face as she placed her in the snow, the sound of her steps crunching and slowly getting softer until there was silence, her father's frantic calls in the darkness, and the fiery sting as they tried to bring her frozen fingers back to life. But it was her second venture into the woods that now had her clutching a tree for support and her breath coming in ragged gasps.

She had barely stepped into the woods and was nowhere near the spot that had changed her life, and yet the horror of that night rushed back with a vengeance.

She took deep breaths to try and clear her mind. Her nightmare would have to wait. She had to press on to protect her son from that dark cloud that taunted her from the other side. No longer could she allow it to continue to reach over and risk what she had spent her entire life trying to hide.

Before the sun began to rise, she had made her way across the field and to the small cabin, knowing her father was away. It was where she hoped to retrace the route that she and Ramona had taken all those years before. She remembered it wasn't a long journey, but at that moment, every inch felt like a stretch.

The hatchet hung heavy at her side, and she hoped it would be enough to do the job she needed. Until she learned of my journeys over to the other side, she had rarely given the bridge a thought, assuming it had succumbed to age years ago.

The path took her through the trees and brush and eventually to the wide bowl of the river. She followed as voices of worry and dread called to her with each step until she was faced with the hill leading up to the crest of the canal bank.

She was there alone with the nightmare of what she had endured. Her hand gripped the hatchet as she scaled the hill, and when she reached the top, a thin line of sun made the water below shimmer. Looking up and down the steep canal, she saw the ropes and boards strung across just up from where she was. After all these years, she had found it, and now she was ready to take it down.

The trees on the far bank opened up right at the bridge, making an entry to the other side. She shook her head as she thought of me making that treacherous climb over the gaping swath of water to be with one of them. She felt she was saving me, and yet, in her heart, she knew destroying the bridge most likely wouldn't keep me away. However, it might give her hope that by removing it, she could clear this reminder of what she had come across that night.

Staring down at the tattered ropes still clinging to the large trees, she marveled that it was still intact. She was horrified imagining me high above the water, knowing if one side gave way, I would either fall into the water or crash into the concrete sides. But the real reason my being there terrified her was something she could never let me know.

As the memories of her own trek across that bridge began to enter her mind, she forced them back and went to the tree with the divided trunk where the ropes were tied. She felt the burn begin to build, and with both hands gripping the handle, she swung and felt the blade hit the knot. She had made a solid strike, but only a small fray was to show for it. Again, she raised it and gave it another solid whack. This time, part of the rope fell away and unraveled. It would work. Instead of taking single swings, she began to hack at the ropes, her mind releasing the pent-up rage that had been tamped down for years.

With an unceremonious drop, the side fell away, making the bridge twist and swing. The side that was still tied was clinging on. Evelyn stood straight and looked down at her work, then quickly stepped to the other side and began her anger-filled hacking again. She made quick work, and in just a few swings, the other rope was severed and fell free. The movement, along with her exhaustive effort, almost had her lose her balance, but she caught herself and watched the entire bridge fall and land against the hard bank of the other side. The bridge was no more. What she had wanted to do and should have done years ago was now done.

She took a deep breath. The sun was now lighting the entire scene. The canal was now a large, impassible chasm. She wanted to feel relief, but seeing the bridge lay there limp and tattered only made her feel tired. Why didn't it feel over?

She wanted the pain and regret to disintegrate along with those ropes. Her furor had destroyed it, but as she stood alone, breathing hard, nothing seemed to have changed.

Angry tears rose up, and she gripped the hatchet, wanting something else she could use it on. She so badly wanted to destroy the memories of what happened along with that bridge, but she knew that even if that were to happen, even if she could remove all that had taken place that night, she would be left with regret. How could she wipe it all away and not remove me along with it? The hate and anger that had stewed were made worse with the guilt that came with it. With no one and nowhere to place the bomb of anger she was holding, my mother wound up and, like a whirlwind, swung around and released the hatchet, hurling it over the canal and to the other side.

When it landed, she could see the metal blade shining on the bank, and a rush of regret washed over her. What if someone traced the hatchet back to her? But who? And what did she care? There was nothing more she could do, so she made her way back down the bank and into the woods.

The ache of memories was still with her as the little cabin came into view. It had been years since Ramona had lived there, and the last time she stepped foot inside was when she learned the truth about her mother. The deception had made her question just about everything her father said and did. What he kept from her was a betrayal she felt impossible to forgive. As she trudged through the field and on her way back home, she began to question her own deception and why she was keeping me from the other side. It wasn't just to keep her secret safe but to keep me from those who could ruin it all.

CHAPTER 53

Mr. Frost put his hand on my shoulder. I believe he thought I felt guilt for my part in revealing that Benji was, in fact, dead. And it's true. Even though they are no longer in a constant state of wonder, I still feel bad that my revelation has removed all hope of finding him alive.

I look up at him and he gives me the most comforting smile he can muster. The weight on his shoulders is obvious as he makes his way toward his wife, who is still in tears over the discovery. It's hard to imagine she'll ever be happy again.

The past couple of days have been a blur. When Old Tom asked where I had found the knife, I took them to the place in the overflow where I had seen the shiny red metal embedded in the bank.

The knife is now back in my pocket, but the weight of what it held in helping to find the Frosts' lost son has it feeling like I'm carrying a bowling ball.

There has been a steady stream of people through the house. Sheriff's officers and mourners of all sorts. Nicole came by with her mother, who brought a warm loaf of bread and their somber faces.

"I heard you were the one who found him," she said as we talked alone in the hallway.

"Who told you that?" I asked, surprised.

"Mr. Frost told my dad that if it wasn't for you, they may never have found him."

I sighed. "I don't know about that. I just found something that was his, so that's where they looked," I explained.

"The overflow, on the secret path," she said. "I guess he wasn't trying to go over to the other side after all." She then shrugged.

Her mother motioned to her that it was time to leave, and Nicole nodded. "I guess I'll see you around. Oh, and I'm glad you're not going to be leaving."

I flinched back. "What do you mean?"

"When my dad asked your uncle how long you'd be staying here, Mr. Frost said he wasn't ever planning on you leaving. Is that right?"

I looked across the room to where Mr. Frost was sitting on a kitchen chair, bent over and petting Rusty. Old Tom was in the chair next to him, watching the exchange.

I turned to Nicole and lifted an eyebrow. I didn't answer; I just gave her a nod.

———

LATER THAT NIGHT, Mr. Frost came back into the house after completing the chores. He still had scraps of hay on his hat and jeans, and a trail followed him from the kitchen. As I sat with Old Tom, watching Mrs. Frost begin to clear plates from the table, Mr. Frost went to her. "We'll take care of this later. Come sit."

She gave him a small smile and put the plate down, and she then stopped as though something spoke to her.

We were all silent as we watched her. Her mind was obviously churning. She then shook her head.

"It makes no sense," she said softly.

Mr. Frost walked back to her, watching her expression and trying to understand.

"What's that?" he asked.

She licked her lips, still deep in thought. "Why would Benji be in that place? It's nowhere close to the head gate or the river. And it's not on the path to the bridge." She squeezed her shoulders and took a deep breath. "I know he was found there, but it makes no sense that he would be in that part of the woods."

Mr. Frost lifted his shoulders. I could see that he wanted to give her answers but was both tired and unsure of what to say.

Feeling it wasn't my place, I sat and watched, but then something spurred me to speak up.

"The trail that goes through the overflow leads to a secret path. It's a shortcut to the hollow," I began to explain.

Mrs. Frost shook her head. "A shortcut? To where? If he had gone to the bridge, or even just back to the hollow, why would he be all the way over there? Where would he have been going?"

"Home," I said. "The path that leads through the overflow is a shortcut to the back pasture and then here."

I felt all eyes on me as they all contemplated what I had just revealed.

"There's no other reason to go that way," I continued. "The path leads here. He was trying to come home."

Her face has me wondering if I've helped or made things much worse. Her brows lower, but her face is more contemplative than sad. She presses her lips together and looks as though she's fighting back tears.

I feel I should apologize, and when she sees my angst, she comes to me. "Thank you, Landis," she says softly and then wraps her arms around me.

CHAPTER 54

BENJI

It was a typical Sunday morning when my mother learned the fate of her attacker. Up until that point, she hadn't known for certain if he was alive or dead. Now, she knew he would never be able to hurt her again, and he could never reveal the secret she had carried. She had spent almost two years with that worry nudging her brain, and the relief came over her like a flood.

For weeks after it happened, she froze whenever someone came to the door. Was it the police there to arrest her for murder? She hadn't heard a thing. There were no reports of a body being found, no whispers about someone from the other side gone missing, and no one to talk to about what went on that night and what might be happening now. She was alone in her fear and in her guilt.

"Killed in action," Gordon read. "The first one from our county. It says he was drafted and sent to Vietnam and killed in an ambush. He was married and had twins about Benji's age."

Realizing what he had said, he looked up, hoping Evie hadn't realized it either.

She was stirring her coffee and seemed half interested. He lifted the paper and turned it toward her to show her the photo. He hoped to distract her from thinking about her brother and the fact that he had been part of the draft, too. Of course, he never made it past receiving the news that he would be leaving.

"This is him," Gordon said as he held it toward her. "His name was Mark Jenkins. It sounds kind of familiar, but I don't recognize him."

There was no response from his wife. They had only been married a year and a half. And while they had known each other since they were children, it wasn't until she began to craft the shirts he and Wesley wore while competing that Gordon began to see her as something other than his best friend's little sister.

He enjoyed his time as she pinned and tucked the shirt to give it just the right fit. He felt odd turning with his arms out and her bent below with shiny pins gripped between her lips. She used her free hand to hold him steady, and when she grinned up at him, he felt his chest fill as he smiled back at her.

When Wesley died, my dad spent every day doing what he could to help out. He took over the chores that Wesley normally did but also spent time filling the massive hole that he had left. It bonded my parents, and even though my mother was only seventeen, they got married just two months later. I was born within the year, which had the local hens clucking as they pointed out the months between the two dates.

"Do you?" asked Gordon. "Recognize him?"

Evelyn sat wide-eyed and frozen, staring at the face in the photo. The eyes weren't leering at her in the shadows, the mouth held no smirk, and the hair wasn't a dark mop. But there was no mistaking who he was.

"Put that down," she said sharply.

He lowered the paper to find Evie in tears.

"What is it?" he asked, already worried he had inadvertently conjured the grief-filled memories of her brother.

"Get it away from me."

She closed her eyes tightly, trying to squeeze the image from her mind. But there was no escaping the horror of that night, and it all came rushing back with a fervor.

Gordon stood and went to her. He was lost as to what to do. This show of anguish was more than what she had shown during the days following Wesley's death. Had it finally all bubbled to the top?

It was him. The one who had left her with wounds that would never heal. He was gone. Her terror-filled dreams of his body frozen in the river behind their home or, worse yet, of him alive and confronting her, attacking her yet again, would never be anything more than nightmares. She would never have to worry about him coming after her or even simply running into him in town. Ever since that night, she never wanted to leave the house, and when she did, she found herself scanning the faces of those she encountered, fearful one of them would be him.

She had never had proof, but she knew inside that he was still out there, still alive. Surely, there would have been news about a missing person, and certainly, she would have heard if a body had surfaced just behind their house. But that never happened. He had survived and was out there somewhere, but not anymore.

Now, he was not only gone but dead. This time, there was no question, and a small prickle of relief made her pause. She looked down into the playpen where I was lying, gumming a plastic toy car. For a moment, she just watched me, and then she took a deep breath and sighed.

"Evie, are you okay?" asked Gordon.

She looked up at him. Okay? She thought. Would she ever be okay? The thing she feared most was now dead, but that didn't mean he was really gone. Her life may have been spared that night, but she harbored something that went far beyond the attack. No matter how much space or time she would be able to put between herself and what happened back in those woods, would she ever really be free?

That night, as her husband and baby slept, Evelyn went to the window of her tiny son's room and stared out toward the dark mass that stretched out farther than she could see. It was out there. The source of her pain began at the edge and continued into the depths of those woods.

Without realizing it, she was rubbing her hands, feeling the invisible ache of fingers lost. Cold, like needle pricks, surfaced in her mind, followed by the sound of dreadful pleas. Then came her heart racing, frantic running, the sound of sirens, and then a gurgled cry. It all came back to her every time she looked back there.

I was her secret. She would keep who I really was from everyone, including me. My father may have had his questions and even doubts, but he didn't want them to be true, so he ignored the thoughts niggling in his mind and refused to accept what might be.

A tiny whimper brought her out of her stupor. She leaned over the rail of my crib and lifted me up and into the cradle of her arms. As she rocked me in the same chair her mother once used, she pressed her cheek against mine and made a vow. Our secret would go to the grave. A secret that, until now, she was the one only who knew. What she didn't know was the grave would be mine.

CHAPTER 55

I had already died when the beams of light came frantically bouncing off of the trees and brush where I lay. They were the flashlights of the searchers and, later, my grandfather as he spent night after night hoping for a miracle.

He came close several times, mostly because Rusty knew that's where I was and continued to stay by me in death as he did in life. It should have been obvious what he was trying to do, but in their anguish and fear, they gave him no heed and instead followed the path they assumed I had taken. The only path they knew.

When I saw that the bridge was destroyed, my hopes of seeing Laura were also ruined. I felt everyone who was against me had won. Not only was I kept from crossing over, but they had made things so difficult that she had given up on us.

After catching Nicole, I wandered the woods in thought. I had no plan and wasn't about to go home and allow my mother to think she had won. I considered going to my grandfather's but knew my mother would most likely go there first. And going to Jeremy's after abandoning our friendship didn't feel right either.

Feeling defeated, I finally decided to take the path behind the farm and wait out the night in the barn.

The fight would blow over, and my being gone, I felt, would make my mother worry enough to forget her anger. I may have threatened to leave and not return, but I never had a plan to do it. I always knew that no matter the conflict, I would always go home.

Along with Rusty, I followed the thin, hidden path I used when I wanted to keep my travels to the river a secret. However, that night was the first time I was surprised when I reached the overflow.

It wasn't the first time the large ditch had water, but I was distracted by my own outrage and didn't expect it to be full.

The spring runoff was larger than it had been in years, and every lake, river, and stream were fuller than they had been in decades.

It was my stubbornness that had me stepping into the water, thinking I could wade the short distance from one bank to the other. The sun had already begun to set, and the glistening ripples hid the strong surge that lay beneath the surface.

I picked up Rusty and had only taken two steps in before I knew I was in trouble.

The water didn't look deep or sound rushing as I stepped in, but the rocks were unsteady, making me stumble back. When I tried to catch myself, I dropped Rusty, and he began to paddle.

I reached down to try and retrieve him, but this only made it worse. My sneakers slipped on the mossy rocks, making me fall backward and even further into the flow. As I tried to stop myself from being swept away, I desperately searched for him but saw nothing. Had he gone under? Had he somehow made it to the side?

I used my hands to try and push myself back up and out of the rush but instead found myself paddling and desperately trying to stay above the water. My feet slammed aimlessly against the rocks on the bottom as I tried to stop myself from being swept down, but the surge made it impossible and kept me rolling and splashing about. Soon, the rush enveloped me, and I was pushed toward a large outcropping of fallen brush. The roots of a large tree at the bank were exposed and acted like a giant sieve.

I saw it as an opportunity to grab onto something and try to pull myself up and out of the water, but just the opposite happened. The force of the flow and the mat of branches pushed me down, and the sharp sticks tore at my arms, side, and legs, eventually taking me under and lodging me against a ragged stretch of roots and debris. The water just kept coming and coming, so strong that my body was jammed into the deep, watery tangle.

I flailed, trying to release myself from the claws of the dead branches, but soon, my frantic fight turned to gasps that brought no air, only the cold sting of water. The blur of sunlight through brush and the faint sound of barking mixed through the muffled whoosh are my last earthly memories.

———

It isn't just the discovery of my clothes or even my bones that brings closure. It's knowing I'm truly dead. My mother's sadness is still there, but instead of being mixed with the guilt over her declaration that I never come back, she now knows I was trying to return. Her pain can now slowly release. Like air in a tire, the loss will begin to gradually subside. It will never completely empty, but at least now that I've been found, the unknowns no longer haunt her. And with that comes the realization that there is no one to blame. My drowning was due to the elements and me. It was an accident. Yes, it was a tragic one because of my age, but it was an accident nonetheless.

There was no malicious monster in the woods looking to snatch those who ventured too far into its depths. There were no murderous acts on the part of those across the hollow. No revenge for the things that happened in the past. It wasn't the act or fault of anyone except me. I was the cause of my demise, and even that is hard to argue.

I misjudged the water, fell victim to the current, and simply drowned. There is nothing and no one to blame but myself. My own actions and the natural occurrence of nature came together and took my life.

My body is where I was at most at peace in that mortal place, and much of it remains where my life ended. What they found was enough to prove the bones and clothes were mine. They were left with no doubt it was me.

Everyone assumed I had tried to make the journey across the bridge and to Laura. Everyone except my mother. She knew the bridge was long gone even before I stormed out of that house, so for her, my disappearance was even more perplexing. I couldn't have gotten far. I wouldn't have been able to get across unless I had waded into the depths of the canal and then climbed out the other side. The thought of this only made her shiver more because she knew it had been done before.

This added to my mother's guilt. Had she tried so hard to keep me away from the other side that her efforts contributed to my demise? She still couldn't help but feel that there was a connection to those who lived there. It was them. It was always them when it came to the terrible things that happened in her life. And there were other reasons to look to them for blame. The talk of Kevin's threats against me, our conflict at school the day before, and Nicole seeing him, hatchet in hand, added to all the fingers pointing his way.

As he stood, with the evidence in hand, he saw Nicole retreat back into the trees. So when the police arrived and questioned him about the destruction of the bridge, he knew his accuser was her. And the hatchet she described, red-handled and small, was found in a shed behind Kevin's house.

There was no other evidence that he had done anything when it came to my disappearance, but Kevin's defensive tone and his prior run-ins with police had everyone convinced he was somehow to blame. He was troubled, and the people in town, especially from my side, had no patience for his bad boy antics, so it was easy to turn their suspicions toward him. He was sent to that home for destruction of property, but the suspicions that stuck were that he was most likely my killer. While there is proof I was nowhere near that bridge, the sideways glances remain.

As I watch, I see signs that Kevin knew more than what he claimed about me and why he wanted me to stay away from his sister. If he did know the truth, then his actions were driven by the same decades-long fear and revulsion my mother felt. This is what pushed them both to keep our two sides separate. It wasn't just Laura and me that this affected; it was anyone who had been touched by the web that stretched out from what took place in those woods that fateful night. The fear of the truth coming to light was far more terrifying than the pain of keeping it hidden.

Now that I'm gone, will her secret still need to be kept? There will be no need to protect me, so will keeping how I came to be even matter? With my loss, I want the burden she held to go with me. The only one who should have carried the weight of what happened was already gone, but he left so much behind that others had to shoulder.

She went to the bridge, knowing what she needed to do. It had to be done. It was a place of pain and the continued cause of her grief. For years, she had tried to push those painful memories out of her mind, and now, my willful determination to see Laura had her make the trek back to the place she had never wanted to see again.

Her darkest memories and nightmares are when the cold and violent attack came racing back into her mind. I had no idea the trauma she had endured until I was free of my physical shell and able to see what had come before. It wasn't until I had left the confines of my earthly home that I knew how little my body was tied to what and who I truly was. It isn't the flesh that connects you but the soul.

Through the pasture and to the trail, she tried to remember the route Ramona had taken on that fateful night. In the daylight, she was able to make her way to the back side of the hollow and to the steep incline of the canal bank.

The dreadful chill of what happened there ran through her, and when she reached the top of the hill, she gasped when she saw that it was still there. Tied across the expanse that separated the two sides was the bridge. Worn and tattered, looking tired and weak, and she shivered at the thought of her son crossing that high expanse on the precarious stretch of boards and rope that had reached across that waterway for years. If, for no other reason, the precariousness of the bridge was enough incentive to destroy it, but of course, what drove her to attack that rundown stretch was more than a desire to impede her son's travels. It was a moment in her life that was embedded in her mind and a fear that went far deeper.

With the hatchet in hand, she went to the base where the bridge was anchored, looking for a good place to land her first swing. She had no time to waste, as I'd be coming home from school and surely planned on making my way to that very spot.

When I eventually did arrive, I was heated and convinced Kevin was the culprit. It only emboldened me, but I knew that night it wasn't meant to be. When I realized the path back home had also been severed, I became even more enraged about my mother's quest to keep me from Laura.

Of course, I was completely unaware of my mother's past with that hidden trail and bridge. What a horror it would have been if I had known the real reason she had tried to keep me from going over there.

I didn't know what she had faced, and I had no idea whose blood flowed through my veins. It was a secret trauma she held close and never planned to let anyone know.

On this side of the veil, I see what happened and how I came to be, and yet it has no bearing on my connection to those I came to love. What still has me here with them, watching and wanting them to go on, isn't blood; that is simply an earthly tie and nothing more.

There was a funeral, and what was found in the overflow was cremated and buried in a plot on the hill just outside of town. My headstone just feet away from my uncle—both of us gone too soon. But my mother wanted to leave some of my ashes at the place I loved.

My father and grandfather were hesitant, but she made it clear that whatever reservations she might have about the hollow, it was the place I had found great joy, and to allow me to forever be a part of it was the last gift she could give.

Following that trail back into the woods to leave a piece of her son had her heart breaking all over again. Could she leave me in the place her mother had left her, the place where she had suffered tragedy and pain?

And yet, as she walked, holding the small box with my remains, I felt her soul lighten. She now knew that even in my struggle to break from her, with anger and rebellion running high, my desire to leave and never come back wasn't what was solid in my heart.

Even with my stubborn ego at its pinnacle, I chose the path back. I wanted to go home. It's not the ending she had hoped for, but at least now she can live knowing even after the raging storm that seemed to break us apart, my desire and intent was to come back to her.

Epilogue

LANDIS

It's the end of spring, and the river is high. I can see Old Tom's graceful arcs just beyond the shaded bend of the hollow. He is unaware I've arrived. I've just returned from taking cattle to the summer range up north with Mr. Frost.

It's my second year of making the trip with him, and while my riding is still a bit unsteady at times, I'm able to herd and can at least get around without issue.

I enjoy being part of what Mr. Frost does. I now call him simply Uncle. He cocked his head the first time I used it but, without saying a word, gave a sniff of approval. Mrs. Frost is now Aunt Evie, and the first time I called Old Tom "Grandpa" felt both odd and warm. He still smiles, and his eyes glisten when I use it.

For a moment, I just stand at the bank and watch him. I think back to the first time I saw him standing in that very spot. I was lost back in these woods, chasing after a note I'd dropped in the ditch. Now I'm here and feeling anything but lost.

The path I take is now well-worn. I feel a fleeting tingle when I cross the overflow, knowing what happened there and what may still remain. For days, they sifted through the sand and silt to find anything they could that was left of Benji.

Like a puzzle, they laid out the bones, scraps of fabric, his leather belt, and shoes on a white tarp. It was a sad and ghastly sight, but it gave the Frosts something to bury. I still see the images in my head as I walk through on my way to the place I know Old Tom will be. I often wonder if that will all fade, but I also hope some part of it doesn't. Even though I never knew him, I want Benji to live on here.

As the horizon begins to turn orange, Old Tom feels my gaze and turns. His face lights up, and I wave. I set my rod against a tree as I adjust my fishing vest. Aunt Evie made it herself. It was not only a gift for my seventeenth birthday, but her unspoken blessing for me to be there in those woods.

My birthday brought a letter from my mother as well. The envelope no longer had the official stamp of the facility where she was being held, and the note was handwritten on blue paper

There was no mention of plans or if I'd ever see her again. "Happy birthday, Landis. Love, Mom" is all it said, but the missing return address spoke volumes.

As I tighten the suspenders on my waders, Rusty's bark startles me.

"Where'd you come from?" I ask as though he might answer.

His tail wags, and he takes a seat. I give him a quick pet, grab my rod, and wade into the shallows of the pool.

I feel the weight and coolness of the water against my waders and find a spot under the shadow of the setting sun.

I release my fly and lift my rod in the high, swooping pattern my grandfather has taught me. My first cast lands the fly lightly on the water's surface, and I still myself as I watch and wait. I'm still in awe of this place, and yet, each day, I find myself ruminating less about where I am and who I am.

I'm still getting used to what is now and will be my home. It has become easy to say, but something I still think about because of how strange a contrast this all is to what I thought my life would be.

The air is still cool, but the days are beginning to warm. The breeze that called to me so strongly when I first arrived a year ago has quieted to a gentle whisper. It tells me there is strength in the trees, consistency in the waters, and what is known as the hollow is my haven.

I no longer have dreams of a lavender farm, and I don't count down the days when my life will change and I can move on. I've found my place, my mind is calm, and my feet are solidly planted.

Books By Brenda Stanley

FICTION:

It Happened in the Hollow

The Treasure of Cedar Creek

The Still Small Voice

Only In Darkness

The Color of Snow

Like Ravens in Winter

I Am Nuchu

About the Author

Brenda Stanley is a former television news anchor and investigative reporter for the NBC affiliate in Eastern Idaho. She has been recognized for her writing by the Scripps Howard Foundation, the Hearst Journalism Awards, The Idaho Press Club, and the Society for Professional Journalists. She is a graduate of Utah Tech University and the University of Utah in Salt Lake City. She is the mother of 5 children, including two sets of twins. Brenda and her husband, Dave, a veterinarian, live on a small ranch near the Snake River with their horses and dogs. You can reach her at her website: brendastanleybooks.com